SEVEN
～SHADES～
OF EVIL

SEVEN SHADES OF EVIL

A MATTHEW CORBETT COLLECTION

ROBERT McCAMMON

LIVIDIAN
PUBLICATIONS
• 2023 •

Lividian Publications
4900 Carlisle Pike #313
Mechanicsburg, PA 17050

ISBN: 978-1-941971-26-0

Cover Artwork Copyright © 2023
by Vincent Chong
Interior Design by Kate Freeman Design

Lividian Publications Trade Hardcover

0 9 8 7 6 5 4 3 2 1

To my Tuesday night friends...onward and upward!

CONTENTS

THE FOUR
LAMPLIGHTERS

AUGUST, 1702

ONE

"IF THIS IS MUSIC," SAID HUDSON GREATHOUSE IN A VOICE NOT SO *sotto voce*, "I'll eat my boots."

His declaration of both melodic revulsion and strange appetite was met with a faint spit of hissing, as if a small nest of snakes had been disturbed in their reptilian raptures. The display of displeasure came not from creatures of the scaly community, but from the females sitting in the audience dressed in as much finery as they could sculpt upon themselves—high wigs, waist-choking bodices and festoons of lace—so that they appeared more like birds of vibrantly colored feathers than the ladies Hudson and Matthew Corbett saw every day in the shops and on the streets of New York.

"Well?" the irritable critic continued, seated beside Matthew. His knitted brows told the tale. "Do *you* think this is music?"

"Hush!" commanded—and indeed a whisper may be commanding, if delivered through gritted teeth—the person sitting on the other side of Greathouse, who this day happened to be Sarah Goodenall, who secondly happened to be a strolling guitarist at Sally Almond's tavern on Nassau Street, and who thirdly happened to be Hudson's romantic interest of the moment. Greathouse returned a scowl that meant the interest was in jeopardy but otherwise kept his next remark in his throat, and Matthew decided to keep his own opinion in silence.

Silence was not the order of the day. This August afternoon Hudson and Matthew sat amid the audience of forty or so citizens—again, mostly women—in the concert room of the Dock House Inn, a chamber offering pews sawn from the best local oak, drapes the color of purple passion itself (chosen specifically by the inn's fastidious proprietor Gilliam Vincent) and an upraised stage upon which now stood the four performers whose musical abilities irked Hudson Greathouse and brought a—necessarily guarded—smile of amusement to the face of Matthew Corbett.

They called themselves the Four Lamplighters, and whose lamps they were currently determined to light were the females in the audience, who by their squeals, giggles and shifting in their seats told Matthew that the wicks were being well flamed. The first song in this performance had been titled "Fishing for Beauties on a Summer's Eve" and after many proclamations of how long and sturdy were the poles of the Lamplighters, things had gone in the further general direction of southern titillations.

But Matthew had to admit that they were quite a sight. The lead singer and guitarist, who had announced himself as Lawrence Love, had introduced the others of this travelling troupe: Rollie Dell on the second guitar, Adrian Foxglove playing the fiddle, and Ben Dover banging away on a pair of drums mounted on stands accompanied by a rather extraordinary cymbal contraption that he operated with a foot pedal. What made them quite a sight, however, was their manner of dress: Love all in burning red, Dell in eye-scorching blue, Foxglove in a shade of sea green and Dover in a nearly luminous purple that put Gilliam Vincent's drapes to pitiful shame.

And then there were the wigs.

Were they wigs, or constructions of powdered cake swirled round and round by a mad London baker to ridiculous heights? No, they were certainly wigs, and what wigs they were! Love's was a bonfire to match his suit and ruffled shirt, Dell's was a blue scream, Foxglove wore the hue of the green-creamed waves that rolled into New York's harbor, and Dover wore the color of the bruises and abrasions that had only recently disappeared from Matthew's body after his fight with the sinister swordsman Count Dahlgren at Simon Chapel's school for young criminals.

It was because of the aftermath of that near misadventure that he was sitting in this audience. Greathouse had come to his doorstep—the little dairy house behind the Grigsby home—not to chide him for being a "moonbeam" or demand that he continue his lessons in swordplay—but to ask him to accompany himself and the lady Goodenall to this musical farrago.

"I wouldn't be caught *dead* at a concert," Greathouse had steamed, "but Sarah's bound and determined and I think it wise to go along. If I don't, what would that tell her of my interest in her music?"

"The truth?" Matthew asked. "That is…nothing at all?"

"I can't admit that! She's too good of a cook and I am very fond of her roasted chicken! Also she affords me a cut rate on my dining at Sally Almond's!"

"So very valuable to you, I'm sure."

"Yes, *valuable!* And I don't like that tone, Corbett! So get yourself to the Dock House on Friday afternoon at two o'clock, as I don't wish to be assaulted by this dubious performance alone! Your ticket has already been purchased!"

Misery desires company, Matthew had thought. Further argument was futile and he had decided it was best not to rile this walking mountain, as there was more training to be done as a new associate of the Herrald Agency and it could be as rough as Greathouse pleased.

But there was another reason Matthew now sat among this audience, which connected with the strange ending of his deeds regarding the elderly woman he had come to know as the Queen of Bedlam. The blood card delivered to him as a portent of death from the hand of the mysterious Professor Fell weighed heavily upon him night and day, burdening his step in the sunlight and blighting his sleep. In truth, Matthew thought of Hudson Greathouse as a bullying lout with only a modicum of intelligence…but a bullying lout with only a modicum of intelligence who could be counted upon to deflect a bludgeon, blade, bullet or choke-rope from one of Fell's hidden assassins, therefore Matthew deemed it wise to tag along whenever the opportunity presented itself.

The Lamplighters were in full voice now, Love's lead singing being supported by the harmonies of Dell and Foxglove. What was amazing to Matthew—and to the rest of the gallery, he was sure—was that the Lamplighters stood for their performance and actually *moved* back and forth upon the stage. It seemed also that they liked to shake their wigs, which brought forth further animation from the ladies while the menfolk sullenly smoked their pipes as if to befog the chamber. The Lamplighters were all young men, in their early twenties the same as Matthew, and all might be called handsome but for the drummer Dover whose leviathan of a nose could be a hook for a tricorn hat…or two, or three.

They had begun a new ditty, with the accompaniment of banging drums and harmonies from the green and the blue:

> *"My name is Love!*
> *(His name is Love)*
> *My name is Love!*
> *(His name is Love)*
> *And I thank the stars in Heaven above, that every time I set my cap, I can lie in any lady's lap! My name is Love!*
> *(His name is Love)*
> *My name is Love!"*

"Groan," said Greathouse, followed by a little whuff when Sarah put an elbow in his ribs.

And another tune followed, or rather tumbled forth:

> *"Oh, the merry month of May, is the time when the ladies lay,*

Down their troubles and their woes,
And feel the grass between their toes,
Oh how I wish I were grass!"

"You're an *ass!* Does that count?" Greathouse suddenly rumbled, loud enough to cause snickers from the men, sneers from the women and evil eyes from the Lamplighters, but the foursome was undaunted and the rhythm never wavered.

"Oh the merry month of May, is the time when the ladies play,
With their trinkets and their toys,
And all the bright and handsome boys,
Oh how I wish I were...but I am! So fiddle dee dee, fiddle dee dee, fiddle
dee dee, sweet ma'am!"

"Good Christ," was Greathouse's twisted-mouth response, though it was delivered in a guttural funk.

"Thank you, fair ladies, and you fine gentlemen who possess good manners, and you know who you are!" proclaimed Lawrence Love when the song and the applause—all from feminine hands—had ended. "We would now like to share a song that has been a great part of our performance since we came together as musicians in Liverpool three years ago! Since then we have played the stages of some of the most majestic halls of England—"

"I didn't know horse barns had stages," said Greathouse directly into Matthew's ear, keeping his volume low and therefore his ribs free from attack.

"—and thus we find ourselves on tour in these glorious colonies," Love went on, "and straight here we have come from a smashing concert appearance in the great town of Boston. So without further pause, here is the tune that one might say put the Four Lamplighters on the path to fame and the wonderful opportunity to meet such gracious, noble and...yes, of course!... beautiful company. Here is 'The Ballad of the Rutting Ram'."

"God save us," said Greathouse, again only for Matthew's ear, but Matthew had the thought that if the man could sing and play a guitar this might be the very kind of tune that would spill forth.

With a wigshake, a strum, a drumbeat, more strumming, and a wide-legged stance that Matthew thought might bring the fair ladies to fainting, Lawrence Love began:

"A ram he stood in the pasture there,
(Oh hi oh hi oh)
Spotted he a dame with long blonde hair,

(Oh hi oh hi oh)
Said the ram to the damsel fair,
Might I have a locket of hair,
To soothe me through the winter nights,
And take my desires to their heights,
For I am a rutting ram,
And I'm horny as can be,
(Yes he is a rutting ram)
And I'm horny as can—"

"CEASE THIS OBSCENITY!" came a shout from the back of the chamber that made nearly everyone—Matthew and Greathouse included—fly up out of their seats. It was followed by the crashing of what sounded like a giant's timber smacking the oak hull of a sixty-cannon warship, and in this caterwaul the Lamplighters went silent and everyone wrenched their necks around to see what parade had just marched into the show.

It was a brigade, not a parade. Leading the pack was High Constable Gardner Lillehorne, resplendent in his own sky-blue suit with clouds of ruffles at the neck and cuffs, his blue tricorn topped by a sunny yellow feather; yet there was no sunshine in his countenance, for his narrow, pale and black-goateed face wore an expression of the deepest disgust, and his hammering at the nearest pew with his ebony cane was summer thunder.

But pounding the hardest with his own evil black billyclub was the vile—at least to Matthew's senses—squat, red-haired and stocky so-called constable Dippen Nack, whose usually rum-sloshed mouth opened to holler accord with his master's voice: "Obscenity! Obscenity! Obscenity!"

As if he even knew what the word meant.

By this time everyone was on their feet and chaos ensued. Some of the women had regained their senses and were screaming their outrage at this intrusion, while the pipe puffers just kept smoking up the place. Coming in behind Lillehorne and Nack were three more burly gents Matthew recognized as constables, telling him that this had been a well-planned attack on the musical talents of the Lamplighters. The performers themselves remained uncharacteristically mute, but for Dover stomping the cymbal pedal once as a last shimmering note.

But one person was far from becoming mute. From the front row of pews there sprang an imp of a man perhaps five feet in height at most, sixty or so years of age, with a single white sprig of hair atop his pate that stood erect to emulate the goatee at his chin, which ended as sharply as a white dagger. His eye sockets were nearly shadowed over by his brows, which met above the bridge of his bulbous nose like a battle between two armies, each conflicting with the other in shaggy combat.

"Here, here!" the imp shouted, with even more vigorous volume than had Lillehorne. "What's the meaning of this outrage!" And before he'd finished that rather needless question he had scrambled up to the high constable and from his low position appeared to be about to bite into Lillehorne's knobby blue-stockinged knees.

"*Obscenity!*" returned the shout of Dippen Nack, who shoved the little man back with his billyclub to the center of the chest and then, grinning, looked around to make sure everyone noted his prowess with the bludgeon.

"Gentlemen, gentlemen!" fretted Gilliam Vincent, who was racing around the chamber doing his impression of the nearest windmill. The shouts and screams of the enraged females were growing to a fever pitch, and Matthew caught sight of two of Polly Blossom's more hefty ladies of the evening who looked as if they were preparing to roll up their lace sleeves and start battering some constables' faces into tomorrow's mush.

"Silence! Silence, I say!" But Lillehorne's command went unheeded, and Matthew was amused to see lighting upon the expressions of high constable and brutish bully a flicker of fear before the advancing petticoated warriors.

Then there glided through the open double doors another petticoated figure, tall and lanky in stature, who lifted up two green-gloved hands and said in his manly tone, "By my order this wretched performance has ended, and anyone who protests may be spending a night behind bars along with these four beasts!"

It was probably the wrong thing to say, and Governor Edward Hyde, Lord Cornbury, likely knew it at once, for here came a wall of women throwing themselves forward even as their hapless menfolk tried to restrain the assaults.

"Home detention, I should clarify!" Lord Cornbury was showing that as a politician he knew how to fry an egg before it was thrown at him, also that he was fashionable in his pale green gown and curly white wig, his makeup and eyeshadow immaculate. "But iron bars for these four purveyors of obscenity!"

"Damn your eyes, lady!" yelled the imp. And instantly, awash in his boat of confusion: "I mean...*man*. They're making music, not—"

"I know full well what they're doing, *sir!*" returned the governor. "And I presume you are their manager? Sidney Sodd by name?"

"And a name known in the entertainment world as a star shines in Heaven! This is a damned outrage I've never seen the like of!"

"Oh, really? You mean you've already forgotten that four days ago you and this bunch of yours were hauled behind bars in Boston for just such depravity as you've displayed here? And a messenger was sent by packet boat from that upstanding town to warn us just what would ensue at this..." The long thin nose wrinkled. "...*event?*"

"If he wants to see depravity," Greathouse whispered to Matthew, "he should come with me on a late-night tour of the taverns."

"I protest this treatment!" Sodd plowed on. "In London these young men are considered artists of the finest merit! The Boston Puritans have no sense of *art!*"

"I have no opinion on that subject, sir, but I do know this is New *York*, not New *London*, and obscenity will never have a purchase in this fair haven! Lillehorne, do your duty and take these offenders away! A night in the gaol should cool their ardors!"

"We are due in Philadelphia in two days! You cannot detain us!"

"Listen to him prattle, Lillehorne! Yes, I've seen those broadsheets you've passed around and I am aware of your schedule. Next Philadelphia and then Charles Town. I'm sure the authorities in those locales will appreciate our adherence to proper social conduct. Away with you!"

"I refuse to be taken away like a common criminal! My charges likewise refuse to be—"

Sodd abruptly stopped speaking. Two men Matthew didn't recognize had come into the chamber behind the constables. One was husky and bear-like, the other smaller with pinched features and a hawk's beak of a nose. They simply stood staring at Sodd, who Matthew saw gave the men a fretful glance.

"All right, then!" Sodd said, in what was nearly a tangle of three words. "We'll go peacefully. Yes, we'll go! Bring your instruments, boys! A night in the gaol won't be so terrible, will it?" And though this inquiry was aimed at Lord Cornbury, Sodd seemed to be speaking directly to the two newcomers.

"All the comforts afforded to masters of perversion will be yours. Lillehorne, take them away! And mind that billyclub, Nack! We want no damage done to our visitors!"

The grin on Nack's face drooped.

As the fivesome were herded out of the hall, Matthew noted the two men spoke quietly to each other and followed at a distance. Lord Cornbury remained behind, his civic duty not yet fulfilled. "Go about your business, ladies and gentlemen! Be aware that I as your governor am always on the alert to provide safety and security, as is my station. These so-called musicians will be out of our town by tomorrow afternoon...and good riddance to them!" His eyes took on a bit of a shine. "Though I have to say I do admire their wigs. Now good day to all!"

Out upon the Broad Way in the rather hot sunshine and humid air, Matthew walked alongside Greathouse and Sarah, who was giving her escort a dose of flaming protestations to this scene that might have served as another charge of obscenities. Greathouse said nothing, showing that he might possess more than a modicum of intelligence.

But Matthew saw the two men following the procession on their way to the gaolhouse, though the pair had a languid, unhurried pace. The smaller one stopped to light a pipe. They both stood watching Sodd and the Lamplighters be taken away, and then they strode off in another direction.

Which wound Matthew's clock of curiosity and set it ticking.

TWO

"IT'S ODD. DON'T YOU THINK?"

"No."

"Meaning you don't think it's odd? Or meaning that you don't *think?*"

Greathouse lifted his gaze from the papers on his desk. He had been scribing the details of a case involving a man who feared his wife was romantically involved with a travelling preacher she was seen several times meeting, but it had turned out that the woman had been trying to persuade the sackcloth-and-ashes fire-breather to cast the fear of God on her husband as a means of stopping his all-too-regular visits to Polly Blossom's house of ill repute. It amused Matthew that Polly's house was free of any obscenity charges, since her donations to Lord Cornbury's "service fund" had helped purchase his luxurious wardrobe. Such could not be said of the Lamplighters, who had spent the night behind bars and would soon be a footnote in the history of New York.

"Listen, Corbett," said Greathouse, in that tone he used to scare little children and wild bulls. "You might be full of yourself after that Chapel incident, and be wearing those fine suits Effrem Owles is sewing for you... *and* getting all those ridiculous stories about yourself in the *Earwig,* but as far as I'm concerned you're still a milksop moonbeam and one slap across the face from me will finish this unwise experiment Mrs. Herrald has foisted upon the world. In other words, shut up."

"Spoken out of true boredom," said Matthew, though he decided it was best not to go any further. Still...one foot further: "I surmise you have nothing else to do?"

"Keep talking. My slapping hand is getting twitchy."

From a far shadowed corner of this upstairs office at Number Seven Stone Street there came a thump and clatter along with what might have been a man's muffled grunt.

"See what you've done?" Greathouse asked, his quill poised over the inkwell. "You've gotten them riled up."

"I think the air of threatened violence has done the trick," was Matthew's retort. The two ghosts that inhabited this space along with the Herrald Agency were perpetually fighting over burnt coffee beans, the earthly battle that had ended with their broken necks down the flight of stairs to the street not being enough to calm the spiritual tempers. "But really," Matthew continued, as Greathouse returned to his scribing, "don't you think it was strange that Sidney Sodd protested going to the gaol until those two men entered the chamber, and then it seemed he was eager to get himself and the Lamplighters behind bars?"

Greathouse finished another pair of lines before he responded. "I presume you've been gnawing on this all night?"

"Not all night. A few hours."

"The waste of a few hours. I care not a sardine's whisker about Sodd, the Lamplighters or the two men. Case closed."

Matthew leaned back in his chair. Though all windows that could be opened were so, the summer's heat in the upstairs loft was oppressive. Noise from the carts and wagons trundling past on the Broad Way rose from the street, as well as the odiferous aromas from the livestock that hauled them. But there was nothing to be done about that, and sweat went with any job that had to be undertaken, even sitting on one's behind with nothing to be done. Except, perhaps, think on something that might have no meaning at all.

To Matthew's surprise, Greathouse was not finished with the subject. "If Cornbury wanted to find obscenities he might walk the docks at any hour of the day. Particularly in the heat of August. I suspect he felt he had to do something because those Puritans up there were watching. And the Lamplighters will get an equal kick in the ass from the Quakers down in Philadelphia. But I agree with throwing them behind bars for a night. Such subjects should not be cast about in front of ladies."

"I think the ladies enjoyed the casting. And wouldn't you say sexual subjects have a long history in the arts?"

"I wouldn't know about that. All I know is, women should be protected from such."

"Really?" Matthew's brows lifted. "How many taverns have you been in where sexual subjects were simply dripping off the walls, and the ladies there were helping apply the glue?"

"That's different," Greathouse huffed. "Women who work in taverns are not what I call ladies."

"I hope Sarah never hears you say that. Your chicken will be roasted well and proper."

"You know what I mean."

"No, I don't. Tighten your noose a little more."

Greathouse slapped down his quill, throwing forth a few black droplets of ink to match his rising ire. But he swallowed what he was going to say first and instead did a little *riposte*: "Have you seen that girl lately?"

"What girl?"

"Oh, come now!" His wolfish grin emerged. "Grigsby's granddaughter! The one who nearly got killed along with yourself!"

"I haven't seen her lately, no."

"I find that hard to believe! You living right in their backyard, so to speak! I thought you were having your meals with them!"

"I've been dining in the taverns lately."

"Wasting your money as well as your hours, then. What changed?"

"Pardon?" Matthew feigned incomprehension, though he knew exactly where this was going.

"What *changed*," Greathouse repeated, as if speaking to a halfwit, "in your relationship with the Grigsbys? Particularly with that girl."

"We have no relationship, other than living knee to elbow."

"Hm. You know, she's not bad-looking. In fact, she's very *good* looking. You saved her from death, you might well claim a reward of some kind."

"Beryl Grigsby," said Matthew, with as much stuffiness as he could conjure, "is an unfortunate bearer of bad luck to whomever she touches. Therefore I'd rather not be touched, nor touch *her*." His frown deepened. "A *reward?* Believe me, if I never see the girl again, that's enough reward."

"Methinks you complain too much," Greathouse said. "You like that? '*Methinks?*' I read that in the *Earwig*, in one of Grigsby's gushing accolades of your prowess as a 'problem-solver'. Since you've got him hoodwinked, you should try to hoodwink the girl too."

Matthew saw no sense in giving any respect to such a statement, so he remained silent and shifted his chair so he might avoid Greathouse's face and view the distant green cliffs of New Jersey, shimmering in the heat.

The truth: Berry Grigsby would hardly speak to him and seemed to be doing her best to avoid him for the two weeks since saving her life on the Chapel estate from bloodthirsty hawks had involved a liberal application of horse manure to the face. Then she'd lately come around to his dairy house with obviously a new attitude and invited him to a social at Sally Almond's, which he'd declined. So now the ice was back frosting the cup. Though it was grand for him to be hailed as such a hero in the *Earwig* he did not feel so heroic in the presence of Berry Grigsby, who easily could have been killed being involved with him in that dangerous situation. *My guardian*, she'd called him. It seemed to him that the best guarding would be to keep his distance from her, lest her impetuous nature draw her into further peril regarding his position as a problem-solver.

He was lost in thought about this when both men heard the door open and close at the bottom of the stairs. Then came the sound of bootsteps ascending. Greathouse set his quill into its rest and said, "A situation, I hope," to mean *more interesting than a fire-breathing preacher, a wronged wife and a whoremongering gallivant.*

Who should enter the office but Sidney Sodd, looking none the worse for a night's rest in the gaol. He was wearing a nice tan suit with dark blue piping, and as he came in, he removed his brown tricorn to reveal the single spike of hair sticking up on his pate like an exclamation.

"Gentlemen," he said, with a nod to each. "I am Sidney Sodd, and I've been given the information that you are in the business of 'problem-solving'?"

"Correct," said Matthew, who stood up as a measure of respect. Greathouse did not repeat the measure. "I am Matthew Corbett, and this is my associate—"

"Hudson Greathouse, and Mr. Corbett is *my* associate," came the interruption in what was nearly a bark. "What do you want?"

"It seems...I do have a problem."

"I can guess," said Greathouse, "but restoring the hearing to deaf ears is not among our abilities."

Sodd looked stunned for a few seconds, and then his face folded in a smile and a quiet laugh came out. "Oh, you're making a joke! Ah yes...I recall seeing both of you at the concert yesterday!"

"Was that what it was? I thought it was an assault by two armies with my head caught in the middle!"

Sodd remained smiling, though the edges of it did fray a little.

"Pardon Mr. Greathouse, sir," said Matthew, "as he's currently scribing the results of a problem that has taxed his brain and given him no rest for at least forty minutes. Would you like to have a seat?" He motioned toward an extra chair that faced his own desk. As Sodd sat down, so did Matthew. Greathouse reached for his quill again but at the last second his fingers denied it.

"All right then," Greathouse said, with a look of anguished resignation. He wiped the heat sweat from his forehead with the back of his hand. "What's your problem?" He drove on before Sodd could reply. "I thought you and that troupe of yours would be gone to Philadelphia by now."

"Yes. Well...the Four Lamplighters and I have booked passage on the packet boat that leaves at three o'clock. I am told that with a fair wind we will reach the town by tomorrow evening and our first concert there is scheduled for the night afterward. So actually our schedule has been unaffected."

"I doubt those Quakers will allow you to finish a single concert, with what I heard. Don't you think the Lamplighters are a bit saucy for a mixed audience?"

"*Saucy*, sir?"

"Yes! Saucy, Sodd! To put it mildly!"

"*Saucy*," the little man repeated, as if relishing the word. Swirls of color surfaced on his cheeks, and he leaned toward Greathouse with what might have been a giddy grin. "Yes sir! You've hit it directly! That is the heart of it, the lungs and the brain too! Saucy! And Christ keep the Lamplighters full of sauce and more in days to come, for then you'll see the fire of it!"

"And here we thought we had a client," said Greathouse to Matthew, "when this gent needs to be led gently to an asylum bed."

"I do think you should explain yourself, sir," Matthew urged, and Sodd nodded with a nearly feverish eagerness.

"What seems saucy today," he said, "is mere pap tomorrow. This is the heart, the lungs and the brain of music, sirs! Of performance! Of the arts themselves! The true artist must keep pushing forward, ever forward! As my charges do…ever forward! Oh, I saw in them greatness, gentlemen! Do you know what I saw?"

"Greatness," said Greathouse, with no enthusiasm.

"I saw…what has never been *seen* before! And that is the crux of it! What has never been seen before is what *must* be seen! What has never been heard before *must* be heard! Their songs, their appearance, their command of the stage and the audience…and yes, gentlemen, their *sauce!* You know they came up with the idea of moving back and forth upon the stage on their own, and let me tell you I have seen dozens of women lose their senses and rush forth simply to kiss a ruffled sleeve! I have seen tears in their eyes, and—"

"Corks in their ears?" Greathouse asked.

"All right, their music is not for everyone! Certainly not for the *elder!* It is for the *young*, as every art begins its journey through mankind, for the young have not the calcified minds and stiffness of sensibilities that impair free thinking and action! If not for the young, the world itself would calcify and crumble to pieces, for the minds of the young keep it fresh and vigorous! So yes, the music of the Four Lamplighters is for the young, and I praise my fate that I am here to guide them along."

"Do you practice this speech before a mirror?" was Greathouse's reply.

"Make merry if you like, sir, but what may be termed obscenities suited Shakespeare well in both comedies and tragedies, and you might look to the Bible itself to find what some might call perversions, as in the Song of Solomon. He owned a harem of one hundred and forty women, later expanded to one thousand. Would your Lord Cornbury place Solomon behind bars for his exuberant tastes?"

"Probably," said Greathouse.

"I'm simply saying that the Four Lamplighters represent the future of music…the mixture of song and performance to stir the emotions of an audience, and thus win their hearts. They *are* the future, like it or not, and their path will continue to evolve from artist to artist long after we are dust in the grave."

"I shudder to think," said Greathouse. "Not of the grave, but of the future of music if that bunch is the vanguard."

"I understand your meaning," Matthew offered to Sodd, "but besides this expounding upon art and the evolution of music…what is your problem?"

"Simply put," said Sodd, "we are in need of a bodyguard. Two would be best, and I have the coin to pay."

"Guarding against whom, exactly?" Greathouse prodded, his interest obviously renewed.

Sodd was slow in answering, his gaze on the floorboards, so Matthew decided to do some prodding of his own. "The pair of men following you. Who are they?"

Sodd's gaze came up from the floor. "Pair of men?"

"You know who I mean. The two men whose presence made you decide yourself and your charges would be safer in the gaol than not. Do you know their names?"

Again, Sodd was slow in his response, but at last he chewed on his lower lip and said, "The larger one is named Graw. The smaller one is Sprain. To answer your next question, they are hired killers."

"Hired by whom?" When Sodd didn't reply, Matthew pressed on: "Sir, we need to hear the whole story or I doubt we will be much use to you. Who has hired the killers, and who is the target?"

"All right. Hired by Edgar Allerby, and the target—I believe—is Ben Dover, our drummer and also one of our songwriters."

"Go on," Matthew urged.

Sodd shifted in his chair. "Allerby owns a number of coffee houses in London, and also in other English cities. The Lamplighters were contracted to offer concerts in several of those establishments. You must know that Allerby is more fond of rum than of coffee, but he is very wealthy. Also that he is a corpulent bully who married a woman twenty years younger than himself…and there is the problem. As things progressed, Ben and Allerby's wife…enjoyed a dalliance. More than a dalliance. Ben has that effect upon women."

"That fellow with the mile-long nose?" Greathouse asked. "That one?"

"You know what they say about big noses, sir," said Sodd, which made Greathouse either consciously or by instinct feel the length and width of his own before he realized what he was doing and dropped his hand.

"To continue," said the little man. "Allerby's wife Alice was so smitten with Ben that she decided to throw aside her marriage and follow the troupe, thus Ben—the others and myself, also—have inspired the undying hatred of the wounded husband. And speaking of dying, Allerby's wife disappeared two weeks before we left England. She was going to make the trip to the colonies on her own, as Ben...well, Ben has a roving eye, and he never intended to take matters beyond a dalliance. He made that clear to her. But her visits to our concerts at other establishments ceased, as did her rather impassioned letters to Ben once he told her we were definitely undertaking this tour."

"Maybe she returned to her husband?" Greathouse asked.

"Knowing Allerby's reputation, I doubt he would've taken her back as—shall we say—spoiled goods. It's possible she returned, yes, but her attendance at our last three concerts was replaced by the presence of the men Mr. Corbett noted yesterday. They followed us to our inn, and we noted them skulking around. Just before we boarded the ship for Boston, we were returning from a performance one night, we heard a cat's squall from an alley—which alerted us to the fact that something was afoot—and an instant later a pistol ball nearly parted Ben's scalp. We could've been fired upon a second time, had not a constable been near. I made some inquiries from associates who might have gotten a whiff of things, their positions being so near to the dirt, and the word was that Allerby had contracted two killers to exact his revenge upon Ben...and, by result of murder, the other Lamplighters as well."

"Did you see them in Boston?" Matthew asked.

"No. They must've taken the next ship after ours. It would be no hard task to follow us, as before the killers entered into this matter I had printed up in the *London Gazette* details of our upcoming tour. Publicity, you know. I thought by leaving England for a while a hot situation with Allerby's anger might have time to cool. I imagine Graw and Sprain went to Boston, found they'd missed us, and located one of the many broadsheets I had circulated around that spelled out our towns of performance. I was shocked to see them here yesterday, and actually relieved that we all might spend a night of safety behind bars. But you see, gentlemen, why I need your services. I am well aware that Graw and Sprain are following our movements, though they might not be seen by myself or the others." Sodd looked from Matthew to Greathouse and back again, his expression dour and the two hairy eyebrows at war. "We do need your help, sirs, to prevent further acts of violence upon my boys."

"Understood," said Matthew. "But why not take a coach to Philadelphia? I think that's probably a faster trip than the packet boat, which has to go around Delaware and up the river."

"Maybe not," Greathouse asserted. "It depends on the ferry boats. Sometimes you have to wait for hours while they get their problems sorted out and everyone across."

Sodd nodded. "And another reason…do you have any idea what damage can be done to musical instruments on a *coach?* Broken guitars, a fiddle and drums would be the devil to pay, and over here I daresay the repair shops are few and far between. No, we must take to a smoother voyage by water."

"Well why didn't you take the morning boat?" Greathouse asked. "It sailed at six."

"We weren't released until eight," was Sodd's answer, "and I had to make haste as it was to find a boat with available cabins. Thus the current situation."

Matthew and Greathouse were silent for a while. Sodd presented the final question: "What is your decision, sirs?"

"I hate your music, if it can be called that," said Greathouse, "but a water trip would be a cooler experience than New York in August. You say first Philadelphia and then Charles Town?"

"And we'd hoped to play Philadelphia, New York and Boston again on the return, but we'll have to see."

"Matthew?" Greathouse asked. He was checking his pocket watch. "Four hours before the packet boat leaves. You'll need enough for two weeks' trip, I'd say. No, better make it three just in case. Why don't you go on home and get ready? I'll stay with Sodd and the 'boys' until you've finished, then we can split the task."

"We're at Mrs. Jorgenson's boarding house," said Sodd, who stood up to his full diminutive height but he seemed already relieved of a heavy weight. "Thank you, gentlemen. You shall not regret doing this good deed."

"Hang the good deed." Greathouse was already pushing aside his scribing of that last and to him crushingly boring case. "We're in it for the money."

THREE

"WELCOME ABOARD! WELCOME, ALL!" WAS CAPTAIN RUFUS Guidenmeyer's greeting to his passengers as they crossed the gangplank onto the ninety-foot schooner *Summer Breeze*, which the red-bearded, gap-toothed and gregarious Guidenmeyer renamed as per the seasons: *Autumn Wind*, *Winter Solstice*, and *Springtime Joy*.

Guidenmeyer's exuberance did not translate well to either Matthew or Hudson; each spending their own short time in the presence of the Four Lamplighters while packing up for this voyage made them both wish not to light the lamps but to break them. The young men without their garish costumes, wigs and a stage upon which to parade themselves were the zenith—or might it be nadir?—of sullen bad manners and taciturn lack of personality. When they did speak among themselves it was a language about chords and melodies, delivered with snorts and sneers, that spoke of how little they seemed to like anything, in particular their own music, Sidney Sodd, each other, and this tour they were apparently forced into taking under threat of the murders of their entire families, if one might surmise so from their behavior.

In Matthew's opinion, the Romeo of this group was the most abhorrent. Ben Dover's arrogance seethed through his skin, in the way he looked with his heavy-lidded eyes down his huge beak of a proboscis at Matthew the way one would look not least of all at the hired help, but also at a toad one might consider smashing under a heavy boot. He uttered the few words he seemed to know in what must be the tar-thick accent of the Liverpool wharf. About the only thing Matthew could make out was the repeated use of the word "mate," which Matthew considered in the present circumstances to mean "friend," if he had any. For the Lamplighters might be bandmates, but their association seemed all business and little camaraderie.

Thus this afternoon the Lamplighters were boarding the *Breeze* with their baggage, instruments and their manager, who seemed to be shrinking even smaller in the fierce heat. Along with this bunch, the boat with its crew of six including Guidenmeyer's wife was taking on as passengers the broomcorn businessman Simms Richmond with his wife Joanna and the lawyer Thomas Brodine: all in all, a full bucket.

As everyone stood on the deck while other cargo was being loaded by the wharfmen, Guidenmeyer set about assigning cabins to those who'd paid the premium. Of the four cabins available, the Richmonds got Number One, Brodine Number Two, Foxglove, Dell and Dover in Number Three, and Love and Sodd in Number Four…which left Matthew and Greathouse consigned to the forward hammock spaces shared by the crew, sure to be sweltering though an afternoon and evening voyage in this weather was considerably more agreeable than Captain Faber's six o'clock boat, by now having cooked its passengers into hard-skinned sausages.

"We'll be gettin' underway," Guidenmeyer announced, "soon as we're loaded up and two more late passengers get here, if they's a mind to travel to…well, here they're comin'!"

And so they were. Matthew and Greathouse heard a gasp from Sidney Sodd, and the Lamplighters looked as if they'd swallowed their instruments, because trudging along the dock with their canvas bags in hand were the two killers, Graw and Sprain.

Before the pair could cross the gangplank, Greathouse's bulk blocked the way. "You're not taking this boat today, gents."

The two pulled up short, but did not retreat. The larger Graw was nearly the size of Greathouse and had a forehead like a slab of stone under a Devil's tangle of curly black hair that hung about his shoulders, while the much smaller Sprain was ruddy-faced, whip-thin and in addition to his hawk's-beak nose had what appeared to be a sand-colored animal's furry pelt laid haphazardly across his scalp, though Matthew realized it was simply the man's unkempt hair. Now Graw took a step toward Greathouse and grunted in a rumbling *basso*, "Move aside, we got our tickets!"

"Toss them, they're no good."

"Listen, you big ox!" Sprain had pushed past his companion and stood looking up at Greathouse, though he might sprain his neck in doing so. His voice was so high-pitched it was near *soprano*. "We're sailin' to Philadelphia and there ain't nought you can do about it!"

"Here, here!" Guidenmeyer had come to Greathouse's side. "What's this about? These gentlemen have paid their way!"

"I say they're not going, they can take the next boat in the morning."

"That's ridiculous! They're here and we've got room in the hammocks! They've paid and we're ready to set sail!"

"We're sailing without these two."

"What's gotten into you, Greathouse?" Guidenmeyer frowned. "Has the heat baked your brain? I'll remind you that I'm the master of this ship!"

"They're not aboard yet," Greathouse fired back, "and they're turning tail if they know what's good for them."

"*Yeah?*" Graw rumbled.

"Yeah," said Greathouse.

"*Yeah?*" It was Sprain's turn to get up under Greathouse's chin again.

"What's this problem?" Thomas Brodine had stepped forward. He was a young man, only a few years older than Matthew, and it appeared that in his cream-colored suit, blue stockings and blue-ruffled shirt he was the very picture of cool command. "Gentlemen, I am a lawyer," he said, addressing the two new arrivals. "Do you need my services to make certain you have not wasted your hard-earned money on a false promise of transportation?"

"You stay out of this!" Greathouse barked. He had already remarked to Matthew that he thought New York was being overrun by lawyers shipping over from England. More than four lawyers and a town is ruined, he'd said.

"I know the law, sir," was the retort.

"And I know that these two men are—"

"*Musicians*," interrupted Sprain, with his hands on his hips. "That's what we are, ya big buffoon!"

"That's a damnable lie!" Sodd had nearly shouted it.

"Oh, I swoon from the heat!" the slim and stately Lady Richmond cried out, hanging onto her husband as if a fall to the deck were imminent. "What is all this turmoil, Simms?"

"Musicians, my tail!" Greathouse sneered. "What do you play, the skin flutes?"

"*Sir!*" was Simms Richmond's shout. "You are in the presence of a lady!"

Matthew thought that this was one hell of a voyage and the ship hadn't even thrown its ropes yet.

"To be more exact," Sprain barreled on, "we write songs! Yeah! Don't we, Graw?" He looked to the larger man for affirmation, but Graw just stared dumbly ahead. "We write songs," Sprain continued, "and we've been trackin' this bunch for a while hopin' to…y'know…get 'em *alone* where they might hear one or two of 'em without bein'…y'know…disturbanced."

"Likely story, you lying villains!" Sodd spouted.

"You ain't thinkin' of *killin'* me, mate?" Dover suddenly asked.

"*Killin'* you? Hell, *naw*! Just wantin' to sell you some songs, if you'll have 'em."

"We writes our own songs," said Lawrence Love, who when not bellowing on stage spoke in a voice that sounded muffled by a heavy glove.

"Well…yes," said Sodd, "but…we could always use fresh material." He shook his head as if shaking off the beginnings of a trance. "Heavens, what am I thinking? No, no, a thousand times no! And I concur with Mr. Greathouse that you should not board this vessel!"

"Gentlemen, I charge by the hour and we shall sue everyone involved!" Brodine's cry had the sound of if not legal triumph then the joy of newfound coinage. "An added suit will address the mental and heat-related harm done to Mrs. Richmond, who wilts away as we stand here in argument!"

"Oh for God's sake!" Greathouse looked about to spray a spit on the lawyer's shiny black boots.

"I have a suggestion," said Matthew, who stepped forward not necessarily to assert himself but to catch a sliver of shade from the nearest boom and furled sail. "Captain Guidenmeyer, am I mistaken that you offer your passengers a small meal in the galley before the bedtime bell?"

"I do. It's biscuits and beef jerky prepared by my Gretchen, along with a little taste of rum."

Matthew nodded. "At this nautical feast, while we are all gathered in the galley, perhaps these gentlemen might present a song or two of their own creation to prove both their aptitude and their intentions?" He raised a hand to silence the protests from Greathouse and Sodd before they could be launched. "I will remind all that Greathouse and I shall be sharing space in the crew's quarters with our songwriters, and thus within distance to prevent any wrong notes tonight. Also that if we wish to reach Philadelphia before the first snowfall we do need to resolve our situation."

A silence descended but for the *skreeling* of seagulls overhead as they fluttered around and around the wharf in white flags of eager hunger.

Greathouse aimed himself at the two targets of the moment. "I'll grant that," he said. "And if you don't come up with something I'm throwing you both over the side. How about that?"

"Please!" Sodd said. "Do you think it's wise to allow them—"

"We've got this in hand," Greathouse interrupted. "Your tickets still good, or not?"

After a short but possibly revealing hesitation, Sprain said through gritted teeth, "They're good." And added: "Ya monstrous hunk'a cabbage!"

Greathouse stepped aside. Graw and Sprain came aboard with their bags, and Matthew noted that all the Lamplighters and Sodd retreated before them as if the two men carried the plague…and possibly they did, if the intent to murder might be called such.

"Thank God we can get underway, then!" said the captain, who motioned the group toward the midships hatch. "Come on, bring your bags and I'll show you to your quarters."

On the way to the ladder Greathouse halted, blocking Matthew's path. Matthew thought that his countenance might have frightened Exodus Jerusalem into true religion.

"Moonbeam, I have a bad feeling about this," Greathouse said. "If anything goes wrong tonight, it's on *you*."

And he punctuated that statement with a finger stab to the chest that Matthew was sure would leave a mark.

FOUR

To SAY THAT THE BREEZE HAD COOLED AFTER THE SUN HAD DESCENDED was a falsity, for it had not. There was enough breeze to fill the sails of the *Breeze* and keep the ship moving—if only at a pace a swimmer might have bested—but it was of the temperature of a dog's breath after a two-mile run and carried with it all the humid moisture of a swamp frog's warty flesh.

At eight o'clock the ship's bell summoned all to the lantern-lit galley, where the evening's repast of the promised victuals and toddies of rum had been laid out upon a long table, and thus to be consumed by the sweating pack of humans who inhabited the belly of this beast. Among them, Graw and Sprain put down their food and drink with what Matthew considered the manners of pigs at a trough, but it occurred to him that Greathouse shared the same. The rotund and apple-cheeked Gretchen Guidenmeyer fussed about offering the guests a draught of lemon water from a yellow pitcher to wash down the sturdy rum, though it was as warm as if recently used to wash the dishes. In any event, along came Sodd and the Lamplighters, with Lawrence Love carrying his guitar.

"Ladies and gentlemen," said the small impresario, "before we hear what I'm sure will be a stunning musical exploit by these two bald-faced liars, and before we witness them tossed into the sea, sure to be devoured by whatever sharks, crabs or mollusks will have them, allow me to present a *pleasing* melody for your enjoyment."

"Do we have to bear this?" asked Greathouse, with a bit of beef jerky and biscuit clinging to his lip.

"For the sake of *comparison*, sir. By way of showing what *real* music can be made by *real* musicians."

Greathouse rolled his eyes, took a slug of rum and kept on eating.

"Thus," Sodd went on, "we present a new song written and to be played this evening by Lawrence Love. And I might add to our other travellers that the Four Lamplighters shall be playing at the Sixth Street Lodge tomorrow night at seven o'clock, tickets I'm sure still available."

"Yes, and make sure you get there early to watch the arrests being made," Greathouse said, and he hoisted his cup toward Matthew sitting across the table in a silent toast to the future difficulties of the troupe.

Love took a chair pushed away from the group and began to strum the guitar. In another few seconds Dover took up a rather quiet—for him, it seemed to Matthew—drumbeat with his palms upon the table.

After a proper few chords Love began to sing not in the bawling manner of their previous display but in what was a more stately, restrained and perhaps more heartfelt attitude:

> "Wildflower girl, looking out the window
> Watching the rain come down.
> She's sad today, but will be glad tomorrow
> When the sunshine comes around.
> Wildflower girl, such a lovely lady,
> Watching the rain come down.
> Her sad eyes, will shine tomorrow
> When her lover comes around.
> My wildflower girl,
> My wildflower girl.

She is my world, and I'll be home tomorrow."

When the last note had been played, Sodd was the first to begin the applause, which was seconded by Thomas Brodine, then the Lady Richmond and all around the table, excluding Greathouse whom Matthew noted simply shrugged his shoulders as if glad to be rid of an irritating canker. But Matthew did think that the song, the music and the singing were all really very good, and perhaps there was a future for the Lamplighters if they survived this tour without being murdered or hanged.

"And *now!*" Sodd drew himself up to his meager height and latched his hands to his hips. "Shall we hear a selection from our two hopeful *songwriters?*" And in that last term Matthew thought the man might well have been sneering *shit-shovelers.*

A few seconds remained stilled in time, as the timbers of the *Breeze* creaked and the lanterns threw their accordant shadows.

Graw stood up. "Gimme that gittar," he said, in a voice like that of a gravedigger standing six feet under.

"Nobody touches me guitar!" Love protested in a rare show of true emotion, but Sodd put a comforting hand on the young man's shoulder.

"Go ahead, Lawrence," he urged. "It's for a good cause. Let's expose this mockery for all to see."

Love muttered what might have been a few inaudible profanities, but he gave the instrument over.

Graw strummed the thing a few times. "Poorly outta tune," he rumbled and proceeded to start turning the pegs, much to Love's loudly renewed objections.

"Sorry, Lovey," spoke up the nasal tones of Rollie Dell. "It *is* out of tune."

When Graw was apparently satisfied with the guitar, he began to not only strum but play his fingers over one string after another to make what Matthew considered a highly pleasing music. Then Sprain got up and stood beside him, and the smaller man added his high voice as counterpoint to Graw's *basso:*

"Mister Green, you have a lovely daughter (Lovely daughter),
She is fair as beauty fair can be.
Oh Mister Green, won't you please hear my plea,
Consent her hand to marry me.
Mister Green, you have a lovely daughter (Lovely daughter),
She walks in grace and all know it's true.
Oh Mister Green, please heed my plea this day,
My happiness depends on you.

Mister Green you have a lovely daughter (Lovely daughter)."

There were two more verses, concluding with the happy fact that the father's consent was indeed given. At the last ringing note, Gretchen Guidenmeyer burst out with "Oh, beautiful!" and in her furious clapping and consequent reddening of the face Matthew feared she was going to pass out upon the spot. Also, the captain, Brodine and the Richmonds showed their appreciation, and when Matthew added to the chorus he caught a look from Greathouse that would've withered a rosebed to a tangle of thorns.

"Well!" said Sodd, who himself had reddened in the face. "Well!" he repeated, as if not knowing whether to draw water or not. And then: "My word! That singing...the two voices, low and high...I must say...the only description I can offer is *righteous.*"

"Does that mean ya like it?" asked Sprain, as Love snatched the guitar back from Graw.

"Yes I do! Quite different...and very surprising! You two have performed together?"

"Weekends at the Scum Bucket and the Old Horsehead," Sprain offered. "Two of the best music taverns in London!"

Sodd looked to Matthew as if he might intend on eating a jerky biscuit and start chewing on Brodine's ear, so confused did he appear. "A moment! A moment! My Lord, I am dazed! You mean...you two are actually *musicians?* Well, of course you are, I've heard it myself! And quite good, really quite good! I mean...you have other songs?"

"A trunkful of ditties," said Sprain.

"Lord, I am thrown off my perch! Are you telling me you are not in the employ of Edgar Allerby?"

"Who?" was Sprain's response.

"I thought...you two were killers...after Ben's hide for his escapade with...well, never mind that!" Sodd swung toward Matthew and Greathouse. "Sirs, I don't know what to say! There's been a huge mistake made!"

"Don't blow your trumpet yet!" Greathouse stood up and lumbered over to face Graw. "The Lamplighters advertised their tour in the London *Gazette.* You two had to know they wouldn't be in the colonies very long. So why take the Atlantic voyage? Why not just wait for them to come back?"

"*Because*, ya giant stewpot," said the pugnacious Sprain, who crowded up so close to Greathouse it seemed he was about to deliver either a kiss or a fist. "How were we to know *when* they was comin' back? They might strike it rich over here and stay on for months!"

"Not happening," Greathouse replied.

"Well it could'a! And anyway tryin' to get close to that bunch in London is like tryin' to fight your way through a mob! And when the mob is made up of screamin' women push comes to shove and you're liable to get a hairpin jabbed in your arse cheek!"

"'nother thing," spoke up the mostly silent Graw, whose tone was like a low vibration in the air rather than a true voice. "Too many music men in London! How was we to have a chance at sellin' anythin'?"

"Well said!" chorded Sprain. His glare defied Greathouse. "That satisfy you, ya big toadstool?"

"No," came the answer.

"I have no idea what is happening here," said Brodine, "but someone *must* need a lawyer."

"They're goin' 'round on a whirlypool is what I can tell," was Guidenmeyer's opinion. He shrugged his heavy shoulders. "Well, I'm quit with the day. Enjoyed the music, though. Up top to check with the wheel-man and then Gretchen and me are gone to the bunk." His wife took his offered arm and they went through the swinging batdoors into the passageway beyond with the happiness of a couple doing in life exactly what they pleased to do.

The others began to drift away as well, but Sodd caught Sprain's shoulder, their being almost face-to-face. "A moment before you retire for the evening. How shall I put this? You two are a bit…um…out of the age range of the performers I normally manage, but…I see great potential in the both of you."

"Are you *insane?*" Greathouse asked, as Matthew just stood aside, content to watch the ongoing rotation of this particular whirlypool. "You don't know these men! And I thought you said your contact in London identified them as killers!"

"We never killed a body in our lives!" Sprain squalled. "Whoever said that is whistlin' up your rear!"

"Yes. Um…well…I think I received the wrong message," said Sodd to Greathouse. He looked past the man at his charges. "Boys, go ahead to your cabins. I'll be along shortly to—"

"Tuck them in?" Greathouse asked.

"See that all is in order for the night. Go ahead, I'll be only a few more minutes."

Before the group left the galley, Foxglove paused to ask, "Any chance we might gets some more rum? Y'know, to wash ever'thing down good and proper."

"I'll confer with the captain." When the foursome had gone, Sodd said quietly, "Heaven knows I try to keep them away from overindulging in liquor. They have an unfortunate tendency to throw furniture out of windows when they are in their cups...and they don't open the shutters first, either."

"I pity your lot in life," Greathouse said. "Now...as I was objecting to what you're about to propose—"

"Listen, ya overgrown meatloaf," Sprain interrupted. "Nobody wants to hear your objections! You ain't got a dog in this run!"

"Exactly so." Sodd gave a curt little nod. "So...might you consider my...um...help in advancing your musical careers?"

Matthew thought it was time for his two pence. "Before an answer is given, may I suggest everyone sleeping on this tonight? And in the morning we could hear another of this pair's musical gems? Just in case, I mean."

"In case of *what?*" Sprain snarled.

"In case of caution. That's what I'm suggesting. Mr. Sodd, you do recall that someone took a shot at you and the Lamplighters from an alley."

"I don't see the need for that, considering the mistake I've made," said Sodd, "but...yes...it does appear that *someone* has a grievance against us, so—"

"A music critic, I'd guess," Greathouse said, with an added *whuff* of disdain.

"So...all right, then. We shall revisit the situation in the morning. Does that suit you fellows?"

Graw gave a shrug, and Sprain said, "I suppose. Mornin' it is."

"We'll be watching you two all night," Greathouse added. "Since our hammocks are nearly one on top of another."

"As you please, Sir Puffball." Sprain gave a mocking little bow, and from the look on Greathouse's face Matthew thought violence was very near. "Come on, Graw," said the offender. "Let's go up and get some air, it reeks down here."

On their way to the crew's quarters where the hammocks were spaced closely together, Greathouse said to Matthew, "Something smells fishy to me."

"We *are* at sea."

"Drop your pearls at your peril," Greathouse warned. A few paces further he stopped in the passageway where a single lantern on its wall hook parted the shadows. "Here." He gave Matthew his pocket watch. "When that pair comes in to take their hammocks, I want you to stand first watch. Or rather, *sit* first watch. I want you in the passageway just outside the crew's quarters, sitting on the floor. Wake me at two o'clock and I'll spell you. And *don't* go to sleep. Hear me?"

"I hear."

Of the eight hammocks hanging in the low-ceilinged and quite stifling forward crew compartment, three were already occupied and one of the occupants was snoring like an off-key hornpipe. Both Matthew and Greathouse climbed into their netted roosts of the evening, and perhaps ten minutes later Graw and Sprain entered the chamber and they too got into their hammocks. A single lantern burned on the wall next to the passageway's opening. Matthew gave the situation a further fifteen minutes and then he quietly got up with the pocket watch in his hand, went out into the passage and sat down on the timbered floor.

Within the hour he realized the heavy heat and the motion of the *Breeze* upon the waves was lulling him to sleep. This was going to be a tougher task than he'd expected. Above him the subtle swaying of the passageway's lantern on its wall hook was an invitation to be entranced and fall into slumber. He kept having to shake the sleep off before it ate him. His attempt at clearing his mind of these encroaching cobwebs was to concentrate on solving several difficult chess problems, visualizing them on a mental board and with pieces that came to life and marched, slinked and slithered around depending on the personalities he assigned them.

Around midnight he was startled by two men coming out of the crew's compartment, but they were two crewmen and they gave him puzzled glances as they passed him on their way to duty. In a few minutes the pair of men they were replacing appeared, coming along the passage and going into the compartment, and then all was still and quiet once more... except for the slight up-and-down and side-to-side motion of the ship, the mewling of the timbers, the sliding of the shadows across Matthew's field of vision as the lantern swayed upon its hook...and the heat...the heat...a stifling heaviness upon every inch of his flesh, the sweat having already bloomed out and dampened his clothes, blooming out again, wetting him further, the heat...the heat...caught in his lungs...almost a further labor to breathe...the heat...

A harsh cough startled him. His body jerked and his eyes opened. For an instant his grogginess denied him recognition of where he was, but then he came to his senses and checked the pocket watch.

Twenty minutes before one. The cough had come from the crew's compartment. Suddenly there came a cough that seemed to answer it. Was this one higher in tenor, nearly a soprano, whereas the first had been basso? A signal, perhaps?

Then...the sound of soft snoring, and nothing more.

Matthew felt a thrust of anger...at himself, for falling asleep, and for this fool's errand. If Graw and Sprain were really killers, why would they kill Dover on the boat? If they did, where would they escape to? The kingdom of the fishes? No, his sitting here "on watch" was ridiculous!

Still...

He decided he'd best get up and check the hammocks, in case anyone had gotten past him while he'd been laid low by Somnus. By the lantern light within, he made out that Graw and Sprain remained in their hammocks, but Graw barely so, both his legs splayed out over the sides.

Matthew returned to his sitting position. There was nothing to do now but try to resist sleep and watch the minutes grind ever so slowly down on the pocket watch.

Promptly at two, which seemed four hours since he'd fallen asleep, Matthew stood up, went to Greathouse's hammock and—careful, careful, the beast might come out of sleep swinging a fist at some ancient or imaginary enemy—tugged at a sleeve, ever so cautiously.

"I'm awake," the man said at once, in a quiet and clear-headed voice. He sat up and swung his legs over. "Any trouble?"

"None."

"The watch." Matthew gave it to him. "Go to sleep," Greathouse directed, and then he went to take his own sitting position in the passageway.

Matthew climbed into his own hammock. He was asleep in the proverbial two shakes of a pig's tail.

And was thrown out of his hammock what seemed like thirty seconds afterward.

Dumped on the floor, he was, as the hammock had overturned. He heard a horrific grating, crunching sound from forward and underneath the ship. Figures rushed past him. Every timber of the *Breeze* seemed to be screaming, a hideous cacophony, and Matthew sat stunned as the world appeared at that moment to be shrieking to its end.

Then...voices from above...a man yelling out...the ship's bell a frantic *ding-dong ding-donging*...the ship still groaning in agony...and it took a few seconds for Matthew to make out what was being yelled...

"Aground! We've run aground!"

And then a closer voice began shouting from one of the cabins along the passageway, and this was the voice that got Matthew up on his feet and moving.

That voice cried: *"Murder! Help! Murder!"*

FIVE

MATTHEW RUSHED INTO THE PASSAGEWAY. THERE WAS NO SIGN OF Hudson Greathouse, but further along the passage there was a knot of people and an obvious commotion going on. Matthew strode toward them, saw they were all in various manner of nightrobes and dressings, and it seemed all their voices were entangled in one dismayed and panicked language that could not at first be deciphered by an educated ear.

Then from the group burst forth Sidney Sodd in a yellow nightshirt and cap the same hue, his face florid and sparkling with sweat, his expression one of sheer terror.

"Corbett!" he said, nearly hollering it. "Graw took the boy!"

"What?"

Adrian Foxglove pushed forward past the manager...or at least it appeared to be Foxglove under the green beauty cream plastered on his face. "Took Ben at gunpoint!" he squalled. "Broke in the cabin, said anyone who moved or called out was gonna get a bullet!"

"Took the boy!" Sodd shouted, wringing his hands. "I told Greathouse! Oh my Lord, murder's to be done!"

The next instant a familiar large figure shoved its way through the human mass of misery and grasped Matthew by the arm, pushing him back toward the crew's compartment as easily as a moving storm pushes a cornstalk.

"What happened?" Matthew asked, knowing it was dumb but there it was all the same. "Graw took Dover?"

"We have to move fast," was Greathouse's reply. He let Matthew go, hurried into the compartment and returned with his canvas travelling bag, which he set on the floor and unlaced. As Sodd continued his dance and wail of despair and the others seemed to have turned into human whirly-tops, Greathouse removed two pistols from the bag. He offered one to Matthew. "It's loaded and primed," he said. "Don't shoot yourself or me."

Matthew took it. His training in gunplay had been secondary to the work at swordsmanship, but he'd gotten to the point of hitting a target two times out of ten.

"Come on!" Greathouse urged, and he used his big shoulders to bull their way through the passage, which was now further enflamed by Brodine hollering he would sue everyone involved with "this travesty of a voyage," the Lady Richmond trying to console her husband who seemed to be going into hysterics, Captain Guidenmeyer futilely trying to calm the harrowing moment and the remaining Lamplighters looking dim and sick.

On deck, Matthew saw that the first hint of sunrise was the beginning of a fierce red line directly ahead, and the *Breeze* had nosed into what appeared to be a boundless marsh with thicket and reeds as tall as a man's head. He judged that the ship had run aground on the eastern side of the Delaware Bay, a veritable no-man's land still deep blue with the departure of night.

"Over here!" Greathouse commanded. A rope ladder over the side led down into soupy brown water. "Mind that pistol when you climb down!"

Matthew sloshed into a waist-deep morass, the mud grasping his boots like iron pincers. He followed Greathouse into the shallows at the bow, where the water receded but the mud only became more jealous of a boot's freedom. "What happened?" Matthew repeated to Greathouse's back.

"Graw took Dover while Sprain went up on deck on the pretense of smoking his pipe. He hit the wheelman in the back of the head with something and before the forward watch knew what was what Sprain steered the ship right into the mud. Damn, this is hard on the legs! But it's the same for them, too! Look there, the mud's got their tracks and they're tearing down the reeds as they go! They shouldn't be too far ahead, so keep that pistol ready!"

Walking was a struggle, but Matthew saw that the mud chose no friends for the imprints of six boots—or rather four boots and two bare feet—could be made out in the blue gloom and were still slowly filling up with water.

"Forward watch said the boy tried to fight them on the deck," Greathouse continued. "So they just tossed him over before they lowered the ladder for themselves. How do you like your music-lovers now?"

Matthew ignored that but had to ask his own question: "How did they get past you?"

It was a moment and a few slogs forward before an answer arrived. "I was just resting my eyes for a minute. It was the heat. Or maybe the rum. Maybe those bastards put something in my cup. You know…to make me groggy." And then, after a few more slogs. "No. I went to sleep. That's all."

Matthew nodded but there was no use in pursuing that track. What was done was done and now had to be undone. He figured Graw and Sprain must've seen the map of Captain Guidenmeyer's route to Philadelphia, which was hanging on the wall in the captain's wharfside office, and planned to get into action as soon as the *Breeze* turned off the Atlantic and started to round the cape. At that point the ship would've been only a mile or so off the marsh, and time for Sprain to take control of the wheel and Graw to break into Dover's cabin. Probably one of them had his own pocket watch and they'd figured out when the ship would be within range of the nearest mudbank. So not only were they passable musicians, but their skills at planning this feat were admirable and their intelligence had certainly been underestimated.

The head-high rushes prevented any long views, though the path these villains were plowing was clear enough. The morning army of frogs had begun to awaken in the wet heat and early crimson light and chirped, burped, thumped and croaked on all sides. Matthew's mud-freighted boots continued to sink to the ankles, and onward the two struggled.

"Give it up!" Greathouse shouted. "We're right behind you! You kill the boy and you're both dead as well! Hear me?"

"Help!" It was Dover's shout from not far ahead and just to the left. *"Please! Help—"* He was interrupted likely by a fist or a hand clasped across the mouth.

"You're both damned fools!" Greathouse tried again. "Where do you think you're going in this swamp? There's nothing out here!"

The hot line of sunrise promised a day of further torment. And now in addition to the frogs arose the flights of biting bugs that the frogs had awakened to eat, yet the insects were more interested in flying into Matthew's and Greathouse's faces, eyes and hair. All in all, not a very satisfactory way to get to Philadelphia.

And not further on…the trio was revealed in the growing light.

Dover must've been knocked down when he'd called for help, for Graw and Sprain were both trying to get him up from the ooze that had seemingly glued him to the earth. One look at the on-slogging duo of Matthew and Greathouse—and the readied pistols in their hands—and Sprain threw up his arms in surrender.

Greathouse's pistol took aim at Graw's slope of a forehead.

"Peace!" Graw cried out. "Peace, for God's sake!"

"Drop the gun or I drop you," was the calm and rather chilling response.

"It ain't loaded! Swear to the Lord it ain't!" Graw lifted his pistol high, which nearly caused Greathouse's trigger finger to add that last fateful iota of pressure. "Peace, I beg you!"

"Don't shoot him, Hudson!" Matthew said, and then to Graw: "Pull the trigger and let fly."

The pistol clicked on empty.

Dover—a wet mud puppy to the tip of his enormous beak—struggled up, fell again and began to crawl laboriously toward his saviors.

"Drop the gun!" Greathouse commanded, and down it plopped. "What were you two idiots planning? To kill him out here? And then where were you going?"

"Kill him?" Sprain's voice had climbed to its highest octave. *"Kill him?* We wasn't gonna *kill* the lad! We're just supposed to bring him back, that's all!"

"Bring him back to where and who?" Matthew asked.

"To London, sir. And to Alice Allerby."

Now Greathouse's gun drooped. *"What?"*

"We ain't killers, sir. We're bounty men! Paid by Mr. Edgar Allerby to bring the lad back to his wife!"

Matthew and Greathouse looked at each other. Dover was still struggling to rise from the muck of his own making.

"Damned if I can make any sense out of this!" said Greathouse. "All right, you can explain yourselves back at the ship! Let's go!"

The five men who returned to the *Breeze* as the sun began to blast its rays across the marsh might have been muddied scarecrows, and to add to the insult of slimy earth the mosquitoes had swarmed in for breakfast. The group went up the ladder as Captain Guidenmeyer and his wife both threw curses at the villains, Gretchen's being the most salty. "Mud all over our clean deck!" Gretchen raged. "You rascally tatterdemalions!"

"Thank God you're alive!" Sodd cried out, embracing the boy, while the other Lamplighters hung back and Love delivered a "You're a muddy mess, ain't ya?" which Matthew guessed served as a *welcome back alive.*

In the galley along with the other passengers and the crew, Graw and Sprain stood dripping mud, their heads bowed as if already standing in the docket.

"Now what the hell is this all about?" Greathouse demanded. "Speak up before we throw you over the side and you can walk to Philadelphia!"

"Just as I said!" Sodd sounded near gnashing his teeth. "They're killers! Tried to shoot Ben from an alley, they did!"

"Naw," said Graw. "That was when I stepped on a cat in the dark and when it squalled I jumped a foot. Me gun went off by accident. I wasn't meanin' to shoot nobody."

"Well if that's true why were you carrying a loaded gun?" Matthew asked.

Graw shrugged. "We was hearin' there was ruffians in that area."

"But you *were* following us, weren't you? And meaning to kill Ben?" Sodd asked.

"What's all this talk of *killin'?*" Sprain offered a frown. "Like we told this big pile a' mustard, we're bounty men. Paid by Mr. Edgar Allerby to return the boy to his wife."

"Heavens, this is more exciting than the horse races!" exclaimed the Lady Richmond.

"Return the boy to Alice Allerby?" Sodd looked as if he'd been punched between the eyes. "What insanity is this?"

"The payin' kind," said Sprain. "It's true, we are musicians. But we're bounty men too, and Mr. Edgar Allerby hired us to bring the boy back to London and to his wife."

"All right, we got that!" Greathouse snapped. "Now why the hell should a man want his wife's lover returned to his *wife?*"

"'Cause," Graw said, "Mr. Edgar Allerby's crazy in love with her, and she ain't been hardly eatin' or smilin' or doin' any damned thing since the boy hopped the ship to come over here. Says the house is dark as a tomb even at midday, and one thing he loves about her—or used to love—is her light and her laughter."

"She does laugh a lot, mate," said Dover.

"You shut your hole!" Greathouse was obviously looking for someone to strike, because it was beginning to appear that something in this situation had gone crazily askew. He returned his attention to Sprain. "You're saying Allerby actually wants the boy to be...I mean...to—"

"Yep, that's what I'm sayin'. Now that's some kind of love, ain't it? That a man loves his wife—and I have to say, she's quite a young looker—so much he wants her back to herself again, and to get her back to herself she needs the 'tentions of that fella there. So the deal as we understands it is that they're gonna work out a kind of sharin' situation, if Dover goes for it. And we was hired to bring him back like immediate-like, to make sure he goes for it."

"Zounds!" said Richmond. "I thought this kind of thing only happened in the worst of novels!"

"Sounds very interesting to me," was his wife's reply.

"Do you go for it?" Sprain asked the big-nosed lothario, whose muddied condition might have affected his appeal to the fairer sex. Or not.

Dover shrugged. "Well...I mean...I ain't a one-woman gent."

"That's been made clear to the lady Alice," Sprain continued. "Hell, she ain't askin' to hitch up with you for *life!* Just maybe on Mondays and Fridays. I don't know, it's to be worked out. All I know for sure is, Mr. Edgar Allerby's sick with sorrow over his wife's sorrow, and the only thing that'll bring the sun back into their lives is *you.*"

Dover seemed to be thinking it over. "Mondays and Fridays, huh? Hm. That could work."

"So you couldn't wait for the Lamplighters to return to London?" Matthew prodded.

"Mr. Edgar Allerby couldn't wait," said Sprain. "We consultuated a map of the cape. There's a little settlement a couple of miles in. Figured we could either buy a horse and wagon there or steal one if it came to that. Then we was to hightail it to New York and get this boy back where he belongs, if we had to tie him up and put him in a trunk to do it."

"I'll be damned." Greathouse's voice was quiet, all the thirst for violence drained.

"I'm still suing someone," Brodine announced. "My neck was pitifully wrenched when I fell from my bunk."

"And we're still stuck in the mud!" the captain lamented. "It's gonna take every one of us out there pushin'! With God's mercy if we fly a distress flag we might get a tow from some other passin' vessel!"

Sodd said, "I am completely knocked to my knees. I thought...well, I can't think! My mind's all raggedy. But at least we can finish our tour without worry!"

"What's to be done with these two?" Greathouse asked. "Put them behind bars?"

Sodd pondered it. He tapped a finger against his chin and looked from Sprain to Graw and back again. "No," he said after a moment. "No...I have an idea. You two...do you really have more songs?"

"Right as rain we do," said Graw. "Good ones, too."

Sodd turned toward the Lamplighters. "Young men, would you have a problem with these two musicians joining our tour? *Not* to be paid from your pockets, but from mine. They're a bit older than I usually manage, but they have a certain appeal and you must admit their voices are quite admirable. I would call them unique. They would be...say...an *opening* act. Yes! The combination of the older with the young! The young teaching the older new tricks, and the old solidifying their place in the halls of music! If they're working *with* us, we will know where they are every minute!" He paused, again in the thrall of this storm of the brain. "*And*," he said, his eyebrows jumping, "when Ben is delivered to the Allerbys, it could be maintained that a speedy delivery could not be undertaken, due to my hiring a pair of ferocious and deadly bodyguards who watched over us night and day! It comes together, you see? Plus our new members will likely find they enjoy being on a *real* stage before an appreciative audience instead of in one of their dubious taverns. And we won't be but a few more weeks here, I think!"

"Dream on," said Greathouse.

"I can see the broadsheet now!" Sodd salivated further. "The Four Lamplighters and...the Bounty Men! How about that?"

There were collective shrugs all around. From Dover there came, "I suppose we can let bygones be bygones, mate. No harm done but a scare and a sore jaw. And anyways...it's a relief to know I ain't gonna be killed... and I have to say, I'll be lookin' right forward to them Mondays and Fridays. Plus every other night of the week I can manage with all the pretty dollies." And here he gave a wink toward Matthew and Greathouse, whose hand once again came up unconsciously to judge the length of his own possession.

"The Bounty Men!" said Sodd to his new musical discovery. "Does that suit you?"

"I don't know," Graw answered. "I kinda think...if we're gonna be professional-like...we should go by our real names. Gordon and Peter."

"Belay it!" said Sprain. "*Peter* and Gordon!"

"See what happens when you give peace a chance?" Matthew asked Greathouse, with a subtle smile. "All works out in the end."

Greathouse gave Matthew a sidelong glare.

"Imagine that," he said.

NIGHT RIDE

OCTOBER, 1702

ONE

⌒⋅⋅⋅⋅⋅⋅⋅◇⋅⋅⋅⋅⋅⋅⋅⌒

MATTHEW CORBETT NOTED THREE THINGS OF PARTICULAR INTEREST in his late-night visitor.

First…the gentleman wore a beautifully tailored gray suit with a ruffled shirt and a dark blue cravat. Matthew had taken notice of such attirements since himself being such a local celebrity after the affair of the Queen of Bedlam during the summer—and the *Earwig* proclaiming him to be so worthy—he had invested in some fine suits tailored of course by his friend Effrem Owles.

Second…the gentleman's fingernails on the long thin hands were sharpened into small knives and curved downward ever so slightly though very carefully manicured. Matthew figured the better to get a grip on whatever he wished to tear with those talons.

And thirdly…the gentleman had brought a strange odor with him into Matthew's dairy-house home. It was up under the man's lemon-scented cologne—a fragrance used quite liberally in an effort to disguise the other—but there it lingered, all the same. *Festered* might be a better word, Matthew thought, because there was something of decay in it. What did it remind him of? He couldn't remember at the moment. His mind was still drowsy since he'd been on the verge of blowing out his candle-clock at just after eleven and drifting into a sleep that was hopefully not haunted by the recurrent mental image of Professor Fell's blood card he'd so recently received.

"I appreciate your giving me the time, young sir," said the gentleman, holding his dark blue tricorn down at his side. "I also regret disturbing you at this hour, but my problem requires immediate attention."

Matthew simply nodded. The gentleman also had a strange accent. Prussian, perhaps? Oh, that was all he needed, to become involved with the escapades of another Prussian! Three candles burned in their holders and a lantern hung from a wall hook. The illumination was sufficient to see that the gentleman had a sharp-nosed bony face under the pallid makeup and cheek rouge he had chosen to apply, and that he had thin streaks of dark eyebrows below his white wig. Below the brows, the eyes were nearly as pale as the makeup, but perhaps were a peculiar shade of gray.

"If I may ask," Matthew ventured, "the hour being so late, can this not be discussed at my office tomorrow?" He liked saying that: *my office*. "It's at Number Seven—"

"I know the location. The clerk at the Dock House Inn informed me when I asked if there was a person here to solve my problem. I explained the situation. He sent me here."

Not exactly, Matthew thought with a slight twist of the mouth. The clerk had sent this gentleman to Marmaduke Grigsby's house. A knock at Matthew's door had roused him and lo and behold there stood in his doorway Berry Grigsby holding a lantern, dressed in her own nighttime flannels—as this October of 1702 had arrived with an early chill—and the lemon-scented, saber-nailed gentleman standing at her side. "You have a visitor," Berry had said, and she'd made a quick face that asked in confidence, *Who is he?*

Too late, Matthew wished he'd at least picked up a shoe from his bedside to whack at one of Professor Fell's minions come to splash blood on the blood card, but again his mind was drowsy from the book he'd been reading on *One Hundred and One Chess Openings*.

"I'll leave you," Berry had said, and of course she knew nothing about the card and Matthew wanted it to stay that way. "Goodnight, Matthew."

"Goodnight," he'd replied, and then the gentleman had slipped in like a shadow, removed his tricorn and stood there waiting until Matthew had decided he couldn't leave his door open all night.

Time to go to work, and display to Sir High-And-Mighty Hudson Greathouse that Katherine Herrald—who if the wind had been providential was now comfortably in England—had not been mistaken in granting him the position of "problem-solver."

"How may I help you?" he asked.

"I must get a message to my brother. It is *vital*."

"All right. That's easily—"

"Not easily," the man interrupted. "Pardon me for not introducing myself. I am Karlis von Eissen. And you are Matthew Corbett, whom I have been reading about in the news sheet. Such as it is," he added, with his own little twist of the mouth. "My brother does not live here. He lives...I will have to show you the map." As von Eissen brought a folded paper from within his coat, Matthew picked up the nearest candle and held it closer.

"You see?" The paper was unfolded and a manicured saber pointed to the neatly drawn image. "This road, what you call the Boston Post. And here, this many miles north along the Post, is another road that takes one to the river. It is a house here where my brother lives."

"Two days ride, at least," Matthew figured. "But why can't you take the message to your brother yourself?"

"My profession does not currently allow travel."

"Hm. What exactly *is* your profession?"

"The shipping of crates," said von Eissen.

"Crates holding what?" Matthew had to ask.

And the answer, given curtly: "More crates."

There was a moment that Matthew nearly thought he had what that aroma—that *smell*—reminded him of, but then it slipped away.

"The message must be delivered as soon as possible," von Eissen continued. He refolded the map into careful squares. "*Vital*," he repeated. "I will pay any amount you request."

Oh ho! Matthew thought. One of his first "cases," if it might be called that! And not only a way to show Greathouse he was up to the job, but a money-maker as well. Did he dare? He did.

"Ten pounds," he said.

"Agreed," spoken with not a hint of hesitation. "I have my purse here." And again he delved into his coat, returning with a black leather purse and an envelope securely sealed with yellow wax. He held the envelope out to the problem-solver, who still wore his beige flannel sleeping gown. Matthew took the envelope and watched as von Eissen unbuttoned the purse and began counting out the coins in a foreign tongue...but not Prussian, Matthew thought...something else. The coins—a sudden wealth—glinted merrily on a table in the candlelight.

"Now," said von Eissen when the money lay out all asparkle, "there are some things you will consider." His tone was different...a bit haughty...the master speaking now to the servant. "You are correct in that it is a journey of two nights, if you keep a sufficiently brisk pace. Which I expect you shall. The first night you will stop at a tavern operated by Joel Beckett and his wife. There will be no other choice, and it is a mile or so from the road that leads to my brother's house." Von Eissen suddenly turned away from Matthew and walked the step and a half to the dairy house's new window, where he unlocked the shutters and cracked them open to peer out into the night. Over the man's shoulder, Matthew could see a silver three-quarters moon in the sky shining like another coin. He would be glad for its light out there in the forest, for the way to von Eissen's brother's house was going to be through some pretty trackless country.

"I regret asking—*requiring*—you to go at this time," said von Eissen as he closed the shutters and bolted them again. "But, alas, the message is—"

"Vital," Matthew finished for him. "What do you mean, 'this time'?"

"Of the month."

"What's the difference? One day is as—"

"I require you to deliver the envelope to my brother at night," came the quietly spoken statement, yet delivered with a compelling authority. "No one else should touch it. Do not tell the Becketts. Tell no one. Only give to my brother. At night. Do you understand that, young sir?"

"I understand the part about giving it only to your brother, if it's so important. But why specifically at night?"

"He has a condition that causes him severe pain in sunlight. *Any* day-light, as a matter of truth. He only goes about at night."

"Do you share this condition? That's why you couldn't see me at my office tomorrow morning?"

Von Eissen didn't reply for a moment. Then he gave a small slight smile that made his mouth for a few seconds look like a razor wound.

"Yes, I do. It is a family condition."

"I'm sorry."

"And why should you be? You didn't cause it. Let me continue. You will leave the Becketts and turn your horse upon the road as it is marked on the map. It will be, by my reckoning, another full day to reach my brother's house. After you give him the envelope, you will accept his hos-pitality, spend the night there and begin your return trip the following morning. Is that clear?"

"Perfectly, thank you."

"Ah. Good. Well…you should make sure you carry a pistol. Two would be better. And prepare them for firing."

Matthew had been staring at the coins on the table. Now he tore his gaze away from the beauties. *"What?"*

"You did hear me."

"The Indians are a danger up there?"

"Indians…bandits…beasts of the forest. Two pistols. Three, better yet."

Matthew swallowed hard and hoped von Eissen didn't hear it. "I think…this may best be a task for my associate, Hudson Greathouse." *Or a militia*, he thought. He hated to say it, but he had to: "I'm not sure I can handle this for you. I mean to say, I don't have as much experience as—"

"Oh, you're joking! Pulling my leggings now, aren't you? After all I've read about you in the news sheet, and what I've heard about you? I wouldn't believe any associate of yours could do the job half as well as you shall!"

"Maybe I should ask Hudson Greathouse to go with—" He stopped himself.

No.

Don't even think that.

It would be like asking Hudson Greathouse to refer to him as a "moon-beam" for time and all eternity. And, in truth, wouldn't he *deserve* the title?

Before she'd left for England, Katherine Herrald had expressed so much confidence in him. Confidence that he could successfully undertake any situation presented to him. Wasn't this a testing of that confidence? And as much for himself as for anyone else?

He had survived an attack by a bear and the ordeal associated with the Queen of Bedlam. Indians and bandits could be dealt with, and if he retreated from this he would be a failure certainly in the eyes of Hudson Greathouse. And particularly in his own eyes.

"Very well," he said, steadying himself. "I'll take two pistols." Which he might rent from someone, using a portion of the coins laid before him.

"Excellent. You will leave by eight in the morning. If you make haste you will arrive at the Becketts soon after nightfall."

"I'll leave at seven," Matthew said. "If I can get sufficient sleep, that is."

"Oh! Of course! You must get your sleep." Von Eissen scanned the interior. "A charming home," he said. "I myself like the smaller spaces." His gaze came back to Matthew and fixed there. "No one but my brother is to take possession of the envelope. No one is to know you are carrying a message. You are to place it into his hand. At night. Do you understand? At night."

"Many times repeated," said Matthew. "First time understood. Thank you for your confidence and your business, and now goodnight."

With the envelope and the map lying on the table alongside the money, von Eissen clicked his heels together, gave a little bow, replaced his tricorn atop his wig and took his leave.

Matthew blew out the candles. He would pack a small travelling bag in the morning and go in search of two pistols he could borrow or rent. Tobias Winekoop at the stable might be able to help...and as a last resort Matthew thought he could approach Gardner Lillehorne and pay him for a pair of pistols from the town's arsenal. But then again he would have to explain why he needed the weapons, so that was only if push came to kick. There was no need to inform Hudson of his impending journey; the money placed into the coffers at Number Seven Stone Street would tell its own tale.

He was about to extinguish the lantern when he realized what the man's smell reminded him of.

Ashton McCaggers' attic of horrors.

Full of dried bones and old odors of tombs.

An aroma of death, if one got down to the essence of it.

Matthew considered that for a moment. Then he left the lantern lit, went to bed and after playing two games of chess in his mind at last he fell asleep.

TWO

NIGHT HAD FALLEN AND THE CHILL THAT CAME WITH IT MADE Matthew glad he'd decided to wear a heavier gray fearnaught coat, a flannel scarf and a gray woolen cap. He was prodding his horse, Suvie, to a canter but the mount had kept up a steady pace during the long day and so he wished not to pressure her too very much…yet the Becketts' tavern must be close at hand, and with it a meal and rest for both of them.

The Boston Post Road was a lonely track this far out from town. He had passed several small settlements, had paused in one of them to water Suvie and wet his own whistle from his leather canteen, then back upon the road once more. He had seen a lumber wagon heading for New York, had seen a coach fly past going south, had been passed by one on its flight north, had seen a couple more riders going to town but otherwise the road belonged to him.

The forest on both sides looked as if God had decided to throw down every huge crooked tree, ugly maze of thornbrush, dangling cascade of vines and wall of impenetrable thicket fashioned from the Book of Creation. It was a forbidding sight, and that was during the day. At night it was just black upon black, a cavern world. The stars were out and the three-quarter moon did shed a little illumination but it was a distant candle in a huge ebony cathedral. At least he was entertained by the hooting of owls along the way, and he saw no Indians, bandits or wild beasts so all to the good.

Matthew caught a whiff of smoke. Suvie rounded a bend and—ah yes!—there stood a small house on the right with yellow candlelight at the windows and smoke rising from two stone chimneys. Behind the house was a barn and a corral and beyond that the utter darkness of more forest. Matthew wasted no time in securing Suvie to a hitching post at the front door. He took his canvas travelling bag—with the two pistols and their necessary implements inside—from where it hung down beside the saddle. Then he knocked at the door, as even if it was a public tavern he found it better manners not to barge in and possibly frighten anyone.

His knock was answered by a gray-bearded and gray-haired gent dressed in brown trousers and a cream-colored shirt and smoking a long-stemmed clay pipe.

"Mr. Beckett?" Matthew inquired. He figured the man to be in his late fifties.

"The same. Come in, come in! Ella, we have a guest!"

Matthew thanked his host and walked straight across the well-kept room to the fireplace to catch some warmth. Ella Beckett, also gray-haired and about the same age as her husband, came in from the back, welcomed Matthew with a friendly smile and bright blue eyes and took his fearnaught to hang on a wall hook.

"Travelling north or south?" Joel Beckett asked.

"North."

"Ah, then. Yes, get yourself warm. Chilly for so early in the season, but we had a light snow this time last year so you never can tell." He looked out a front window at Suvie. "Take care of your horse for you. Thought we'd have coach passengers stopping with us by now, didn't we, Ella? But again you never can tell. Likely broken down somewhere, as they do. Going so fast they throw their wheels. What will you drink? A cup of mulled wine?"

"That would be very excellent."

"I'll fetch it," said Ella. "I have chicken in the pot, boiled turnips and cornbread. Does that suit?"

"Perfectly, thank you."

Matthew found himself in the delightful and comfortable presence of two people who seemed to thoroughly enjoy being of service to travellers. He told them his name and that he was from New York town, that he was heading north…and that was all. The envelope and map were buttoned in an inner pocket of his suit jacket, where he meant for them to stay until needed.

At dinner, as a small polite fire crackled in the kitchen's fireplace, Matthew took further delight in a meal that easily ranked with the best of Sally Almond's cooking. During the meal—which really was a feast, with the amount of food supplied—there came a knock at the door and Joel excused himself. Matthew expected it to be coach passengers, and was surprised when Joel returned to the kitchen in the company of two Indian braves wrapped up in blankets. They both eyed Matthew quickly, making some judgment about him, and then Matthew watched as Ella wrapped a large wheel of cornbread in a piece of cloth and gave it to one of the braves, who nodded his approval. They left without a word, and Joel returned to the table.

"Our Indian friends," Joel explained. "Their village is some distance away, to the south. But they travel far to get some of Ella's cornbread, and we're happy to oblige them."

"It's a compliment," Ella supplied. "Sometimes they bring us venison, and they make a kind of beer that Joel likes but when I tried it I thought I had tasted fire." She shrugged. "It's nice to know they accept us as friendly."

Indians…bandits…beasts of the forest, Matthew thought. Well, at least the Indians were not a concern.

"You spoke my name," said Joel as he lit his pipe from a candleflame.

"Pardon?"

"At the door. You spoke my name. Who told you about our tavern?"

"Um…another traveller who evidently stayed with you."

"Oh? And what is *his* name? Ella and I both have good memories."

Matthew hated to concoct lies, but where to go from here? "I didn't catch the name. It was in a tavern in town." Amazing how easily a lie slipped out, even though one detested it.

"Are you a pipe smoker? I have several extras I offer to guests."

"No sir, but thank you all the same."

Joel smoked for a moment in silence and Ella offered Matthew another helping of everything, which he gladly accepted.

"So you're heading north?" Joel asked. "Where to?"

Boston, he thought he should say, but that seemed a lie too far. Besides, what matter if these two people knew his destination? But of course *not* about the envelope…never that.

"Actually," said Matthew after he'd taken another drink of the equally excellent mulled wine, "I'm visiting someone. I understand it's another day's ride. I believe the road is a mile or so ahead, on the right?"

Joel had been steadily puffing his pipe. Now he ceased the puffing and took it slowly from his mouth. "Matthew…if I may…*who* are you going to visit?"

I have been sworn to secrecy, Matthew thought he ought to say. But then again…what matter that these people should know? The name wasn't going to hurt anything.

"A gentleman named von Eissen," he replied.

Joel glanced quickly at Ella and then returned his attention to the young man from New York town. "If you're talking about the road that takes you to the river cliffs, and I believe you are…no one named von Eissen lives there. Do you mean the Vyden house?"

"No, I…well, I mean…I was told a von Eissen lives at the end of the road."

"Who told you that?"

Matthew felt himself sinking into a swamp. To tell, or not? "His brother," he decided to say, just to try to clear up this clouded glass.

"Vyden had no brother. In fact, he died many years ago. When Ella and I had our farm along that road."

"Who," said Matthew, "is—*was*—Vyden?"

"Nicholas Vyden," Ella said, her expression gone to stone, "was an insane Dutchman who made his money in the shipping business in Holland, or that's what we heard. He built that house—that great scab upon the earth—and then went about trying to control the shipping on the river below."

"Control it? How?"

"By building a huge barrier out of logs," said Joel. "A thing that worked on chains and pulleys, meant to be raised to block boats if a toll payment wasn't arranged. We understood he had an engineer come from Holland to build it for him."

"And it *was* built?" Matthew asked.

"Something went wrong. There was an accident of some kind. The engineer was killed and the barrier was wrecked. So it turned out that the cliffs below Vyden's house had splintered logs just beneath the surface and no boats could be docked there. A couple of supply boats from New York town tried, we understood from one of his servants, and they got their bottoms torn out."

"Hm," Matthew said. He frowned. "You say Vyden is dead?"

"Many years ago, when we still had our farm," said Ella. "We watched the funeral wagon pass by, and later the wagons carrying the furnishings away. No one lives in that house now."

"And hasn't for a very long time," Joel added. He blew a curl of smoke toward the ceiling. "So this supposed brother has foxed you, Matthew. Why in the world were you intending to travel down a cursed road to a dead man's house?"

Matthew may have touched the outside of the buttoned pocket. He wasn't sure, because everything seemed to be slowly spinning and out of focus and it wasn't the mulled wine. He heard himself speak: "A cursed road?"

"That's what the Indians say." Another curl of smoke ascended. "They wouldn't go down that road if it was the only place on earth to get Ella's cornbread. And we had our own experiences."

"Joel!" She reached out to cover his hand with her own. Her bright blue eyes were suddenly dimmed and watery. "Don't!"

He looked at her and smiled, and it might have been the saddest, most heartbroken smile Matthew had ever had the misfortune to witness. Matthew shifted in his chair, thinking that something terrible was coming.

"It's all right," Joel said quietly to his wife. "Really. That was a long time ago, too. We haven't told anyone for…years, have we? I think we should tell this young man, otherwise whatever we say…he might just leave here and go down that road anyway, just to see for himself. Yes. I think we should tell him."

Ella said nothing more. She got up and began clearing the plates away. Matthew saw that her mouth had become a grim white line and her face was equally grim and pale.

"You don't have to tell me anything," Matthew said.

"I do. It might save your life, if you're the stubborn and stupid type." Joel reached for a deerskin pouch and began to refill his pipe. When the pipe was fired and going again, he said quietly, "Our farm. A few miles from here, along that road. Our home. Ella, me, and our son. Will. A fine boy, he was. Seventeen years of age when…seventeen years of age," he repeated, and he was silent for a little while. Dishes clinked together in Ella's hands as she put them into the wash basin and the kitchen fireplace spat a few sparks on a hard oak knot.

"It was after Vyden died," Joel continued. "All of a sudden…something started getting at our cattle. Tearing them up at night. Going for the throat, just awful bloody. We started hearing the howling from the deep woods. Wolves out there. Coming in at night to kill our cattle. But…a strange thing. I started a journal, keeping track of when we lost an animal. It was one attack a month. I mean to say…maybe two or three nights one right after another, but then it was not until the next month. I realized the things were coming in under a full moon, or nearly full either waxing or waning. Maybe they were roaming the land and their pattern brought them to our farm the same time every month. Who's to say? Wolves are smart. They're a thinking animal. Oh, we went out looking for them with our muskets, Will and me, but we never saw a one."

"He was a good boy," Ella suddenly said, her back to them as she washed the dishes. Matthew didn't want to see her face, because her voice was tortured. "Our Will," she said, like a sigh of wind in a graveyard.

Joel leaned forward in his chair, his dark brown eyes as intense as gun barrels aimed at their guest. "I reasoned out when the wolves would come again. I told Will we were to wait out in the pasture with the cattle, our pistols ready, each of us with a shuttered lantern, and when we heard a noise of something coming—and we would know when that happened, because the cattle would let us know—we were to open our lanterns, pick a target and shoot. So we waited. First one night, then the next. The wolves didn't come. I figured they smelled us there…smelled where we'd walked… smelled our presence. But then, the third night…they were hungry, you see. They couldn't keep away."

"*Please*," Ella said softly, as if begging her husband to cease the telling.

"On the third night…under a waning moon…the cattle started low-ing. Moving, being agitated I guess would be the right word. But what Will and I heard all of a sudden was something hitting the wall of the barn about fifty yards away, and the horses in there started screaming. Well, the barn door was latched…the wolves couldn't get in at them, but one of them—more than one—was throwing itself against the boards. Will started running toward the barn. I shouted out for him to wait, but he was a fast runner. He unshuttered his lantern. I saw something moving…figures… blurred shapes…big things. I saw his powder flash and in the noise of the shot I heard a whine of pain. Only…it didn't sound exactly like an animal. It was…I still don't know."

Beckett had to pause. He put aside his pipe and ran a hand over his face. Matthew saw it tremble.

"I saw…something jump at him. Two or three of them. Will's lantern fell. I ran toward him, and…as I unshuttered my lantern…I was hit from behind. And when I say hit…I mean to say it felt like I was knocked down by a cannonball. When my face struck the ground I lost two teeth. Something—heavy, so heavy—was on my back, bearing me down. I could feel claws in my shoulders. My pistol…lost. And I heard my boy scream."

"*Oh*," came out of Ella, who stood frozen at the wash basin.

"I was trying to get up, but I could hardly move. And then…I felt the breath of the thing on the back of my neck, and I swear to you…I swear before God," said Beckett, "that it made a noise that was nearly human. Almost a voice, if you could make a voice out of muscles and razors. And it said '*No.*' I fought, but later I found out my right arm—my gun arm—was broken. I was a pitiful shell compared to that thing on my back. And I had to hear my boy being torn apart. Thank God…thank *Holy God*—he didn't live too long."

Again, Beckett paused and this time tears glistened in his eyes.

"They took down two of the cattle," he went on, when he could. "Left my boy…scattered. Do you know what it's like to be in a nightmare that you can't wake up from, and you try and try and scream behind your teeth but you can't wake up? That was me out there." He drew in a long, pained breath. "It was all over by the time Ella got to me. All over, and they were gone. She had to see what those things had done to Will before I could stop her. She couldn't speak for nearly two weeks. Couldn't utter a word. That's what living on that road did to us, and to our boy."

"*Damn*," Matthew said quietly, shocked at this story. "My God, that's terrible!"

"Yes," said Beckett. "Those things…they could smell us, and they were trying to draw us away from the cattle. I think…if Will hadn't shot one, they wouldn't have killed him. That one on my back…it could've finished me in an instant, but it didn't. Like I say, smart. *Cunning*. But oh my God… what killers they can be, when it pleases them. Well…we buried Will and we left the farm. We were going to move to New York but the couple we knew who owned this tavern were putting it up for sale. Ella didn't want to stay so near to where it happened, but…I do go out there every so often to his grave. I just stand over it and speak a few words. But I only go in the daytime and I make sure I can get back here by dusk. We have a good life now. We enjoy being of service to the travellers, and we make a good coin. We keep plenty of candles lit. I'm sorry, Ella," he said to the still-frozen woman, "but I thought it best I tell this young man." He stared across the table at Matthew with red-rimmed eyes. "It was near twenty years ago. Sometimes it seems like it happened last night. Do you understand that?"

"I do, certainly. But…you kept referring to what attacked you as 'things.' Not 'wolves'."

"Because I don't really know *what* they were. I'll tell you also…I've been able to pick up some of the Indians' lingo. There's one who comes occasionally who speaks pretty fair English, too. The Indian word for 'cursed' also means 'diseased.' That's what that road is. Diseased. And to travel to the river cliffs to that empty house—and you wouldn't reach it before nightfall, even if you left at first light—would be an act of insanity. Or suicide," he said. "No one lives there, but the Indians still hear howling at night from the woods around it, under the full moon. Those things are still out there, after twenty years. So now you know."

Matthew couldn't find any words. The envelope in his buttoned pocket suddenly felt as heavy as a gravestone. And all the coins that remained in a small bag under Matthew's bed at home…payment to Charon?

"A fine feast, wife of mine," said Beckett, his good nature if not entirely returned then somewhat recovered. "Matthew, let's go sit by the fire in the front room and tell me exactly why you intended to go to that house."

"That great scab upon the earth," Ella remarked.

As Matthew sat with Beckett in the agreeable light and warmth of the front room's hearth, he was torn by his obligation. To go, or not to go? To tell, or not to tell? "I am employed," he decided to say, "by a gentleman asserting himself as brother to a von Eissen who is supposed to be living there, and to deliver a message. I cannot say what the message is and further than that I can't reveal any details. Other than I'm required to deliver the message at night."

The pipe had returned to Beckett's mouth. He removed it and blew a thick cloud of smoke that curled upon itself, reached toward the hearth and slinked up the chimney.

"That's a death sentence," he said. "If you venture to the river cliffs, you won't come back alive."

THREE

AT FIRST LIGHT, MATTHEW FACED A CHOICE.

The day promised to be sunny and bright. Birds chirped in the trees. There was not a cloud to be seen. By sunlight the surrounding forest looked more inviting than dangerous, yet Matthew knew only an Indian could make his or her way through that wild tangle of vegetation.

What to do?

He had spent a restless night in an otherwise comfortable featherbed in one of the tavern's guest rooms. He had shaved, washed his face, changed his shirt and stockings and then breakfasted on ham and eggs with the Becketts, who went about their pleasantries as if not a word about their son or the cursed road had been spoken last night. He had repacked his travelling bag and put on his fearnaught for the morning was yet chill. He had paid for his stay with a coin from von Eissen's fee, and was now sitting astride Suvie in front of the tavern with Joel and Ella saying farewell.

What to do?

"We hope to come to New York town soon," said Joel. He put his arm around his wife. "A woman does like to shop."

"Yes," Matthew said, but he was asking himself *what to do?*

"Good journey to you," Ella said. "So nice to have your company."

And another question Matthew had to consider: *What would Hudson Greathouse do?*

This was over his head. *Far* over it. He didn't have enough experience for something like this. *Hell's bells!* he thought. Get back to New York as fast as Suvie will—

Hudson's gravelly voice, speaking: I knew you were a weak-minded moonbeam.

Joel stepped forward and rubbed Suvie's neck. He looked up, squinting in the early sun. "You're going through with it, aren't you?"

"I…" He stumbled over this question that might mean life or death. But he had two pistols, and he would get them out and ready by nightfall! Still…Joel and his son had had two pistols as well, hadn't they?

And then it came out, as Matthew knew it must. "I have to," he said.

"I tried," Joel answered. He gave Suvie a final rub and stepped back alongside his wife. Both their faces were blank. They had tried. "Good luck to you," he said, and with that they turned away.

Matthew urged Suvie onward, heading north.

In time he came to the road.

It was a track hardly wide enough for a post coach. On both sides the forest was so thick it tried to bully the very sunlight into submission. As it was, the daylight was dimmed to a green haze speckled with the orange and red bursts of hardwood trees that locked arms twenty feet above Matthew's head. The air itself smelled not of fresh growth but of old rot, wet in its decay of roots and vines. He pulled back on the reins and paused at the entrance to this tunnel of threat, for a tunnel is what it appeared. It curved slightly to the left a distance ahead and climbed upward.

Suvie grumbled underneath him. She felt it too, but what Matthew felt he didn't fully understand. It just was a sensation of gloom as heavy as ten fearnaught coats draped around his shoulders.

He had to go.

Didn't he?

Hudson Greathouse would.

Wouldn't he?

Before Matthew could start going down that road in his mind, he flicked the reins and started Suvie along the physical road. He would stop further on and prepare his pistols. He thought he was stupid and should have turned back for New York because he wasn't ready for a task of this nature...but then again, he'd survived other dangerous situations...deadly situations, in fact. He bore the scar of a bear's claw on his forehead to prove it.

And what really made him go on was that his curiosity—that devil!—had awakened and taken flame. If no von Eissen lived in the house at the end of this road, then who was supposed to accept the envelope? Ten pounds was a great deal of money. He hadn't been paid such an amount to take an envelope to an empty house, that was for certain! So who was waiting at the river cliffs for the message...in a dead man's house...a great scab upon the earth....

Who?

The day wore on.

Matthew stopped several times to let Suvie rest and take water from his canteen. He prepared the pistols and hooked them to a rope he'd brought so that the guns hung on either side of the saddle in front of him.

Then in mid-afternoon, following a road that curved back and forth as if drawn on a map by a town's drunk, and rising and falling in equal measures, Matthew came upon a huge oak tree on his right that had two words painted on its massive trunk in red, the words faded by time and nature but still frightfully legible.

Go Back.

Matthew reined Suvie in as if a puppeteer had jerked his arms.

He sat for a while, staring at that sign with one hand on a pistol grip. He realized it had been some time since he'd heard birds singing. All here was silence but for the sound of the wind moving through the interlocked branches above.

"Suvie," Matthew said, keeping his voice low as if the forest might hear and sprout fiends to attack him then and there, "I am one damned fool. Don't you think?" To her credit she didn't answer. "I don't think that was written by an Indian or a wolf, do you?" Which begged another question and threw more logs into the fire of his curiosity.

He went on. Not a quarter mile further he passed a road that turned to the left and approached what appeared to be a ramshackle farmhouse, a barn broken by the hard hammer of weather, the remnants of a split-rail fence and a pasture overgrown with weeds. Somewhere over there was a grave.

Another hour, another fall and rise of the road, another curve, and Matthew noted that the sun was dropping through the trees. Had the sun ever dropped so fast in New York before? He felt the dark edging in, and with it a deepening chill.

Then he came upon the hanging man.

This time it was in his face as Suvie rounded a bend, and he would never tell Hudson Greathouse that he wet the breeches of his fine dove's gray suit a little bit before he realized the figure hanging from a branch down upon the road at his eye level was made of straw and dressed in dirty rags.

Once more he stopped Suvie and this time she gave a nicker and a snort and wanted to back up. "Easy, easy," he said, speaking as much to himself as to the noble mare.

The straw man was caught by a breeze and swung slightly back and forth, twisting as it swung with an old, discolored rope around its neck.

Matthew suddenly felt himself being watched. He was sure of it. The nape of his own neck prickled too much. He turned in the saddle and looked back. Nothing there but road and forest, forest and road. Dare he call out? He did: "Anyone there?"

An Indian, maybe? Watching there from the woods? If so, you never saw an Indian unless they wanted to be seen, and this one—or more than one—did not.

Matthew again took stock of the hanging figure. Eyes were on him, he had no doubt of it. He aimed his voice toward the forest on his right and said loudly, "I have business ahead! I mean no one any harm, but I have to go on! Do you hear? A straw man is not going to stop me!"

Of course there was no reply, and Matthew had expected none.

"I'm going on!" he said. And something he immediately wished he hadn't said: "Mark it, I'm carrying two pistols!" Then, that foolish statement out in the air revealing his limitation of two shots if one or both of the weapons didn't misfire, as often happened, the problem-solver from New York gritted his teeth against the Fates and made good his intent to continue, even going so far as to give the straw man a knock as he passed it which of course made the figure swing back into his own self before he got clear.

As Suvie carried Matthew further on, the dark descended through shades of pale. With the nightfall, which cast a nearly absolute ebony blanket upon the road, Matthew grew more and more tense and Suvie seemed more and more agitated. He could see a little bit, as the waxing moon glimmered through the high branches in lighter puddles on the dirt, but he was aware that if Suvie made a misstep it was finish to this journey with possibly fatal consequences.

He had no idea of the exact time, and wished there had been some way to bring a lantern to bear upon the way ahead but there was not. He began to seriously wonder if ten pounds was too cheap a price to pay for a horse's broken leg and the life of—

His musings were very suddenly interrupted as Suvie rounded a bend and there stood in the middle of the road a figure holding a torch.

Matthew reined Suvie in. It was a man—a large dark-bearded man, husky with wide shoulders—wearing what appeared to be stitched-together blankets as clothing. On his feet were wrappings of cloth laced up with vines.

"Off the horse," he commanded, in a voice that only needed a strike of lightning to go with its low growl of thunder.

Matthew hesitated. One hand had already gone to a pistol's grip. Then he was aware of more figures emerging from the forest all around him, some with torches and others standing just at the edges of light. He quickly counted six men and four women, all of whom appeared to be dressed in rags and in a wretched condition of cleanliness.

"You'll never live to cock that pistol," the first man said, and the tone of that voice told Matthew no truer words had ever been spoken.

He got down, noting with some small measure of gratification that no weapons were in sight. But some of these men and women in their dirt-stained and ragged condition, all hard sinews and jutting bones, looked to be deadly weapons enough.

Thunder Voice approached. Matthew nearly shrank back, for the man had a bestial face with a low sloping forehead under a dirty mop of dark hair, heavy dark brown brows, eyes black as cinders of sin, and gray streaks in the coarse bristle-brush of beard. The man held the torch out so close to Matthew's own face that the younger man feared ignition. Others in this strange group were coming forward, ringing him and Suvie, who strained and nickered against the bit Matthew was holding.

"Jack, take the horse," the man said, and another bearded brute came forward to do so.

Matthew and the first man stared at each other, until Matthew found a shred of his shrinking courage and said, "Good evening."

"Who are you?"

"Matthew Corbett, from New York. And you?"

"Have they forgotten how to read in New York?"

"Pardon?"

"You passed a sign. Painted on a tree. Is your eyesight in danger?"

"Only from the torch you're holding too closely to my face. Do you mind?"

The torch did not retreat. Matthew felt someone come up behind him and pluck at his coat, and he looked around to see a thin black-haired girl of about twenty years or so staring at him as if she'd never before seen another human being.

"Corbett," the man repeated, as if rolling it around in his mouth for the taste. "Where do you think you're going?"

"I am on my way to—here! Stop that!" He had realized one of the other men had plucked his travelling bag down off Suvie, and that one and another were pawing through it. "Those are my personal items!" he protested into the torch.

"We have no personal items here," came the reply. "On your way to *where?*"

"I think that's my business. I don't care to be mauled in the middle of the night. Who *are* you people?"

"The only place you *could* be going," said the man, his face and voice impassive, "is the Bodenkier house. So...why?"

"Bodenkier? Who is that?"

"Take his pistols," the man told another. "Tie the horse here." And to Matthew, "You're going to take a walk with us. Cause us no trouble. If you try to run, I'll break both your legs." He motioned toward the woods with his flame. Matthew noted that he glanced quickly up through the trees at Selene's growing orb. The man pressed his free hand against the back of his neck and shivered, and at the same time Matthew thought he heard one of the women give a small whimper of pain.

"Move," said the man, and Matthew had no choice but to obey.

FOUR

AN HOUR'S WALK IN THAT FORBIDDING TANGLE WAS A TEST OF THE legs, the balance and the spirit itself, because as soon as Matthew freed himself from one creep of vines or claw of thorns he was attacked by another. All around him strode the strange people with their torches, moving as if upon an uncrowded New York block, so sure was their footing. In fact a few ran ahead, which Matthew would have thought an impossibility. He plodded onward with the evident boss of this troupe at his back and the raggedy girl with black hair traipsing around him and grinning in his face like a lunatic.

"I'll tell you that people in New York know where I am," Matthew lied, to save his hide; in this case a lie might be a lifesaver. "If anything... unfortunate...happens to me, they'll—"

"Quiet," growled the man. "Don't make things worse for yourself."

At that, Matthew really did start sweating.

A little further on, one of the men out on his right gave a guttural cry and fell to his knees. Matthew imagined he heard the cracking of a bone. At once one of the others picked up the man's fallen torch but no help was offered to the fallen individual. Everyone kept walking, as the man curled up and shivered in the brush.

"Aren't you going to help him?" Matthew asked the boss.

"There's no help for him."

"I understand there are wolves in the forest."

The boss stopped and gave a terrible grin that was intensified in its ferocity by the torch flame. "He says," he announced to the others, "that he understands there are wolves in the forest." Then his grin shattered into an equally terrible laugh echoed by one and all.

"What's the joke?" Matthew asked.

"You are. Move on."

The raggedy girl suddenly capered in and sniffed—actually *sniffed*—at Matthew's throat. As he drew back, the girl bent down and sniffed at his crotch.

"Perla! Stop that!" the boss snapped, and she scampered away. "She's in heat," he said to Matthew.

This was the damnedest group he'd ever seen. As they continued on into the woods, Matthew thought that they were certainly not Indians nor wild beasts of the forest, and they could not be bandits for what band of brigands would be out here on a road no one travelled? So...another log on the curiosity bonfire...who *were* they?

The glare of more torches appeared ahead. They came to an area that was not so much cleared as it was that the vegetation was somewhat thinner. A rock face jutted upward, a stacking of ancient boulders like a throw of God's dice. Matthew saw other figures crouched around a central fire. There stood a few haphazardly cobbled wooden shacks, and at the base of the rocks the entrance to a cave. Torches had been driven into the earth and cast shadow-edged light. The people of this strange congregation—obviously as poorly lived as the most wretched of creatures on the earth—came around to stare at the new arrival. The boss gave him a hard shove toward the cave's entrance. He passed men and boys, women and girls, all in rags and as dirty as muck. Over there stood a woman with leaves in her wild blonde hair, an infant suckling at one breast. Before he was pushed again into the mouth of the cave Matthew judged this group of tribal savages to number between thirty and forty individuals. Then he was in a darkness broken only by the glow of a few candles, and the man behind him had given his torch to one of the others and now commanded, "Sit down over there."

A hard floor was no compliment to Matthew's behind. The man took a seat on a flat rock somewhat higher than the floor, with candles on either side. He was joined by two other bearded bulls of the woods and a thin-faced woman with long gray tresses who settled themselves also on either side. Matthew noted uneasily that the woman did not sit; she crouched, her tattered dress barely covering her body and her feet bare, and there was something about her that looked terribly hungry.

"Matthew Corbett," the boss said. He laced his dirt-stained fingers together. "From New York. A long way from this place."

"Too long, I fear." Matthew had decided he could approach this situation one of two ways: either begging for his life, or showing some courage that he definitely did not feel. But false courage or not it would have to do, for he felt begging was a short trip to a grave. "To whom do I have the dubious pleasure of speaking?"

"You can call me Murdo."

"That suits."

Murdo grinned again. This time it wasn't as fierce, but a grin on that face had something of a snarl in it. "Listen to him!" he said to the others. "At our mercy, and he shows an admirable bit of courage! We can smell your fear sweat, boy."

Matthew chose his next words carefully. "I think I'm entitled, don't you?"

"Yes, I suppose. Daniel, fetch him some water." One of the other men instantly got up and loped out. "Now…let's get down to business. Why are you travelling to the house of Walloch Bodenkier?"

"That's the first I've heard of the name."

"But it's not the first you've heard of the *house*. What? Did someone in New York employ you to be his servant?"

"May I ask a question?" Matthew went ahead before a *no* could be given. "Who are you people and what are you doing out here?"

"That's two questions!" the woman snapped. She had eyes like holes bored in metal. "And two questions too many!"

"Forgive my curiosity, madam. It's my nature."

"*Madam!*" she cackled. "He called me 'madam'!" Her crooked smile faded to a sad slant. "It's been so long since anyone addressed me as such. I can hardly recall."

Matthew decided these people must have escaped from an institution for the mentally deranged. Perhaps a wagon broke down, and they all fled to the protection of the—

A skull was suddenly thrust into his face. It was turned upside down— an animal's skull of some kind, the openings sealed up with dried mud except for the cup that held a portion of liquid. The one called Daniel was offering him a drink.

"Go ahead," said Murdo. "You must be thirsty."

They were all watching him. Did he dare refuse the offer? He really was thirsty...but to drink from the skull of a beast? Ashton McCaggers with his collection of bones might have given a gut-laugh over this situation. Matthew felt he had to do it. He took the skull in his hands and yet paused with his mouth over the brainpan.

"It's only water," Murdo said. "We get it from a spring up the way."

Matthew drank. Only water. Then he returned the skull to Daniel's waiting hands and realized one of the hands had a patch of bristly hair at the base of the palm. The skull and the hands withdrew into the dark.

"Walloch Bodenkier," said his host. "Why?"

The moment of truth. What the *hell* was this all about? He still considered himself to be keeping the confidence for von Eissen, but...yet...things had taken a decidedly sinister turn, and he felt his life at the moment not to be worth ten pounds nor even ten pence.

"Waiting," Murdo said. Matthew saw him give a quick wince as if something had suddenly pained him, and the man rubbed the mound of his left shoulder.

"I know nothing about Walloch Bodenkier," Matthew answered. "I was hired by his brother for a mission I am not at liberty to tell you."

Murdo remained silent for a few seconds. He ceased rubbing his shoulder, locked his fingers together and leaned forward. The candlelight played shadows across his face. "Not at *liberty*? Liberty. Now there's an interesting word. If Bodenkier had his way, the idea of liberty would be an ancient dream. It would be *nothing*. We are the only prevention of New York... Boston...Philadelphia...Charles Town...everywhere in these colonies... losing their liberty. Or rather, having it stolen from them, by night. If you truly know nothing about that...*creature*...and I think I believe you...then I will inform you that we—as you see us—are soldiers, of a kind. We are fighting a war against a bitter enemy. This war...has been going on for generations. There can be no end to it until the Bodenkiers of this world—of *their* world—are totally destroyed. We are here to—" He suddenly had to stop, because Matthew had seen his lower jaw seemingly jump out of its sockets. As Matthew watched in a kind of stupefied horror, Murdo took both hands and popped the dislocation back into place.

"You never should have come along that road," he said, his voice harsher than before. "This is no place for your kind."

Matthew had so many questions he didn't know where to begin. His expression must have betrayed him, because Murdo went on. "We have contained him in that house. We think he must not be able to use the river, or a boat would've already come to take him out. Oh yes, we know he has associates able to roam freely, but Bodenkier is vital to their plans."

That word again, Matthew thought. *Vital.*

"He cannot use the road," Murdo said, "or we would catch and kill him. The whole of his sect. So the best we can do for the moment is containment, and we have kept him trapped in that house for..." He paused, thinking, measuring time. "Over twenty years," he said.

Matthew's voice was a quaver. *"Twenty years?"*

"We survive. You say you have a mission? So do we. Now...what is it you've been sent here to do for him?"

"I...really...I..." It spilled out: "Are you people *insane?*"

"What would be insane, young man, is for that monster to get out and into civilization, such as it is. We watch the house but it's a large estate. We know he prepares traps on the grounds, and we've found that out the hard way. If we were to discover where he and the others sleep by day and kill them, before they were extinguished they would send out screams that could be heard not by the human ear, but by their kind even across the ocean. That would bring hundreds of them. Thousands, maybe, to join the war against *us.* If we could get to him—and all of them—by night, that alarm mechanism they have is negated. They die silently by night...but then again, they hardly ever die."

Escaped from Bedlam, Matthew thought. All of them. Living out here twenty years. Their belfries were cracked. Talking about killing people who could scream across an ocean? It was utter madness!

And here he was, sitting in a cave in the midst of them!

"You were sent out here as a sacrifice," Murdo told him. He stared at the back of one of his hands and flexed the fingers, again and again. "To be food for them. We believe they survive on small animals they catch on the estate, enough to keep them from shriveling. Whoever sent you was offering them a meal they could make last for a year or more."

"Let me," Matthew said carefully, "go and bring help for you."

It happened so fast Matthew had no time to react. One second Murdo was up on his throne of rock and the next—a blurred shape, impossibly fast—he was in Matthew's face with a fist clenching the front of the young man's coat. And Matthew's own mind was losing its grip on reality because he imagined he saw a patch of hair ripple across Murdo's forehead and then be absorbed back into the flesh.

"You know *nothing*," Murdo whispered, as a thick musty animal odor assailed Matthew's nostrils. "Nothing. Your entire world is one room. But we do know...all those rooms in the mansion...so many...and so many are deadly dangerous. We are fighting for humanity. Everything we are...there's a purpose to us. Can you even begin to grasp it?"

But in the silence that ensued, with Matthew's heart pounding and the New York problem-solver smelling his own fear sweat, Murdo released him, drew back and said bitterly, "No, you cannot."

"Are you going to kill me?" Matthew asked, because the time had come for him to prepare…fight and flight, the only chance and not much of one against these lunatics.

Murdo crouched down upon the ground. He sat there for a long while, brooding, his shadow thrown huge against the wall of rock at his back.

Then: "Daniel, you and Micah escort this young man back to his horse. Take Judd with you. Return to him his pistols and his bag. If Perla tries to follow, strike her down. She has designs on him." Murdo's hooded gaze came back to Matthew. "No, we won't kill you. We'll let Bodenkier have that honor. Go on now, and make haste."

Matthew was never so glad to stand up in his life. The gray-haired woman still looked like she wanted to tear him apart and then into further small pieces.

"Farewell, young man," said Murdo, who remained seated. And to the others escorting Matthew: "If it starts on any of you, understand I forbid him to be touched on penalty of castration. Being *neutered*, I might say," he said with a thin-lipped smile toward Matthew. Then his expression darkened as fast as any storm might move. He growled, *"Get out!"*

FIVE

WAS A NIGHT EVER SO LONG, OR AS MUCH SHROUDED WITH MYSTERY as with darkness?

In Suvie's saddle with his pistols and his travelling bag restored, Matthew had gratefully left his two escorts about forty minutes ago. Two only, because the third had suddenly lifted his eyes into the chill moonlight that filtered down through the branches, had given a piercing cry that made Matthew think a beast of the forest was about to devour them all, had dropped his torch, clutched his hands to his face and, doubling over like a hunchback, had run staggering into the woods.

"Keep moving," Matthew had been told. But the voice that spoke it was so harsh it sounded strangely inhuman. "Just keep moving."

Matthew would have paid ten pounds and ten to get to the road faster, but for him it was again a long and hard trek. As soon as Matthew swung up into the saddle with a breathy *whoosh* of relief, the two men and their torches moved away through the thicket at running speed.

And now onward to the house on the river cliffs, that great scab upon the earth where dwelled people who could—ridiculous!—scream across the ocean.

Twenty years in that self-made prison. Of course they were all insane. And he was beginning to fear for his sanity as well, on this haunted night. He prided himself on his intelligence. He considered himself well-read and knowledgeable about the world, with all its bizarreties and strange happenstances, but all this strained the mind. Still…he thought it odd—extremely so—that the period of twenty years included the death of Will Beckett by wolves, yet that group in the woods seemed untroubled by wild beasts. In fact, they seemed much like wild beasts themselves. And all that about killing Walloch Bodenkier, and some kind of war that Matthew failed to understand…he couldn't make heads or tails of it.

He was still pondering the situation when the road ended. Moonlight shone upon a black iron gate and a fence topped with spear points, all of it at least seven feet high. He dismounted and found a chain and large lock securing the gate. Beyond the fence a weeded-up path led upward. There stood more darkness of trees and underbrush, with no house in sight.

But there! An iron bell and a pullcord attached to the gate.

You were sent out here as a sacrifice, Murdo had said.

The ravings of a madman. And yet…Matthew spent a moment fitting one of the pistols into the waistband of his breeches, under suit jacket and fearnaught, and then the other was secured in his travelling bag. Satisfied at least with this precaution, he rang the bell.

The hollow sound of it was startling in the silence. He rang it again, and waited. When no light appeared beyond the gate and no one emerged from the dark, he steeled himself for that noise and rang it a third time.

Was someone there? For suddenly a figure emerged from the dark, and moonlight through the bars of the gate touched the pallid face of a thin young girl with long dark hair.

She stood without speaking, staring at him with strangely luminous eyes. Dressed in a long gown of some kind, Matthew saw. A sleeping robe?

"My name is Matthew Corbett," he said. "I've come from New York with a message from Karlis von Eissen. I had supposed his brother lived—"

He need say no more, because she was reaching toward the lock with an ancient-looking key. The lock clicked free, the chain rattled away, and she pulled the gate open on rusted hinges that made a shrieking noise so loud Suvie almost jumped loose of Matthew's grip on her bit.

"Tie the horse here," the girl said when he started to bring Suvie through. Her voice was as soft as if spoken from a dream. "The way is dangerous for an animal."

"Dangerous? How?"

"The master has set traps for the beasts that roam these woods. Sometimes they are so insolent they scale the fence. Tie the horse here," she repeated.

Matthew hesitated. Murdo had mentioned the traps. This night ride should've never been taken, not for ten times ten pounds.

"Are you coming, or not?" the girl asked. He noted she seemed to be scanning the woods over his shoulder.

"Don't you carry a light?"

"I know the way. Coming, or not?"

Not, he wanted to say. But he was supposed to stay in the house until morning, and truth was he and Suvie had just about ridden themselves out this night. Also, it was a long way back to the Post Road and he'd have to go past those lunatics again in the dark, which he despised to do. A damnable choice to be made!

"Sir?" she prodded, her voice still soft…dreamily so.

He tied Suvie to the gate. She locked it at his back. "Walk directly behind me," she instructed. "Do not deviate from my path."

"I wouldn't dare deviate. You can make your way with no light?"

She was already walking, if that strange cadence of a glide could be considered a walk. Matthew got right up behind her, and in so doing he caught the faintest whiff of that same odor he'd detected from von Eissen… the dried bones and musty death aroma of McCaggers' attic museum. It was then that he thought he had made a terrible mistake, that he and Suvie should've immediately turned back, sore butt and tired horse legs be damned, and take their chances with the Bedlam Bunch, because something was at work here that made the witch hunt at Fount Royal seem like the plaything of a child.

"Watch your step here." The girl pointed down at the ground on his left. "Keep directly behind."

"I can't see a thing. What kind of traps are set?"

"Pits with stakes and broken glass at the bottom. Wires that when disturbed swing spiked planks down from the trees. Other things."

"Lovely," Matthew said. "Your master made these things?"

"He is quite clever in using what is at hand…the metal window frames, the window glass and such."

"You're his servant?"

"We are all his servants. Duck your head here. *Lower*," she commanded.

By the time they went up the stone steps of a large turreted house that had not a glint of light in it nor it seemed any glass in the windows, Matthew was sweating bullets and thinking it was a wonder he hadn't been smacked in the face by a spiked plank. At the huge yawning hole of the entrance—no door, either? Used for the traps, he supposed—the girl said, "You will wait here," and then she merged with the dark.

Matthew realized that now he couldn't make his way back if he wanted to, and he wanted to in the worst way. New York seemed the distance of another world from here. And he had begun to think that the forest lunatics were better hosts than people who lived in total darkness, in some kind of weird castle taken apart to create animal traps.

One light began to show beyond the entrance.

A single candle, it looked to be, and a stub at that. As the small glow neared, Matthew saw that it was carried on a flat piece of wood by a frail-looking little boy maybe ten or eleven years of age, wearing what might be called a youngster's sailor suit, darkened with grime and sagging on his frame. Atop his head was a white wig also suited for a child, sitting somewhat crooked on the scalp.

"Hello," the child said, and managed a smile that showed teeth far past the need for dental correction. "Please come in."

Matthew didn't. "I have a message from Karlis von Eissen for your master, whom I understood was his brother." He reached into his coat, unbuttoned the pocket, removed the envelope and held it out at arm's length. "I am to deliver this only to your master."

"That would be myself," said the child. "I am Walloch Bodenkier."

Matthew couldn't speak. This was the "creature" the madmen wanted to kill? And a *child* had devised those traps? It was total insanity!

Bodenkier just kept grinning.

A thought ripped through Matthew's brain. Murdo said they had contained Bodenkier and his "sect" in the house for over twenty years. Had he meant this boy's *father?* When he could find his tongue, what came out was: "Where are your parents?"

"Unfortunately, long extinguished. Come in and meet the others."

Extinguished. Murdo had used that word. "Who else is in the house?" Matthew asked, and heard his voice tremble but the truth was he was beginning to feel strangled by a kind of cold fear he had never experienced before.

"No need to be afraid, young sir," said the boy. "One step across the threshold and you will be among lifelong friends."

Matthew was aware of movement behind Bodenkier, there in the dark. And an instant later he realized that the hand holding the piece of wood with the candle on it bore the curved claws of Karlis von Eissen. "Just take the envelope," he said shakily. "Then I'll ask your girl to lead me back to the gate."

"I fear she's indisposed."

Another impression…that grime on Bodenkier's clothing…particularly around the neck collar, and in splotches down the front…grime…mold…or bloodstains?

The boy's eyes had taken on a crimson glint. He lowered his light. "I can't quite reach the envelope. Hold it nearer, won't you?"

"Here." Matthew dropped it at the boy's dirty bare feet, the nails also long and curved. "I want someone to lead me out."

"Impossible at the moment. I think you should—"

There came a thudding sound followed by a strident scream from back toward the gate, and then the scream changed to a mangled, high-pitched howling.

Every hair on Matthew's head and body stood up. *"They're here!"* Bodenkier shouted, in no longer the voice of a child but a voice ancient and aflame with rage. His face changed—lengthened, contorted—as if the very bones behind it were in motion.

With a single move the boy had lunged forward and swept Matthew aside like a wheat straw, using one arm. Matthew went down upon the steps. The candle was dropped and went out. Bodenkier stood at the threshold giving a bellow into the night that made the iron bell sound mute, and as Matthew struggled to get up, a shape massive and gnarled hurled itself past him and smashed into the boy, who was whirled backward like a dried leaf. Then another and another massive shape rushed in, and more and more, an animal smell in the air, the smell of fury, frenzy and violence beyond Matthew's ken. He crawled away, tried to stand again, heard shrill cries and the tearing of flesh, eerie keenings, crashes upon a floor.

He was picked up. In his state of dazed horror he felt claws dig into his back. He had lost his travelling bag. He was being carried, faster and faster, away from the house. Something made a whining noise, there was a rush of air and an object of some kind hissed past his ear. Whatever was carrying him jumped from side to side, a leap here and a leap there. Matthew felt coarse hair pressing against his face. Then he must have been at the gate because he heard Suvie screaming too, kicking and jumping in an effort to get loose.

"I'm throwing you over." It was Murdo's voice, but changed. Harsh, guttural, hardly recognizable as human. "Don't look at me!" he rasped when Matthew tried. "I thank you for showing us the way."

"What?" Matthew said stupidly. *"What?"*

"Through his traps. We followed your scent. Their reek…everywhere…your scent, fresh. Poor Daniel…a misstep. Listen to me. Get on that horse and ride like hell, for Hell will be after you." Murdo's body shivered. Matthew felt the arms that held him grip harder, as if the man's power was on the edge of explosion. "Some I can't control…they hate your kind." And the last word, a snarl from the depths: "*Over.*" With that he flung Matthew upward and out.

Matthew's fearnaught caught on the spear points. He dangled there, thrashing, until he tore himself out of his coat and dropped to the ground. Then it was a matter of untying Suvie and holding on, trying to get himself up in the saddle as she—no fool, that mare—broke into a wild gallop away from that great scab upon the earth.

Matthew rode like hell. Whatever was going on back there, he was quits with it.

SIX

COLD WIND WAS IN HIS FACE. THE PUDDLES OF MOONLIGHT SWEPT past. Matthew leaned forward and let Suvie fly. She was in charge now, and he simply the hanger-on.

What had been during the trip an easy walk for Suvie punctuated at times by a trot was now a wild headlong race for survival. He thought one mile had been galloped through, then a second, and Suvie was lathering and straining and he feared she might fall dead beneath him but still she rushed on, until at last…at last…she staggered and stumbled and he had to fight the reins to draw her in before she did kill herself.

He got her down to a canter, but still she shrieked and snorted and turned in confused circles. "Easy, easy," he kept saying, though he was aware they were still way too far from the Post Road and way too near that scene of demonic destruction. When Suvie finally slowed herself to a walk in a straight line—definitely *away* from the river cliffs—Matthew dismounted, still carefully holding her bit in case she bolted, and gave her a few handcups of water from his canteen, then took a long swig himself.

He let her rest for an anguished fifteen minutes, and then he climbed back into the saddle and started her off again. She kept straining against the reins and he kept holding her back until finally she accepted his command to trot, even though he again feared her earlier exertions might burst her heart. But there was no respite for either of them out in these woods, on this road, on this night.

They passed the hanging man, which Matthew didn't see until straw scraped his shoulder. Not much further on, he heard distant howling from the forest on his left. Two calling, one answering, it sounded like. With that noise, Suvie gave another start and he had to fight her once more. Matthew thought that if he ever got home he was going to kiss the dirt of his floor and he would buy Suvie golden horseshoes, if there was such a thing. If not, there ought to be.

"We're getting out of this," he told her. "Yes, we are. Getting out of this. God grant it, we are."

The sounds of howling faded. Matthew reined Suvie in from her trot and she settled on a walk, which he knew she didn't like and he surely didn't like but a dead horse in this case probably equaled a dead man.

They had gone on at this pace probably another hour when Suvie at first grumbled deep in her throat. Then a moment later she gave a high whinny and Matthew felt her flesh crawl.

By that, his heart nearly stopped...because he knew Hell was coming.

He needn't look over his shoulder. He wouldn't see it coming, and the monster—yes, *monster*—would likely be attacking through the woods. It would come silently, would leap through the shards of moonlight, would first rend him to pieces and then Suvie. He dug his pistol out and cocked it, the cold sweat rising on his face.

Suddenly Suvie made the decision for him.

She bolted.

The mare's panicked strength rocked him back and almost out of the saddle. He lost the reins. She ran, faster than before, faster than ever he would've believed the horse could run. Her heart surely must explode at this, or her legs give way. He grasped around her neck to keep from being thrown off by her forward momentum, and then he did make the mistake of looking back.

The fright of it made the flesh of his face go so tight his teeth were exposed in a macabre grimace. For a massive hideous shape had burst from the forest on the left and with horrible speed and leaping bounds was gaining on them. He fired stupidly, without aiming, but aiming was impossible aboard a galloping horse. The smoke rushed away and the monster was still there, now so much closer than before.

"Go go go go!" Matthew shouted, but Suvie was at her limit. And now that shape was clawing toward Suvie's hindquarters and in another few seconds it would make its leap up the mare's back and fall upon Matthew Corbett, rest in pieces.

He didn't think, he just threw the pistol at it, and it was hit but slowed only a claw's length. Now he could sense more than see it tensing itself to jump, and he in turn twisted his body while still hanging on to Suvie's neck for dear life to kick at the beast when it came.

Now...it was coming...now...

A flame shot through the night from the other side of the woods. The flaming arrow lodged itself in the beast's side and the creature twisted almost as if to pluck it out with its front claws. A second flaming arrow...missed over the body. A third...right into the thing's neck, and by the flame Matthew had an instant to see that the beast had gray hair and, in its malformed, elongated head, eyes like holes burned in metal. Then, in the following instant, it had turned away and with what Matthew might have described in better circumstances as a graceful leap silently reentered the forest.

And was gone.

But another figure ran out of the woods, rushed into the road and hurled itself at Suvie. Matthew had a clench of renewed horror, until he realized the figure had feathers in its hair and was draped in a blanket. The Indian had hold of Suvie's bit and was fighting the horse to a stop. He was dragged a distance but he hung on, and Suvie tried to rear up but failing at that started kicking like an enraged mule. Still, she was more or less under control enough for Matthew to reach for and grasp the reins, and then he had to hang on as she bucked a couple of times. Totally exhausted, she gave a shiver and a snort that blew one of the Indian's feathers out of his hair... but at last she stood at some measure of calm, her head bowed forward as if to find blessed sleep right then and there.

Matthew slid out of the saddle. His legs wouldn't hold him. He sprawled out on the cursed road. And pushing himself up to a sitting position he saw three more Indians approaching him, all with bows and quivers of arrows, the brave in the lead carrying a lantern in which burned a pair of tapers. The one with the lantern was a tall, rather gaunt man with three feathers in his mound of hair and was wearing not a blanket but a pair of dark breeches, boots and a soldier's redcoat jacket.

"Stand," he said. "Can you?"

"Yes." Then: "Not yet."

"Foolish, to travel that way."

"Yes," Matthew agreed.

The brave with the lantern spoke to one of the others in their language, a nearly musical sound. A piece of something grainy was offered to him. Cornbread, he realized. He took it and ate. "I saw you...at the Becketts'," said Matthew.

"Not me. Two of the others. We don't come for the bread only. We come, this period, to see Joel and Ella are safe." He spoke again to the others. A small pig's bladder was unstoppered and held forth. Matthew took a drink of beer that seared the back of his throat and brought tears to his eyes. He had a second sip, same as the first. Damned good.

"What are you...what are you doing out here?" Matthew asked, and with the help of the strong beer he got to his feet.

"Watched you leave yesterday sunrise. If you returned at all it might be…in a *haste*, you English would say? Decided to wait until next sun, just to see. I am…" He searched for the proper English word. "Curiosity," he said. He took the bladder and returned it to its keeper. "But we go only this far, not wise to travel on."

"I wholeheartedly agree with that, sir. Thank you for saving our lives… myself and my horse." Matthew felt near collapse, but he was hanging on. "You said…'this period.' What did you mean?"

"Moon time," said the brave, and motioned toward the orb with his lantern. "They prowl at moon time. Like you would say…*clockwork?*"

"Yes," Matthew said. "Clockwork."

"Walk from here. Will walk with you. Horse needs rest."

"How far?"

"Sunrise, not far."

Matthew nodded. He didn't exactly understand, but he thought the brave was saying they would reach the Becketts' tavern at dawn.

"English word," the brave said. "*Advice?* Joel and Ella should not know. We watch for them. They have good lives."

"Yes," Matthew replied. "They do." And not only was there to be no word about this to the Becketts, but there would be no word to Hudson Greathouse either. That beast of a man would either laugh himself silly or have Matthew chained up and carted to that lunatic asylum down in Pennsylvania where he could join the Queen of Bedlam for lunch and checkers. No, better to make up a story about the ten pounds…which was going to have a dent in it, to pay for two lost pistols. Better to say he'd delivered a message to the King of Siam rather than to…

…Walloch Bodenkier…whatever that creature had been. He doubted he would ever see Karlis von Eissen again, but if he did…message delivered, sir, if not exactly to his hand, thank you for your business and here's a kick in the nutsack to go with it.

Matthew thought he was going to forget this night ever happened, if he could. He was going to blot it from his memory, if he had to find an Indian and buy seventeen bladders of beer to make it so. No one should know. *Ever.*

And the people in the woods? Mad wretches, all. Yes. Leave it at that.

From the distant forest came howling. But different than before. There was no violence or anger in it, no rage, no cry for war. A chorus of voices, soaring up and up, twisting and twining, a strange and oddly beautiful symphony of the night.

"They sing," said the brave with the lantern. "I wonder why."

Matthew just gave the faintest of smiles.

He was looking at a patch of moonlight there upon the earth. He could hear Greathouse saying *you're a moonbeam now, and always will you be a moonbeam.*

It seemed to Matthew that there was an awful lot of power in a moonbeam. More than Greathouse would ever know.

And Matthew's answer would be *I try.*

He took Suvie's reins, and he and his horse walked with the Indians toward the dawn.

THE HOUSE AT THE EDGE OF THE WORLD

SEPTEMBER, 1702

ONE

⸺◦⸺

"YES SIR, YOU HEARD ME CORRECTLY," SAID THE MAN IN THE PURPLE peruke. "A monster is roaming the woods of Briartooth."

"Ah," Hudson Greathouse replied, for though his ears had clearly absorbed this information the gentleman's strangely colored wig—lavender? periwinkle? lilac?—had snagged his attention more than what was issuing from the mouth, which itself was full of teeth that seemed the size of tombstones. In fact, every dimension of the man appeared to be either too short where length was required or too long where shorter was better. Hudson suspected his own faculties were at fault, and that third tankard of ale at the Trot Then Gallop last night was still distorting and discomforting his senses. But that *wig!* Lilac, he decided. Perhaps a homespun attempt at dyeing a wig that had gone over to yellow or a silvery-gray, and here was the sorry result.

"Are you *listening*, sir?" the second man asked.

"I am!" The answer had come a bit too quickly and too sharply. Hudson pulled his gaze away from the shiny sheen and focused on his questioner, who was the younger of the two by at least thirty years, the elder lilac-wigger being in his early sixties.

"That's good to hear, sir," said the second man, speaking from a crimped mouth in a meaty, ruddy-complexioned face whose display of pockmarked cheeks and battle scars at the corner of the left eye and across the chin spoke also of a life lived hard. "Mayor van Dekker and I wouldn't care to think that we'd ridden nearly fifty miles to tell our tale in the presence of a daydreamer."

Hudson shifted ever so slightly in the chair behind his desk, hardly making it squeak. His expression was cool but a fire had been stoked. He didn't think he'd ever been so insulted in his life. Call him a gadabout, a ruffian, a rascal, a ne'er-do-well, a soldier of fortune, an opportunist, a bully (when it suited him to be so), a lecher (also the same), an intemperate rogue, a foul wind, a loose cannon, a gentleman of three ins and three outs, a goosecap, a pudding-head and a bachelor's son, but a *daydreamer?*

Such an insult might call for a duel, if these two had not come to this address offering money to solve their problem. And so, as this was the entire purpose of the Herrald Agency's newly founded New York office at Number Seven Stone Street, here in the year of 1702, it behooved Hudson not to behave as a scapegrace or a hobbledehoy, but rather to draw in his horns and observe the tact.

"All right," said Hudson, letting the errant misspoken word exit his mind like a grimy beggar kicked from a kitchen. "Let's start again, shall we?" He had before him on the desktop a sheet of white paper. He dipped a quill in his inkpot and held it ready. It occurred to him that a peal of distant thunder on this rainy day in the second week of September could be an omen of things to come...or, it just meant a pair of muddy boots on the evening walk back to his room.

They had told him their names and positions when they'd arrived a few moments before, and also the manner of their arrival at Number Seven. The purple-pated Willem van Dekker was the mayoral eminence of the town of Briartooth, in New Jersey, and rough-faced Dirk Sleet the head constable. They had reached New York last night. This morning they had gone to City Hall for advice on their problem. A quick audience with Gardner Lillehorne had ensued, during which New York's own strutting and preening master of constables had told them their situation was regrettable but out of the hands of the law because nothing could be proven. Lillehorne at least had had the decency to direct van Dekker and Sleet to the Herrald Agency, and thus they now occupied two chairs before Hudson's desk and began the recitation of their problem anew.

"A monster is roaming the woods of Briartooth," said the mayor, whose face seemed to ripple with a flinch even at the mention of it. His voice carried a nasal Dutch accent that was hard on Hudson's English ear. "The creature has committed murders and cannot be captured or contained. We need someone to find this thing and rid us of it, before it kills again."

"A *monster,*" Hudson repeated. His charcoal-gray eyebrows went up, first the left one that was split by a jagged scar, and then the right. His quill had not moved a fraction of an ant's leg. "In your woods."

"Yes, in our woods," said Sleet, who obviously was coming to the end of his charming demeanor. "You have the same look in your eye that idiot Lillehorne gave us this morning. This is a serious matter! As I say, we haven't ridden—"

"Nearly fifty miles to be scoffed at, I'm sure," Hudson offered a quick but tight smile and drew the desk's candle a bit closer to his paper, as a thickening of clouds had cast a darker pall into the room. A steady rain peppered the window glass. Beyond the windows hovered a gray gloom. Hudson wondered how Matthew was faring. The moonbeam had done quite well at that affair he'd termed "The Queen of Bedlam"; he'd escaped with his life after turning a lot of important teacups over. Indeed, sweeping them off the table and smashing them on the floor. Hudson had thought the harrowing experience would send Corbett into a fast and permanent retirement from the rigors of problem-solving, no matter what Katherine said about him, but the boy had solved that incident involving the Eternal Maidens Club and even now he was across the river helping a man who'd been swindled out of his horse in a crooked game of Jingo at a roadside tavern. Hudson had offered to go with him, as he knew those tavern dogs could bite most savagely when roused and challenged, but Matthew had said he needed to do this on his own and so Hudson—against his better judgment—had shrugged and let the moonbeam float off to recover a horse from a den of thieves. Good luck to him, and here was hoping Corbett came back in one piece...was that why the extra tankard of ale went down at the Trot last night? Because Hudson was actually *worried* about the boy?

No.

Of course not. After all, the boy had acquitted himself fairly well in that more recent mess with the Four Lamplighters last month, curse the memory.

It had gone down because he was extra-thirsty. End of story.

"Description of so-called monster, please," said Hudson, his quill now ready to scribble down at least *something*.

"We have no proper description," van Dekker replied.

The quill went into its resting place beside the inkpot. "Gentlemen," said Hudson, who put his large hands upon the desktop and laced his fingers together as if erecting a personal fence against fools. "Are you telling me that no one has ever *seen* this monster?"

"Someone has seen it," said Sleet. "A young girl, aged eleven years. Her description of it to her father and mother was nearly incomprehensible. Then she went into a state of terrified sobbing, was put to bed in a doctor's care and has not spoken or hardly eaten since...and that was five days ago, and the last straw as far as the citizens of Briartooth are concerned."

"The last straw? It seems you're giving me a haystack before the barn is built. What's the beginning of this story?"

"A history," said van Dekker, "of Briartooth, if you please. I'm sure you would not be surprised to know that less than fifty miles westward of New Amsterdam is the edge of the world as we know it to be."

"You mean 'New York,'" Hudson corrected.

"I mean what I say. New Amsterdam it shall always be to myself and the descendants of the great Dutch families who retreated from the treacherous English after our colony was stolen in return for a few islands of doubtful worth." A spray of spittle issued from the mayor's mouth and dappled the paper atop Hudson's desk, and the old man's face under the purple wig became further contorted. "We were betrayed by our own. Scoundrels all! We should have rightly stood our—"

"The matter at hand," said Sleet, who in speaking put a hand on van Dekker's arm to restrain the mayor's embers from breaking into an orange flame. "What Willem is getting at, is that Briartooth is situated in the wilds. Five years ago it was a single trading post and a small fort. Then came the discovery of the hordes of beavers in and around Black Oak Swamp, and suddenly Briartooth exploded with new wealth, new citizens, new businesses, and everything it takes to grow a *real* town. The going price of beaver pelts continues on an upward climb."

"Hm," said Hudson. He frowned. "What do the Mohawks think of their land being taken by industrious white traders?"

"We have an agreement with the local tribe. They are paid a yearly sum and a small token on every pelt."

"Very Christian of you. Also playing with a damned devil's fire. If you think paying Mohawks an extortion fee to keep them from coming into town one night and slaughtering every man, woman and child in their beds will work forever, you don't know their whimsical ways."

"Our agreement has so far been unsullied," said Sleet, with a slight lift of his slablike chin. "There's no reason to expect a breakdown in what is profitable to both Briartooth and the tribe."

"Here's hoping," Hudson answered, with another tight smile. He picked up the quill again and redipped it. "All right, so Briartooth is becoming a wealthy town due to the pelt trade, and it sits...as you say, Mr. Mayor, at the edge of the world. Where does the monster enter in?"

It was a moment before van Dekker spoke, for it seemed he was gathering his thoughts and organizing them enough to continue. "We have had, for the past five years, at least two hunters and trappers every year who have disappeared without a trace in the vicinity of the swamp. The same as for, most recently last month, a young man who arrived in Briartooth to take stock of the town for a potential business opportunity. Mrs. Harmon at the boarding house warned him not to go out into the woods alone, but she says he had an interest in the local botanicals and he unwisely disregarded her advice. He too has vanished, and his wife has visited Briartooth demanding to know what's happened to him. So you see—"

"I do see," Hudson interrupted, for he thought he could already solve the problem. "You're attributing the presence of a monster to explain the actions of a bear, a wild boar, a panther, a highwayman or a Mohawk who has decided not to play by your rules." He shrugged. "I'm sure every hunter and trapper in that area understands the risks."

"We have considered all those factors," said Sleet, who Hudson noted laced his fingers together in his lap to make his own foolproof fence. "But Mr. Greathouse…if any of those things befell our friends…where are the bodies? Yes, I know Black Oak Swamp—the area around Black Oak Lake— is large and extremely dense, but there's no trace of anything. We've sent search parties out and they have remained in the woods for many days and nights, finding nothing. These men are well-suited as trackers, with much experience. We've even paid the Mohawks to search…but, again, nothing."

"Not quite," said van Dekker. "The footprints, if you please."

"Ah yes, the footprints." Sleet nodded, his face grim. "In the case of the young man who disappeared, footprints were found in an area where there appeared to have been a struggle. There was a spillage of blood but no body. There were other marks where something—the young man, we conclude—was dragged through the brush a distance. The body was dragged into the lake. We searched as best we could on the other side, but the tangles of briars in that swamp are fearsome and some places are simply impossible to comb through."

"Footprints," said Hudson. "You mean 'boot prints'?"

"No," van Dekker answered. "The prints of bare feet. I see you are quite a large man, but I'd wager the size of the prints we found would burst even your boots."

"So this monster is in actuality a good-sized man?"

"Well…" van Dekker darted a glance at Sleet and then continued on. "The footprints, sir, are strange."

"How?"

"Four toes on the left foot," said Sleet.

"Six toes on the right," said van Dekker.

Hudson remained silent.

Distant thunder echoed across the town. Hudson looked down upon his paper and saw that his hand and the quill had been at work in the last few seconds without his fully realizing such. Scribed before him was *six toes on the right foot*, followed by a pair of question marks.

"Interesting," Hudson said, when he returned his gaze to the two visitors. He felt himself gaining strength and purpose for the challenge. He said, "Tell me about the child."

"Her name is Andra van Otten," Sleet answered. "As I said, eleven years old. She and a number of her friends were dared by another group of children to walk through the woods to Black Oak Lake and back. There's sufficient high ground to keep out of the bogs. Andra and the others went,

THE HOUSE AT THE EDGE OF THE WORLD

it being broad daylight and the children carrying sticks to defend themselves with."

"Sticks," Hudson said. His eyebrows lifted once more. "I presume these children have heard stories of this monster from their elders?"

"Whenever another person vanishes, it's the talk of the town. Children can be foolish, as you know if you have any. Andra's parents tell me the child and her friends were supposed to bring back swamp roses to prove they'd gone all the way to the lake. The most experienced trapper in Briartooth won't go into that area alone and without a blunderbuss, but here you have a group of six children with sticks wandering around out there. In any case...after a time all of them lost their nerve and went back to town...all except for Andra."

"Can you tell me what she experienced?"

"Ah...well..." Sleet tapped a finger against his chin a few times. "The tale—as disjointed as it may be—is that Andra was coming back through the woods, the sun was lowering, and suddenly—this is all according to what her parents have said—Andra felt the presence of something behind her. She heard a heavy movement—again, their description—and she turned to see...the creature, coming at her with terrible speed. She ran, and thank Christ she's small and fast. The worst part...is that the creature is also fast, and when it was nearly upon her Andra went to ground and winnowed into a hollow log. I daresay that saved her life. According to the parents, the monster picked up one end of the log and began to drag it back toward the swamp. She crawled out the other end, got to her feet and ran again, and she did not look behind her to see if the thing was coming...she just fled for her life. When she told her parents what had happened they came to see me at once."

"Understandable. Quite an experience for a young girl." Hudson had written down *heavy movement* and *terrible speed*. Obviously the thing's malformed feet did not impair its mobility. "You do have *some* kind of description?"

"It makes no sense," said van Dekker. "Even in describing a monster such as that abomination."

"Sense or not, I'd like to hear it." Hudson redipped his quill and waited.

Sleet said, "The creature as Andra described it—again speaking with her parents—is that it's man-shaped, but large and bulky. As to it possibly being a man, it wore no clothing and its flesh had been raked by the briars."

"White flesh?"

"Yes, it's no Mohawk," said Sleet. "Now here...we get to the part that in our minds makes it a monster. The face of the creature as Andra has described it was—as she put it—'mostly mouth' and full of jagged teeth. She says it was bald and had a dark beard. And...the strangest thing...is that Andra has attested it had only a single eye."

"Blind in one eye? That's strange how?" asked Hudson.

"One eye," said the mayor, "in the center of its face."

"A cyclops," said Sleet.

Hudson digested this information and realized as he scribed it onto the paper that young Mr. Corbett would be gnashing his teeth to get at this case, and so it prided Hudson to be able to look across the desk at the two men and say, "I believe I should accompany you to Briartooth. Twenty pounds up front, and fifty pounds if I find and remove your problem. What say you?"

"We say we welcome your interest, and that the future of our town is imperiled if this condition continues," van Dekker answered, "so we find your fee to be reasonable."

"Glad to hear it." Hudson said. "I should tell you that I don't believe in monsters. There has to be a logical explanation for this, which I intend to—" He was interrupted by a quick sound of something tumbling on the staircase just beyond the office's closed door. "—find," he finished calmly.

"We appreciate that," said Sleet, "but what in the name of Heaven was that *noise?*"

"The ghosts that haunt this building." Hudson put his quill aside. "On rainy days they throw each other down the stairs."

"Ah," said van Dekker, as if this made all the sense in the world, but his eyes had narrowed and shifted toward Sleet, questioning a man who did not believe in the torments of a monster yet held regard for the pranks of ghosts.

"I'll be ready to leave in the morning at first light," Hudson said. "If you gentlemen wish me to be an affable travelling companion, you may take me to dinner this evening at Sally Almond's tavern over on Nassau Street."

"Our pleasure, sir," announced the mayor of Briartooth, who had regained his composure yet could not help turning his lilac-wigged head to gaze at the closed doorway beyond which romped the restless spirits.

Hudson smiled and nodded. *Yes,* he thought, *call me ruffian, gadabout, a soldier of fortune, a foul wind and a loose cannon...fine...but also call me quite hungry and desirous of someone else to foot the bill, and therefore I have solved my first problem of the day.*

TWO

HUDSON HAD ARRIVED AT THE EDGE OF THE WORLD. HE STOOD ATOP A gray rock on a hillock looking toward the vast unknown.

It was many shades of green and brown, a wilderness thicket extending many miles out to the far horizon where the sun was beginning to burn red and sink toward its day's end. To his left and to the southeast could be seen the houses, the church, the schoolhouse, and the trading post of Briartooth, all tightly arranged on a number of short dirt streets. To his right and to the northeast about two miles distant he could make out a clearing where blue smoke rose amid the wood-and-dried-mud dwellings of the local Mohawk tribe. He saw they had a corral there with a number of horses, which meant they had greater mobility and most likely used those to trade with other tribes. Before him and slightly to the right he could see the oval of Black Oak Lake, its smooth surface mirroring a perfectly blue and cloudless afternoon sky. At this distance the swamp that surrounded the lake appeared to be a morass of boggy puddles, patches of woods and tangles of thorn, yet in this pleasant light it appeared no more sinister than someone's overgrown garden graced with a few muddy footprints. Several blasts of wildflower colors and a carpet of pearly-white flowers in a small clearing almost at the base of the hillock he stood upon was truly inviting. Hudson could see how one might walk into that territory simply for the experience of enjoying its wild beauty.

And that, he reasoned, had been the end of the young botanist, John Stoddard.

Hudson had arrived last evening with van Dekker and Sleet after a ride of three days. A conversation with Mrs. Harmon at the boarding house this morning had told him that Stoddard and his wife were makers of soaps and medicinal ointments. The young man had come to Briartooth as part of a sales trip to the more outlying localities. A bowl of fragrant swamp roses on Mrs. Harmon's front desk had piqued Stoddard's interest, and in spite of the woman's warning not to venture into the swamp alone he had set out likely with the brash surety of youth that he was immune to all dangers, yet he did have the sense to carry with him a loaded pistol.

Hudson wondered if Stoddard had not stood exactly as he was standing now, with Briartooth at his back and the tantalizing—and, yes, very beautiful—unknown before him. A soft breeze brought to Hudson's nostrils the heady aroma of the flower garden, yet beneath the fragrance lay the odor of brackish water and depthless bog. That subtle warning had not been enough to turn John Stoddard away from his fateful appointment with the so-called monster; neither would it turn Hudson Greathouse away, though he still believed this cyclops creature—if it really did exist, and not just in a child's fevered mind—was a manufacture of this earth and not of the realm of Greek gods gone mad.

He was dressed for a camping trip, wearing brown breeches and supple brown boots, a close-fitting gray shirt and a light canvas tan-colored jacket, with a black woolen skullcap upon his head. In the haversack strapped to his back was a supply of pemmican, a flask of water, his tinderbox and the makings of a fire, two pistols and ample ammunition. At his right side was a knife in a leather sheath. A canvas bag at his feet held a blanket and a one-man tent he could set up and take down with no difficulty. He was ready for a night in the realm of the cyclops, and to see what he would see.

But…a *moment*.

What is *that?* he asked himself, and from a side pocket of the haversack he removed a spyglass. He opened it to its full length and trained it a few degrees to his left and down into the woods.

There…amid the sheltering trees.

A house.

And not *simply* a house, but quite the two-storied, gable-roofed mansion. It was made of dark stones mortared together with white seams, like a chocolate cake with vanilla icing between the layers. The spyglass showed him a few windows, some shuttered and some not; many sections of the walls were simply blank, and his impression was that—oddly—whoever had built that house did not have much of an affinity for the outside world. He counted four chimneys. The house was fairly well-camouflaged amid the surrounding forest. Looking back and forth at the town of Briartooth and the dark-stoned mansion, Hudson realized the house was perhaps half a mile more westerly than the town, likely connected to it by a road he could not see, and was thus half a mile more at the edge of the world than Briartooth fancied itself to be.

He kept watch on the house for a moment more through the glass. Nothing moving there, except a flock of birds passing over. He collapsed the spyglass and put it away, but still his gaze remained on the roofs and the chimneys. A large house, built with great effort and certainly great expense. Built to last for a hundred years…but why here, even further west than Briartooth? Why was it not nestled within the relative safety of the town itself? It seemed to Hudson that whoever lived in that house was tempting fate, because surely one day the Mohawks were going to tire of playing parlor games with the settlers and take their land back by bow and tomahawk. He was amazed they'd turned a blind eye on the construction of that huge

domicile, but probably they were amused by the eccentricities—and fool-
ishness—of the white man.

It was time to go down into the swamp and earn his pay.

He descended from his rock on the hillock, mindful of small depres-
sions in the earth that might cause a misstep. He had come too far in his
life and circumstances, he mused, to break his neck walking down a hillside.
Before him was the carpet of grass and small white flowers. Birds sang in
the trees. There was a soft drone of insects all around. Yellow moths flew
up from the vibration of his boots upon the ground. Dragonflies flitted
about, hovering for a few seconds in the darkness of his shadow. The sun
was warm, the breeze carried a slightly cool breath that announced the end
of summer, and all seemed right with the world.

This was the kind of day, Hudson thought, that could kill a man. It
lulled the senses to sleep. Better to be on the cannon-cratered battlefield,
where the crack of the musketeers' weapons, the clash of swords and the
hurrahs of fighting men created a thunderous symphony, as bitter as it may
be. He was aware that all life—just as all soldiers—struggled to survive, and
this stronghold of nature was no different; there were many wars going on
all around him, most of them unseen. It was the world: a constant battlefield with life or death as the stakes, no matter what the façade.

Hudson continued across a clearing about a hundred yards wide, with
weeds and grasses up to his knees. He was following a map of the area he'd
received from Dirk Sleet, who'd told him several of the local hunters had
volunteered to come out with him to help him set his trap for the monster
of Black Oak Swamp, but Hudson was having none of that; he preferred
not to be responsible for the lives of anyone else, and it seemed to him that
this was his own battle to fight.

The subject of wars and battles had been much on his mind since his
first meeting with van Dekker and Sleet, and made more so by his inland
excursion to what was essentially a Dutch enclave. Of course there were
many Dutchmen in and around New York; there were whole towns in New
Jersey made up of Dutchmen, but Briartooth was different in that he had
the impression the Dutch here were still at war with the English, at least
in their own minds. They had settled this town so far from any other not
only for the purpose of the beaver pelts, but as if to create their own small
world, and one of the first things he'd seen upon entering Briartooth was the
windmill built of orange-painted clapboards at the edge of a pasture where
a herd of cattle grazed.

He wondered how van Dekker and some of the other Dutchmen
he'd met would react to the knowledge that at sixteen years of age Hudson
Greathouse had left the hovel where his mother had perished of bloody
coughing fits—his hard-edged and cruel soldier father having fled the family

long before—and joined the English army in time to serve in the last years, 1677 and 1678, of the Franco-Dutch war, the enemy being the soldiers who marched under the tricolor orange-white-and-blue *Prinsenvlag*. Hudson had noted that same banner on display on a flagpole beside Briartooth's town hall and also beside its schoolhouse. His limited knowledge of the Dutch language had come from bloodied prisoners of war begging for their lives, which he had not been inclined to favor in those turbulent and impassioned days of carnage.

He trudged on, coming upon soggy earth from which sprang tangles of briars. Yet there was higher ground, as Sleet had said, and Hudson's boots for the present remained dry. The woods line was just ahead. Hudson saw that the sunlight would be dramatically cut within what appeared to be a formidable thicket this side of the true morass of Black Oak Swamp. A bird flew up shrieking at his approach, a sudden jarring noise that in spite of his sturdy fortitude put his nerves on edge.

As he neared the woods his thoughts returned to the war. This shadowed place reminded him of a scene in which he and a band of other mercenaries fighting for the English-allied French had hunted down a half-dozen Dutch soldiers who'd escaped the carnage of the battle of Cassel. Their instructions had been to bring the soldiers back alive…but in the bloodlust that war and the pursuit of revenge awakened, such aspects of civilization perished on the point of the sword. Six heads placed on a table in the commander's tent had told the tale.

Hudson entered the woods, following a trail that likely had been cut by the boots of many hunters and beaver trappers. Ponds of brackish water festered on both sides, and the swirl of insects around him made him glad he'd applied peppermint oil to his face and hands before leaving Mrs. Harmon's boarding house.

His intent was to find a place near the lake where he could make camp for the night. A large fire might serve to keep away any roaming animals, but might also serve to invite the so-called monster in for a closer inspection. He forged onward, aware of the coils of briars that now grew in such abundance that they twined up the trees and formed thorny canopies above his head.

He was the last of the League of Eight. The eighth man, the only survivor of the mercenary band that after Cassel had volunteered for the most dangerous jobs. At the conclusion of that war, the League of Eight had made a decision. They had bound to each other by document and blood to continue their services for any country allied to England. It was, in essence, a military corps of problem-solvers. If war plans must be stolen, assassins foiled or the order of a kingdom put to wreckage, the League of Eight was presented the honors. Over the years the young Hudson Greathouse had seen his companions fall...Reejer, Windom, Bartlesby, O'Meara, Nevirosky, Tallman, and Keifer. They had died in various ways, by Dutch or Spanish bullet or sword, by hangman's noose or executioner's axe, by dagger to the heart or poisoned kiss. He alone lived to tell the tales, but like the six heads on the commander's table he was obliged to silence.

After that, the desire to dance in the hellish ballroom of warfare left him. But it was hard for a soldier to find peace in the world, especially if soldiering was his world and especially if the world was always in need of soldiers, which was always true. He could not go to blacksmithing, or becoming a stablemaster or the owner of a grist mill or a tavern where memories of the challenging and precarious past gnawed at the soft and uneventful present. What, then? In the fugue of an aftermath of aimless wenching and drinking at the end of his second marriage, his eye had wandered over an advertisement in the London *Gazette*. *Needed, Adventurers With Keen Minds and Hardy Spirits. Inquiries to The Herrald Agency, Number Twelve Raphael Street, Knightsbridge.*

And so the world had continued its turning from dark into light, and Hudson Greathouse had found a new place in it. But...ever the same...a problem-solver, though in this incarnation he was expected to use the wits and the mind more than the sword or bludgeon.

On he went, deeper into the tangles yet following the tamped-down trail. His boots began to find mud. Spears of sunlight penetrated the overhead foliage and tendrils of heated mist wafted about, giving the scene a phantasmagoric bent. Though the sun was strong and the sky was blue, Hudson's rapier injury of the ninth of October, 1686, was bothering him; the two ribs that had been broken on his right side and healed back in their own knotty way foretold rain by three days.

Within twenty minutes he came out of the swampy woods upon the vista of the lake. Numerous streams radiated from it. Along their lengths he could see the beaver dams in them; obviously the hunting and trapping had not caused the beavers to head out in search of safer territory. Smaller ponds sparkled with sunlight, but the air had become heavy with the pungence of the swamp. Hudson pushed on, meaning to follow the curve of the lake, but it became hard going with the profusion of thorns and the black mud bogs that appeared nearly underfoot. He crossed several of the streams and noted that they were all shallow, maybe calf-deep at most, and it occurred to him that whatever "monster" lurked out here—if one lurked at all—it could follow the streams in order to hide its tracks and its direction. But that would mean it had the intelligence of a man, wouldn't it? He shook his head as he roamed onward, and caught a glimpse of a good-sized buck and doe just an instant before they crashed away into the foliage.

After another forty minutes of exploration Hudson found a small, dry and high-ground clearing on the western side of the lake and, since the sun was sinking ever more toward the horizon, he decided this was the place to make camp. Moving with a purpose and surety born of experience, he took off his haversack and went about setting up and staking down his tent. Then he made a circle of stones about four feet in diameter and gathered up pinewood kindling and larger pieces of wood for his fire. He settled himself to wait for nightfall. As the sun sank down and the dark began to crawl over the world he used his tinderbox to strike a flame. When the fire was going to his satisfaction—a large, smoky fire to lure all monsters in the immediate vicinity—he ate some pemmican and an apple he'd purchased at Briartooth's general store. He drank a few sips of water from his leather flask and sat cross-legged before the crackling flames, which he had to admit were ridiculously high and a waste of good wood for one person, especially on a pleasantly warm night such as this. Even so, there was no shortage of available firewood out here, so he didn't concern himself with wastefulness very much.

A waxing half-moon made its appearance in a star-filled sky. Hudson listened intently to the night's symphony: the *chirrup* of crickets, the entrancing *sirrus-sirrus-sirrus* of insects calling back and forth in the trees, the hooting of a distant owl. The sounds relaxed him, but not so much that he didn't keep the two loaded pistols close at hand, one to the left and one to the right.

He continued to feed the fire to keep it high. He had no doubt it had brought a scouting party of Mohawks out to find the source of the smoke; they had likely seen the foolish white man they'd expected to see and gone back to their dwellings. Hudson lay back and looked at the stars for a while, contemplating the many other nights he had done so when time and circumstance allowed. He took a moment to wonder how the Chess Boy was doing on his own expedition into the dark territory of crooked gamesmanship, then he got up and walked a distance away to relieve himself, returned to the tent and built the fire up again, drank some more water and took the pistols with him when he slid into the tent upon the blanket he'd laid down.

His eyes closed, but he did not sleep just yet. He listened to the hooting of the owl. A breeze stirred the treetops. The bass rumbles and higher-pitched croaks of the frogs built to a crescendo, silenced as if on cue, and then began to build once more. Far away a pair of dogs started barking, probably from the Mohawks' settlement.

And just that quickly Hudson sensed that he was no longer alone...or, at least, he was no longer the only creature in the swamp and these woods that walked on two legs.

He heard the crunching of weeds behind the tent. At once he grasped both pistols and sat up, his head just grazing the tent's canvas. The fire was still burning brightly. He waited, hearing the sound of someone—some *thing*?—slowly and with seeming caution approaching his refuge.

And then, a voice.

"Pardon? You, there. Pardon, please."

A civilized and very polite monster, Hudson thought. Still, he took his pistols with him when he pushed himself out of the tent and stood up to face his visitor.

"I am unarmed, sir," said the man, who took stock of Hudson's weapons but stood his ground. He lifted his triple-wicked lantern a bit higher to illuminate his own face. "May I ask what it is you're doing here?"

"Hunting," Hudson said.

"Hunting *what*, exactly?"

"The monster. Are you it?"

The man's face was impassive. Hudson judged him to be in his late thirties, in good health, tall and slender and with a sharp-boned facial structure framed by a neatly trimmed black goatee and mustache. His hair, tied back in a queue so tight Hudson thought it must have been painful, was also black or very dark brown, with just the beginning traces of gray at the temples. His eyes appeared to be the same ebon or darkest shade of brown, and his nose was slim-bridged and flared slightly at the nostrils. He was wearing an expensive-looking leather waistcoat with mother-of-pearl buttons over a pale yellow shirt, a pair of black breeches and boots the same. Hudson had caught what to him was a twang of the Dutch accent in the man's voice that was as irritating as the mosquitoes and other insects that swirled around and around in the lantern's light.

Then the man laughed.

It was a polite laugh and it disappeared quickly enough, but it left the man's face in an attitude of true amusement. "Me, the *monster?*" He gave an additional chortle. "What tales have they been feeding you?"

"*They?*"

"The fine citizens of Briartooth. Surely they've been filling your head with their confused pap of fears and suppositions?" His black eyebrows went up. "May I ask your name, and how you come to be camping at near midnight on my property?"

"Your property? Not the town's?"

"The entire town and this expanse of land up to the Mohawk settlement is my property. Belonging to my family, I should say, and deeded to us by the English over twenty years ago. Now…your name and situation, please?"

"Hudson Greathouse. I've come from New York on behalf of Mayor van Dekker to—"

"Oh, my Lord!" said the man, with a quick scowl. "He and Sleet, I presume, have dragged an *outsider* into this? Are you a constable of some regard?"

"Not a constable, but I do hold myself in some regard." Hudson gave a wry smile. "Obviously van Dekker and Sleet hold me in regard, too." He nodded toward the dark line of the woods behind the man. "I'm guessing that's your house I've seen through my spyglass? Very well-constructed to be out here in the wilderness. What's *your* name?"

"August van Remm. Yes, my sister and I live there. It was built when Briartooth was a simple trading post. Then the hunters and trappers moved in, much to our discomfort."

"Discomfort?"

"Our father," said van Remm, with a chill in his voice, "would not have built so far from the nearest village if he hadn't wished privacy. There was no keeping the intruders out when the rush on the beaver pelts began." He stopped speaking, and Hudson could tell that the younger man was studying him from head to foot. "Well," van Remm said after a moment, "at least they found a gent large enough to fight this imagined monster, should one actually appear."

"You do know it appeared several days ago and attacked a little girl by the name of Andra van Otten?"

Van Remm shook his head. "I didn't know. My sister, Leopolda, and I do not associate more than is necessary with the townspeople. But...I am distressed by all this talk of beasts and monsters in these woods...it is utter nonsense, to be sure." The lines in his forehead deepened. "The little girl... is she all right?"

"I haven't seen her, but I understand she had a terrible experience. Or... at least, what she's described is harrowing. As far as being physically harmed, she was fortunate in that regard because she was able to outrun the thing."

"She described it?"

"She did. A large-sized white man, bald and dark-bearded, no clothing...and a cyclops to boot."

There was no response from van Remm for a few seconds. He looked stunned, as if all the air had been sucked from his lungs. Then he drew a breath and said, quietly, "A cyclops."

"One eye in the center of its face. I guess that makes it a cyclops."

"I...I've never...I've never *heard* of such a thing in real life, outside of myths and fables! You seem to be a reasonable man. What do you make of this?"

Hudson shrugged. "It seems that every year for the past five at least two men in this area have disappeared. I suppose you know about those?"

"I do. No one has ever said these woods were free from danger."

"The last was a botanist named John Stoddard. And now this supposed sighting by the little girl. I'm being paid to investigate." Hudson held up his pistols. "As you can see, I came prepared."

"I saw your fire from the window of my study," said van Remm. "I had to come and find out who was foolish enough to pitch camp here. I *knew* it had to be..." He searched for a conclusion to his statement. "An *outsider*," he said. "No citizen of Briartooth would be in these woods after dark."

"And here I intend to stay," said Hudson. "Whether this is your property or not, there's a job I've been hired to do and I'm going to finish it to the best of my ability."

"What? By killing the monster and dragging its body back to town to be skinned and hung up on the wall of the trading post? How much money are you charging these simpletons? I don't know what Andra van Otten thinks she saw, and I don't know what happened to those hunters and trappers, but...a *cyclops*? Really, sir!"

"That's what she described," Hudson said. "But I can see you're not too concerned about stumbling into a monster in the dark. How far is it to your house? A quarter of a mile? And you out here unarmed? Don't you have a healthy respect for the dangers of Black Oak Swamp after nightfall?"

"There's a path from here to our house. I know it very well." He motioned toward it with the lantern. "Leopolda and I enjoy walking in the forest. It is a peaceful and beautiful place. Let me tell you that in our twenty years of living here, neither Leopolda nor I have ever seen anything in these woods more dangerous than a rutting stag with a formidable set of antlers. Yes, there was a large black bear roaming out here at one point, but I understand the Mohawks killed it. There are treacherous bogs one might step into and be taken down without a trace, if one doesn't know the lay of the land. As far as there being a giant cyclops in the vicinity that steals away hunters and terrorizes little girls...well, enjoy your lucre from the townspeople over a nice bottle of wine at their expense, won't you?"

"The night is still young," Hudson replied. "And there's always tomorrow, and the day after that. I'm settled in until I can come up with an answer."

"Some questions are born of imbecility," van Remm said. "To which the only answer can be nonsensical." He gave a slight bow. "I wish you well in your quest, sir. I will also offer you a drink of good Dutch ale, if sometime tomorrow you wish to follow the path to our house."

"Thank you, I might take you up on that."

"A pleasure. Good night, then."

"Good night."

Hudson watched as van Remm turned away and, following the lantern's beam, crossed the clearing to enter the woods and regain the path home.

Hudson remained watching until van Remm's light was gone. Certainly the man was not very fond of the townspeople of Briartooth; in fact he seemed to resent the entire existence of the community. Hudson thought that van Remm's father must've been a fanatic for privacy, building all the way on the frontier twenty years ago when the nearest trading post then was probably equally twenty miles to the east. Why in the name of Queen Anne's hairpins would someone with such obvious wealth want to *hide* out here?

Hide was the right word, Hudson decided.

My sister and I live there, the man had said.

Why? What was the van Remm family hiding *from?* Especially if the father who'd built the house was gone, either deceased or departed back to the Netherlands. Why stay way out here, wearing his leather waistcoat and mother-of-pearl buttons with no one to impress and shunning everyone in Briartooth?

Hudson heard himself give a slight grunt. It was a mystery that could not be solved tonight. There were still many hours before the dawn, and as the supposed monster might just as well attack by daylight, he would have to always be on his guard. Maybe he could get a little sleep, though. Maybe.

He returned to his tent with his pistols in hand. He fed the fire one last time. Then he crawled into the tent, situated himself with the guns on either side, and drifted into a territory that was somewhere between true wakening and true sleep, but was the safest state for a soldier.

THREE

BY THE AFTERNOON OF THE FOLLOWING DAY, THE ACT OF COUNTING the butterflies and watching the beavers at work on their dams had become to Hudson only a little shy of torture. He had wandered around making his way as best he could through the briar thickets. He had waded through ankle-deep mire and probed the bogs with a long stick. He had examined snake holes close-up and wasps' nests at a distance. He had watched the crows fly and seen the gray-bellied clouds begin to slide in from the west. The way his ribs were aching, there was going to be one devil of a storm either tomorrow or the next.

He had entertained the idea of accepting van Remm's offer of ale, but that was for later. He was acutely aware of being watched as he moved about the forest and the swamp. Mohawks would never let themselves be seen by his white eyes, but they were surely present. If they were skulking in the area they might know something of this "monster" that would be of value, and just for the general principle of the thing they might not care to share their knowledge with the pale hunters and trappers out from Briartooth. Hudson considered that someone in the tribe must speak English, unless they were being communicated with in the Dutch language. Nevertheless, it was worth the walk.

He left his tent up but packed his pemmican, water flask, pistols and ammunition into his haversack. He strapped it onto his back and set off to see the Mohawks.

They would know he was coming long before he reached the settlement. That was fine with him. If they didn't want him in their camp they would let him know in some form or fashion, and if they were curious about his presence they would let him come on in without interference.

His walk through the dense forest was no jaunt along the Broad Way. Nearly two hours passed before Hudson saw the Indian symbol of a stylized bear on a tree trunk, applied there in chalky red paint. It meant this was one of the boundaries of what they considered their territory. He pushed on, crossing a small stream and then climbing up a rocky rise, at the top of which he saw the cooking fire smoke of the Mohawk settlement a few degrees to the right and only a couple of hundred yards away. When he started down the rise he became aware that he'd been joined by two figures moving in a crouch on either side of him in the underbrush. He saw only quick glimpses of their shapes; they made absolutely no sound in their forward progress.

As Hudson found himself on what was more or less a narrow path smoothed down by the passage of hundreds of Mohawk travellers, the escort on his right let out a cry that was part birdcall and part dog bark and altogether startling enough to raise the hackles on the back of Hudson's neck. The cry echoed off toward the village and caused the real canines there to raise a caterwaul of barking. An answering human cry came back as sharply as an owl screech. Hudson kept on going, and in another moment realized that about twenty feet behind him walked a bare-chested Indian with three feathers jutting up from his topknot and an array of small bones and trinkets dangling from both ears. The brave's sinewy arms and shoulders were covered with the blue swirls of tattoos and he wore a deerskin loincloth and calf-high deerskin boots. He looked fierce enough to chew leather into custard. Hudson noted the lack of body paint and considered it a good sign that he wasn't going to have to fight his way out of here to save his hair.

He continued onward, with the brave behind him and the two others on either side. When he came out along the path upon the wide clearing in which the village was situated, he became the center of attention of a half-dozen dogs that jumped and yipped around him, though the human population gave him only passing regard before they returned to their chores. A few children came running up, but the brave behind Hudson spoke harshly to them in the native tongue and they scattered. Then Hudson stood amid the well-constructed wood-and-dried-mud huts and the drifting blue cookfire smoke like a stranger in a strange world, nearly invisible to all but the yapping dogs. He looked to the tattooed brave, who motioned him to keep moving with what appeared to be a disdainful flick of the hand. The other two who'd escorted him in ran past, and in another moment a three-feathered brave with jagged lightning-like tattoos across his bare chest and intricate symbols on his face came stalking through the smoke. He stood before Hudson like an immovable chunk of rugged brown rock.

"Speak English?" Hudson asked.

"Fair," came the reply from the impassive and quite fearsome face.

"I'm—"

"Set roots by lake," the man said. "Little child's hut."

"My tent. I'm here to—"

"God's glory!" cried a ragged voice. "An Englishman!"

Hudson looked to his left, at what was certainly a sight.

The man who'd given this exclamation was rail-thin and bare-chested, every rib showing. He wore a pair of dirty, much-patched brown breeches and moccasins. His hair was blonde, nearly white, and hung in nasty tangles around his shoulders. His scraggly blonde beard was decorated with blue and red beads, among other bits of things Hudson did not wish to examine too closely. It appeared to Hudson that this gent had not bathed since the last time his mother had lifted him from his cradle, twenty-something years ago. He came toward Hudson on long gangly legs, his gaunt hook-nosed face grinning, his blue and bloodshot eyes aflame. He wore a small wooden crucifix on a leather cord around his neck, and Hudson instantly knew what he was: one of the frontier preachers who thought it was their duty to God to bring Christianity to the heathens. Hudson understood that most of those Johnny Baptists wound up either broken by the tests of faith the Indians presented—otherwise known as torture—or as nutty as mincemeat pie. This one fit the mold; he was missing the middle two fingers from his right hand and his left was bound up in a blood-crusted wrapping.

"To hear the English language is a delight!" the man said. Hudson saw tears well up in his eyes. "A damned delight!" the wilderness reverend proclaimed, and he wiped his face with a scabby elbow. "I am James Davees, late of Boston. Forgive me for not shaking hands, brother. I would hug you, if you would allow."

"No," said Hudson.

"Ah. Understandable. I am currently not in the best of condition, I realize." He underscored this statement by scratching fiercely with the jagged nails of his remaining fingers at a bloody place atop his head, where Hudson figured the fleas had pitched a permanent camp. Davees finished the task of further raking his scalp to the blood and then he squinted at Hudson as if seeing him for the first time. "What is your business, brother?"

"My name is Hudson Greathouse. I'm here from New York on behalf of the town of Briartooth, I'm investigating the tales of this 'monster' that's supposedly snatching away hunters and trappers. Do you—"

The Mohawk brave interrupted Hudson by firing a rapid stream of tongue-twisting lingo at Davees, who answered in the same fashion. The Indian seemed to be pondering Davees's reply for a few seconds, and then he gave Hudson a look that would have stabbed to the brain had it been a dagger. He shrugged, abruptly turned and stalked away.

"Where's *he* going?" Hudson asked.

"He knows why you're here. They all do. There's only one reason you'd be camping out by Black Oak Lake. He says it's all white man's nonsense and he wants nothing to do with it."

"Is that the chief?"

"The chief's eldest son. Tomuwae won't see you, it's no use to ask."

"It might be nonsense to the Mohawks," said Hudson, "but to the people of Briartooth it's very real. Or...at least, they believe it to be."

"I suspect you've seen nothing of this creature?"

"Nothing."

"I've been here a long time," Davees said. He wore a crooked grin and his eyes held a wild gleam that Hudson thought might be edging toward madness. "How fares Boston?"

"I haven't visited there for a while. I'm sure it grows apace."

"I had a wife and daughter," said Davees.

Hudson remained silent.

"I am now a messenger of God," the man went on. "It is important work."

"I'm sure. Well...Mr. Davees, I—"

"*Brother* Davees," came the correction. He took another step toward Hudson, who steeled himself to bear a nosegay of commingled odors of dried sweat, rancid oil, old urine, clotted excrement and other items of fetid repulse. His hard steel was nearly melted to soft pewter by the foul flames of Brother Davees's body, but he stood his ground. "Please...it's been so long since I've conversed with an Englishman. Briartooth is mostly Dutch, you know, and white men don't often come here. Won't you...*please*...allow me the pleasure of your company in a drink at my hut?"

How could one refuse the pleading of a soul who had given up everything to come out into the wilderness and play fool for the Lord? Hudson thought that the Mohawks were using him as a medieval court might use a jester, otherwise he would already be bones. He was nearly bones, at that. Maybe one of his tests of faith was the starvation treatment.

"I have a pig's bladder of blackberry wine," said Brother Davees, as if this were a grand inducement for further company.

Hudson looked up at the gray clouds that nearly covered the sun. The rain was still a distance off. He decided his two-hour journey here had to be useful to someone. Why not to James Davees, lately of Boston?

"Lead on," said Hudson, and the other man gave a shiver and all but gasped with relief.

They crossed the village with a contingent of dogs and children following behind, the dogs yapping and the children shouting and running about. Around Hudson and James Davees the daily life and chores of the village went on as if both white men were already ghosts and walking through the unseen world, perturbing only the restless canines and the uncomplicated minds of the young. To stop this discord a rotund woman with long gray braids suddenly came charging at the children, clapping her hands together and hollering like a brass band, and the youths scattered like birdshot.

Hudson followed Davees past the corral that held a dozen fine-looking horses and a few colts. Further along, next to a crowded pigsty that smelled equally as bad as the preacher, was a small hut set far apart from the others. It appeared to Hudson that the wood of the hut was not chinked by mud, but by dried horse manure.

"Here we are," Davees announced, as if his guest had not already known.

They entered through the folds of a thin blanket fixed across the opening. Within the dank interior, Davees with some effort by both his injured hands struck a flint to spark a wad of dirty cotton. From that small flame he lit a pair of candles stuck with melted wax on a table that looked as if it had been constructed by a blind carpenter using far fewer fingers than were available to Davees. The spreading light illuminated a single stool before the table, a pitiful arrangement of filthy blankets on the dirt floor and two buckets to hold drinking water and waste. On one wall a small wooden crucifix was attached by an arrangement of knotted vines and just beneath it stood a piece of uprooted tree trunk supporting an open, water-stained and much-battered Bible. The only other furnishing in this miserable hovel was a wooden box on the ground, and it was this that Davees bent down to open.

"Please," he said. "Sit, won't you?"

Hudson shrugged off his haversack, put it aside and eased himself down upon the stool, which groaned and trembled under his weight. When he was fairly certain it wasn't going to collapse, he relaxed...but not before he'd repositioned it so he was facing the way out.

From the box Davees brought forth a dark brown, oily-looking pig's bladder that had a cork stuck in it. This he set upon the table before Hudson, and then he produced from the box a pair of wooden cups with the bark still on them. "Would you open that for me?" Davees asked. "I can do so, but it does take some time."

Hudson uncorked the bladder. From it he poured into the cups a nearly black liquid that looked thick enough to be chewy. He caught the strong aroma of fermented blackberries and thought that one drink of this would be enough to have him seeing monsters behind every tree on the trip back.

"To your health, brother," said Davees. He took up a cup and drained it.

"The same," Hudson replied. His sip was what a mouse might've caught on its tongue, but even so his lips burned like the blast of Judgment Day and the fire went all the way down to his cellar.

"The spirit of the Lord is in this," said Davees, who was already pouring himself another shot of redemption. When his eyes had ceased to water, he sat cross-legged upon the ground and grinned up at Hudson with a mouthful of teeth that, already green to begin with, now were stained as dark as if he'd been drinking ink.

They sat in silence. It seemed to Hudson that Brother Davees was so starved for the company of another white man that the opportunity for feast had robbed him of speech. Hudson took another small sip of the deadly wine, cleared his throat, and asked, "How long have you been here?"

"Years," came the reply, along with a little giddy laugh. "Years and years. I am making progress, believe it or not. Or rather...the Lord is making progress, through me. I am His hands among the savages."

"I'd guard the remainder of my fingers, then. What have they been doing to you?"

"Oh...little tests. Little cuttings and burnings, here and there. At first...it was terrible, but now...I am the stronger for it. They make the wine for me. I have tried to hold communion, but it becomes a..." He was still grinning, stupidly, though a small ripple of disturbance seemed to pass across his face. "A rather uncontrollable event," he said. "You can understand."

"Yes." Hudson started to drink again and then thought better of it. He shifted uneasily, for Brother Davees just kept grinning and staring at him with those wild, glinting eyes as if he expected his visitor to speak some kind of profound revelation from God. Hudson felt the pressure to say something...anything. "Do you ever intend to return to Boston?"

"Hm," said the preacher, and now his brow furrowed and he peered into his cup as if the future could be read there in the grainy bits at the bottom. "A good question. The answer would be...if God intends me to return, I shall."

"Don't you miss your wife and daughter?"

"Oh, yes! Of course I do. You know, I started out as a schoolteacher. I had great designs to become an administrator at the school…but…I was passed over for the position several times. Then…well…I became a shade bitter, I suppose. I began to drink a little. A very little, at first. It is amazing, brother, how God works. I thought I was falling into a pit…striking out at my family…becoming angry that others were stepping into the role and responsibility I thought I should have, but…all that time, the Lord had His eye upon me. He told me what I must do, to make up for what I did to Hester that night, when she'd found what I did with her father's money. They were going to take me to court, I had no way out. A Sabbath night, at that. Cold outside, very cold."

Hudson worked the hard bark of the cup around in his hands and stared at his knuckles.

"Would you fill me up again?" Davees asked, and lifted his own cup in his mangled right hand.

"Surely," said Hudson. He filled it to the brim and returned it.

Davees gave a heavy sigh. "I do miss my…our…house," he said quietly. "A fine dwelling, that was. Built upon a leafy street, among other fine dwellings. I had a study…a fireplace…a fine porch to sit upon, and think of the world and our future." He smiled sadly. "But…I have a new purpose now, and I shall carry it out to the best of my ability, God willing. I shall bring the love and laws of Christ to the savage heart, no matter how long that takes. So…as I say, if God intends me to return to Boston, He will show me the way there."

"You have your work cut out for you," Hudson said, and Brother Davees nodded. Something else had been stirred in Hudson's mind when Davees spoke of the fine house he'd left behind in Boston. "Tell me…what do you know of August van Remm?"

"The van Remms? Well…they were living in that house long before I came here. They keep to themselves. I have never seen the sister, and only rarely have seen *him*."

"What? You've seen him in town?"

"Oh no. I've seen him here in the village. But very rarely, as I say."

"Here? What business does August van Remm have with the Mohawks?"

"He buys their horses." Davees lifted his cup once more and licked his darkened lips. "Just another touch, if you please."

Hudson held his next question until after he'd poured another small amount from the bladder and returned the cup to his host. "Buys their horses," Hudson repeated, to return the preacher to the proper track. "What need does he have of horses?"

"I don't know. Particularly the ones *he* buys."

"Meaning?"

Davees paused until he'd gotten some more of the blackberry fire down his gullet. "He buys only the horses that have become lame or infirm in their old age. The cream of the herd is sold to other villages at what they consider an auction. I've seen van Remm here when he comes to negotiate prices with Tomuwae. The chief is what you might call a canny business-man. He has seen that van Remm has a desire for the horses that no one else wishes to buy, and he raises his prices accordingly."

Hudson was silent for a while, taking this all in. "Why," he asked at length, "should a gentleman who seems to have no desire to travel or associ-ate with other persons wish to buy infirm and aged horses? Does that make any sense to you?"

"It is not my place to ask any questions concerning the tribe's busi-ness. I will say, from what I gather, that Tomuwae commands more money from August van Remm than what he earns on the beaver pelts. And Tomuwae doesn't want beads or trinkets, either; he demands the payment in good English gold. It buys them seeds for their crops, feed for the horses, handtools and whatever else they've decided they need from the trading post in Briartooth." Davees finished off the last of his drink. His eyes had become more shiny and even more bloodshot. "Sir?" he asked, his voice just a bit slurred. "Are you a religious man? Do you walk at the side of God the Father?"

"Never mind that," Hudson answered. "I want to know why August van Remm buys lame and worn-out horses. You say Tomuwae wouldn't see me?"

"Absolutely not. If he wished to see you he would've met you when you first walked in, and if you tried to approach his dwelling without an invitation you would be refused at the threat of violence."

"I think it's worth a try."

"I wouldn't push my luck, brother. They have given you respect because you've spent a night in the creature's territory and you seem unafraid. That's why they let you come here in the first place."

Again, it took a few seconds for Hudson to digest this information. "Hold," he replied. "Just a moment. Are you saying that the Mohawks be-lieve there really *is* a monster of some kind in Black Oak Swamp?"

"Several of the braves have seen it," came the answer. "I've heard them talking about it. They stay away from that area when they're hunting."

"I am told," said Hudson, "that the town of Briartooth used Mohawks to try to track this creature, but it was a failure."

"Not a failure. The Mohawks can track anything alive. In this case they didn't wish to find its trail."

"Why would that be?"

Davees shrugged. "I don't know, but from my understanding the command to lose the thing's trail came from Tomuwae."

"So the Mohawks don't think it's just white men's nonsense?"

"Not at all. As I say, the creature has been seen, but it's the business of white men. The Mohawks want nothing to do with it. Now…please, sir… let us talk about your relationship with the Lord." His grin presented the wine-stained teeth. "I think you should consider it, if you plan to spend another day and night seeking the monster of Black Oak Swamp."

"I do, and I will," Hudson said, "but I'm still not sure I believe in monsters." He stood up. Though it was only two miles back to his tent, it was a hard trip. "I'd better get moving."

"Please!" Davees scrambled to his feet, though when he had reached his summit the power of the wine staggered him. "Don't leave yet! We have much to talk about!"

Hudson hefted his haversack and put it on. "I regret I can't stay. I have a job to do."

"Can't you remain a few minutes longer? Please…let me hear what you know of Boston. The Thunder Man can wait, can't he?"

"The Thunder Man?"

"That's what the Mohawks call him. Those who've heard him cry out have remarked on the volume of his voice. Please, brother…stay a bit longer and tell me of Boston. Of what news from our England, as well. I'll escort you out when you're ready, but…I ask you…*God* asks you, through me… please indulge a sinner with a few crumbs from your table."

Hudson had made up his mind to leave, but he paused. What would it hurt, to give this wretch a few moments more? "All right," he said, and he took off the haversack again and put it aside. "Of Boston, and news from England." He took his place on the stool once more, and Brother Davees sat at Hudson's feet, his tortured hands clasped together as much as they were able, his tortured eyes upon his visitor with hopeful expectation of being delivered back to civilization for just a short time, his tortured soul eager for balm.

Hudson decided he would paint his "news" of Boston and England in the colors of the wildflowers that grew around Black Oak Lake, and by this he might leave James Davees with the fragrance of swamp roses here in this dismal hovel, that all was right with the world and no man need worry about the future of God's kingdom here on earth. The bitter truth of hatred and wars, of greed and inhumanities that seemed to be the true nature of Man had no place further burdening the heart of this servant.

Being a gadabout, a ruffian, an intemperate rogue, a foul wind, a loose cannon and all the rest of it, he thought it was the least he could do.

FOUR

A LOW RUMBLE OF THUNDER AWAKENED HUDSON FROM HIS STATE OF semi-sleep, and as he sat up in his tent to greet the dim gray light of morning the ache in his ribs told him that the predicted storm was fast approaching.

He peered out from the tent and looked up at the ominous clouds. No rain was yet falling, but the atmosphere had turned muggy, the smell of it wet and coppery. He roused himself to go pee and do his business in some distant weeds, then he withdrew back into his shelter, ate a piece of pemmican and drank some water. The noise of the wind was for the moment a polite whistle that came and went. Hudson listened to the sound of it rustling through the treetops and wondered where the owl that had hooted for most of the night was now hiding itself. He debated what his actions today should be; soon his only option would be to hunker down in the tent and wait for the rain to pass, and how long that might be was difficult to tell.

He had tended the fire until the early hours of the morning. The same as the night before, no monster had troubled him. His only frets had been the hooting of that damned owl and the humming of mosquitoes in his ears, though a fresh treatment of the peppermint oil to his exposed flesh kept them from biting.

Last night he'd stretched out to sleep with one question on his mind: why was August van Remm buying worthless horses from the Mohawks?

It was time, he reasoned, to trek along that path out of the swamp to the van Remm house and accept the offer of Dutch ale, which suited him for this early hour of the morning as well as at any other time of the day. If the van Remms were late sleepers, a heavy fist on the front door would get them moving. His curiosity about the horses would keep no longer.

Hudson hefted his haversack again and headed westward, as the wind tossed the treetops above his head and weak rays of sunlight struggled to pierce the clouds.

To call what he was following a "path" was being entirely too gracious, but at least the weeds were trampled down enough to show him the way. He entered the darkness of the forest, the oaks and elms towering over him by some forty feet, the whorls of briars and other malicious underbrush crowding in on either side. A long slow rumble of thunder gave speed to his pace, and he felt the first cold spit of raindrops on the back of his neck.

The ignoble forest path curved him to the left. A new shudder of wind brought green leaves tinged with autumn's yellow spinning around him. Shortly a wall of dark stones similar to those used in the construction of the van Remm house materialized before him; the wall was veined with green creepers and briar vines, was about eight feet tall, and appeared to block any further advance to the mansion. Still…there had to be an opening somewhere. The path continued to the left adjacent to the wall. Hudson followed it, as the next peal of thunder came as a high, sharp *crack* not unlike the report of a musketeer's flintlock.

He found an open archway and started to enter through it, but he paused to note what appeared to be a rusted gate of iron bars lying mostly obscured by the brush nearby. He saw where the gate had once been fixed to hinges in the archway, but had been removed—torn away, actually, it looked to him.

Well, he thought.

Something of considerable strength had done that, no doubt of it. He didn't think he himself could've done it, and he was the strongest man he knew. He passed on beneath the archway, and found that he was a short distance—maybe thirty yards or so—behind the looming shape of the dark-stoned, many-gabled van Remm house. To his right beneath the overhang of several large oak trees was a weathered barn in serious need of painting, and beside that a corral for the exercise of the horses. Attached to the barn was a shed in which stood a carriage adorned with a large V and R painted in gold leaf. The carriage had been painted black with gold ornamentation and trim, but it had definitely seen better days and was nearly as weathered as the barn. Hudson decided he might take a look at the horses before he announced his presence to August van Remm.

A bright and startling flash of lightning preceded the next crack of thunder. Again the wind spun leaves from the trees, yet only a few raindrops were falling from the turbulent sky. Hudson approached the barn, lifted the latch and entered.

Within the dim interior were bales of hay and canvas sacks of oats for the horses along with the usual array of buckets, coils of rope, and implements that might be found in any barn. He noted the absence of any saddles. There were four stalls, two of which held sad-looking, swaybacked horses blotched with sores. Hudson doubted they could pull a handcart, much less carry a rider or be hitched to a carriage. Toward the rear of the barn was a wooden gate that, when opened, appeared to offer a high and wide enough aperture for a horse to be led through. Hudson walked to it, unlatched the gate and pulled it open.

The smell of dried blood was nearly overpowering. This caused him to catch his breath and stop in his tracks. He heard the high, insistent buzzing of flies. The chamber he had entered seemed darker than the rest of the barn, with small cracks between the boards letting in only the faintest wraiths of outside light. He doubted that this chamber was ever well-lit even on a day when the sun was strong. He waited for a moment as his eyes became accustomed to the gloom. When the thunder spoke again one of the suffering horses gave what sounded like a moan from a human throat.

Hudson made out a heavy-looking chain hanging from the ceiling, with one devil of a wicked hook on its bitter end. The chain was attached to a wooden winch mechanism operated by what appeared to be the wheel of a sailing ship. A fly flew into his face and another landed on his lower lip; he quickly brushed both away, and took stock of the chamber in which he stood.

It occurred to Hudson that neither August nor Leopolda van Remm—or whoever did the work in this room—were very much concerned with keeping the place clean. Then again, of what use was there to clean a slaughterhouse, when obviously it was used with such regularity?

The floorboards had seen an ocean of blood. Gore had stained them nearly black. Flies whirled about in emulation of the storm-torn leaves. But there on one wall was an indication of someone's desire for organization: the killing and gutting instruments of heavy mallets, axes, saws and cleavers of many sizes and shapes were arranged on blood-stained shelves, ready for further use. At the center of the room was a large table, also black with dried blood. Someone had scattered handfuls of a white substance—sugar? salt?—upon the table. Hudson walked to the tableside and dared to wet an index finger with his tongue, dab it to the stuff and taste it.

Yes. *Salt.*

There was something else upon the table, stuck in the matted mess. Hudson reached out and ran his hand across it, and wondered how many aged and infirm horses had been gutted and hacked to pieces here, to leave so much of their manes and pieces of hide plastered in all that grue.

He retreated from the table. He stepped away from the chain with its hook used to impale and elevate a horse while its belly was cut open to let the intestines slide out. The floorboards offered an uneven footing; perhaps he was walking on the crusted remnants of some of last year's offal, for surely this chamber had been in use for a very long time.

The thunder boomed, shaking the place, and now both of the horses moaned.

The van Remms, Hudson realized, were buying old horses from the Mohawks and slaughtering them here. As for the salt...a preservative. They were cutting up horses for the meat, salting it down and storing it somewhere.

So...they liked horsemeat. Many did. But still...the way they were going about this...it didn't sit right in Hudson's craw. Surely they didn't hire a professional butcher to do the task; a professional would never have allowed the chamber to remain in this frankly wretched condition. And the way van Remm shunned the townspeople…no, this was being done by amateur hands, but practiced enough to know what they were doing.

He was a tough-stomached bastard, but with all this reek up his nose and the flies whipping into his face he needed to get out of here, fast.

He pushed the gate closed and relatched it. On the way out he saw the two swaybacked horses turning around and around in their stalls as if the human presence had made them more aware of their eventual fate in that dismal chamber. He cast his gaze away from the beasts, and as the lightning flashed white and the thunder roared again with a noise like a giant awakening from its sated slumber he walked out of the forlorn barn, paused to secure the latch and then stood under the oaks with the wind pulling and pushing him in opposite directions.

It appeared to him that most of the windows of the van Remm mansion were shuttered. That was no surprise, with this storm coming on. But…had there been a movement at a four-paned glass window high up in the house? Hudson thought—or imagined—he'd seen such, just a quick glimpse of something there and then gone. He debated his next move, whether to return to his tent or follow the carriage path around to the front door.

He'd been invited for a drink of ale. He was thirsty, after having all that odor of dried gore up his nose. And, his curiosity needed to be slaked as well. He considered that Matthew Corbett would most likely go around to the front door and knock for entrance. He decided he was not going to back off something the moonbeam would do, therefore his debate was ended on a point of honor.

On his way to the front of the mansion, Hudson considered also that Corbett was still pretty much of an impetuous fool, but so be it.

He ascended a set of dark stone steps to a spacious porch that sheltered a formidable oak door. He took hold of the plain brass knocker and gave it two poundings.

He waited. Lightning flashed once more and the thunder boomed. No one answered his request. Rain began to hiss through the trees and wind swirled across the porch. Hudson gave it a moment longer, then he reached out to grasp the knocker again.

There came the sound of a bolt being drawn. The door opened a crack. Hudson lowered his hand.

"*Ja?*" It was a woman's voice, low and smoky. Nothing of her could be seen.

"Good morning," Hudson answered, as cheerily as he could manage. "Are you Leopolda?"

"I am the *Madam* van Remm," she replied.

"Ah. Well, I'm—"

"*Meneer* Greathouse," she said curtly. "Yes, I know. August has told me about you."

"Did he tell you he invited me here for a drink?"

"He did." There was no movement to open the door any wider.

"I've come to claim it," Hudson prompted.

There was a pause. Then she said, "It is a bit early for visitation, don't you think?"

He was about to answer *Not so early that a glass of ale wouldn't be welcome* when the bottom dropped out of the lowering sky. With one more sizzle of lightning and crash of thunder the rain came down in torrents. Hudson looked upon the storm and saw that the world beyond the van Remm house had grayed out. Rain smashed upon the porch's roof with unsettling violence.

Hudson returned his attention to the door. Its crack had not widened a fraction, but neither had it diminished the same. "Nasty weather today," he remarked.

"It will pass."

"Is your brother at home?"

"He—" She stopped speaking. Hudson could hear the voice of August van Remm beyond the door, talking quietly to his sister in Dutch. She answered the same, the only word Hudson recognized being *Nee*, for the English *No*. The male van Remm spoke again, with a more insistent tone in his voice.

Then…silence but for thunder and rain.

The door opened.

August van Remm stood foremost, as his sister had retreated a distance. "Pardon, sir," he said, with a slight nod. "Please come in."

"Thank you. A little wet out here." Hudson walked into the house, van Remm closed the door, and *thwak* went the bolt. "I'm glad you didn't make me walk back to my tent in that deluge," Hudson said, as he took off his haversack and lowered it to the glossy, black-painted floorboards.

"We wouldn't be so cruel," said August, with a thin smile illuminated by the short candle he held burning in a small pewter holder. He wore a white shirt with ruffles on the front, plain black breeches and black shoes with silver buckles.

"You might catch your death," Leopolda added. Her smile was exactly the same as her brother's, though the glare in her dark eyes told Hudson she wouldn't care if he did.

Hudson's first impression of her was distinctly chilly; the second impression was that she was very beautiful. She was tall and slender, the same body type as her brother. She had long, lustrous ebony hair that fell about her shoulders and was touched with gray at the temples. Her face was strong-jawed and aristocratic, with the same thin-bridged nose and slightly flared nostrils, in her case nearly a sign of defiance. Her eyebrows arched above the haughty and rather disdainful eyes. Her skin was as white as delicate china, but Hudson had the feeling she was not in the least fragile. She wore a dark purple dress, more of a straight-hanging shift than a full-skirted gown as might be worn by the English ladies of New York. Around her neck was a string of black pearls alternating with purple stones that Hudson thought must be amethysts, or whatever they were called. Hudson's appraisal of the woman included the simple gray slippers she wore, and on her hands were—a strange bit of fashion—ebony leather gloves.

"Come, sir," said August. "The parlor is this way. Leopolda, would you bring us two glasses of the very fine De Hooiberg that arrived last month?"

"As you wish," she said, and she moved away down a corridor next to a set of stairs that ascended to the upper floor.

Hudson thought he might carry his haversack along, if only for the comfort of knowing that within it were two pistols. His ribs had ceased their ache, now that the storm had arrived, but what had begun to gnaw at him was his sense of impending threat. Such gnawings had saved his life more than a few times on the field of battle, both in war and at work for Katherine Herrald. He picked up the haversack and followed van Remm along the corridor to a set of sliding doors. He could not fail to notice, before they reached the doors, that here and there the wooden walls of the corridor were scarred with broken places as if someone had struck several blows upon them with a heavy mallet.

"Here we are," said van Remm, as he slid the doors open. They entered a high-ceilinged room with a fireplace whose mantel was formed of a checkerboard of orange, white and blue ceramic squares that signified an affinity to the Dutch flag. The colors were jarring because everything else in the parlor—sofa, a small round table beside it, two chairs, a writing desk, the carpet, paintings and framed items on the walls as well as the walls themselves—were of dark and muted shades, mostly of swampy grays, damp purples, and muddy browns. A small fire crackled in the hearth and hissed like a nest of snakes when raindrops found their way down the flue. From the ceiling on a long chain hung an iron chandelier that held six burning tapers.

August van Remm put his candle down upon the table. He sat on the sofa and motioned Hudson toward a chair. Hudson took it, while putting his haversack on the carpet beside him. The parlor had two windows but both were shuttered. Rain was slamming against the shutters and above the house the thunder crashed.

"We do get some wicked storms here," van Remm remarked. He opened a small silver filigreed box that was situated upon the table and drew out a thin black cheroot. "Smoke?" he asked, offering the box to his visitor.

When Hudson shook his head, van Remm lit his cheroot at the candle's flame, blew a stream of smoke toward the dark oak ceiling, and closed the box. "So," he said, "how goes your investigation into the monster of Black Oak Swamp?"

"I've seen nothing yet, but then again it's only been two days."

"You really believe this tale, then?"

"I believe I'm being paid to investigate what the townspeople believe."

Van Remm nodded thoughtfully. He exhaled smoke and watched it drift toward Hudson Greathouse. "I assume then," he said, "that you are here to stay for some duration?"

"That's right."

"How would you react if I said you were wasting your time?"

"I have time to waste as long as I'm being paid."

"Ah!" Van Remm grinned. "A true mercenary! And obviously a man of intelligence. A *reasonable* man, as I've said before." He drew on the cheroot again and stared at the burning tip for a silent moment. "Sir, let me ask you a...a rather delicate question."

"Ask away."

"What are you being paid?"

"A nice sum."

"You won't tell me, exactly?"

"I would rather that remain between myself, Mayor van Dekker and Constable Sleet. You understand. It's business."

"I expect," said van Remm, "that you're being paid a—" He stopped speaking as his sister entered the room, bearing two glasses of pale ale on a wooden tray. "Here's our repast!" van Remm proclaimed, and then he winced as a particularly loud clap of thunder seemed to blast the sky directly over the house. "My, that was a shout from God, wasn't it?"

Leopolda did not serve the men. She put the tray down on the round table and then she sat on the sofa a short distance from her brother. August reached over for his glass, and Hudson rose from his chair to retrieve his own. While he was up, he decided to take a closer look at some of the dour paintings and woodcuts that adorned the walls.

"You were saying?" Hudson asked. He took a drink of what was very excellent ale, at least to his own undiscerning taste, as he wandered over to the nearest wall.

"I was saying I was going to ask you a delicate question." August sipped his ale and put the glass aside. "Mr. Greathouse, if we—my sister and I—were to double whatever sum you're receiving for this endeavor, would you consider going back to New York and forgetting you've ever heard anything of this?"

"Of *this?*" Hudson prompted.

"The creature," said Leopolda, speaking as if her lips were the strings of a tightly drawn purse.

If Hudson's interest in the van Remms had not been sharp by now, it was further forged into a dagger's blade by both the brother's question and the sister's comment. Hudson gave no outward indication of this, but examined a grouping of small paintings that all depicted landscapes of what he thought must be Holland, since in two of the pictures were windmills. "Tell me why your father built this house so far from civilization," he said. "And what became of him?"

"He passed away seven years after we arrived," said August. "We came here in 1682, at the end of the war. He died in 1689 at the age of fifty-nine. His heart gave out, pure and simple. Our mother, bless her soul, had passed away several years before we left Amsterdam."

"That was the answer to my second question," Hudson said. "What about the first one?" He heard a distant boom that sounded as if the storm were moving away, but then the thunder crashed over the house once more and if anything the noise of the deluge increased.

Leopolda spoke up. "Our father wished *privacy*. Is that so difficult to understand?"

Hudson glanced at her and saw that she'd moved closer to her brother on the sofa. Their shoulders were nearly touching. "I can understand privacy," he said, "but not isolation. It must have been difficult for you two, leaving Amsterdam to come live not only in an English-governed country but out here at—as Mayor van Dekker put it—the edge of the world. Another thing: I'm sure building this house cost your father a fortune, carting all the materials out and sheltering the workmen."

"Leopold could afford such," she answered. She gave a slight lift of her pointed chin, and her dark eyes glinted. "He could've afforded a dozen houses just such as this. We came over from Amsterdam in our own *ship*."

Leopold, Hudson thought. The daughter named after the father. And the son? "What was your mother's name?" he asked.

"Augustina," August replied.

Hudson nodded. He took a drink of the ale and continued on to a small woodcut contained in a polished pinewood frame. He heard another distant slam of thunder…and then he realized with a jolt that the noise was not coming from outside the house.

Before him on the wall was the woodcut of a large cannon on wheels. Below the rendition was a small brass plaque that read *Briartooth*.

"Our great-grandfather's first cannon," said August, in a quiet voice. "Forged in his foundry about the year 1548. The first of many. The cannons of the van Remm family helped our Netherlands become the great sea power that it is…or…*used* to be. It was the Golden Age. Our cannons were without equal. They made that era what it was."

Hudson glanced back again at the pair, and saw now that one of Leopolda's black-gloved hands was clasped by one of August's pale white hands, and she was sitting nearly in his lap.

"Your family," said Hudson, "forged land cannons for the Franco-Dutch war?"

"Hundreds," came the reply. "It was not the fault of the weapons that we were overpowered, but the fault of the weak-willed politicians."

Something banged toward the back of the house. It was definitely not thunder. August released his sister's hand, stood up and retrieved the candle in its pewter holder. "I think a shutter's been blown open. Pardon me a moment, I'll take care of it." He started for the sliding doors and then paused. "Mr. Greathouse, you haven't answered *my* question. If I were to double your sum—*nee*, triple it, let us say—would you consider returning to New York and forgetting this matter?"

"I'll consider it. As you've said…I'm both mercenary and reasonable." Hudson lifted his glass in a mock toast to the idea of so much gold, but he had no intention of giving the proposal more than mockery. To be standing in the presence of the members of a family whose Dutch cannons had been responsible for the dismemberment and horrific deaths of so many of his fellow soldiers was one thing, but to renounce his word and his duty was something else entirely.

"Excellent," said August, but his voice was curiously empty. "I'll return shortly." He gave a slight nod and smile to his sister, and when he exited the room he left the sliding doors open.

"You should never have come here," Leopolda said after August had gone.

"I was invited."

"I mean to Briartooth. It was a dark day when you made that decision."

"I do remember it was somewhat cloudy," said Hudson. A muscle jumped in his jaw as he looked again at the woodcut of the cannon. Leopold van Remm must have named the trading post Briartooth in honor of his grandfather's work and the family's legacy, and of course the name had continued on with the town as it prospered.

Hudson turned to face the woman. The time for games had ended. "Who's eating all that meat from the horses you slaughter? Surely not just you two." She didn't reply, but looked at him calmly and steadily. Hudson took a couple of steps toward her and said, "There's someone else in the house, isn't there? Who is it?"

She simply continued to stare at him, her expression impassive.

Hudson heard the creak of floorboards behind him, the noise all but masked by the sound of rain pounding the roof. Before he could turn, a pistol's barrel was placed against the back of his head.

"You are correct, sir," said August van Remm. "Leopolda and I do not live here alone. In our cellar is the monster of Black Oak Swamp."

FIVE

"OTHERWISE KNOWN," AUGUST CONTINUED, WITH THE PISTOL'S BARrel making an impression on the back of Hudson's head, "as Zukor van Remm, our younger brother."

Hudson heard the pistol being cocked.

"I'm afraid I don't believe your half-hearted conviction to take my offer. I knew when I first met you that you would be a stubborn fool. You simply look the part. Leopolda, open his haversack. In it will be two pistols. Please draw them out, and be careful. They're likely loaded."

Leopolda went to work. In another moment she had both pistols in her black-gloved hands.

Hudson heard a slamming sound from the back of the house. It was the noise of a heavy fist or a shoulder beating against a door.

"He is agitated by the storm," August said. "Zukor has fought his way out several times, and as I am not the most able carpenter by now the doorframe and hinges are severely weakened."

"*Zukor*," said Hudson, whose outer demeanor was still calm though he was desperately trying to think of a way out of this. Sweat had already begun to blossom in his armpits. "Who was he named after?"

"Our father's favorite hunting dog. Leopolda, put one of the pistols atop the mantel. Then aim the other at our guest's belly and remove the knife from the sheath at his right side."

Hudson was calculating seconds and inches. Did he dare try to twist his body and throw the rest of his ale into August's face? No, he was sure the man would blow his brains out the instant he made a sudden move. He watched as Leopolda followed August's instructions. The barrel of his own pistol took aim just north of his navel, and his knife was placed on the table.

Thunder spoke once more, a hollow echoing sound...and then it was followed by a similar noise, but more ragged and enraged. It went on for several nerve-shattering seconds before it died away.

The Thunder Man was crying out, Hudson thought. "Would you mind," he said, as calmly as he could manage, "telling me what's going on here?"

"Take him into the woods, kill him and let's get this done with," the woman said, as she bit upon her lower lip. "August, it was foolish to invite him here!"

"Not at all, dear heart. *Meneer* Greathouse was going to cause us a problem. I knew that at once, as soon as I met him. He was not going to leave until we…" August hesitated, shaping the rest of the sentence. "Until we made him disappear," he finished. "As far as taking him into the woods to kill him…I don't think that is the solution to our problem."

"What, then? We can't let him *go!*"

"Of course not." August was silent for a moment. Hudson could hear Zukor battering at his door over the tumult of the storm. "Our brother," August said, speaking to his captive, "is in one of his states. They come and go, but in the last five years they have become uncontrollable. Leopolda used to be able to soothe him. Now the only thing that calms him is…unfortunately…murder. He must spend his rage somewhere. You see?"

"Not really," said Hudson, figuring he must stall for time though it appeared his hourglass was fast running out. "Enlighten me."

"Let's finish him, August! The quicker the better!"

Hudson slowly lifted his half-full glass of ale. He gave Leopolda the best smile he could construct, though it seemed to tighten his mouth to the point of tearing his lips at the corners. "At least let me finish *this* first. It would be a shame to let such Dutch liquid gold go to waste."

"It won't waste. I'll drink it over your corpse."

Hudson decided what he wanted to do. His heart was beating hard. He heard the sound of splintering wood from further along the corridor.

"He's near breaking out!" True fear brimmed in Leopolda's voice.

"I'm going to sit in that chair and drink the rest of this," Hudson said. "If you want to shoot me, August, you have my blessing. It would be a mess to clean up, though. You didn't have to clean up the other bodies, did you, because Zukor killed those men in the swamp. You just had to *hide* the bodies. What happened? Your insane younger brother broke out and went off on a rampage?"

"Insane?" August gave a small laugh. "If that were only *all* of it. Leopolda, go speak to him. Try to calm him."

"He's beyond that."

"Go *try*," he insisted. She hesitated a few seconds longer, her dark eyes filled with pure hatred for Hudson—and also perhaps for the entire population of the town named after her great-grandfather's first cannon—and then she left the room.

Hudson slowly walked to the chair and sat down. He sipped his ale as August stood a few feet in front of him and held the pistol aimed at

Hudson's forehead. In his other hand was the short candle burning in its holder, the yellow light giving August's face a demonic cast.

"Would you really murder me?" Hudson asked. "From what I gather, Zukor is the murderer in this family. You and Leopolda have just been burying the evidence."

"You don't understand."

Leopolda was shouting in the corridor, speaking Dutch. Hudson could only fathom fragments of it: *"Zukor! Zukor...listen...sing to you!"* Then she began singing, again in the native tongue, what sounded like a child's nursery rhyme. The noise of the beatings against the door ebbed.

"Make me understand," Hudson said. Thunder boomed, but distantly now, and the Thunder Man remained silent as Leopolda crooned her tune.

August's gun hand was steady, but when he spoke his voice trembled with emotion. "We never asked for anyone else to come here! It was a trading post, yes, but...it was so far away from everyone and everything! How were we to know it would become a *town?*" It was a question that August did not expect to be answered. "Our father came here to be *alone*. For all of us to live here and be *left* alone. Yes, we had a tutor but she was old and she'd been with the family for many years. Zukor was four years old when we came over. Leopolda was nineteen and I was seventeen. We were on our own ship, so no one knew about Zukor beyond *Dokter* Elzewoort."

"Knew what about him?"

"Don't you realize...he wasn't supposed to live," August said, nearly imploringly. "He was supposed to die within the first month. But...he lived. And on and on he lived. Such as he...*Dokter* Elzewoort said he had never seen the like, but he knew such had been born before and they died early because...because life itself would not accept them."

The flesh at the back of Hudson's neck was beginning to crawl. Leopolda was still singing in the corridor. The noise of the rain had lessened. The next peal of thunder sounded some miles away.

"What was wrong with Zukor?" Hudson asked, but he already knew.

"He's gotten worse," said August. "Much worse. In the last five years... two or three outbreaks a year, when not even Leopolda can calm him." The pistol drifted a few inches to the right, and when Hudson's gaze followed it August corrected the error. "The first time he broke out...he was gone for two days and nights...and when he came back, he brought the mangled body with him. To show us, you see. Like an animal might, proud of its conquest. A loyal hunting dog, *ja?*"

"Wasn't there someplace he could be kept?"

"Where?" The word was released with such vehemence that it was nearly a strike to Hudson's face. "Who would take him? After he brought back the third body...we thought...should we kill him ourselves, and end it?

But by then…we had buried two others in the woods behind the barn. And by then the Mohawks knew, and we had to have meat for him—much meat—so we had to strike a bargain with Tomuwae. As long as we bought the horses at a price he demanded, he would keep his silence and help us obscure Zukor's trail and the evidence when such was needed."

"A nice business arrangement," Hudson said, with bitter sarcasm. He was watching the drift of the pistol and thinking of the second gun up on the mantel.

"Tomuwae wishes the town would disappear as much as we do. We have been fortunate that Zukor has never killed anyone after there's been a fall of snow so he would be more easily tracked. In fact, during the winter he sleeps most all the time. Like an animal, as I've said."

Hudson took another drink. His glass was getting mighty low, and so was his hourglass. Leopolda was still singing quietly, though every so often there came the fierce bang of a large fist on weakened wood. "You could've taken him somewhere," Hudson said. "A hospital…a church…some—"

"No, we could not!" August shouted, and red whorls surfaced on the gaunt cheeks of his pallid face as red cinders burned in his eyes. "If we did, then the outside world would know!"

"Know what? Your brother's condition?"

"More than that. They would know…our family's *preference*."

Hudson was almost afraid to hear, but even with the gun aimed at his brainpan he had to ask. "Meaning?"

August van Remm simply stood staring at Hudson for what seemed an eternity. Then he called out, "Leopolda! Come here, please!"

Her singing stopped. "August…I can't…I have to—"

"This gentleman is desirous of an answer to a question. Please come here."

She returned to the room, with the pistol still in her right hand. As soon as she entered, the rough banging started up again. The Thunder Man cried out with such terrible force Hudson thought that alone would blow the door off its hinges and destroy whatever lock was keeping the monster from rushing out into the corridor. Once there, in his animalish rage he would crash his fists wildly against the walls as he had done many times before—leaving those mallet-like marks in his wake—and fight his way out of the house until his urge to kill had been satisfied.

Leopolda stared blankly at her brother. "What do you require of me?"

"Nothing just yet, dear heart. Let me ask you…who do you love?"

"You…of course."

"And I love you, sweet one. Come here, let me hold you."

She went to him. He put the candlestick down upon the table and pressed her body tightly against his, as he looked over her shoulder at Hudson and the pistol looked at Hudson from the woman's side.

"Together forever," he said to her, in the hushed and reverent voice of a true lover.

"Yes," she answered, and when she looked at him her eyes were soft with either remembered dreams or those she'd constructed. "Forever and ever."

"Show him, my angel," said August, and from her he took the second pistol.

"Darling, I don't—"

"He's going to die. Show him, so he will realize what our family has known of love for generation upon generation."

Leopolda nodded. She turned toward Hudson and fixed him with a solemn glare.

The beautiful woman began to remove her gloves. First, the one on the right hand.

The sixth finger that had been pushed in with the fifth was exposed to the candlelight. When the left glove was removed, the sixth finger there came to light and so did the warty stub of the seventh further down on the otherwise marble-smooth hand. She spread her fingers out to Hudson, and all of them curled.

It took Hudson a few seconds to gather his wits enough to respond. He rubbed his nose, sniffled, took the last drink of his ale and then said to August, "What's *your* trick?"

"I have a tail," came the reply. "Also other specialties of a more personal nature."

"I should've known not to ask."

August returned the pistol to his sister. She took hold of it and aimed it at Hudson with both hands, all thirteen fingers.

"Stand up," August directed. While keeping his focus on Hudson, he reached back to retrieve the candle. Along the corridor, Zukor bellowed again and hit the door with power supplied by ferocious rage.

"I think I'd rather remain here a while longer."

"The next sound you hear will be the shot that at the very least will break your right shoulder. I became an expert marksman at thirteen years of age."

"Get up," said Leopolda, and she motioned with her own weapon.

Hudson drew a long breath, exhaled it and stood up. Beads of sweat ran down his sides. "Have you two never heard of chains? They are known for their ability to restrain."

"He can tear a chain out of the wall, as he's done several times before. And to have to put chains on our own brother? Distasteful," August replied. "You are now going to walk along the corridor ahead of us."

"What are you going to do, feed me to him?"

"He doesn't eat human flesh. He destroys it. With your disappearance and the description offered by Andra van Otten, the end of Briartooth will not be much longer in coming."

"All right, but what then? You remove Zukor's potential victims, and... what? Who will he go after, if he can't—" Hudson stopped speaking, because he'd had a realization. "I see. You want him to go after the Mohawks, so they'll kill him for you. Would that absolve you of all guilt?"

"Do as I've told you. And yes, Zukor would make his way to the Mohawk village if he could find no other victims. He does have limited intelligence, and I—we—believe he has heightened abilities to smell his prey, again like a good hunting dog. They would put him out of his misery long before he reached there, of course. *Meneer* Greathouse, please go into the corridor before I have to harm you."

"Heaven forbid," Hudson answered. He was in what he would term "a tight." His heart was battering at his chest with nearly the same force as the monster of Black Oak Swamp beat at his prison door. It sounded as if any second the thing were going to get out, or Hudson's heart was going to stutter and stop. That might be a mercy, he thought. He was frantically looking for an escape; there was none. Rushing either one of these two would only serve him at least one bullet. Did he dare risk a mortal wound?

He fixed upon something that might at least give him some kind of chance, depending upon what happened from this point on.

"*Move*," said August van Remm, and this time his order was final.

Both brother and sister stepped back to let Hudson pass into the corridor. Quickly, August got behind him and put the pistol's barrel to his spine. Another burst of rain hit the roof. Thunder growled from the west. The storm was not yet done.

"Stop and stand still," Hudson was told as he reached a battered-looking door near the end of the hallway. A thick oak reinforcing plank was set across it on metal brackets nailed to the cracked wall on either side. Leopolda reached past Hudson and with a seven-fingered hand plucked a key from its hook on the wall.

Something slammed hard against the door in front of Hudson's face. He watched the door bulge outward, even with the plank securing it. The wood around the brackets popped and cracked. Hudson could see the holes where other nails had already been expelled. The frame around the tortured door had begun to splinter.

"Zukor!" said August, and again Hudson could understand only bits and pieces of the language. "Step back!...sending someone down...hear me?" He glanced over at his sister with a sheen of sweat on his face. "Tell him."

"Zukor! Can you hear me?" Leopolda leaned her face toward the door. "I know you can." The pressure on the other side of the door eased. The house at the edge of the world gave a noise that sounded like a groan of relief.

"...sending someone..." she said. "A bad man, Zukor. Bad. Yours to destroy. Go down...bottom of the stairs...wait there. Go on, now. Go. Bottom of the stairs."

"Give him time," said August, and Leopolda nodded. Both the van Remms seemed as fearful of their deformed brother as Hudson was. Which was no comfort to Hudson, because he was the only one going into that deathtrap of a cellar.

"All right," August said at last. "All right, I'm ready."

"...open the door now," Leopolda said to the creature within. "Stay... bottom of the stairs."

Leopolda fitted the key into the door's lock and turned it as Hudson watched with the pistol pressed against his back. She lifted the oak plank from its brackets and put it aside. She reached out, turned the door's handle, and pulled the door open. It came with a sharp protest from its battered frame.

The stub of the candle August held illuminated only a flight of rough stone steps leading down into a pool of utter darkness. A wave of fetid smell came rolling up. Hudson thought it was an odor akin to an animal's spoor.

Now was the moment, he decided. He had to play this right, or he was lost.

"*Please*," he said, trying to sound as if he were nearly broken. It was not that much of an effort. He looked into August's face. "At least...let me have some light. Please. Don't make me go down there in the dark."

"You won't last long enough for it to matter," said the bitch with a baker's dozen digits.

Hudson ignored her. He had to make her brother ignore her too. "I'm begging you, sir, for all that's holy and honorable. Please let me carry the candle down."

August blinked. His mouth crimped, and in that instant something of pity came upon his face. He started to pull the candle stub from the small pewter holder.

No, Hudson thought. *No!*

The man's hand stopped. Hardly two inches of candle were left, for it had burned down almost into the holder. He hesitated a few seconds more and then handed it to Hudson. The thing in Hudson's grip had the weight of sea foam. "If you think you can use the candleholder as a club, you will find that impossible," said August. "The pewter is hollow. But there's your light, what there is of it. Go down the stairs now, let's have no more dawdling."

"Thank you for this," Hudson answered. He imagined the woman was wishing him an agonizing trip to Hades. He had nowhere to go now but down. The pistol's barrel prodded him. Van Remm was correct, Hudson knew. As a club the holder was useless; it had no weight and it would give no power in the striking. But that was not why he'd wanted it.

He had no choice but to take his chances.

He went through the door. As he started down the stairs the door was closed at his back. The dark closed around his little candle. He heard the lock click, then the sound of the plank being secured.

He could hear ragged breathing below him, a breathing that sounded like a bellows at work. At any second the monster might charge at him.

Hudson gritted his teeth. With the back of his hand he wiped away a bead of sweat that clung to his right eyebrow, and he descended to his fate.

SIX

Midway down the stairs, Hudson stopped.

He pulled the miserable little candle stub from its socket and held it before him at arm's length so as to watch for any movement below. Moving quickly, he placed the pewter holder on the step beneath his boot. He crushed his foot down upon the socket as hard as he could, and then again. His candle made out a wall of equally rough stones to his left. He transferred the candle to his left hand, bent down and picked up the holder with his right. Its socket had been flattened into an edge. He scraped the edge back and forth across the wall, again using sufficient strength for the task.

Then he had a jagged knife blade as well as a candle. Neither one of them were going to necessarily save his life, he knew, but being able to give the candleholder a slashing edge gave him at least a bit more than the proverbial snowball's chance.

So be it.

"Zukor!" he said, in the strongest commanding voice he could summon, and the next two words he snarled in Dutch: *"Stap terug!" Step back!*

There was no reaction from below, only the continued noise of the bellows breathing from the darkness beyond. Hudson hoped that speaking to the thing by name would serve to confuse it, maybe slow it down. How he was going to get out of here with his skin still on, he didn't know. There were no windows, the place was a beast's cave. He could never get through that locked and reinforced door, and even if he did—which would be impossible—he would still be facing two pistols.

Nothing could be gained by standing in the middle of the stairs. He had the feeling that one or two more steps down, and Zukor van Remm would be there in his face.

"Zukor!" he shouted again. *"Stap terug!"* He was almost to the floor. He heard thunder crack above the house, a muffled sound but still powerful. Two more risers and he would be at the bottom. He made them, stood on the dirt floor and held the candle out, his improvised knife up against his side and ready for a slashing strike.

Dripping wax stung his fingers but Hudson paid that no mind. His candle, in all senses of the word, was burning itself out. He was tensed so hard breathing was an effort. Again, he could not stand in one place waiting to be attacked; he had to move, but he wanted to keep that stone wall at his back. He slid along the wall and kept going until he came to a corner. His meager light revealed a water bucket and a pile of hay where Zukor must sleep. Littering the floor were a few horse bones they'd given their brother to gnaw upon. On the wall behind the hay pile was fixed a metal plate where a few links of rusted chain remained.

In silent fury the monster lunged at him from the dark.

Hudson had just a quick and terrifying glimpse of the thing before a thick arm hit his wrist and sent the little candle flying. He saw a bald head and a dirty, black-bearded face. He saw a gaping mouth full of broken teeth. He saw the single glistening black eye that was almost at the center of the face just above the thin-bridged, aristocratic nose that both his brother and sister shared. On the right cheek almost down to the mouth was a crater that held a second eye the size of an infant's, but this one was dead and dead-white as cold stone.

Then the light was gone, a four-fingered hand that was nearly a claw gripped Hudson's throat, and Hudson was lifted off his feet with awesome power. The other hand grasped his jaw and started to tear his face apart. The beast was almost as tall as himself but broader across the shoulders. Hudson struck out with his blade. He felt it dig into flesh. Again he struck, back and forth at the hideous face as the claw threatened to crush his throat and his own face was twisted to the breaking point.

With an ear-splitting bellow the Thunder Man threw Hudson aside like a straw poppet. Hudson hit the earth on his right side. Breath burst from his lungs. He had the sensation that all his ribs had been newly broken because that area felt like a sack of sharp nails, but there was no time yet to count the costs; he squirmed across the dirt back to the safety of the wall, where he got into a crouch ready to meet another attack.

It came. Hudson's right arm was grabbed. It would have been torn from its socket if Hudson hadn't shot to his feet as if his legs had become catapults. His blade hand was trapped. He hammered his left fist into where he thought the beast's face should be, going for the cyclops eye. The thing was maddened by whatever furies that governed him, but he was intelligent enough to guard his single light. The grip on Hudson's right arm weakened enough for Hudson to pull free, though at the moment he thought his shoulder had been dislocated. He did everything he could; he swung wildly back and forth with the blade, kicked with both boots into the naked shins and stabbed out with the rigid fingers of his left hand seeking the vulnerable eye. Whether he hit it or not he didn't know, but Zukor gave another thunderous cry and struck Hudson a blow on the left shoulder that took him off his feet and sent him flying head-over-heels into the dirt. In falling he lost the blade.

Hudson felt the cold chill of death. Zukor was strong enough to rip him apart. It was simply a matter of time. With blood in his mouth Hudson crawled in what he thought was the direction of the wall, but he couldn't find it. His brain was rattled and he was lost. It came to him, crazily, that the generations of inbreeding of the van Remm family had created a human cannon.

He could hear Zukor's rough breathing, like a wounded beast.

No…no…that was his own breathing.

On his knees, Hudson searched for the wall with his bruised hands. Suddenly his right hand brushed what he thought must be one of Zukor's knees. Without hesitation he twisted his body around and kicked at it with both boots. There was a solid *crunch*. Zukor gave a satisfying grunt of pain and staggered away but the monster was far from retreating, for in the next instant a sledgehammer of a blow parted the air past Hudson's left temple and the jagged nails of a groping hand grazed his cheek. Hudson rolled away across the dirt, and then he lay on his belly as muffled thunder spoke over the house and the deadly dance in the dark went on.

He had no chance. If Zukor could smell him, the creature knew where he was without having to use that horrific eye. Hudson thought it was useless to fight; he would never get out of here alive, and resistance simply delayed the inevitable.

But he was a still a soldier in heart and mind, and though all sense said he should give himself up to the judgment that Fate had prepared for him, his inner fighter would never surrender.

One advantage, if such was possible, was on his side. He doubted that anyone had ever given Zukor a battle, and if the blade, the fist and the boots had done any kind of work even a maddened monster would be wary of earning any more pain.

He was thinking that when Zukor crashed down upon his back.

He caught the claws an instant before they tore his eyes out. Teeth snapped at the nape of his neck. He twisted, struck back with his elbows and slammed with his head. Hudson got himself turned around with a desperate and mighty effort. They fought in the dirt, now truly both like enraged animals. He could hear the teeth cracking together as they sought flesh. The thing was bearing him down again, was flailing at him and crushing him into the ground. In another second a fist was going to knock his brains out. He realized that to live beyond his next breath he would have to equal Zukor's ferocity.

His hands found Zukor's ears, one normal-sized and one a gnarled nub.

He heard himself growl like a beast, and then his head struck forward and his teeth closed upon the aristocratic van Remm nose. He bit deeply and shook his head back and forth as the blood spurted into his mouth. Then Zukor was trying to get away from him but he didn't let go; the hot fever of battle had taken him. His teeth crunched together through the flesh, and with a final jerk of his head he tore the mangled nose away from the monster's face.

The Thunder Man roared, but the sound now was more of pain. Hudson was tossed aside and he lay in the dirt dazed at his own violence and spitting out blood and flesh.

Now come on, Hudson thought. *Finish it, by God. Come on!*

He heard Zukor throw himself against the door at the top of the steps.

The creature had had enough of the man who fought back equally as viciously. But if anything Zukor's ferocity had been stoked to a higher conflagration. With a bellow that had blood in it Zukor began to crash against the door, again and again, as if only one thing mattered in the world and that was getting out of this dank prison even if it meant breaking his own bones to do so.

"Zukor!" Leopolda shouted from the other side. *"Stop it!* Do you hear me? *Stop!"* Crazily, she began to sing the Dutch nursery rhyme song to him in a terrified voice, but the baby of the van Remm family was no longer listening.

Three more strikes, and Hudson heard the nails that held the brackets pop loose like little gunshots. Another three strikes, and the door burst open from its shattered frame. Zukor shambled out, a massive naked figure in the doorway. Hudson heard Leopolda scream.

Her scream trailed along the corridor. Hudson heard August shout "No! Zukor, stop!" from the front of this tormented house.

Something crashed over. August gave an unintelligible yell. Leopolda screamed again. The scream was followed by the crack of a pistol. Then Leopolda's scream turned to a mad rush of babbling, and it was then that

Hudson pulled his two hundred and twenty-seven pounds of pain out of the dirt and, wobbly like a man of eighty years, got to his feet.

He climbed the steps as fast as any man who'd just survived a carriage wreck could move. In the parlor he found Leopolda pressed up against the far wall with one of his pistols in her hand. Blue smoke still hung in the air, but it was curling from the gun that lay next to the man on the floor whose neck had been broken so severely his head was turned nearly backwards. August's face in death was a study in shock.

The monster of Black Oak Swamp was on his knees. The noseless, bloodied and one-eyed face stared at his sister. Hudson saw the eye blink. In his chest, just above the heart, was a blue-edged bullet hole that was spooling dark blood.

Zukor stood up. He put a hand to the bullet hole and held his cup of blood up before the single eye. He made a rumbling noise deep in his throat, and then he lurched toward his sister with his arms open, whether to embrace her or crush her never to be known.

She fired.

The bullet went into his forehead and out the back of the bald skull.

Zukor took two more steps, as Leopolda cringed against the wall. Again he fell to his knees.

He went down on his belly, and amazingly he began to slowly crawl toward his sister.

She was transfixed with horror. Zukor's right claw came out as he reached her. The four fingers curled around one of Leopolda's ankles...and then he shivered once and was still.

The smoke of Leopolda's shot rose up toward the iron chandelier with its six burning tapers. Hudson realized the sounds of thunder and rain had quietened. For now, at least, the storm was over.

But not quite.

"*You*," Leopolda said, her voice dripping venom. She looked toward the remaining pistol up on the fireplace mantel and moved to get it, but she could not because the monster's dead hand was holding her fast.

Hudson walked across the room, past the two bodies, and retrieved his gun. When he tried to speak he couldn't find his voice. His face felt warped out of shape. He didn't think he had any broken ribs after all and his shoulder was still in place, but he was going to have so many bruises he would be known for a time as the Mottled Man of Manhattan.

He tried again. It was more of a croak than a voice, but it would have to suffice. "I don't believe you want to do what you're thinking."

"You've destroyed everything!" she said fiercely. "Damn you to Hell, you've killed us all!"

"A matter of opinion, Madam van Remm. I'm leaving now…if I can walk. I'm going to see Constable Sleet as soon as possible. I'm sure he and Mayor van Dekker would like to pay you a visit."

"Destroyed it all!" she raved on. "Everything!"

"Hm," he said. The table had gone over. His knife lay on the floor. It hurt like fiery Hell to bend down and pick it up, but that was why they paid him the money. "You might do better," he advised, "to go see Sleet yourself, and tell him everything."

"Better?" she asked. "What, will I deserve a better quality of *rope?*" She stared down at August's body for a few seconds, and she began to cry… silently at first, and then with horrible, gasping sobs. She tried to reach him, but she could not get her ankle free from Zukor's death grip.

Such is family, Hudson thought. The ties that bind.

He thought also that if he didn't get out of this house in the next minute he would become a jibbering idiot. His haversack was too much of a burden; he would leave it for Sleet to collect.

"Good day," he said, and that sounded to him like the most stupid two words that had ever been spoken in the history of the world. Leopolda paid him no attention; she was trying to pry Zukor's hand loose, so she could curl up on the floor beside her August, but not even thirteen fingers could do the job.

On the way out, Hudson noted that Zukor's blood and brains had splattered upon the old woodcut of Briartooth. He spat a piece of nose flesh from his mouth, and then he all but fled the house. If his legs had been working right he would've run as fast as a racehorse, but less than twenty yards from the house he fell down and it was a minute or so before he could gain his footing again.

The rain had stopped but the woods were dripping wet, the earth spongy underfoot. On the walk to his tent Hudson's legs gave way once more, and he fell into a puddle of mud. He lay there under the moving clouds thinking how close this particular soldier came to seeing it all end, and how precious every moment of life was even in the worst of storms.

On an impulse Hudson rolled in the muddy water, over and over as if to cleanse himself of death and blood and the evil that men often did to hide secrets that had chained them to darkness from generation to generation. He had solved the problem and earned his money. He had stopped the killings. He had survived it.

As for answering the questions of ultimate responsibility…that was beyond him. And he liked it that way.

After a while, he rose up from the mud.

He walked on, feeling cleaner than before.

THE SCORPION'S EYE

June, 1703

ONE

Across the table from Minx Cutter sat a man with the word *Love* ornately tattooed on the scarred knuckles of his right hand and *Hate* on the scarred knuckles of his left.

He kept them in full view atop the table so that she might appreciate either their beauty or brutality. She thought that he, of the rest of the men assembled in this mean little room, might try to kill her…and so her knife was ready beneath the table, slipped slowly from its place under her dark green riding jacket—her "joseph"—and held in a firm but casual grip in her right hand, the better to pierce his gut if he lunged at her. Then it was a leap out the window behind her if the other three took up his bloody cause.

The man who was torn between Love and Hate took a drink of bitter red wine from the tankard before him and cocked his head, dark eyes narrowed, his weather-seamed face appraising her in the yellow glow of the candles. His eyebrows were flame-colored thickets and he had a burning bush of hair that stood up in wild cowlicks at front and back.

"So," he said, in a husky but quiet voice that told all he was the leader of this gang of devil's grenadiers, "you wish us to catch a thief for you."

"Not catch, exactly," the woman replied, just as quietly. They might have been friends meeting in this backroom of the Iron Cock tavern at the end of Water Street where harbor water actually rolled up onto the street in curls of white foam and the moored ships groaned in their uneasy sleep; they might have been true companions or lovers, but in fact were none of these. They were, instead, business associates of a sort, and looking to profit from each other this night in June of the year 1703 in the Puritan-hallowed town of Boston. By day the Puritan ethic of hard work and diligence being an honor to God ruled the town, but by night the rules changed. Minx Cutter knew well that all rocks when overturned revealed the insects that hid beneath them, and so it was true even of Boston, this foundation rock of Puritan creed in the New World; beneath the solid stone was another world, and at night the crawlers came out to play.

"Not catch," Minx repeated, keeping her steady gaze fixed upon the man who was split between Love and Hate, and whose name was Dylan Bandy. "*Find*, yes. I will handle the rest of it, thank you."

"Very sure of yourself," Bandy replied, with a hint of a sneer.

"I am," said Minx, her face remaining emotionless.

"Ha," said Bandy, but this was expressed without a smile. He took another drink of wine and watched the woman from New York with a heightened sense of curiosity and not a little measure of awe.

Minx Cutter had arrived in Boston two days before, on a packet boat that had suffered the wave-tossed indignities of two rainstorms and had a near miss running aground on the hard edges of Massachusetts colony rocks. She had been sent from New York on behalf of her new employer the Herrald Agency, on a mission that Katherine Herrald had thought Minx might find of interest, and so it was that Minx on this muggy eve sat in this smoky tavern where refined women dared not venture. Far be it for Minx to claim refinement, for she had walked her share of dirty streets by night and known the heat and smell of blood upon her hands, but if anything she considered that her experiences in the world—and as part of Professor Fell's criminal underworld—had prepared her for her new line of work: a "problem-solver," as much as her compatriots Matthew Corbett and Hudson Greathouse.

Perhaps neither Matthew nor Greathouse trusted her completely yet, but Minx shrugged this off; she understood that Madam Herrald had sent her here as the best person for this job, and she was content to have the madam's trust. She intended to earn it…and yet, she didn't fully know what she might think when she had the scorpion in her hand, and when she felt the free wind blowing and heard the trumpet call of ships about to cast off their moorings for England. She wondered…when the scorpion was in her hand…would she return it to its rightful owner, as was the stated plan…or would she cast off her own moorings, and would the gleam of all those jewels bring to her eyes the bright promise of the freedom they would purchase? It was a question she wondered if Katherine Herrald had asked herself, as well.

Freedom, Minx thought, and her lip slightly curled.

She had betrayed Professor Fell and escaped him. She had caused the Professor's own dream of riches born from warfare to explode on Pendulum Island, little more than three months ago. And so where might she travel, to find freedom from Professor Fell's wrath? For surely it was coming at her, as surely as it was coming at Matthew; even now she could sense the fist tightening beneath the glove, and she knew it must somehow strike at both of them.

Freedom. Not even the scorpion could buy that for her.

But for now she *was* free—or enjoyed an illusion of freedom—and she sat confidently in this tavern with her right hand gripping a knife under the oaken table, with a peaked cap the color of a summer forest perched jauntily atop her curls of blonde hair, her once-broken and yet-crooked nose smelling the thick air of the world of insects beneath the rock, and her intelligent, light brown eyes directed at a man who might try to kill her in the next few minutes. Dylan Bandy, the king of this particular rock garden, had already killed two men and a woman in the nine months of his self-imposed exile from England to this Puritan stronghold. He did have quite the raw and ragged temper. This was according to talk in other taverns she had visited, and the talk included stories of equal violence and ferocity concerning Bandy's band of night stalkers: the long and thin-limbed Scotsman McGill who had a face as pale as a crater-marked moon, the burly brown-bearded and barrel-chested Bronson, and the dandily dressed and powdered-wigged Wampanoag Indian called Nip for some name that made a tangle of the white man's tongue. All save Bandy were standing, or leaning against the planked walls as their nature willed. From Nip's clay pipe puffed blue fumes of smoke that rose up and hung like seething spirits at the ceiling, the Indian's narrow eyes nearly hidden behind the clouds. McGill cleaned his fingernails with a curved knife that Minx imagined had found other more gruesome uses, and Bronson's arms were crossed over his chest like small trees, his beard still holding bits of buttered cornbread he'd recently engulfed into his cavern of a mouth.

"You," said Bandy, "must be a female lunatic. Coming in here—into *my* territory—and seating yourself like the queen of the world. I am not used to having conversations with *women*."

"I can tell," Minx answered.

"It is *unheard of* for a woman to be in here."

"Well," said Minx, with a quick glance around at the Sir Fart Blossoms, drunken louts and Lord Lobcocks who occupied the larger room beyond Bandy's gang, "I should hate giving this place a bad reputation."

"Your quail-pipe will get you in trouble yet," Bandy warned.

"Woman," came a low, harsh voice from the center of the smoke, "holds knife under table."

"You think I don't know that? Bleeding Jesus!" Bandy shot Nip a red-eyed glower, then returned his attention to Minx. "That's another thing. Holding a *blade* on me, and thinking you're so sharp?" His cheeks had begun to show swirls of red, and he took another drink of wine that Minx hoped was meant to delay the burst of temper tapping at his window. "Well, you're scared of me—of *us*—so I'm supposing that's a good sign," he said when the tankard was lowered again. "Just don't do anything you'd regret."

"If I do," Minx answered calmly, "you'll regret it first." And deciding that a show of ability was needed, she brought the knife out from beneath the table, took perhaps two seconds to aim, and let the blade fly.

The knife pierced Nip's wig and pinned it to the plank behind him. White powder flew like a snowstorm and scattered across the shoulders of his jet-black coat. To the credit of the Wampanoag's nerves, however, Nip did not blink nor remove the pipe from his mouth; he simply stepped forward a pace and left the wig hanging on the wall like a small dead dog with slightly yellowed curls. His own pate was bald save for a black topknot that had been neatly tucked beneath the topping.

"*No*," said Bandy, speaking to McGill. The Scotsman had readied his own knife for action, and Bronson had started forward to lock an arm around Minx's throat. "Let her be. No harm done. Right, Nip?"

"Got other wigs," Nip said, with a resigned shrug.

"Quick with a blade," was Bandy's next comment to Minx. He allowed himself a shadow of a smile, which made his weathered hatchet of a face look more ominous than ever. "All right, then," he said, as if finally accepting the woman's presence and appreciating her abilities, "you've come from New York to find the scorpion and you wish us to *help*. For whatever reason, you've sought myself and my comrades out for the undertaking of this task. And, I have to say, shown quite a bit of bull's balls for a female. People don't just find us, you know. And usually they don't like us to find *them*."

"You have earned the respect and the fear of many good Puritans," Minx replied. "Also your last murder, of a constable, has frightened the law—whatever there is of it here—into leaving you be."

"The constable beat a friend of mine nearly to death a few weeks ago. I don't let something like that pass."

"From what I hear," said Minx, as she leaned slightly toward him, "you have—shall we say—influence in many different areas. And also knowledge of many things that happen in this town, both by day and night. Ears to the ground, one might say. That's why I've sought you out."

"To help you find who stole the scorpion, as you've said," Bandy replied, with a nod. "But were you thinking it was done by myself and my crew? I'll have to say, we do have experience with cracking tools and we *have* done the occasional job, but this...no."

"I already know who took it from the Sutton house. A maid by the name of Elisa Rhodes. She worked there for two months and then vanished on the same night as the scorpion's lockbox. The problem I'm facing, Mr. Bandy, is that it appears Elisa Rhodes was not her real name and there is no record of her anywhere in or near Boston. She had concocted an elaborate story of her family and background, complete with forged letters of reference from London. Where is the thief who calls herself Elisa Rhodes, and who obviously entered that employ to steal the scorpion?" Minx let this sit for a few seconds before she went on. "I was wondering, sir, if your ears had told you anything?"

"Hm," came the man's quiet response. The fingers of his *Love* hand drummed the table. At length he said, "Tell me what you know of the scorpion."

"I know that it's a fabulous piece of jewelry. A brooch pin in the shape of a scorpion, fashioned of silver and its spine studded with eight stones... two emeralds, two rubies, two sapphires, two diamonds and at the center of its head an oval blue moonstone the size of a man's thumbnail. They call that particular stone the 'scorpion's eye.' The brooch has been in the Sutton family for as many generations as Oakes Sutton can recall, and he is nearing his eighty-third year. Who made it and how it entered the family, he doesn't know. But...he and his family desire it returned to the Sutton hand, and that's what I intend to do."

"And what else do you know about it?" Bandy prompted, with a lift of the fiery eyebrows.

Minx was silent for a moment, for she knew in which direction he was headed. "It is...the family believes," she answered, "capable of mystic powers. The word *mystic* being the elder Sutton's own."

Bandy grunted. "From what I hear, the word *mystic* hardly does it justice. From what I hear, the scorpion has the power to curse to madness whoever possesses it. Oh, it's no secret here in Boston! You mention that thing, and everyone's heard of it. Why do you think it's never been stolen before *now*? It's kept in its lockbox and never worn...never *looked* at, what I hear. The Sutton family themselves fear it, but it is—as you say—a fabulous and very valuable piece. So they've held onto it lo these many years, brought it over from England with them when they came." He took another drink to wet his dry whistle. "But only a fool would steal the thing, and for sure it wasn't just this woman's idea. Someone hired her to do it, of course. Set her up with false papers and everything she needed."

"Of course," Minx agreed. "Any idea who that someone might be?"

"The collector," said McGill, who stopped speaking as soon as Bandy raised a finger from his hand of *Hate*.

"Before we go on," Bandy said, "what's the Sutton family paying you to recover the thing? And tell me true, woman, because I can smell a lie on a skunk's breath."

"One hundred pounds," was the reply, and the truth.

"Ah!" Bandy's smile was broader now, and almost festive. "Well...you'll never get it back by yourself. Even if I tell you the name and where the

scorpion likely is…you won't get to it, not alone. You won't even get to the front door, not through that iron gate. And the house itself…a fortress."

"You may underestimate me, sir," said the princess of blades, who had another knife ready in another hiding place of her joseph.

"I may. But…if the scorpion *is* inside the fortress of Xavier Dreadson, which it probably is, considering the man's interests…then it will have to be stolen *back* from him. No one person can do that."

"His *interests?* Meaning what?" Minx prompted.

"Tell her, McGill," said Bandy.

"Xavier Dreadson," McGill said, with a heavy Scottish burr, "collects *death*. Or…that is to say…items deadly and dangerous. I've heard stories of what lies inside that house of his—we all have, and maybe it's the truth or not—but if anyone has arranged to get the scorpion, it will be him…and *because* of its reputation."

"His house is a fortress?" Minx returned her attention to Bandy. "But surely it has a weak point, as all fortresses do?"

"Possibly. A couple of breakers I know—*knew*—tried to get in. That's the last I heard of them. He was a shipbuilder in England, came over a few years ago, bought and sold a shipbuilding company here. Then he bought an unfinished mansion house about three miles up the coast and disappeared into it when the work was done. He's rarely seen in Boston anymore. As I say…he's made his place into a fortress. He brought the workmen over from England, kept them housed on the estate and sent them back when the last stone was laid." Bandy nodded. "Yes. Dreadson must have the scorpion. It suits his…shall we say…oddness. And no, he's not going to open that gate for you, or answer your knock at his door if you got that far. If the Suttons want the damned thing back, it has to be *stolen* back."

"What's in the house that's so deadly and dangerous?" Minx asked.

"His collections," Bandy replied. "From around the world, the stories go. Those from workmen at the harbor who took his crates off the ships. Occasionally a crate would fall and break open. It's said dozens of human skulls rolled from one. Another revealed an army's worth of swords and battleaxes. Some of the crates had air holes for living creatures inside. One tidbit I've heard: Dreadson values his collections enough to let loose a tiger at night to roam the grounds."

"Impressive," said Minx, with a lifting of her eyebrows.

"And hungry. It's said two men from a village up there arrive in the morning to feed the thing with horsemeat and lead it back to its cage. Oh… and this I know for certain: the windows of Dreadson's fortress are covered with iron shutters that are bolted at dusk and opened at dawn. *Every* window. From six in the morning until six at night the place is patrolled by several men with muskets, but the gate is always locked and the iron fence around the estate is ten feet high. Dreadson pays his guards very well, so they're beyond bribery by common thieves. Or even *uncommon* ones, like us," he added.

"Intriguing," said Minx.

Bandy finished off his wine and listened for a moment to the babble of other drinkers from the front room. He examined his tattooed knuckles and then narrowed his eyes at Minx. "Some say there are gold statues from ancient Egypt in that house. Diamonds as big as a man's fist. Daggers and swords in sheaths covered with jewels. Gold coins by the bagful. And another thing…deadly traps to catch thieves who get over the fence, past the tiger and through the iron shutters."

"Do you believe that?"

"He's had some servants who talked when their cups were full. But as I say, no one knows for sure…and the fellows who found out what's what in that house never came back to tell."

Minx frowned. All this was impressive and intriguing, but was it impossible? Still…a job was a job and a challenge a challenge, and she felt herself compelled by this one.

"I see your wheels moving," said Bandy. "Mine are moving too."

"Are we moving in the same direction?"

"Mine are moving this way: you need help, and to get it, you—and the Suttons—are going to have to pay for it. I'm not saying we can get into that house or *if* we get in find the scorpion…but I think I may know at least *one* thing to try." He let this sit for a few seconds before he continued on. "So this is where I'm going: we want fifty pounds and anything else we care to take out of the house. Fifty pounds up front. We agreed on that?" He was asking the other members of his crew, who nodded…all except Nip, who gave a shrug that spoke volumes for an Indian who had seen much of the white men's madness and had decided their madness was a way of life.

Bandy returned his gaze to Minx Cutter. "Bring me the money tomorrow night, here at ten o'clock. Then you can go back to wherever you're staying and—"

"Wrong," Minx interrupted. "I'll talk to the Suttons and bring you the money, but I'm going with you tomorrow night. How can I be sure you'll even *try*, if you get the money and I'm not along?"

"How can you be sure we won't take the money, ride you out in our wagon a mile or so, cut your throat and throw your body into the weeds?" was the rather chilling response.

Minx gave him a faint smile and stared forcefully into his eyes. "Would you really *want* to do that?" she asked.

Bandy paused. He flicked a glance at McGill, Bronson and Nip as if asking their pardon for ungentlemanly manners. "No," he allowed. "But

I'm damned if I ever had a woman speak to me in this way, and force herself into my business."

"I'm not forcing, I'm guiding," said Minx. She stood up from her chair. "Tomorrow night at ten you'll have your fifty pounds. Then I'm going with you to Dreadson's fortress…and perhaps we'll find out if five uncommon thieves can crack their way in?"

"I count *four* of us," said the brown-bearded Bronson.

"Without me," Minx answered, still staring into Bandy's eyes, "you're just *common*." She advanced on Nip, said, "Stand aside," and when the Indian obeyed she pulled the knife from the wall and deftly twirled it into its pocket within her jacket. "Goodnight," she told them, and she left the room and the Iron Cock.

"Woman moon-touched," said Nip, the blue fumes floating around his head. He picked up his fallen wig and stroked it like a favored pet. "Brain broke like clay pot."

"Damnedest woman I ever seen," said Bronson. "Dylan, we ain't *really* gonna try to crack the Dreadson house, are we? I ain't one for gettin' et by a tiger, no matter what treasure's supposed to be in there."

Bandy didn't answer for a time. He decided he needed another tankard of bitter red wine, for at least when he was completely drunk he would feel less like a fool tempted into action by a beautiful—and maybe deadly?—woman.

"We *are* going to try to crack the house," he said, and his voice carried a hard edge. "Call it a point of pride. Never been done before, and I'd like to say the Bandy crew can do it."

"Or die trying?" asked McGill.

"I've got some ideas. Maybe they'll work. Got some things to find and put together before tomorrow night. Whoever's not with me can walk out of here right now, no hard feelings…but you're done with me, and you're on your own. So…what's your say?"

None of the other three men spoke, but none of them left the room either.

"That's my boys," Bandy said, and he grinned. But he was thinking that this Minx Cutter had caused him to not only put his reputation on the line, but also the lives of himself and his stalwarts. So falls a man, he thought. Then again…if they could get past the fence and the tiger and the iron shutters and locks and whatever else might lie in wait in that devil of a house… they might come out rich, and as true kings of the night in this fair town.

Hell of a woman though, he thought. Ought to slit her throat for talking to him like that…but he had the feeling that tomorrow night they would need her…if only as bait for a hungry tiger.

TWO

A DAY PASSED, A DUSK SETTLED, A NIGHT CAME ON, AND THE DARK deepened.

Out of Boston on a narrow dirt road a wagon trundled onward in the silver moonlight, its destination past two small villages that had taken root north of the town. Dylan Bandy had given Minx the dubious honor of sitting beside him on the driver's plank, while the others had settled into the back. The team of horses pulled them forward while Nip's pipe puffed blue clouds in their wake. The Indian wore another curly white wig, and whether it had a knife hole in it or not Minx didn't know. She'd seen a canvas bag in the back, along with two coils of rope fixed to iron grappling hooks. She'd noted that preparations had been taken to tie sheepskin noise-dampers with leather cords around the prongs.

She was also prepared. She wore not the movement-inhibiting gown of a lady but the working clothes of a thief: a short-tailed velvet black jacket over a gray ruffled blouse, black breeches made for a man, black stockings and black leather gloves, with a dark gray cap fitted tightly over her hair. The others wore similarly dark clothing, but for Nip's wig. In Minx's jacket were two throwing knives, and a third in the calf of her right boot. Therefore she was prepared not only for the task of stealing into Dreadson's fortress, but for the event that Bandy had changed his mind now that the fifty pounds had changed hands and might be tempted to do upon her some violence he would regret.

They passed through woodland and across pastures, and left the two sleeping villages behind. An owl hooted from a tree and a bat flew across the moon, and Bandy said quietly, "We're almost there. Haven't lost your nerve, have you?"

"No, and I'm here to make sure you don't lose yours."

Bandy might have bristled at this comment, but instead he took in a long draught of the night air, looked up at the stars and then gave Minx a sidelong glance. "What world do you come from?" he asked. "What's your story?"

A world beyond your knowing, she thought, but she answered, "My world is likely not so different than yours. I expect you've had to learn to survive the best you can. The same as myself."

"Yes, I expect so," he agreed. "Ever been married?"

"No. Have you?"

"I had a wife and a son in London. Left them buried there, after one of the plagues swept through. I almost died myself, in a swoon of sweat and shit, but for some reason…God said I should not follow them to their reward, but I should continue on in this…" He paused, summoning the right words. "Vale of *opportunities*," he said. "That I should continue on, to whatever lay ahead. But when one loses what one loves, very dearly…where does one continue on to? What is the destination, and what the reason?"

"Life," said Minx.

"Ah. Of course." Bandy nodded. "One must be always strong, always in command of oneself. *Life*," he repeated. "One dies of it, eventually. After the passing of my wife and son, I realized what I had not before, and what wrecked me so for many years. What caused me to beat my fists upon the wall, and cry out to be heard when no one was listening. I realized…life is not fair. Just that. And therefore I presumed to spread the unfairness of life to as many unfortunates as possible, and broaden their knowledge for the benefit of their education."

"Admirable," said Minx.

"I was a professor of economics in London. Oh yes, a real brain at business. When I lost my position, due to my…mental state and my rather interesting addictions…I became a professor of another kind. I taught the lesson of not turning a back to a man like me in a dark alley, lest a cudgel across the skull result in an empty pocket. But *your* story, now. How is it that you've never married? Because you've never found a man worthy enough?"

Minx was silent, watching the moon follow them above the trees. "I nearly did," she answered, thinking of a daring young blade named Nathan Spade. She said, "But the time and the man are gone," and she was shamed for a moment by the wistfulness of her own voice.

"And we are *here*," said Bandy, who reined the horses in and pulled the wagon to a halt. "Light one up," he told the others in the back as he planted the wagon's brake. Bronson opened the bag, brought out a small punched-tin lantern, and flaming its candle with his tinderbox he handed the illuminator to Bandy.

"The gate is a little further around that bend," Bandy told Minx, with a motion of his lamp toward the gravel road ahead. "Let's get to it, boys," he said, and Minx caught in his voice a note between cocky confidence and grim resignation.

Bronson took charge of the ropes and grappling hooks. Nip removed his wig and left his pipe to cool, and then he took up the canvas bag, which looked too heavy for the thin-limbed Scotsman to handle. Bandy walked in the lead with Minx a few paces behind him. They rounded the bend, curving between ancient oaks that locked their limbs together across the road, and in another moment the meager light fell upon a massive iron gate and fence that blocked the way. Both gate and iron-barred fence were topped with spear tips that looked sharp enough to not only snag clothing but tear flesh.

"Look here." Bandy approached the gate and angled the light. Minx saw a heavy chain secured by a fist-sized lock. "Nip, what do you make of this?"

The Indian came up to the gate and set his burden down. He spent a moment examining the lock, nearly caressing it with his sinewy fingers. "Give try," he said. From the inside of his tobacco-brown coat he brought out a thin metal tool. He shook it once, and it opened up like a peacock's plume to display an impressive number of even thinner metal lockpicks in various sizes and shapes, three files and what appeared to be a drill or two. As Minx watched and Bandy aimed the light, Nip the lockpicker went to work on the keyhole.

"This may take a while," Bandy told Minx, as Nip tried several of the picks in the hole and met with no success. He spat into the keyhole on his next attempt, but once more the lock defied him.

Minx caught the movement of a light in the darkness perhaps a hundred yards beyond the gate. It was up in the air maybe thirty or forty feet, and she realized what it had been. "Someone's walking with a candle in an upper floor of the house," she said quietly. "I thought all the windows were covered with iron shutters?"

"Supposed to be." Bandy gave the further darkness his full attention, but the light did not return. "Sure you saw something?"

"I'm sure. At least one upper window is not shuttered. There! See it?" Again the light sparked, moving to the right.

"I see it. *Strange*. I've sat out here a few times looking at that house and I've *never* seen a light at night before. Usually those shutters are sealed tight."

"Ah!" said Nip, as he worked with another implement in the depths of the keyhole. "Some move!"

No one urged more speed from the Indian. Minx realized they held his abilities in this area in respectful regard. All they could do was wait while Nip worked the lock. Minx kept watching the dark blocky shape of Dreadson's house, but was unable to see any more movement of a candle. From the black tarpit of night, with the aid of the silver moonlight streaming down, details gave themselves up to her eye. She saw towering roofs topped with chimneys, a widow's walk at the uppermost of the house, and stone slabs holding the place together. She had the impression that it looked more like a prison than a house, and she thought that perhaps Xavier Dreadson had done something in his past to make him desire to imprison himself without fully knowing why.

Click!

The lock was sprung. Bandy drew the chain out and tossed it aside. "Good work," he told Nip, who simply nodded his head. Then Bandy pulled the gate open, and it gave a horrendous shriek at its hinges that seemed to be a cry of alarm—either for the master of the house or for the tiger, if such a creature roamed the grounds.

"All right," said Bandy, who sounded to Minx as if his teeth were gritted. "Stay together and stay sharp. Keep your heads on swivels. Light us another one, Nip, and give me the bellows."

From the bag Nip brought forth a second lantern and lit its candle with his own tinderbox. Then he reached into the bag again and gave to Bandy a small fireplace bellows. "You hold this," Bandy said, giving his lantern to Minx. "I'll need two hands, if that thing finds us. And whispering from now on, if you please."

They moved on along the gravel road, toward the ominous bulk of Dreadson's fortress. Minx had the feeling of being watched, and by more than the man in the moon. She kept not only her head on a swivel but her arm too, moving the lantern back and forth. She noted that the grasses on both sides of the road had grown almost to hip height; usually a person of wealth kept sheep or horses on such an estate to trim the lawn, but with a tiger about that would be a doubtful proposition. "Tell me," she said to Bandy, "have you ever seen this tiger? Or is it a myth spread to keep thieves away?"

"Never seen it, no. Just heard about it. Myth or not, I'm taking no chances." He didn't offer to explain that last statement, and Minx didn't pursue it. She was too busy moving the lantern and scanning the dark beyond its range, while also watching for a light in motion in the house that was growing more massive before them as they approached.

"Let's try the front door first," said Bandy. "See if Nip can get us through before any climbing's done." Up the front steps and to the door, they found another iron gate and large lock barring access to the door's lock, which doubly complicated the procedure. "No need to try a back entrance," Bandy decided. "To the northeast corner. That's the easiest way up."

"Up to what?" Minx asked. "An unshuttered window?"

"No. McGill goes up. He's the best snakeman I've ever seen."

"Thank you, sir," McGill replied, his voice a little shaky.

"Ah," said Minx. A snakeman…a thin-bodied thief who was talented in getting himself into small places. But what small place was there to get into? And then as they neared the northeast corner of the house she looked up and could see by the moonlight what the snakeman's entry likely was. "A chimney?"

"Exactly. Those grapples are going to make a soft bump, but Bronson's got a good arm and a knack at lodging the things."

"Hey!" McGill suddenly said in a strained whisper. "You hear somethin'? Moving in the grass on the left!"

Both Minx and Nip swung their lanterns in that direction, but they could see nothing other than the high grass.

"Steady," Bandy cautioned after another moment, when no snarling beast leaped out at them. "Let's don't start hearing and seeing what's not there. Bronson, can you make a toss from here?"

"I can." Bronson was already getting one of the ropes ready for a throw. "Stand back," he said, as he whirled the grappling hook around and around. When he was ready, he let fly. The grapple soared up, taking the rope with it. There was a quiet *thump* as the grapple landed, and then Bronson pulled it downward to seek purchase on one of the lower roofs. He yanked it hard several times to test the weight. "Got it hooked, first try," he said, with a measure of pride in a job well-done.

McGill was putting on a pair of deerskin gloves. He had removed a third lantern from the canvas bag and tied it to hang from his neck and down upon his chest with a leather strap. "Up you go," Bandy instructed, and Bronson held the rope taut as the snakeman began to climb up with a speed and agility that Minx had not expected.

From her own criminal past, Minx knew it was the snakeman's task to find a way in for the others if the lockpicker couldn't do the job, and if time was of the essence. And here, time was definitely essential. She kept imagining she heard movement in the grass behind her—the long heavy skulking of an animal's body, it might have been—but her lantern showed nothing and the sweat that had broken out on her face was for naught.

Still, an alarm had begun to chime at the back of her brain, and as she kept watch on the darkness around them she thought, *Hurry*.

McGill had almost clambered up to one of the lower roofs. Nearby stood a chimney that might accept a snakeman, unless all the chimneys of this strange house were blocked up. Another candle suddenly appeared at an upper and unshuttered window. Minx could see an indistinct figure in white seemingly pressing its face against the warped glass panes. A hand came up and clawed at the glass. The figure remained there, in what appeared to be a position of torment, for perhaps three seconds before it moved away.

"Damn," Bandy whispered. "What was *that?*"

"Should we call this one off?" Bronson asked, as up above McGill was removing the grappling hook from its hold and reeling up the rope to use on his chimney descent.

"I don't know," Bandy answered. "We've come this far…but I don't know. Didn't expect anybody to be up and about in there."

McGill was waiting for a signal to proceed. Bandy wiped a hand across the back of his mouth and looked at Minx. "What say you?"

Minx's eyes searched the other windows, most of which did appear to be sealed by the iron shutters. There was no further sign of a moving candle. "You're asking the opinion of a *woman?*"

"Yes, and I want it *now.*"

"We've come this far," she agreed. "We should go on."

Nip gave a mutter and Bronson shook his head, but the Indian lifted his lantern and moved it quickly up and down. McGill fixed the grappling hook to the chimney's rim and lowered the rope. He lit his lantern, and then the snakeman began his descent.

Minx smelled it before she saw it.

It was the heavy, musky smell of a wild beast. It was pungent and sour, and she knew what it was because she had been born into a circus family and she had smelled the territorial scent of a big cat before. She turned and shone the lantern into the high grass, and catching the brief glint of a pair of eyes she felt her stomach clench and she knew Dreadson's tiger had found them.

The creature came forward, as silent as death, low to the ground and magnificent in its sheer size and power. Minx felt herself almost helpless to move at the tiger's approach, its gaze seemingly fixed upon her, its maw already opening to expose the fangs ready to rip meat from bone. She heard Bronson give a startled cry of terror, for likely he had never seen such an animal before and to him it was a true monster. The big cat tensed, about to launch itself at her, and for one of the few times in her life Minx Cutter felt the cold hand of fear grip the back of her neck.

Bandy broke his own trance of terror. He stepped forward, toward the danger, and blew the bellows into the tiger's face.

A blizzard of small black grains burst out and spun in the air. The tiger blinked and sneezed, backing away from what Minx realized was an attack of crushed and ground-up peppercorns. But in the next instant the beast snarled and righted itself and rushed forward, into another fireblast of pepper as Bandy stood his ground. The tiger began to sneeze and shake its head back and forth, trying to clear the burning in its nostrils and eyes, and Bandy took the opportunity to make one more dangerous stride and give the beast a third burst of hot spice.

With a growl that seemed to shake the earth and a fearsome snap of its teeth the tiger turned tail and rushed away into the high grass, wisely deciding that it did not wish pepper with its meat this night, nor perhaps any other.

Minx let loose the breath she'd been holding. Her eyes watered too because the pepper was still flying about. Her hand had gone to one of the knives within her jacket, and now she released it because thankfully the danger had fled…at least for the moment.

"All right," said Bandy in a hoarse voice, as if consoling himself. "All right." In spite of his bravery, he couldn't suppress a tremble. "The thing's gone. Good Christ…what a beast!" He tried for a grim smile that would not hold. "Well, at least we know *that* story's true." He turned his attention upward once more, toward the chimney that McGill had entered, while Minx couldn't help but keep her lantern aimed at the high grass behind them. Bronson and Nip had both pressed themselves against the wall during this encounter, and neither one seemed to be wanting to be peeled off it.

The uncommon thieves waited.

"He's got to be down by now," Bandy fretted. "Unless he's stuck somewhere in there. He should've opened up one of these bottom windows and signalled by now."

They waited a minute longer, and then Nip said flatly, "*Trouble.*"

"Yes," Bandy agreed. "Something's gone wrong."

"What're we gonna *do?*" Bronson asked. "Leave him?"

"We can't leave him. Damn…we need another snakeman! Hell, I'll go! Bronson, toss the other rope up!"

"You never snaked down a chimney in your life!" Bronson said. "You're *way* too big!"

"Toss it up, I said! I'm not leaving him in that house!"

"Bronson's right," Minx said, because she realized what had to be done if there were going to be any chance of finding the scorpion. "You're way too big. So is he, and so is the Indian." She looked up at the chimney that had taken McGill. "*I'm* the only one who can fit down that." There was no time for indecision. "I'll go. Toss up the rope."

"You can't go!" Bandy protested. "We don't know what's happened to McGill in there! He could be—"

"Wounded or dead, yes," she agreed. "But unless you want to leave him, someone has to go in and at least find out. And I am not keen on leaving the scorpion, either."

"We don't know for sure if it's in there! We never knew!"

"Well," said Minx, "whoever's floating around in there with a candle should be able to tell us. That's what I'm here for. Bronson, toss up the rope."

The grappling hook sailed up. This time it didn't snag perfectly and Bronson had to pull it down and try again. On the second effort the hook held firm. "Ready," Bronson said.

Nip reached into the bag, brought out another leather strap and approached Minx. He looked her in the eyes as he tied the lantern around Minx's neck. "Woman cracked pot," he said.

"Take this, if the candle goes out." Bandy handed her his tinderbox to tuck into a pocket. "It's a good flint, you should have no trouble." His mouth twisted. "*No trouble,*" he said with a dollop of sarcasm. "Look what you've gotten yourself into. Haven't you heard that when you lie down with dogs you get up with fleas?"

"I was flea-bitten long before I came to Boston," she answered, with a thin smile. "Besides, I've always liked dogs."

"Got your blade?"

"Several."

"Of course you do. All right, then. Be careful. If you can get to a lower window and unbolt the shutters, give us a signal. Nip has a tool to cut the glass."

"I won't wait for that. I'll break the damned window myself."

"As you please," said Bandy. "I would imagine that by now the element of surprise has been lost. I'm just hoping McGill didn't walk into something he can't walk out of. Up you go."

Minx nodded. She took hold of the rope as Bronson held it taut, and she began to climb. She recalled that the last time she'd done any climbing was with Matthew Corbett, going up a sturdy vine on the side of Professor Fell's gunpowder fortress on Pendulum Island. Compared to that, this was an easy venture. She reached the lower roof and found that her candle was still burning in the punched-tin lantern. The chimney was just ahead, the grappling hook still attached to its edge and the rope trailing down. When she looked over, she saw no light from below.

It was time, she thought, to earn her money. If the scorpion was in this house, she wasn't leaving without it.

Then again, she might not be leaving at all.

But danger was her drug and triumph her motive, and so Minx eased herself over into the chimney's maw and began to descend the snakeman's rope.

THREE

HALFWAY DOWN, IN THE SOOTY WORLD OF THE CHIMNEYSWEEP OR THE thin-limbed thief, Minx felt the black bricks constricting about her shoulders. One might believe the house was a living thing, and had decided to slowly contract its chimney and squeeze her until her bones broke. As she continued downward she thought the fabric was being scraped from the shoulders of her jacket and soon the flesh would be at risk.

Down and down she climbed, a slow descent in the narrowing confines. Suddenly her boots puffed old ashes that spun about her like a gray shroud, and she was standing in the fireplace. She ducked her head under the mantel, stepped out onto a planked floor, removed the lantern from around her neck and shone it around.

It was an inner room with no windows. A sitting room, it looked to be, with black heavy furniture, the walls painted charcoal gray. And lining the walls were part of Xavier Dreadson's celebration of death and the implements that caused such. Mounted in rows upon black shelves were dozens—hundreds?—of human skulls. Some were toothy and some were toothless, some appeared unblemished and some broken upon the face or upon the crown, and as death brooked no favorites there were many skulls of small children and infants as well.

In spite of her fortitude, Minx gave an involuntary shudder. There was far too much yellowed bone in this room for her. A pair of closed, black-painted doors beckoned her from across the chamber. Her first task was finding McGill, but caution must be observed. She approached the doors, slowly and carefully cracked one open, and peered out with the aid of her lantern. What she would have done for a triple-candle lamp, but this sorry stub would have to do!

Beyond was a hallway and a set of stairs going up. The light did not travel far enough to see much, but upon the walls of this hallway—also painted ebony—were fixed a multitude of swords, axes and spears. One would not be lacking for a weapon here, which Minx decided might be a good thing for her.

She heard a gasp and a groan to her left.

Was someone lying on the floor there? Yes, she thought so. "McGill?" she whispered.

There was no reply for a few seconds. And then came a whisper tight with pain, "Who is that? Cutter?"

"What's wrong? Can you move?"

"Ahhhhhh….my right foot. I stepped in a trap. Piece of the floor… opened up. Stepped on a pair of blades, went right through my boot sole. Damn it!"

From upstairs somewhere came a shriek, followed by a bout of unholy laughter and gibbering. A woman's voice.

"What in God's name is *that?*" Minx asked, mostly to herself, but the fallen man answered, "Been goin' on like that…since I got in here. Can you help me?"

She eased out into the hallway and saw that McGill was lying on his left side, his face pale and sweating. The blood had flowed out of his boot, but the piece of floor planking that hid the thief trap had closed itself, probably on springs when McGill had worked himself free. McGill's lantern lay nearby, but its candle had gone out in his fall. Again from upstairs, a woman shrieked and laughed, though the sound was distant. Minx had new respect for McGill, having to lie in the dark and listen to that without knowing if anyone was coming to help him or not.

"Can you move at all?" she asked him.

"Can't put any weight on that foot. I can crawl...but I don't know what else is in this floor. Mind your step out here...the trap's about three feet from where you're standin'."

"How far to the front of the house? Any idea?"

"No. And...listen...if there's one trap in this floor, there're bound to be others."

"Agreed," said Minx. She was already scanning the planks, looking for what might appear to be extra-wide cracks where hinges or springs were placed. She reached up to a wall and removed from its position what might have been an ancient Greek or Roman spear. It would do well now as a probe for hidden dangers. She carefully stepped out into the hallway, pressing the spear's tip with some force against the planks ahead of her. Still...such a trap might not work without a certain amount of weight triggering it. Whatever Dreadson had done or had collected to warrant such defenses, she had no idea. It occurred to her that Dreadson had taken the kind of precautions someone might conceive in order to protect themselves from Professor Fell, whose revenge in matters large and small made puny the ferocity of a tiger.

Upstairs, a woman laughed and the laughter turned to sobbing and her ragged voice cried out, *"Never! Never!"*

Minx had a decision to make. She made it in a matter of seconds. "McGill, I want you to stay where you are. I'm going upstairs."

"What? Are you *insane?* We've got to get out!"

"I came for the scorpion," she said. "Whoever's up there...that's not Dreadson." But, she thought, it might be a woman who had used the name Elisa Rhodes. There wasn't time to go wandering through this house and find a window to break for the others to get in, certainly not with possible thief traps hidden about. And upstairs? Would there be traps up there too? She doubted it; most likely only the ground floor was defended thus. "I'm going to light your lantern before I go up," she told him, thinking it was the least she could do. "Just stay right where you are."

She probed with the spear and moved forward. Nothing opened up to pierce her boot sole with a blade. She spent a moment with the tinderbox and got McGill's lantern going, and then she set the lamp down next to his hand.

"Don't go up there!" the Scotsman said. "Please! Don't leave me!"

"I'll be back," she answered, noting the puddle of blood on the planks. Time might be precious for McGill as well.

Minx started up the stairs, probing before her with the spear and the lantern's light. On the wall to her left were what appeared to be African tribal masks painted in various colors and decorated with feathers, and she could not help but note that some had human teeth and looked to be covered with dried and wrinkled human skin.

About three-quarters of the way up the stairs, the spear tip disturbed a thin wire that disappeared into the wall.

There was the clicking of gears in action. The risers in front of Minx sprang open like a coffin's lid, and exposed within were perhaps fifty knife blades pointed upward to kill. She realized that if she'd hit that wire, her next step would've taken her tumbling onto the blades. It was not a way in which she wished to leave this earth. She pushed the slab of risers down again with a boot until she heard something click once more, a satisfying sound that she hoped locked the mechanism. Then she carefully stepped over the tripwire and continued up, both spear tip and lantern light still searching for more hazards.

She reached the second floor. The woman's eerie and crazed laughter was somewhere near. Minx followed a twisting hallway where a dozen suits of armor stood on either side. Again here knives, swords and battleaxes decorated the walls. She found dried human excrement on the floor, which was not a good sign.

Around another bend in the hallway, her light fell upon a woman who lay curled up in a corner. To term this person "wretched" would have been a compliment. The woman had wild and dirty black hair, and nearly equally dark were the hollows into which her eyes had retreated. She was skeleton-thin, barefooted, and wore a filthy gown that might have once been white, but was now matted with indescribables. The woman was staring fixedly at a candle in a holder on the floor beside her, her foam-whitened lips moving but making no sound.

Minx spoke. "Elisa Rhodes?"

There was no reaction to Minx's presence. The woman babbled something a little louder, but then began to speak again only in what was obviously a ravaged mind. Minx wondered how long it had been since this woman had eaten anything; the madwoman was starving herself to a shadow.

"I've come for the scorpion," Minx said. "Where is it?"

"No, no, no," whispered the woman, still staring at the candle. "No, no, no. Never. Never." She began to laugh, even as tears streaked down the gaunt and dirty cheeks. The laugh ended on a choked sob.

"Does Dreadson have the scorpion?" Minx prompted. "Where is he?"

"Dreadson, Dreadson, Dreadson," the woman answered, in a singsong voice. "Has it. Yes. I have to leave this place. I have to—" She suddenly seemed to realize she was no longer alone, and her eyes struggled to focus on Minx. "It's the scorpion," she whispered. "Pulls at you. Can't leave it alone. Never. Never, no...not like that."

"Where is Dreadson? Here?"

"Where am I?" the woman asked, and she looked at her thin, filth-clotted fingers. "What year is this?"

"1703," Minx said.

"There are *things*," the woman said. "In the air. Things…different… everywhere." She began to work at a fingernail as if desiring to pull it loose. "Dreadson, Dreadson, Dreadson. It pulls at you, it won't let you be. Every time you look…something strange. Something changed. Never, no. Not like that. The world will not end like that."

"*What?*"

"In a fireball, and all is gone. Don't look through it."

"Look through what?"

The woman stared blankly at Minx, as saliva drooled from her mouth.

"The scorpion's eye," she answered. "It shows you things. And…rather…you should burn out your own eyes…to keep those sights away." She picked up the candle holder.

"Where is Dreadson?"

"Here. He has it. Dreadson, Dreadson, Dreadson, my lord and master. Rather burn out your own eyes…God help me." The woman leaned forward and brought the candle's flame to her right eyeball.

At once Minx had knocked the candle aside and out with the spear. The woman curled up more tightly in her corner, and she began to rock herself and cry softly and whisper, "Never, never…not like that…"

Minx went past her, and not much further along the corridor she found an open door into a bedchamber that rewarded her lantern light with the shine of gold.

Xavier Dreadson had indeed amassed treasures. On a table were small golden statues of various strange beasts—mythical animals perhaps, or the totems of ancient religions—that may have come from any corner of the world, and on the wall glittered golden masks in the shapes of sun and moon and stars. The room smelled hideous, and in the bed among the vile sheets lay another wretched and skeletal creature, this one male, with long, ragged gray hair and a gray beard. As Minx entered the foul chamber, the man gave her no notice. He was holding the scorpion brooch, with his right eye pressed against the moonstone. Minx heard him gasp and mutter, and for a moment he pulled his face away and lay his head back against the dirty pillow, and it seemed he was resisting his desire because sweat gleamed on his face and he shook his head back and forth as if to deny his need…but then he gave in to it once more, and once more he seemed to be looking through the moonstone at something Minx Cutter could not see.

"Mr. Dreadson," Minx said quietly, "I've come to take the scorpion back where it belongs."

He either did not hear her or he did not care, and she may as well have been a ghost of the long-dead past.

Minx approached the bed, careful not to step on any dried pile of repugnance. In this room the chamberpot was a distant memory, and so also might be the dinner plate. She stood next to him, and watched him peer through the moonstone and heard him whisper and groan at some mystery that had revealed itself.

She reached out, took hold of the scorpion and pulled it loose from his fingers.

Xavier Dreadson first looked at his hand, as if the scorpion brooch had vanished of its own accord, and then his dark sunken eyes found Minx's lantern and her face and he opened his mouth to show the stubs of dirty teeth and he screamed like a man whose life has been jerked away from him in an instant.

"Give it back to me! Give it back!" he shouted, and he tried to get out of bed but his legs were shrivelled and nerveless, and he fell naked to the floor as Minx backed away.

"Give it to me! It's mine! It's *mine!*" the madman demanded, dragging himself through the filth on the floor as he came after Minx, who continued to back toward the doorway.

A pair of spindly arms grabbed Minx from behind. She fired an elbow into the face of the woman who had been known as Elisa Rhodes, and was now barely human. The woman fell away like a dead leaf. The master of this hideous domain was still coming onward, crawling to grasp at Minx's ankles. He had become a true snakeman, his flesh gray and mottled with bedsores, the bones jutting out from the skin. Minx had to get out, before this creature could touch her. She stepped aside, out of his grasp, and had a moment to think like a real thief before she left the room. She picked up two of the small gold statues and put them into her jacket. Payment due to her partners in crime.

Dreadson crawled forward, sobbing. "It's mine...it's mine...*mine...*"

She had seen before those crippled by the power of drugs or liquor, or many other things that might destroy a human being. Never before had she seen a man—and a woman—destroyed by a jeweled brooch. But destroyed they were, and no help could she give them but to tell a local constable in the nearest village to come here and clean up this mess and the human debris.

Dreadson was almost upon her. He reached out, about to grip her ankles with his hideous long-nailed hands.

Minx thought she might pierce him with the spear if he touched her, but murder was no longer her game.

She turned away, and with the scorpion in a pocket and the two gold statues—heavy, to be so small—lodged in her jacket she got out of the room and past the fallen weeping woman and to the dangerous stairs, and as she went down them with as much caution as she could manage she heard them both screaming up there, and then squalling like infants deprived of their precious rattles.

It occurred to her, as she reached the bottom of the stairs without incident, that working for the Herrald Agency was going to give her as much as she could handle in the future, and perhaps more than she *wished* to handle.

She went to McGill's side, helped him up and said, "Lean on me. We're getting out."

FOUR

To the east across the harbor, the sun was coming up.

Minx Cutter sat in a chair in her room at the Waterbury Inn and let the sunlight touch her face.

Before her, on a table, sunlight also touched the silver scorpion and blazed the eight stones along its spine...two emeralds, two rubies, two sapphires and two diamonds. It made the scorpion's eye burn vividly blue.

Minx looked out across the water, at the ships resting at their moorings.

Freedom, she thought. She *was* free now. She sailed under no flag but her own, but what was her destination? What was her future?

That was always a question held in great regard and great mystery: if one might only know the future, what would one do with the present?

Presently, she intended in a few hours to return the scorpion brooch to the Sutton family and book passage on a packet boat back to New York. But that journey might wait a few days, for this night she was supping with her new comrades, her band of uncommon thieves. Dylan Bandy had invited her. All that gold...it made a man hungry and thirsty and in need of company. It did the same for a woman.

And she needed laughter and a light spirit after the events of the night. She and McGill had gotten out of the house by opening the iron shutters of a front window and smashing out the glass with a chair. Bandy had been about to try to climb up to the chimney himself or smash into an upper and unshuttered window, but had been restrained by both Bronson and Nip.

When Minx had handed over the golden statues, Bandy had asked, "Is there more of *this* in there?"

"Yes," she'd answered. "But…Dylan…it's not worth it. Take what you have and let that be enough."

"Gotta get McGill some help," Bronson had said. "He could lose that foot."

"We go," said Nip. "*Now*, if you please."

It seemed the desire for thievery had been satisfied. On their way out, they heard the tiger moving in the high grass like a roving wind but it did not attack again, and Minx thought that the smell of McGill's blood was not strong enough to entice the beast to suffer another pepper attack.

They had closed the gate as best they could and then Bandy stood looking back at the house, which was as black as sin.

"You'll tell me the whole story?" he'd asked Minx on their way to the wagon.

"If you want to hear it."

"It was bad?"

"It was…eye-opening," she'd answered.

She stared at the silver scorpion, there on the table in her sunlit room.

At the scorpion's eye, burning blue.

A mystic power in that brooch, it was said. A curse to drive its possessor to madness.

It's mine…mine, Dreadson had sobbed on the bedchamber's floor.

And from the woman who had been known as Elisa Rhodes: *Every time you look…something strange…something changed…*

What exactly? Minx wondered. What power did this thing hold, to attract and destroy? To cause a man and a woman to withdraw from the world and become as animals themselves, needing this thing more than *food?* What drug was it, that tempted so?

She picked up the scorpion.

And put it down again, for today it felt oily to her fingers.

Might she have one look through the moonstone? It *was* just a moonstone, after all. A large one, the size of a man's thumbnail, centered on the scorpion's head.

Might she have just *one* look?

But as Minx picked it up again she thought that this *was* the kind of object that should be locked away and never worn, never looked at, never seen. Who had fashioned this thing, and for what reason?

One look?

Minx drew the moonstone to her right eye, and peered through its blue opacity toward Boston's harbor.

In the moonstone there was nothing but blue.

She waited…for what she didn't know. The scorpion's eye showed her nothing. Nothing. After thirty more seconds…nothing still.

And yet...

She thought an image was there in its depths, and it was becoming clearer. As she concentrated on it, it became simply the image that showed through her window, of the peaceful harbor and the sailing ships docked there.

That was all.

And yet...

Something...*something*...was different.

There were more ships than she recalled seeing. She pulled the scorpion's eye away—it did seem an effort—and she viewed the scene beyond her window. Then she looked through the eye again. More ships? Yes...*many more*...which was *impossible*. Wasn't it?

And then she felt what was nearly a cold wind blow through her, on this sunny morn, and the scorpion's eye began to show her a moving picture, of more and more ships sailing into the harbor at a speed beyond reckoning, and everything was speeding, even the clouds and the sun across the sky and the moon following and the sun after it again, and more ships and stranger in appearance, and some now spouting black smoke and sparks from funnels, and now thousands of them and across the bay...across the bay...buildings going up at rapid speed, and falling down again, and new buildings going up, and bigger and bigger, and the ships had paddlewheels and multiple funnels and they were beyond anything Minx had ever seen... and faster and faster and—

She pulled the scorpion's eye away. This time it seemed more difficult, and required more effort. Her hand was shaking. She looked out upon the harbor and saw it quiet and peaceful, a few new ships coming in to dislodge their cargoes, stately ladies all.

"*Oh,*" Minx whispered. Had that been a whisper she'd heard from the mouth of Xavier Dreadson?

No more of this! she told herself.

But the scorpion spoke, and to her mind a devil's voice said, *See what is to be, if you dare.*

The scorpion's eye came up to her own without her fully realizing it. She found herself turning away from the harbor, and suddenly the wall between her and the world was gone, and possibly as well the wall between the present and the future—if she was not herself going mad. For the scene of the colonial town was changing...faster and faster...a dizzying, sickening speed...and in the space of seconds fires burned wooden buildings and brick buildings came up and fell down and the sun and the moon sped across the sky and in the streets were carriages of different design than she knew, and in another instant those were swept away and now...stranger and stranger...came things with wheels that were neither wagon nor carriage...

and larger they grew, and more people, a buzzing beehive of people, a madness of humanity, a crush and a bellow. And at night lights that were not candles, and many colors and pulsing, and now things in the air that *flew* and also had lights…blinking…blinking…towers going up to impossible heights, red lights blinking that were not candles…and machines moving on the streets with lights before them…and everything changed, and everything strange…

She told herself to put this down, to put it away. Before the images drove her over an edge she did not know she was balanced upon, because she was not ready for these sights…these visions…and no one she knew could ever be ready for them.

With an effort that seemed a contest against invisible and infernal forces she might not win, Minx put the silver scorpion down upon the table.

She sat still, her heart beating hard, and stared at the thing. Her hand wanted to grasp it once more, her eye wanted to see. But her mind said, *no*. That there was a time for these things, and if this was true and not a madness she could not explain, she and everyone she knew would be long dead ere any of these changes came to be.

And that, perhaps, was the most dangerous and compelling part of this drug: the desire to know what lay beyond—far beyond—one's own life.

She could not deny what she had seen, though she would never tell a soul. Not even Dylan Bandy, not Oakes Sutton, not Katherine Herrald. Illusions? False images of what *might* be? A trick of the mind and the light, and the fact that she was tired and needed rest?

Yes, call it that.

Her hand wanted to pick up the scorpion again.

Never, never, Elisa Rhodes had said, from her filthy corner in the Dreadson house. *Not like that. The world will not end like that…*

Minx remembered asking, *What?* but she chose now to forget the reply.

For would it not bring on madness to really see the future, to know how the world must progress with you a memory in the grave? Or when all who kept your memory are to be forgotten, in that long line of years? Everything strange and changed, and to know such things as should not be known before their time…and even, possibly…things to be known after time itself ceases to be as men understand it?

Her hand moved to the scorpion.

It was a deadly, dangerous thing.

Minx picked it up and wrapped it in a brown cloth. She wrapped it very tightly. The sooner she returned it to the Suttons, the better. She would not touch it again.

She hoped.

But for now she was a young woman, vibrant and alive, and she was going to dinner tonight to eat and drink and laugh, because she had done her duty and would report a success back to Katherine Herrald, along with one hundred pounds. She had made peace with herself, and she knew where she was going.

Her own future, and she would live it as anyone should…moment by moment, and to the full.

SKELETON CREW

JULY, 1703

ONE

TWO WOMEN—ONE WHITE, ONE BLACK; ONE WEARING A PEACH-HUED dress from the famous seamstress Evelyn Crabtree in London, the other in a brown shift sewn by its owner's hand with a colonial needle—sat at a table playing what was in New York town the popular tavern game of Jingo, the cards being laid out before the players under the lantern's yellow glow. Beside the white woman's right hand on the table was a loaded pistol. The black woman kept looking nervously toward the window to her left, two panes of glass remaining and the other pair covered from the elements by waxed paper.

This night there was no concern about the elements, if weather was the subject. Here in the middle of July the air was warm and sultry, a full moon ashine behind wispy clouds, and through the window and the chinks between some of the cabin's logs came the sounds of the New Jersey summer forest: a soft *chirruping* of insects swelling and ebbing and the distant hooting of an owl.

When the woman of color glanced again toward the window, the white woman said casually, "No need to rush. All is in order."

"Yes ma'am," said the other, and returned to inspecting her cards.

"I will say again…my name is Katherine and I'd like you to refer to me as such. Look there, you have a run of diamonds in process totaling thirteen."

"Yes…Katherine," came the reply, and then, earnestly: "It's hard for me."

"It shouldn't be."

"Such is as it be."

"Well, Katherine is my name just as Miriam is yours, but as I am present in your home you may call me *mud* though I would prefer the name I was given at birth."

Miriam Lamb let a small smile pass across her face. One more glance toward the window and then she cleared her throat and sat more upright in her chair, her focus returning to the cards before her. But in another few seconds she said quietly, "Might I ask a question?"

"Anything."

"How old are you?"

"I turned fifty-three in April."

"I got eight years on you," Miriam said. "But I recall fifty-three! Four years after that was when the master—"

"You have no master," Katherine Herrald reminded her.

"But I did then. Master—" She stopped herself. "Mr. Stanwyk," she amended, "passed away that cold January. Lord...bitter cold. But we always had us a good fire, all of us and Stepper and me. It was a sad thing, Mr. Stanwyk wastin' away like he did."

"I'm sure it was."

"You have to know that Mr. Stanwyk was a good mas— A good provider to his help. I think about him sometimes. Him and his wife. She used to like to swing on the tree swing Stepper hung up for her, and Mr. Stanwyk there pushin' her up and up, and her happy as a lark. It was nothin' like bein' at...that other place I told you."

"You've got your run of diamonds, let's see your next cards," Katherine said, and took a drink of the excellent apple cider from the earthenware cup just beside the pistol.

"Yes...Katherine." The next four cards drawn were two hearts, a club and the ace of hearts which added one point, but which might have brought forth a cry of *Jingo* if Miriam had been playing like the cunning gamblers in New York town who considered this game of reaching twenty-one in the same suit as the "castle card"—currently a diamond—nearly a religion. Both women were waiting for the Mad Queen to show up, which had the power to destroy the "castle" and divert it to another suit. Miriam said, "You're at sixteen and I'm at fourteen, and I'm thinkin' you're goin' to win this game too."

"We'll see. You just have to be patient."

"And *lucky*, I reckon. Then again, I'm mite the luckiest woman I know. Wish Stepper could see this, he was lucky hisself at cards."

The luckiest woman, Katherine thought. An admirable attitude from a woman who'd been a slave from childhood, whose boychild had been taken from her and her husband Stephan Lamb at his age of thirteen, and who had survived a series of "providers" to whom the slaves were either animals to be worked to the point of near death or items to be sold at the next auction to the highest bidder. And here she sat in this cabin she and Stephan had together built back from a ruin, with a run of diamonds before her on the scarred table Stephan had crafted. She had come a long way, but Stephan had not made the journey with her these last three years. The man had taken sick and like Gerrard Stanwyk—a Dutch fur merchant as well as a gentleman farmer whose estate, now passed to another owner, was perhaps forty miles from where they sat—wasted away in the bed in the next room, and was buried in a clearing in the woods behind the cabin a few yards from where Miriam had buried the dog.

So now the luckiest woman was on her own, and Katherine Herrald had come from New York town to make sure her luck did not run out.

Surely Miriam Lamb was made of sturdy timber, Katherine mused. The woman being sixty-one was showing some frailties, as her back was somewhat bent and her body thin. Her whitening hair was pinned with small bone clips and her seamed face was the nearly blue-black of pure African heritage. In the lantern's light, as well as the glow from the lantern on a wall hook beside the door, Miriam's eyes fascinated Katherine because though they were as black as any ink ever dipped from a Herrald Agency inkpot they were also luminous, energetic and intelligent. True, Miriam was behind in their rounds of card play four to Katherine's fifteen, but she was just learning the game and she already had a good sense of its flow. Katherine had decided early on, when she'd broken out the deck on her arrival yesterday afternoon, not to pretend with her: learn the game, persevere through the losses, learn to win and don't expect an easy time of it, which was the way Katherine Herrald had herself been raised.

Of equal importance, however: it gave Miriam Lamb something to concentrate on while they waited.

Last night they had not come. This night?

Perhaps, though the hour was growing late.

Still…it was not quite the witching hour, and wasn't that the time the skeletons rose from their graves and roamed the night?

Katherine's next four cards yielded a jack of clubs—offering one point—and the rest were useless so she was currently stalled at seventeen.

"Lordy, looka here!" said Miriam with a little rush of excitement as she drew her hand of four, and in it were the king of clubs adding one point as all face cards did, the ace of spades giving one point, a nine of clubs not applicable in this case, and the six of diamonds equaling twenty-two: success!

The first thing Miriam had shown Katherine two days ago, when she had come up the stairs into the office from Stone Street, was the yellowed document signed by various officials who Katherine was sure looked down their snuff-powdered noses as they pressed their pens to parchment.

It was called the Order of Manumission, and by its writ had freed Miriam and Stephan Lamb from slavery. In Katherine's experience it was not written very often, but it did serve to emancipate slaves, indentured workers and convicts. The reason for this order to be in Miriam's hand was that—as she'd stated—she was the luckiest woman. To be bought by a good "provider" from a bad "master" was a lucky thing, in a manner of speaking, and for both Miriam and Stephan to be sold together was another element of luck. In the end, Gerrard Stanwyk had presented in his will his desire that all twelve of his slaves be freed upon his death, and so the lawyers had arranged for twelve souls to go out into a world that could be a double-edged sword for the unwary white and a hanging dagger for the black. Thus Katherine found herself here, somewhere in the woods between the three villages of Chamberlin's Crossing, Edenborough and Suylandt, determined to keep that dagger from falling.

Hold! Was that the thump of hoofbeats upon the earth?

Miriam tensed. One of her hands settled down upon the spread of diamonds, as if she wished time to backtrack and the moment never to arrive.

But the moment *had* arrived, and with it the night's visitation.

A bell rang. It was low-toned, Katherine noted, to sound like portending someone's funeral.

And then came a shouted voice, harsh and muffled: *"Miriam Lamb! Come out and pay your toll!"*

"Stay exactly as you are," said Katherine, her voice easy. She noted also that the luckiest woman made of sturdy timber had begun to tremble, just a little.

Katherine Herrald stood up, picked up the pistol and walked to the door as if she were ambling toward a nice quiet lunch at either Sally Almond's or the Dock House's Rose Garden Cafe. She opened the door and lifted the lantern from its hook.

Then she cocked the pistol, and she walked outside.

TWO

THERE WERE FOUR, AS MIRIAM HAD SAID THERE WOULD BE.

One who held aloft a small lantern had guided his horse just slightly ahead of the others. *He who bellows*, Katherine thought. The leader of this bagful of bones.

For they were all skeletons, sitting astride skeletal mounts.

Or so they wished to appear. It was a neat trick, dressing up in black robes, gloves, hoods and masks with skulls and skeleton bones painted upon them. Even the horses were gowned as skeletons to their hooves in the manner of the ceremonial dressings used in medieval knights' tournaments.

Only these riders were not here to offer chivalry, but to proffer chicanery. Katherine noted with interest that both the lantern held by the central rider and the shine of the full moon caused the paintings of skulls and bones upon both riders and horses to glow with a faint greenish-white sheen, and she tucked the observation into a place where her brain might get at it later.

Before the skeleton crew could speak, Katherine said, "Miriam Lamb is not paying a toll this month. Nor the next. In fact, she will not be paying a toll ever again, so continue on to your graves and fall into them, if you please."

There was a moment of ominous quiet, broken only by a *whuff* from one of the horses obviously irritated by the eye-holed hood it was made to wear, and by the distant owl hooting in search of a midsummer night's romance.

The leader leaned forward on his saddle, for either it was a man or a woman whose voice had dropped to her cellar along with her sense.

Behind the painted skull the man spoke with a sneer: "Ain't *you* the fancy dance!"

"And here's my dancing partner." She held up the pistol. "I'll show you the black powder hop, if you like."

"*Ha!*" he answered, though in it was a note of caution. "Now who the hell are *you* and where'd you come from?"

"Gentleman first. Same questions."

"Whoever you are, you're playin' with fire."

"You might notice I seem to be holding the match that would burn you quite severely."

"Hell with that!" he snarled. "No goddamn woman can handle a pistol!"

"It's true," Katherine said, "that there are four of you and I only have one ball in my firearm. So if any trouble erupts here in the next short while I shall be compelled to put that ball through the left eyehole of your ridiculous mask. I'm surprised your horses can see where they're going and you all haven't broken your necks yet."

"Keep talkin', missy! Just dig yourself down deeper!"

"If you're on your way to a masquerade party," Katherine said, "don't let me stop you, but I don't think those costumes will win any ribbons tonight."

Here befell an ominous silence, and Katherine thought for a moment that she had played her hand too unwisely and not well. Behind her calm façade her heart was beating hard and she felt sweat at the back of her neck, but her parents—her father a professor of history at Eton College and her mother a poetess and artist who had garnered some fame for her landscape watercolors—had emphasized to her the importance of finding inner peace in any storm and so projecting that image to the world. In this moment their teachings were highly prized.

"You know," said the lead skeleton, "we might have guns too."

"I'm sure you do," Katherine replied, still calmly though she realized she was balanced on a razor's edge. "How else would you have killed Mizz Lamb's dog?"

"A yappin' bitch," he answered. And to the others: "Just like we have here."

If he expected a laugh he did not get it, for all knew the gravity of the situation. Even the insects of the forest had silenced.

"We could kill you," he went on, "drag your body off and nobody would give a care."

"I believe my associates in New York town would. Before I left I wrote a letter directing where I was going, so that action might result in your neck being stretched."

"I could shoot you down in a damned minute, you fancy piece of dried-up ass!"

Katherine managed a thin smile, because with this creature's discomfiture she knew she had at least won this round. She levelled the pistol at the painted skull. The barrel did not waver. "Do your damnedest," she said. "I assure you I'll do mine."

Once more silence fell upon the battlefield.

"We got places to be," said one of the others to the leader, the voice equally gruff and muffled by the black material.

The skeleton man with the lantern dropped it slightly. Katherine took this to be also a good omen though she was watching as much as she could see of the black-gloved hands; in this case the faint glow was a helpful aid.

"Miriam Lamb is payin' her toll," he said. "You can mark that as a vow. And I won't forget this night, Fancy Dance."

And so vowing he wheeled his mount away, the others followed suit, and the four skeleton riders went pounding off under the full moon along the quarter-mile of dirt road that led to another quarter-mile of dirt road and then to the choice of direction between Edenborough, Chamberlin's Crossing and Suylandt.

Katherine waited. Her heart was still pounding and she could feel it at her temples.

I won't forget this night, he'd said. Did that mean there would be no return *this* night?

And well they did *got places to be*, Katherine thought, because for the past seven months the skeleton riders had been terrorizing the neighboring farmers and landowners into paying what they termed a "toll"...essentially, a payment to live on the land they had settled upon. That had been the gist of Miriam Lamb's visit to Stone Street, and her plea to give whatever help might aid in unmasking these scoundrels and putting an end to it.

I cain't pay much, Miriam had said, *but I brought along somethin' for the minute.*

And thus had been set upon Katherine's desk a brown jug of the really delicious apple cider Miriam brewed. Behind the ramshackle cabin, past the outhouse, the barn and the chicken coop, were several acres of apple trees, and this is how the woman made her living. It wasn't much, but she paid her way—and the unnecessary "toll" of ten shillings every full moon—by selling to the locals, apples in season and in other seasons apple jam and jelly, preserves, fried apples, pickled apples and her specialty of fermented applejack that Katherine was sure would wet the whistles of every liquor aficionado in New York if the taverns could get their hands on it.

Ten shillings wasn't much to Katherine but it was a lot for Miriam and also for the other victims. It was one hundred and twenty pence, or half a pound. One victim on a nearby farm had refused to pay for two months, and before the third was out his barn was burned to the ground and his horses slaughtered. So this skeleton crew could play rough if they were denied.

Katherine was bound to deny them, and to make sure no harm came to Miriam Lamb or any of her holdings.

Those glowing painted skulls and bones…she recalled something of interest she'd read in the London *Gazette,* but it had been long ago—years?—and she couldn't remember exactly what it was. More advice from her father, rest his soul: Always keep learning, for that is as much of life as your blood and your brain.

She didn't think they were turning their horses around and coming back. There was only the one road in and out, and everything else thick forest no masked hoodlum or horse could get through. But she was certain it wasn't over. Oh, no; it was just beginning.

She uncocked the pistol and returned to the cabin, where Miriam was still sitting at the table.

"I heard," the woman said. "Think they'll be back tonight?"

"I don't think so." Katherine sat down. "Still…I'll stay up awhile after you go to bed."

"Wasn't you scairt?"

"Every second," she admitted. "But it's part of what I do."

"Bein' scairt?"

"*Overcoming* being scared. You are within your rights to deny paying anything to live on this land. No one owned it before you and Stephan settled here. You rebuilt the cabin and planted the orchard. You put your heart and soul into it. You are a free woman, and you have a right to live freely."

"Yes ma'am...I mean, Katherine...but it could all be gone in one night, just like at Jesper Sallow's farm."

"I'm here to make sure that doesn't happen, and I intend to find out who is behind this criminal indignity."

Miriam nodded. For an instant Katherine thought she saw tears glistening in the older woman's eyes, but they were blinked away.

"I shuffled the cards for us," Miriam offered.

"Good. Let's have another—" Katherine abruptly stopped speaking. Cards for us.

For us.

"Ah!" she said, as the memory came back. "*Phosphorus.*"

"Pardon?"

"What makes the paint glow," Katherine said. "The painted skulls and bones, I mean. There's a substance called phosphorus that I believe is mixed into the paint." She did not go into the details, that she recalled from the *Gazette* that phosphorus had been discovered by a German alchemist who was working with evaporating human urine into salts—the reason she remembered the article, for its bizarre nature—and from the thickened urine hoped the paste could be condensed into gold. What he came up with was a waxy white substance that glowed in the dark and burned brightly. More recently in 1680—the real thrust of the article—a London scientist named Robert Boyle created the substance and was marketing it to ignite small sulfur-tipped wooden sticks that had not yet caught on with the public, but might have some use in the far future.

"Tell me more details about the towns around here," said Katherine to Miriam's puzzled expression. They had gone over this in rudimentary fashion already today, but the realization that what was likely a very costly substance was being used in the paint for the simple purpose of adding to the fearsome costumes intrigued her. "Start with Edenborough."

"Nothin' much there no more. Few years back—before Stephan and me came—I heard it told one of the men who lived there shot an Indian brave, was a chief's son. Well, the Indians came in their droves and there was a mite rough fight. Ended up with most of the cabins burned down and a lot of dead folk. I believe Edenborough's just a name now."

"And that's what...four or five miles to the west?"

"I'd say so."

"All right. About Suylandt."

"A Dutch town. Most there are Dutch and they fly their flag. Got a few cabins and a general store, and that's about the like of it."

"And that is five miles or so to the north?"

"Five or six, yes..." Miriam paused and tried again. "Yes, Katherine."

"About Chamberlin's Crossing, then. Three miles to the east, is that correct?"

"Three would be 'bout right. Well, Chamberlin's Crossin' is a fair-sized town. Got over a hundred people there. Two nice churches and a school for the children. New cabins goin' up. Well, I'd call 'em *houses*, 'cause they a whole lot more sturdy than what you're sittin' in. I'd say they was…what's the word when somethin' is meant to be there in a forever way?"

"Permanent?" Katherine supplied.

"That would be it."

"Does Chamberlin's Crossing have an official of the law?"

"Oh, yes! They got 'umselves a sheriff!"

"Hm," Katherine answered. "Have you not told this sheriff about your situation?"

"Yes, I have. I know others around have told him too. He say he lookin' into it, but them skeleton men are mighty hard to catch."

"Not if you're really trying. What's this so-called sheriff's name?"

"Mr. Dawgett. I mean *Sheriff* Dawgett. Able Dawgett is the full of it."

"I presume the name of the town comes from the bridge we crossed yesterday?" Katherine had followed Miriam up from New York, the former on a horse and the latter driving her horse and wagon. They had crossed the Pompton River on a covered bridge that looked and still smelled of new timbers. With that bridge, the ferryman in this area—whoever he might be and whatever his hours and proclivities to work—was out of business.

"It does and it's a Godsend," Miriam said. "Me and the others on this west side of the Pompton don't no more have to pay the ferry to get to the general store on the east. Mr. Hutcheson, you know, he buys my goods. Or I mean…he *used* to, 'til 'bout two months ago. Says my last batch of cider was bad, but that cain't be true. Well, the town used to be called Greenfields 'til Mr. Barton Chamberlin moved in—'cause of the meadows and such, I reckon—so after that bridge went up they honored him by changin' the name."

"Mr. Chamberlin?" Katherine's finely trimmed brows went up. "A wealthy man, I suppose? And also an educated man?"

"I would think, from the big house I heard he had built on that land of his. I got that from Mr. Hutcheson at the store. I hear he paid for the second church to go up, and the schoolhouse, and they got a whole street neat and nice as you'd ever see."

"Neat and nice," Katherine repeated. "I'm sure. What business is this Barton Chamberlin in that has made him so wealthy?"

"I wouldn't know, I've never seen him or that place of his."

"But it's not far from here?"

"I believe it's just past the bridge. The road to get there, I mean."

Katherine nodded. "You realize the skeleton men have to come across the bridge, don't you? They might know of a more shallow ford but it's pretty obvious they're coming from the direction of Chamberlin's Crossing."

"Well why in the world would anybody there be dressin' up and ridin' out like they're doin'?"

After a pause, Katherine answered with a smile. "I am thinking aloud. The hour is late. You should get to bed."

"You're sure you won't take the bed tonight? Lot more comfort than the floor and a blanket."

"The floor and a blanket were fine last night and it shall be equally so tonight."

"More of that Jingo tomorrow? I think I'm getting' the hang of it."

"We shall play," said Katherine, "until we drive the Mad Queen to renounce her throne."

Miriam gave a little chuckle. "You sure talk funny."

Katherine considered it a good sign that Miriam had taken this night in stride, and seemed no worse for worrying about the consequences. Which meant she trusted the New York problem-solver. Which also meant that the New York problem-solver had to live up to that trust. Tomorrow would bring the second test in this strange contest between the skeleton crew and their defiers...and Katherine had to wonder not a bit fretfully what might come of it.

"If you'll fetch in the firewood in the mornin'," Miriam said before she retired, "I'll fry us some eggs and I can bake us up some apple cakes."

"I'll look forward to that." Miriam's kitchen was the fireplace where her cooking utensils and pans were dependent upon a good flame...not so much different, actually, than the best houses in New York but for size and variety of available items.

After Miriam's door had closed, Katherine walked to the window to survey the moonlit night. The forest sounds had returned, a soft chorus beckoning sleep. Did the skeleton men lurk out there, preparing another assault? Katherine decided to sleep with the pistol close at hand and her nose searching for any smell of smoke, if the torches were thrown as they'd been at the Sallow farm. From what Miriam had told her, three other settlers had been scared off by the skeleton crew after Sallow's barn went up in flames and the horses were killed, but two more along with Mizz Lamb remained in their holdings.

What was the point of it? Ten shillings a month...quite a lot for these farmers trying to wrest a living from the land. But the purchase of the phosphorus would be expensive, if whoever was behind this didn't personally make it and that would demand some scientific knowledge and equipment. And the costumes themselves...who sewed them?

It seemed to Katherine that a number of people were involved in this, but again...to what point?

She intended to take her horse—Alexander, a sturdy steed—to Chamberlin's Crossing after breakfast to converse with this so-called sheriff, whose excuse in not catching these marauders sounded to her very suspect.

In the meantime, as she lay on the floor trying to find sleep with the pistol beside her, the night moved on and—after much listening and in truth much trepidation—the problem-solver from New York gave herself up to what dreams might come.

THREE

KATHERINE REINED HER HORSE IN.

She had paused at the midpoint of the covered bridge to take stock of the workmanship involved. The bridge was about fifteen yards in length, spanning a relatively narrow portion of the Pompton, and wider than a coach and two. In fact, she deemed it wider than two coaches to pass alongside each other. An interesting width, she thought...and why was it so wide? From her saddle she cast her gaze along the joints and fittings and determined that professional hands had crafted this span between east and west. Had Barton Chamberlin employed engineers and carpenters from New York? Or...had he paid for the expertise of the craftsmen from London? If so...again...why?

A bridge might be simply a bridge, she mused, though in this case it seemed to her more than a crossing for whatever traffic might use the connection...but to the west were only the few farms including Miriam's land and her apple orchard. It was quite an expensive endeavor for apparently little use and gain. But there must be some gain to be had from it, for Katherine doubted that Barton Chamberlin had financed this very fine and particularly sturdy bridge simply for the poor farmers to bring their goods to town.

She urged her mount onward, determined now to find out exactly what that gain might be.

It was a clear, warm morning and the surrounding forest was lush with many shades of green and sweet with many varieties of birdsong. For this outing Katherine wore a simple cream-colored blouse, a pale blue vest with gold-toned buttons, a blue peaked cap and in the French style of *devantiere* a split skirt of royal blue to allow riding with both boots in the stirrups instead of the usual female's posture of side-saddle, which she not only disliked but considered both rather patronizing to the woman rider—though it was certainly the style that had endured for more than a century—and dangerous if one had to get up to speed in a hurry. She would rather be thought of as a *female flagrante* than finding herself thrown from her horse in the pursuit of looking like an equestrian rather than being one.

Not far past the bridge she noted the road to Chamberlin's property that branched off to the left. There was nothing remarkable about it, only a simple dirt track cut out of the surrounding woods. It curved to the right and disappeared amid the foliage. She continued on, thinking that on the way back it might be of interest to follow that road and have a look at the man's domain.

Within ten minutes Katherine had reached corn and bean fields that presaged the town, and in another few there stood a wide area cleared from the forest in which were arranged several well-painted houses surrounded by white picket fences and other various structures. Two with small steeples nearly across the street from each other. She saw a haywagon pulled by oxen trundling slowly along, a brown-bearded man on a horse clopped past her and gave her a look one might grant the very Devil, and two women talking in front of one of the churches suddenly stopped in open-mouthed wonder to watch Katherine's approach. Before the New York problem-solver could hail them and ask where she might find Sheriff Dawgett, they scurried inside and the door shut behind them like an exclamation of God's disapproval.

Katherine shrugged. She had seen a structure up the way that displayed the red-painted sign of *GENERAL STORE*, so perhaps Mr. Hutcheson might be useful this morning.

He was, but there was something grudging about his demeanor. He was a slim man in his fifties with thinning sandy hair and round-lensed glasses that perched low on his nose.

"Do I know you?" he asked from behind his counter with a squint of the eyes, after Katherine had inquired if he was Mr. Hutcheson.

"I am Miriam Lamb's friend," Katherine said. "She told me you used to buy her wares until the last two months. Some tale about a bad batch of cider?"

"That's between Mizz Lamb and me," he said curtly. "Other than bein' her friend, who are you?"

Katherine introduced herself. "And I am currently involved in aiding Mizz Lamb in her problem. I'm sure you know what I mean."

"The riders." Hutcheson nodded. "I know. And I'll be sorry when Mizz Lamb leaves, but I don't see her stayin' too much longer."

"That's to be determined. May I ask if these riders torment anyone who lives east of the river?"

"I couldn't say."

"Do they torment you or anyone else but the farmers who live on the west side?"

"Not me. About the others, I couldn't say."

Katherine brought up a rather thin smile. "I find that hard to believe, sir." She motioned toward the nearest window, where two women—the same from the church—and an older white-haired gent were peering at her through the dimpled glass as if she were a denizen of another world, which she thought she likely was. "In my experience a general store in any town is where people gather to gossip and spread whatever news is available. Surely you can say if anyone but the farmers on the western side of the river have been tormented by this…let's call them…skeleton crew."

Hutcheson took his time in answering. His voice was gravestone heavy when he did: "No ma'am. I couldn't say."

There was nothing more to be said on that subject, since what ought to be said could not be spoken for whatever unspeakable reason. Katherine shifted the focus. "I'd like to see Sheriff Dawgett. Where might I find him?"

"He's around."

"Sir, I'd appreciate at least one straight reply. Or I could go back to New York town and return with a magistrate who might ask these questions in a more forceful manner."

Hutcheson was again silent and Katherine could tell he was sizing up the situation. At last he lifted his chin in what was possibly a thrust of defiance, yet the mention of a magistrate had done its work. "Able's likely out at his farm. Follow the main road, you'll see his house and his fields couple of miles along."

"Thank you for that direction. Good day." On the way to her horse, Katherine made the two women and another two who'd joined their survey scurry away from the store as if they really had somewhere else to go, while the white-haired man still stood there agawk. A small boy about ten or so came running past Katherine and plucked at her skirt as he sprinted by, to the shrill cry from one of the women of "Malcolm! Malcolm, you come *here!*"

Katherine swung herself up onto her steed and left Malcolm to the mercies of his mother and the others eating a little July dust.

The sun was warm, the sky was nearly a cloudless blue and the birds darted back and forth over Katherine's head as she followed another road sliced through the forest. It would be a full moon again tonight, she mused as Alexander trotted onward. Would the riders make a second attempt at Miriam's? She felt they would, if simply because men hated to be called down by women even if the particular woman did not hold a pistol.

In time she sighted a small white-painted farmhouse on the right, surrounded by a corn field, a barn, a corral holding two horses, a chicken coop, outhouse, smokehouse and other utilities necessary for operation. She guided Alexander off the main road onto the track leading to the farm-house's door, and on that ride in closer she saw a man walking amid the bountiful stalks of corn.

She dismounted and as quietly as possible moved through the cornfield toward the figure. She got around behind him, so he jumped when she said, "May I have a word?"

He spun around, sputtering. He was a short, heavyset gent with curly gray hair and a grizzled lantern jaw, his skin burnished by the summer sun. His dark brown eyes widened and for a second his entire face contorted. He said, "What're *you* doin' here?" which was absolutely the wrong thing to say, since it acknowledged knowing her in some regard. Also, the voice...harsh and gruff...very likely the same voice muffled by a skeleton mask yet she could not be certain. But then he stammered and corrected himself and she had a sure feeling this was the man: "I mean to say...who *are* you?"

"My name is Katherine Herrald," she answered, though she considered that introductions had already been made by moonlight. "You are Sheriff Dawgett?"

"I am. What're you doin' sneakin' around in my cornfield?"

"Pardon my approach. Some say I have a quiet way of walking."

"You can get shot that way! What the devil are you wantin'?" He was still flustered and spittle flecked his lips.

"I have come from New York town to aid Miriam Lamb in her prob-lem against the...well, I'm sure you know."

"How should I know?"

"As sheriff you ought to."

"You're talkin' about the riders? How the hell can *you* aid her? Two women standin' up against that bunch? You're takin' your life in your hands."

"Possibly." Katherine offered a fleeting smile as chilly as December. "So inform me, just for my interest, what you have done as sheriff to catch these marauders."

"I don't have to tell you my business."

"True. But as I told Mr. Hutcheson at the general store, I can certainly bring a magistrate here to ask about your business, and I'm also sure this magistrate would wish to see a signed judicial certificate identifying you as a sworn sheriff and not a farmer playing as one."

"You threatenin' me, missy?"

"I am *warning* you," Katherine said, and Able Dawgett fell silent.

From the house there came a woman's call: "Able! Able, answer me back!"

Alexander had been seen from a window and the horse was not rec-ognized, Katherine thought. They likely didn't get very many visitors here.

Dawgett gave a loud whistle in reply, evidently a signal that he had not been swarmed upon by some corn-devouring insects. Then when the woman called "You all right?" he answered back, "Go on in the house, I got business!"

He gave her a few seconds to do as he asked, and then he aimed his musket-barrel eyes at Katherine. "Why do you want to come up here and cause trouble?"

"I'm seeking to end trouble."

"You don't know anything about it."

"I have time to hear what *you* know." When that was met with more sullen silence, Katherine said, "It's obvious that the riders are only tormenting those farmers who live on the western side of the river. They're likely—more than likely—using the bridge recently built by Mr. Barton Chamberlin to come over from the eastern side. I intend to visit him after our current unproductive conversation."

"Mr. Chamberlin ain't home," Dawgett said, his arms crossed over his chest. "Took his wife and gone to New York town for a few days."

"Oh? Is he procuring a new shipment of phosphorus?"

"Of *what?*"

"Phosphorus. The element used in the skeleton costumes' paint to make it glow. A nice effect, if fear is what you're after." She noted very smooth and tight cloth patches sewn onto the elbows of Dawgett's sweat-stained shirt. The knees of his trousers were also patched by an efficient seamstress. "Did you wife apply those patches?"

"Maybe she did."

"I presume she might make a little extra money by using her needle and thread?"

"Woman, what the *hell* do you want here? I can't stop the riders! People 'round here are scared to death of 'em! I suppose Mizz Lamb told you what happened at Sallow's place!"

"She did. Let me ask…if you know the riders go out under the full moon every month, and I understand from Miriam they've been demanding this extortion money since March, why don't you station men on the bridge during those nights to catch them?"

"Nobody 'round here wants to get killed for rabble like that over the river. You want me to ask 'em to risk a pistol ball for a *slave?*"

"Miriam Lamb is no longer anyone's slave."

"She should move on. Woman, we've got a good town here. A growin' town, and I plan to see it keeps growin'."

"What do the farmers across the river have to do with preventing the town from further growth?"

"I'm done talkin'," he said, and in those three words Katherine heard the snarl of the skeleton crew's leader, mask-muffled or not. "Get off my land," he told her, and then he stood with his hands on his hips and his stocky upper body inclined toward her a few degrees as if he might rush her and drive her to the ground.

Nothing more could be gained here. As Katherine rode away she looked back and saw Dawgett and presumably his wife—another thick-bodied figure—standing before the house watching her. She rode on.

And passing through the town where she was again greeted by persons standing stock still and surveying her as if they feared an attack of the New York bloody black blister plague if they breathed the same air as herself, she came to the road in the forest that would take her—if she chose to follow it—to the Chamberlin property.

Without hesitation, she turned Alexander upon that road and continued on toward what sort of investigation she did not know, yet she had to see for herself.

A few hundred yards forward, and the forest cleared for a huge white house set atop an area of rolling hills, the house adorned with three chimneys and a glass-enclosed cupola atop the roof. And Katherine instantly saw what could be seen from that cupola, for in a fenced pasture before the house were—how many?—perhaps four or five hundred head of cattle grazing upon the good green New Jersey grass. It was a huge expanse of land, and upon it as well stood several outbuildings all—as the street of town had been—"neat and nice." She saw three workmen moving around near the outbuildings, one of them pushing a wheelbarrow and another two carting what looked like burlap grain sacks. Again she cast her gaze across the pasture and presumed she might have undercounted the herd by a hundred. All in all, it was quite an impressive scene.

Katherine dismounted before the house, went up four stone steps to the white-lacquered door and used the knocker. In a moment it was opened by a short gray-haired woman with heavy lines on her face and wearing what must have been a housekeeper's black uniform with silver buttons and a blouse with ruffles down the front.

"Yes'm?" she asked.

"Is Mr. Chamberlin in?"

"I'm sorry, no."

"Ah! My misfortune! I've come up from New York town to discuss some business."

The woman looked Katherine up and down. "Business, ma'am?"

"Yes, and very important business that I thought Barton—I mean, Mr. Chamberlin—might appreciate. When do you expect him in?"

"Not for several days, ma'am. As a fact, he and the missus have themselves gone to New York town just yesterday morning."

"Oh." Katherine brought up a frown. "I wonder if he was going there to see me. We have a profitable arrangement in…" She hesitated only an instant. "…the shipment of a certain supply from England he's been receiving. Let me ask…is he staying at the usual place?" She ventured a guess, as it was the best—and most expensive—inn in New York and she herself knew that from experience. "The Dock House?"

"Yes ma'am, the same."

"A creature of habit, he is. I'll go visit him there." She gave the woman her most courteous smile and turned away.

Before Katherine could descend the steps, the woman said, "Oh, ma'am! I would save you the trouble! The missus is staying at the Dock House, but the master will be found at his gaming club!"

Katherine turned around again, holding her smile. "Oh, of course! His club! But I forget the name of it."

"The Fine Fellows, ma'am."

"Ah, now I recall!" It was one of several gaming clubs in New York. This one catered to gents with heavy purses and wild extravagances of every sort. The club was available to members who held gold keys and was several—she had heard—luxurious bedrooms around a central gambling parlor, all this on the second floor of Patrick Tawney's Red Lion Tavern at the corner of King and Queen streets. "Yes," Katherine said, "I'll visit there first thing, but of course being a woman I shall have to ask a gentleman to go up the stairs for me."

That brought a small return smile, a glint in the eye and a little twist of the lip. "Men can be a bit…if I may say…outrageous, can't they, ma'am."

"You may say, and well said," Katherine answered. "Thank you for your help, and good day."

She returned to her horse, rode down to the portion of the road where she could again have a view of Barton Chamberlin's holdings and there she sat for a while under the sun, contemplating what she was looking at. A huge herd of cattle. A wealthy and perhaps reckless gambler. A new bridge built at quite an expense and a town that the false "sheriff" Able Dawgett said he intended to "keep growing." And of course the poor farmers on the western side of the river, Miriam Lamb with her apple orchard and her brave defiance…

…of the skeleton crew, who if Katherine knew anything about the outrageous nature of men would return tonight as soon as the moon rose and their cloaks and masks took on the glow of the element she believed Barton Chamberlin was purchasing in New York as well as ditching the wife to kick up his heels with the other Fine Fellows.

She continued on, crossed the bridge over the Pompton and steered Alexander back to Miriam's cabin to wait for nightfall and what the full moon might bring.

FOUR

"JINGO!" MIRIAM ANNOUNCED ON SIGHT OF THE ACE SHE'D JUST BEEN dealt. Her decision was much more confident now that she'd enjoyed a few victories. Katherine thought it was a good call, since Miriam's point total stood at six while her own was eighteen. The following castle card was a three of hearts, which banished the current castle card of spades and gave them both three points. Their hands were discarded and the next new hand of four cards was dealt. Miriam had among them a six of hearts and the jack of diamonds, which added up to ten, and this time around Katherine was looking at a measly two of hearts as her only card of value in the deal. The contest to twenty-one continued.

"Tell me," Katherine said as they played on, "might you ever wish to leave this place?"

"Leave? Wherever would I go?"

"Possibly to New York. I think you might find a farm and apple orchard close to town. I believe the taverns would offer a pretty sum for your applejack, and the market there is thriving."

Miriam nodded, but she was looking at her four cards under the lamplight. The king of clubs, the jack of spades, a two of clubs and a four of hearts: in total, six points to add to her previous ten. "I couldn't leave Stepper," she said.

Katherine waited. Her own cards: a nine of diamonds, a four of clubs, a five of hearts and two of hearts. Twelve points to Miriam's sixteen. But she sensed a Mad Queen coming, as they did with a maddening regularity.

"Sometimes," Miriam quietly said, "when it's bitter cold out and all the world is ice and snow…I feel like I can warm him by goin' out to his side and…y'know…just sayin' a few words. Like…tellin' him what my day was, and how I'm doin'. Just small talk, y'know, but I feel like it warms him. And then…in the hot days…the dog days, they call 'em…well, I kinda think my speakin' to him cools him a bit. Keeps him comfortable. You see?" Her gaze came up from the cards.

"Yes," Katherine said.

"And that orchard. Anybody look at it, think it's just trees. Row after row of just trees. But oh no. It's the heart and soul Stepper and me put into them. All that hard work, and gettin' everything just right. I guess…'cause I won't have no more children…I guess they're like that to me. Children. Have to be watched and cared for, and some don't turn out right no matter what you do for 'em. But others…oh, they amaze you. They don't look like much at first and you think that one's done for, won't amount worth the seed, all scraggly and not wantin' to bloom, and maybe one season passes and another and you don't get much a'nothin'…and then, Mizz Katherine…then the miracle happens. Then…you see the blessin' that was given to us. Given by God to me and Stepper, with this land." She smiled so very faintly. "Oh, Mizz Katherine…I couldn't leave Stepper to shiver in the cold and suffer in the heat, and I couldn't leave the children we've raised. I think you understand that."

"I do," said Katherine. "I understand it very well."

The next four cards Katherine dealt to Miriam were the ace of clubs, the seven of diamonds, the eight of spades and…there it was…the ten of hearts.

Eleven points in that hand. Plus the sixteen she already possessed. Twenty-seven. And as the magic number had been reached there was no further hand dealt to Katherine, who felt sure that the next card out of the deck would've either been an ace—to which she could cry "Jingo" to possibly sabotage Miriam's leading position—or a Mad Queen which would have changed the castle card once again.

"Lucky that time," Miriam said. "Can I get you another little sip of the 'jack?"

"Possibly later, but thank you." It was high quality and highly potent applejack, best taken in a cup the size of a thimble. They had shared a sip over supper of corn soup and biscuits with a small side portion of salted and peppered turnip greens.

"Whenever you like. The jug's always—"

Miriam abruptly stopped speaking, because they both had heard the *whuff* of a horse's exhale from outside and they realized the visitors this time had not stormed in, but crept in.

"Miriam Lamb!" called the mask-muffled voice. *"Come out and pay your toll!"*

Without a word Katherine picked up the pistol on the table beside her right hand and cocked it. Her heart was beating hard but she steeled herself. She went to the door, opened it and then retrieved the lantern from its hook…but she'd already seen that tonight there were only three skeleton riders. She walked toward them and stopped as the leader brought his horse forward a few paces, his own lamp lifted high.

"We're not givin' this up," he said.

"It seems one of you has. Did he shy away from a return engagement? Or did his wife simply refuse to let him out of the house two nights in a row?"

One of the others turned a laugh into a cough when the leader—and Katherine thought it was near certainly Able Dawgett—shot a skull-faced glare at him.

"This isn't about money," Katherine said. "Tell me how these farmers on the west side of the river have anything to do with the growth of your town."

Dawgett—it must be him—paused a few seconds before speaking. Then: "Lady, just get on your horse and go back to your own life. You think you're gonna keep that black crow here? And them other poor rags on them other farms too? Well, how're you gonna do that? We'll just come back next full moon, and we'll be wantin' twenty shillin's. So unless you plan on stayin' around here and plantin' your flag, you ain't got no chance in hell of headin' off what has to be done."

Katherine simply stared up into the mask's eyeholes. "What does the bridge have to do with it?"

The skeleton man shook his head. "My God, you are a damn nuisance!"

"Damn me if you wish, but I think anyone who plays at sheriff by day but embraces being a bandit by moonlight should be doubly damned."

That comment must've scraped his flint, because his voice was tight when he answered: "I'm done talkin'!" He made a motion to wheel his horse away.

"I've already heard you say that at your farm today," Katherine said, but even as she spoke it she realized she had gone a scrape too far, for in the next instant the skeleton head twisted toward her, the black clad shoulders hunched forward, and she saw the metal gleam of the pistol his gloved hand was whipping forth from the robes.

He fired.

Crimson sparks flew. The ear-splitting *crack* of the shot silenced all the forest's midsummer music. But Katherine had already dodged to one side. The ball hissed past her left ear and *whack*ed into the cabin's timbers behind her. Before the blue smoke could fog the short distance between herself and her attacker she lifted her own weapon and fired.

It was done not because she wished to kill Able Dawgett, since his one shot was gone unless he had another gun, but as a statement to those present that she was not to be trifled with, and that a woman could very well handle a pistol as her departed husband Richard had taught her. These things whirled through her mind in the hot second before her ball struck the skeleton crew's leader. Dawgett gave a howl of pain, dropped both lantern and pistol to clutch at his collarbone on the left side and nearly toppled from the saddle.

Before his cry went twenty yards the others had wheeled their horses and bolted for home. Dawgett's hooded head turned this way and that, looking for aid, and seeing that he'd been abandoned by his bony brothers he kicked his heels into the flanks of his horse and away they dashed as if pursued by real phantoms of the night.

"Lordy!" someone was saying—a high, excited voice—into Katherine's ear, but the violence of the moment had dazed her. "Lordy! I saw it all from the window! Near 'bout shot you!"

Miriam Lamb, she realized. Yes. And back to the moment she came, though the small beads of sweat at her temples remained.

"I got him," she said. "Not mortally, I think. I *hope*. Damn it! Dawgett was a fool to fire that gun!"

"*Who?*"

"Your sheriff, who is not a sheriff at all but is leading that bunch."

"But...why would the sheriff be tryin' to—"

"I just *said!*" Katherine turned on her not without heat, for it was coming clear to her how close she had come to being buried back there beside Stepper and Scruffs the dog. "Dawgett is not really a sheriff! Maybe he *tries* with others, but to you and the farmers on this side of the river he is an enemy! Do you understand?"

"No, I don't. Why would he be dressin' up in skeleton robes? And dressin' up them horses too? What's the aim of it?"

"That I don't know," Katherine admitted, "but I intend to find out." It was obvious that someone had spent time in planning these scare-and-power tactics to move the western farmers off their land, as well as spending a great deal of money. Her mind was circling around Barton Chamberlin. But if the aim was driving what might be termed "squatters" off the land so claims of abandonment could be brought to the local court—whatever that might be—then why not just *pay* the farmers to move? What would be the terms? Possibly thirty pounds to each household? Was that too much for a wealthy gambler to offer?

"Looky here," Miriam said, and she came back from where she'd picked up the pistol Dawgett had dropped. She held it at arm's length, as if it were a copperhead snake, and offered it to her heroine of the night.

The New York problem-solver took it and instantly saw that this pistol was far beyond Able Dawgett's means. It was a beautiful burnished silver with scrolled engravings, the grip was pearl-white ivory...and there upon the grip was embossed a small red diamond.

A small red diamond from a suit of cards. Embossed on both sides by an expert and obviously meticulous craftsman.

"What do you make of that?" Miriam asked.

"I make of it...that I *will* accept another sip of applejack tonight," Katherine replied. "We'll hold onto this and see what comes of it." And it occurred to her that one sip might not be enough to soothe her to sleep, for that bullet from her gun might wind up killing Dawgett. Though he'd likely meant to put her into the forever sleep, the idea of killing someone was abhorrent to her. Therefore…tomorrow…she must return to Dawgett's farm, and see what harm she had done.

At a little past eight on another warm and sunny morning, Katherine knocked at Dawgett's door and when it opened was greeted by his heavyset wife aiming a blunderbuss into her face.

Katherine didn't move.

"You dare to come here?" the woman challenged, her blue eyes ablaze.

"I wished to know what his injury is."

"Broke collarbone. In terrible pain. That make you happy?"

"Is there a doctor nearby?"

"Saw him last night," was the answer. "Took the ball out and made Able as comfortable as he could." The woman frowned, which was nearly as much a forbidding sight as the business end of the blunderbuss. "What the *hell* are you doin' here?"

"I told you. I came to—"

"Not *here*. This town. Come to give aid to that slave woman and them trash farmers over there? All of 'em squattin' on land that—" She stopped speaking.

"On land that what?" Katherine asked, but as easily as possible.

"I could kill you right this minute," the woman said.

As she spoke, two children—a boy about ten and a girl twelve or so— peeked warily out from either side of the woman's wide-hipped, many-times-patched—and very adroitly patched—skirt.

"You could," Katherine agreed, "but I don't think your children would appreciate watching a cold-blooded murder."

There was a tense moment of silence. Then the woman snapped, "You two go on in the house. Go on, I said! Don't you dawdle!"

They obediently withdrew.

The ugly muzzle of the blunderbuss lowered, but only by a few inches.

"Did your husband tell you that he fired at me first?" Katherine asked. "If he didn't, I'm telling you now. I'm also telling you that this business with the skeleton riders is going to end very badly. Before it's over—if it's not stopped—there's no telling whose blood will flow."

"Maybe yours'll be next!"

"It's possible. I'm going to make a guess, if you don't mind: you sewed the masks and costumes. Did you also apply the paint, or was that done somewhere else?"

To this there was no response, but at least the blunderbuss did not rise again.

"This situation," Katherine continued to the woman's stony glare and silence, "does not need to involve violence. It does not need to involve burning farmhouses and slaughtering horses, and it certainly does not need to involve gunplay. I regret your husband's injuries, but I have to be truthful and say I would be regretting mine more."

Slowly...very slowly...the blunderbuss went down to the woman's side.

"Get out of here while you can walk," she said.

"I'm going. But one request from me, if you please. Would you inform whoever is behind this that I am willing to negotiate?"

"To *what?*"

"To meet and talk," Katherine explained, but gently as befit the current atmosphere. "To come to some kind of agreement."

"I don't know what you're jabberin' about, or who I would be informin'."

"Very well. I wish your husband a quick recovery." On her walk to Alexander, Katherine realized Dawgett's wife had not yet left the doorway, and the tingling at the back of her neck and along her spine told her that it was a foolish thing to turn your back on an angry woman with a blunderbuss and a score to settle. But as she mounted her horse she heard the door close, yet only when she was off along the road with the farmhouse dwindling in both view and threat did she allow herself an exhalation of bated breath and a shiver as if someone had just walked over her grave.

FIVE

THE DAYS CAME AND WENT.

Sunny one more day, then cloudy and rainshowers the next two, sunny once again and all the birds in full flight amid the lush green trees.

"How long you gonna stay?" Miriam asked over their nightly Jingo. "I mean...not pushin' you out 'cause I enjoy the company. But...Katherine...they ain't gonna be comin' back 'til next full moon."

"Oh," Katherine answered just before she turned over a Mad Queen, lost her advantage of ten points in spades and was only a few more hands away from losing the game eight points to twenty-one, "I think we'll see something develop long before then. Soon, I believe."

The wait continued. Katherine wished to make herself useful and took her turn at chopping wood for the cooking, which left her with hands raw from the axe handle and shoulders and back wailing for mercy. She was better suited to feed the chickens and tend to the horses, though shoveling the manure out of the barn was not to her liking. But she did it anyway. Also she accompanied Miriam in the wagon to the nearby hamlet of Suylandt and to the more distant villages of Guilford, Lancaster and Pattawatomay to sell her cinnamon-flavored apple sauce, her cider and baskets of apples at the general stores there. The trip took more than two hours each way, on a trail through forbidding wilderness. Pattawatomay fascinated Katherine because it consisted of a few cabins, a trading post, and a number of either strong-willed, God-protected or just plain foolhardy settlers, since it was situated right on the edge of a Delaware Indian tribe encampment. But it appeared that the meeting of men from different worlds was at the moment a peaceful accord, since Indians came to the trading post for goods and the settlers bought various items from the Delawares. According to the gray-bearded and coonskin-cap-wearing Mr. McDuffie at the post, both Delawares and the Pattawatomay whites were very fond of Miriam's cider.

Also, as soon as the Delawares realized Miriam's wagon was at the post, a throng of them emerged to stand and watch her and Katherine as the two women rode away. As Miriam explained and as had been explained to her by Mr. McDuffie, the Indians got some kind of pleasure from observing a human being who was the color of night.

All in all, the day's profits: four shillings, eight pence.

But the day had been profitable in other ways as well. For the first time Katherine had dared to ask Miriam about her life as a slave, and learned that at the age of six she had been captured after a massacre by a warring tribe in her homeland, sold to Portuguese traders and then to Dutch slavers, bought by an Englishman and served as a house slave and farm worker to a succession of owners until brought across the Atlantic by Mr. Stanwyk to his estate south of New York town. *And what about your life?* Miriam had asked.

Her life.

Coddled in so many ways, Katherine thought. Of course always mentally challenged, for that was the bedrock of the Arness family. But born into comfortable wealth and always accepted into whatever corridor of society she chose to enter. Certainly there were obstacles, being a woman, and she was not quite the illustrious firebrand as her artist mother, but she had learned the art of communication, of determining the correct word or phrase at the correct time, of reading faces and postures—the unspoken language—and using that to her advantage. So to compare her life of relative ease, horseback riding, mental puzzles, shopping holidays in London, society balls and such to one who had lived their existence from the age of six to the age of sixty-one as a slave…how could she even comprehend such a thing?

"I know your life was way different," Miriam said, as if she was also adept at reading faces and postures, as Katherine had shifted uneasily on the wagon plank and not only because it was rough on the bottom. "Tell me. I'd like to see it. Y'know…in my head."

Katherine did. There was no need to be ashamed of her upbringing and her education. It was simply a fact. And in the telling of it Katherine got the sense that Miriam had "in her head" transported herself into the skin and history of the woman at her side, and though their worlds could never be the same, perhaps at this one moment there was a convergence of very different lives.

"Was you ever married?" Miriam asked, as the two horses trudged on and the wagon's wheels creaked ever toward the bridge at Chamberlin's Crossing.

"I was. I met Richard at a social event. A ball, really, given by a friend of my father. Richard was a young lawyer. Well…a lawyer in training with a large firm of many lawyers. When we got to know each other, he told me he longed for—as he put it—more adventure in his life, beyond a lawyer's desk and office. But he still wished to be of help to people, and thus in time he founded the problem-solving agency."

"What happened to him?"

Here on this warm and sunny late afternoon Katherine could not help but feel a chill. She didn't wish to go into the details, that Richard had been executed in the most grisly manner on orders of the monstrous Professor Fell.

She said, "He passed away in the line of duty," and that was all that needed to be spoken.

The wagon's wheels kept rolling on.

And Katherine suddenly realized that she was offering her face to the sun as its rays streamed through the branches overhead, that she was listening to the many different birdsongs, that she was smelling the sweetness of the air and enjoying the moment of just being…*here*. She was a woman of London and of New York, accustomed to crowds and noise, to the chaos that was part of life amid the bustling streets and buildings always being hammered and nailed together, the incessant growth of human ambition. She would never have dreamt that along this dirt track surrounded only by untamed wilderness would she feel a sense of peace…a sense that she had long forgotten what it was not to have appointments, or a schedule, or anything pressing upon her that had to be accomplished lest she feel like… what?…a failure? If she was not industrious every day, if she had no places to hurry in and out of, she was not living up to the standards of her family?

For it seemed to her that, though she was waiting on some kind of development after the shooting of Able Dawgett, she looked forward with a great sense of calm to a lamplit supper of fried eggs and apple fritters, of turnip greens and boiled okra, and afterward the...yes, say it...fun and camaraderie of their nightly play at Jingo.

And sitting here beside Miriam Lamb, on this hard wagon plank with miles yet to go and summer's eve just beginning to cool the air, she felt sure she was exactly where Richard would have wanted her to be.

"If you like," she said to Miriam, "I'll take the horses the rest of the way in."

It happened the following morning, while Miriam was out in the orchard and Katherine was on her way to feed the chickens.

Katherine saw the rider approaching. He was a man about thirty or so, dark-haired, wearing a nice gray suit and mounted on a fine-looking dappled steed. He reined in as Katherine walked forward to meet him carrying her bucket of grain and seeds.

He looked at her askance, as if he had mistakenly arrived at the wrong place, but she said, "I'm who you've come for."

"Ah. Mr. Barton Chamberlin would ask that you grace him with your presence for supper tonight at seven o'clock. He understands that you know how to get there."

"I do." Katherine was aware of Miriam cautiously approaching from the side.

"If you'd prefer, a coach can be sent for your convenience."

"No, I'll ride in."

"Excellent." It was said with no emotion. The man's expression was equally impassive. "May I suggest dressing for the evening? I have to ask... do you own a better gown?"

"This is just my chicken-feeding get-up," she said, and she gave Miriam a quick wink. "I've brought along my emperor-meeting gown as well."

"Yes." The man showed a fraction of an inch of teeth. "Then I shall report to Mr. Chamberlin that you accept his invitation."

"Do report," Katherine said.

The messenger nodded, turned his horse and both women watched him out of sight.

"What does it mean?" Miriam asked.

"It means...I should get cleaned up before I meet Mr. Barton Chamberlin." It didn't need to be said that what lay ahead promised to be a very interesting—and possibly dangerous?—evening. Katherine walked back to scatter feed among the chickens, debating whether her *devantiere* skirt could hide a pistol.

SIX

THE YOUNG MAN WHO'D BROUGHT THE SUPPER INVITATION WAS WAIT-
ing at the foot of the front steps to take Katherine's horse when she rode
in. Without a word he took the bit and guided Alexander toward the barn.
Katherine ascended the steps, used the knocker and in a few seconds the
door was opened by the gray-haired housekeeper, who this time gave a
quick curtsey but kept her face downcast and eyes averted.

As Katherine crossed the threshold into a foyer with white walls and
a floor of red tiles, she was greeted by another man also outfitted with the
silver-buttoned uniform of a servant, this one a slim older gent wearing a
white wig and white gloves. "Madam," he said, giving a bow, "please follow."

Through a hallway and many rooms they went, it not being lost upon
Katherine that the furnishings, hanging tapestries, glass-shaded lamps and
carpets were all of the finest quality and of course purchased at the greatest
expense, though a vivid, bright red predominated throughout the house
and jarred her eyes at every turn.

Then Katherine followed the servant through an arched doorway and
there was the dining room with a huge table, a crystal chandelier above it,
and the walls a throbbing crimson, and coming into her face with a square-
mouthed smile was a man wearing a white suit and a red ruffled blouse
nearly as screamingly loud as the room itself.

"There is our guest!" he said, or rather boomed it as if addressing an
audience in the distant town. "Madam Herrald, so kind of you to join us
for supper!"

"Thank you, I'm pleased to be here," she replied, her ears ringing. Her
impressions of the man: he resembled a boiled and shaved bulldog, the
pock-marked flesh of his face beyond ruddy to nearly a reddish glow, the
bulbous pug nose tinged blue with broken veins, his scalp a plain of the
color she imagined Egyptian sand to be. He was probably around her age
or perhaps a bit older. Below the red hairy centipedes he called his eyebrows
the eyes were deep-set, pale blue and nearly frightening in their intensity.
Barton Chamberlin was quite the formidable figure...even though the top
of his Egyptian sand only reached Katherine's chin, and the man made three
of any other man she might name, so large around was his body. Her host
was almost square in build and the thickness of his neck could likely snap a
hangman's noose, if it ever came to that.

"Ah!" Chamberlin said, with a big-toothed grin. The eyes gleamed.
"What do you make of me?"

"Well-fed," she answered.

"And right you are, madam! You have hit it directly on the button! Come, come! Sit down, we'll have some wine!"

At the near end of the table three silver place settings had been readied, along with crystal wine glasses. Chamberlin motioned toward the chair on his right and showed he was at least part gentleman by waiting until Katherine had seated herself before he squeezed his bulk down in the chair at the head of the table. She noted that his chair creaked in a cry of true distress.

"Another guest is coming?" Katherine asked.

"My wife Lily will be along soon. I must tell you, she is thrilled to have your company this evening. It's not often—well, hardly *ever*—that we entertain guests who can carry on a decent conversation. By the way, did you bring my pistol with you?"

Katherine showed no surprise at this query, though it was difficult to control her expression. "It's in my saddlebag. I'll return it to you before I leave."

"Oh, Michal's likely found it by now. I instructed him to go through your belongings, I hope you don't mind."

"My pleasure," Katherine said, "but I assumed you'd made a present of it to Dawgett for doing your dirty work for you. Shouldn't it be returned to him?"

"It was *loaned* to him," was the reply, still made with a square-mouthed smile and a booming voice. "And tossed to the ground like any old piece you might buy at a tinker's back alley? The tragedy of it! Anyway, Dawgett won't be *able* to use half of his body for the next few weeks. Ha! Did you hear the joke I just made?" Before any further comment could be made yea or nay, Chamberlin brought out from some kind of sleeve under the table a wooden clapper device which he struck together twice so loudly Katherine feared her teeth might crack. Instantly a male servant emerged from a door on the other side of the room bearing a bottle of wine on a silver tray. As the wine was uncorked and poured—deep red, of course—the master of the manse plowed on: "A beautiful pistol, you must admit. One of a set I bought after I won a very large pot at my gaming club a few years ago. You know, on each grip the...well, you do know. And I understand you also know the name of my gaming club, since you bamboozled dear Esther into believing you were a business associate. Manners, Madam Herrald, manners!" He took a drink of his wine. "Ah! Not the best I have ever sipped, but it shall do for the evening. Does it please you?"

She drank a small swallow. Rich and peppery. "Nice," she said.

"There are more bottles where that came from, so drink up. We don't go for half-measures in this house! Oh, look who's joined us! The lady Lily!"

Entering the room was a slim young woman probably in her mid-twenties, very lovely, with light brown eyes and blonde hair. She was dressed in a magnificent white gown trimmed with red and with red designs in swirls along the sleeves. She might have been the epitome of style in London, except for the hat she wore atop the pinned-up pile of hair: it was a garish mass of peacock feathers going this way and that anchored by a round purple cap.

"We're just at the wine, dearest," Chamberlin told her. "Now sit down and catch your breath, you'll have plenty of time to converse with Madam Herrald."

When the "lady Lily" took her chair—and Chamberlin did not rise for this event—she simply sat grinning across the table at their guest with what Katherine thought was the air of an imbecile.

"I don't know what your meals have been like at Mizz Lamb's," said the behemoth of the table, "and I dread to imagine, but here we eat in courses." So saying, he chop-chopped with the clapper and here came the servant bearing a tray of huge black sausages with little cups of what appeared to be different sauces.

"Good hearty blood sausages!" Chamberlin looked to Katherine as if he'd become more red and swollen with the anticipation of this dubious dish. "Wonderful for the vitality!"

The servant cut the sausages into pieces and forked them onto the plates. Katherine noted that Lily got only a beggar's piece while her husband received an entire sausage, which he promptly doused with a dark brown sauce. "Hot spices!" he exclaimed. "The hotter the better, I say! Care to give it a try?"

"I am content," Katherine replied, and regarded her hunks of sausage with loss of appetite. Though the outsides were burned black, the raw insides were bleeding onto the plate.

"My dirty business," Chamberlin suddenly stated, and at first Katherine thought he was referring to the sausages. "That's what you said, isn't it?" He cut and speared a black-and-bloody piece and jammed it into his mouth. Then as he spoke around his mouthful crimson flecks gathered on his lips. "So little you know."

"Enlighten me."

"Do you like my hat?" was abruptly thrust into the conversation by Lily Chamberlin, in a high, frail voice fairly trembling with excitement. She repeated it to Katherine's silence. "My hat? Do you like it?"

"Very becoming," was the diplomatic answer.

"Becoming what?" the young lady asked, with a puzzled note and expression.

"It's very fashionable." A white lie, perhaps.

"I think so too. What do you like about it?"

Katherine could sense that Chamberlin was watching her very careful-ly. It seemed to Katherine that Lily's eyes were glassy and she hadn't even taken a taste of her wine yet. "It fits your head well," Katherine said, and Chamberlin boomed a laugh that almost lifted her out of her chair.

"It's one of my favorites," the young woman said, continuing on as if no laugh had exploded in the room though her glassy eyes had widened a bit and were more shiny still. "I collect hats. I have three hundred and fourteen."

She had said this with the pride of a child over a bagful of marbles. Katherine's impression was that Lily Chamberlin's hinges were not quite fastened tightly enough...or perhaps they were so tight one or two had sprung loose. "A lady must have interests," Katherine replied, with as warm a smile as she could muster.

"May I?" Lily asked her husband, and once again there was something of the child in her voice but also of the fearful dog in the way she stooped her shoulders and seemed nearly to be begging. He waved a corpulent hand at her and she was up and out of the room like a shot.

"Her hats," said Chamberlin with a sturdy drink of his wine, "would fill this house if I allowed it." He leaned toward Lily's untouched plate, speared her blood sausages and brought them over for his own appetite. "My dirty business, you said."

"Correct."

"What did you see when you came up the road?"

"A rich man's grandiose statement of wealth."

He laughed again but it was more of a burp around his mouthful of sausage. "Yes, that if it pleases you to hear it. But the cattle, Madam Herrald! The *cattle!*"

"I did notice those."

"Well you should!" He wiped his mouth with the back of a hand. "*Beef* cattle, madam! The finest money can buy! Of course some died on the voy-age over and by necessity fed the sharks but I have more on the way...and when the breeding truly begins, my herd will rival any in Europe! A thou-sand...two thousand...three thousand...and more and more as the years go on. Do you see what I'm getting at?"

Katherine nodded. "You're going to need more pastureland."

"Exactly! And that takes years to develop properly! The land must be cleared and seeded. A great endeavor, madam! And forthwith the name of Barton Chamberlin will be known as—" He held up both hands as if seeing something miraculous written in the clouds by the quill of God. "—the Baron of Beef!"

Katherine was about to comment on that ridiculous title when two things happened at once: Chamberlin used his clapper to deafening effect and Lily came back into the room wearing a moss-green hat adorned with metal sprigs and twine attached to multicolored glass balls that clicked and clacked as she regained her place at the table, her still-dazed eyes fixed upon Katherine for some sign of approval.

Again before Katherine could think of something—anything—to say, the servant reappeared bearing a huge pot of what turned out to be creamed beef mounded upon more mounds of biscuits, apparent when he spooned the thick brown matter upon Katherine's plate.

"Beef, madam!" said Chamberlin as the servant gave a brief bow of respect to the table and went away. "The future of these colonies!" He dug into the mess before him with ravenous relish, the stuff gathering in the corners of his mouth as he spoke. "You know of course that pork is currently the meat of choice, and I was in that business in London, but here I have the opportunity to begin an endeavor that I believe will feed the growth of these colonies for a hundred years. Beef, madam! Yes, *beef!* And I will be the first to begin the herd of the future! In fact as you can see it is already begun!" His reverie was interrupted by a frown as he regarded her plate. "What's wrong, don't you like good solid beef?"

"This is not exactly solid," she answered, watching it drool from her fork. She in turn regarded the small mountain of food Chamberlin was tearing into. "Do you always eat like this?"

"This is my newest hat," Lily suddenly said. "Is it not the finest thing?"

Correct, Katherine wished to say, but when she opened her mouth it came out as, "Very unusual. I would call it *daring.*"

With that Lily gave a glowing grin and clapped her hands together in what appeared to be nearly an ecstasy.

"So," said Katherine, in order to steer the subject back to the subject of steers, "you had the bridge built for your cattle to cross over to these imaginary pastures."

"Not imaginary!" A thick forefinger went up. "In the planning stages and well along, I assure you. I have a young lawyer in New York town handling the paperwork. Do you know Thomas Brodine?"

"I know the name but I've never met him."

"A fine, brainy fellow. You see, I've purchased the land that lies south of my estate through the New Jersey court, but I cannot purchase the land *north* of me because it has been bought by an ironworks currently preparing to start operations. The town lies to the east, therefore I must go west across the river and that rabble over there must abandon their hovels so a claim of ownership can be made."

"You call them rabble," Katherine said, putting a chill in the air, "but I have a feeling one might find a bit of rabble in your own family history."

This statement brought a thin smile to Chamberlin's greased lips but his eyes had taken on a fierce and rather frightening glint. "How right you are, madam," he said quietly. It was the quiet of dark weather building before a storm. "But I have pulled myself *out* of the garbage my family called *life*. And I did it by strength of will and what's up here!" The forefinger tapped his skull. "I fought tooth and nail for what you see before you, madam! And I'll not let trash like that over the river stand in the way of my progress! I mean to say, the progress of these colonies! Beef will be the life's blood, can't you see it? It will give force to the hammer and the plow with equal measure! So what does the measly stand of broken-down farms and one apple orchard have to give that can compare with my offerings?" He drained his wineglass but he was not yet done. "Oh, I have given my all for this project, you can bet on it!" His face seemed swollen and had reddened to a degree that Katherine thought a pin prick to the forehead would draw a shot of blood across the room. "My sons want none of it, by the way! Sons of different mothers, they are, and both like *those* darlings! Caswell remains in London where he—yes, get this—formulates soaps and perfumes and thinks that's an honorable man's business, and Dade…he is the dumbest of the pair! But I must say he has the gift of persuasion, for he's persuaded some contact of his to do business with the Spanish, and—now this is hilarious—he has paid several hundred pounds for land in the *Florida country!* He has bought swamps and scrub and sand-choked beaches! How the hell will that nightmare of a land ever show a profit?"

Lily raised her hand. "May I?" she asked.

"Yes, go on!" There was a snarl in the voice. "Wear a dozen at once if you please, just stop needling me!"

She scurried away.

"Speaking of needles," Katherine said in the silence—but for the gobbling of creamed beef and biscuits—that followed, "I presume Dawgett's wife sewed those costumes for both man and horse?" She waited, but Chamberlin just kept eating. "It would've been on you if Dawgett had been killed. Were you prepared for violence?"

"Certainly not!" His fork clattered onto a nearly empty plate. "Dawgett took that upon himself! I didn't wish him to burn anyone's barn or slaughter any horses, and that's God's truth! I should say he got a bit heady over the job to be done."

"And nearly got his head blown off for it. Two things I don't understand. Number one, why not just pay them to leave? Say thirty pounds for each?"

"I don't pay squatters and rabble!" The blood flushed back into his face. "Not one pence for laziness and…" He sought the next objection. "…the stubborn hindering of progress that would benefit these entire colonies!"

"You equate laziness with lack of your kind of money."

"Well, it's a fact of life, is it not? Show me a lazy man and I shall show you a failure! Which all those across the river are, and don't try to tell me otherwise!"

"I will tell you that Miriam Lamb is far from lazy, and in fact one of the most industrious persons I have ever met. But to my second question: why not simply demand…say…a pound from them at the beginning? Why drag this out with the business of ten shillings a month?"

Chamberlin spent a moment pondering his answer, during which he finished off the last creamed beef-damp biscuit and the final stomach assassin of blood sausage. "I wished them," he finally said, "to know both fear and pressure. Two things that quite impressed me at an early age, I might add. They either break a man, or build him. Oh yes, they broke that weakling who called himself my father, but they built me!" He went so far as to thump his chest, which put a grease mark upon his white suit jacket. "I deduced that they might be afford the ten shillings, but no more than that and even so it would be a hardship. Then I wished them to fear the coming of the skeleton riders as they had never feared a moment in their lives! To see those creatures on their horses was enough to scare some of that rabble—pardon me, 'industrious success stories'—off at once, but I knew some would hang on because they're stupid. Therefore they had to be worn down. And you can bet that those who ran off first will spread it far and wide that skeletons on skeleton horses roam the woods around here, so I'll have no further competition for land. Even that ironworks might pack up and go if they can't get the workmen. Yes…fear and pressure…that's exactly what I wished to give them."

Katherine said, "Are you sure you're not reliving some moment in your own life that you dread to recall?"

"I am living a fine life, thank you very much! And with finer things to come, I can promise! Ah, here's our Lily with her most recent acquisition!"

The woman entered the room with a glow about her, and Katherine considered that for Lily compliments were likely few and far between. But upon her head this time was a hat that appeared to be an emulation of a bird's nest…in fact, it *was* a bird's nest, complete with a stuffed robin and two blue "eggs" that were likely polished porcelain. The thing must be heavy, for it seemed she was having trouble balancing her head upon her neck. When she managed to lower herself onto her chair without spilling either bird or eggs she looked to Katherine for an obvious further stroking.

"*Ha*," said Chamberlin in a humorless voice, and clapped with the clapper.

"May I ask," said Katherine as the servant appeared with a rolling cart and began to clear away the plates, "who makes these hats for you?"

"Oh, yes. Aurora Flinders of New York town. You might know her?"

"She has a reputation." Katherine answered. There was no need to say that Aurora Flinders had the reputation as a rather peculiar resident of Windmill Lane who supported herself by concocting so-called—and dubious—medicinal potions for every ailment under the sun but also indulged in making these swoon-worthy hats.

The servant loaded everything up and rolled the cart away. "So here we are," said Chamberlin, with a self-satisfied smile. "You might say the future well-being of these colonies depends on that riffraff packing up and moving on. When is Miriam Lamb leaving? I have the sense that when she goes the rest of them will follow."

"She's not leaving unless you pay her thirty pounds. Plus I would insist you add another ten pounds for the murder of her dog. I would also remind you that I can easily bring a real sheriff here to stop this bullying criminality once and for all."

"Really?" The smile became a smirk. "Bring your sheriff on, then! He'll find himself tarred and feathered and gone swimming in the river, because I would remind *you* that everyone in town is on my side of this."

"You speak of further violence rather flippantly. If this continues someone is bound to be hurt...possibly killed...and I can't allow that."

"THEN GET THEM OFF THAT LAND!" The shout came so quickly from the strained and reddened face that both women jumped in their chairs and for an instant it seemed that Lily's eyes cleared as if she'd been dashed with cold water. "IT'S THE ONLY WAY, DO YOU HEAR?" Sweat had risen on Chamberlin's face and scalp, his mouth contorted with anger and the eyes blazing. "A refined white woman in the employ of that *filth!* Dear God! How could you stoop so low as to spend a single minute speaking for her?"

Katherine considered that at the moment silence was the best reply. By the current statement of lawful procedures, a "squatter" had the right to claim land if he or she either built upon it, cleared it or farmed it, and Chamberlin could not move on his own claim until abandonment was proven. Thus the stalemate, with Katherine seeing no good options.

"I have more beautiful hats," said Lily in a dreamlike voice, but no one was listening.

Chamberlin wiped his sweating face with both hands. His smile jerked on and off, on and off. "Pardon me," he said thickly. "A thousand pardons. I do get carried away. Don't I, dear?" There was no answer from the dreamer.

Chamberlin breathed in and out a few times as if to calm his body as well as his nerves. "Let us be civil," he said. "Let us enjoy our dinner and put this problem to rest."

"For the moment," Katherine replied. Chamberlin simply nodded and finished off the bottle of wine.

Out came the servant carrying what appeared to be folded white sheets. These had attached cords, which the servant went about tying first around Katherine's neck, then the master of the house and finally Lily. Katherine realized they were huge napkins. She soon saw the need for them, for the servant went away and returning rolling the cart on which were three platters of the largest pieces of beef Katherine had ever seen, though the rinds of fat upon them were substantial and again the meat was bleeding onto the plates.

"Ah!" said Chamberlin. He was beaming. "Now here's some *real* food!"

Katherine noted that though all the steaks were large, the one given to Chamberlin was the largest, next was her own and a smaller piece for Lily. Katherine sat looking with some distaste at the bloody, fat-thickened thing as Chamberlin began to saw his knife across the meat before him.

"This is the future of colonial meals!" he said before he stuffed his mouth. And with his mouth stuffed: "Eat up, madam! It is history in the making!"

Katherine used her knife to cut away the fat before she took her first bite.

"My God, woman!" Chamberlin said. "That's the best part!" And so saying, he reached across with his blade, stabbed the slab of fat and drew it, dripping grease, onto his own platter.

The sound of Chamberlin's voracious eating turned Katherine's stomach, though she did try to eat as much as she could put down and not be sick. Lily picked at her food like a bird at seeds. And while this was going on Katherine recalled two things Chamberlin had said.

I have given my all for this project, you can bet on it.

And you can bet that those who ran off first will spread it far and wide…

An idea came to her. It was as insane, perhaps, as was this dinner and Lily's hats, but still…an idea.

She said, "You enjoy your gambling."

Chamberlin stopped chewing, at least for the moment. "What?"

"The Fine Fellows. Your club. The pistols you won. You enjoy gambling. Yes?"

"Yes, and I'm very good at it. What's your point?"

"I may have a solution to the problem," Katherine said. "I would have to speak to Miriam and the others. Some arrangements would have to be made that could take…oh…a week or more. But…perhaps a solution might come out of it, if you're willing."

"Willing to do what?"

"I will speak to the others first. Then…well, we shall see."

Chamberlin grunted. His face had bloomed ruddy again and his napkin was spotted with history in the making. "I believe you need more wine, madam," he said, and returned to the hunk of beef he was rapidly devouring. Katherine watched him start on the thick piece of fat she had rejected.

"Yes," she said, averting her gaze. "I *will* take another glass."

The clapper went into action again, and Katherine saw Lily wince at the sound as if she were being whipped.

SEVEN

THE NIGHT HAD ARRIVED, AFTER A SPAN OF NEARLY TWO WEEKS, AND all was in order.

Lanterns glowed yellow in the main barn—one of several—on Barton Chamberlin's estate. A table had been set up, with two chairs facing each other and the dealer's chair set to one side. In attendance were the young Thomas Brodine in his fine pale gray suit, the older lawyer David Lattimore Katherine had hired for the event, the dealer Jerome Merrick from the New York Lion's Club who all had agreed upon after much negotiation, Chamberlin himself, Lily, two representatives from the town, Katherine, and those whom Chamberlin had grudgingly said could attend. Because of their "odious presence" the game would have to be played in the barn: Miriam Lamb and the others who still held their ground on farms across the river. There were eight more people in that group, missing just one mother who it was decided best stay with her two young children on their farm, lest the little ones cause a distraction to the gamblers.

And quite a gamble it was going to be. Katherine's studied countenance was outwardly calm but the butterflies in her stomach were at war. Chamberlin in his bright crimson suit and red-checked waistcoat kept staring at her with a crooked smile meant to topple her confidence before the game had begun. Of course it was true that Miriam Lamb and the others were going to win no matter what—if having to be uprooted from their farms could be called winning—but Katherine wished to make a good showing, and she was far from an expert at this sort of thing.

Still, it was the only sensible plan. If she won, Chamberlin would pay each of those he despised as "rabble" thirty pounds to leave their holdings, and if he won Katherine would pay an equal amount. The sticking point in the negotiations had been the extra ten pounds from Chamberlin for the murder of Scruffs, and that had been a hard go but finally had been settled because according to the rather pompous Thomas Brodine, "my client does not expect to lose, having played and won at this game perhaps fifty times in as many visits to the Fine Fellows."

So be it.

Wooden benches had been supplied for the lawyers and for the town's representatives. The rest would have to sit upon bales of hay, and Lily—in her hat topped by what appeared to be a small tree branch with colored bits of leaf-shaped paper decorating the thing—had her own cushioned chair, as red as raw beef. The spectators would all be sitting facing the dealer several paces away, and thus the stage was set for the night's contest.

Katherine glanced at Miriam, who gave her a nod and the show of a clenched fist for support. Then Katherine took her seat, Chamberlin sat down opposite her, and the two lawyers spent a few moments both inspecting the contents of one of the three sealed decks of cards Merrick had brought. When they were done and Merrick was seated, the deck of cards was set before him. Brodine opened his cow-hide valise and brought out the document that had caused such argument between himself and Larrimore the last few days.

"I have here," said Brodine, "the final agreement to be signed by both parties. I can assure both that Mr. Larrimore and I consider it fair and equitable, as the situation demands." From the valise as well came two quills and an inkwell, which he set at the middle of the table. He drew the inkwell's stopper out, dipped one of the quills and offered it to Katherine. "Madam Herrald, will you sign?"

She did so without hesitation. Larrimore picked up the second quill, dipped it and held it toward her red-suited opponent. "Mr. Chamberlin, will you—"

"*No*," was the reply, his stare fixed upon Katherine.

"Sir," said Brodine, who immediately stepped to his client's side. "All is in order. We do need you to sign the—"

"Why should I sign *anything*? This is a laughable farce! I'm going to win and everyone knows it! So why should I waste the ink and the effort?"

"It's the principle of the thing, sir."

"Hang the principle! If I can't beat this woman at Jingo the Fine Fellows should put me in a tar barrel and roll me into the sea to catch the next tide back to London! And I want it made clear that I take no responsibility for killing anyone's dog!"

"Noted, sir, but…it's a legal thing, you see. Please."

Chamberlin cast a dagger-eyed glare at the young man. *"Legal thing!"* he spat. He withdrew from inside his jacket a red-and-white-striped handkerchief, which he used to mop a light sheen of sweat that had risen on his brow. "Damned warm in here already, isn't it?" he sneered across the table to Katherine. "I hope the smell of hay and horse manure doesn't offend you! Too *very* much, I mean."

"Sign the agreement," said Larrimore, "or we call this off. The next step, sir, is a visit to you from a reliable and official sheriff."

Chamberlin breathed in and out a few times and began to fold his handkerchief. "Keep your threats under your wig. I shall sign the agreement if I *lose*. Is that good enough for you?"

"No."

"Well, it'll have to be. All here are witnesses. If I lose, I sign. But I will not lose, and I expect Madam Herrald to stand sturdy to her part in this farce...though why she would wish to spend her money on *these*," and here he ran a dark gaze across Miriam and the group sitting on their haybales, "I have no inkling. Shall we proceed or shall we continue haggling over nonexistent issues?"

"Proceed," said Katherine, and Brodine removed the quills and inkwell.

From his cloth bag Jerome Merrick produced a small abacus specially made for two-player Jingo and set it atop the table beside his right hand. The abacus held red and blue beads on wires in two frames one atop the other, the topmost representing fives and the bottom ones.

"I shall outline the game for benefit of the assembly," Merrick announced, and continued: "There are five hands to a match, the winner reaching the value of twenty-one in each hand. The deck is shuffled and I draw the top card, the suit of which becomes the first castle card. The value on that card is awarded to both players. If the first castle card is a royal card or an ace the value is ten to both players. The purpose is to reach twenty-one in that suit.

"Four cards are dealt face-up to both players in the initial hand," he went on. "In the deal, royal cards and aces are worth one point...but for the Mad Queen, which is every queen in the deck. When her card is dealt to either player, she destroys the current castle card and calls for another castle card to be dealt. If the same suit is drawn as already the current castle card, the player who drew the Mad Queen earns the points on the card and play continues. If a different suit is drawn, the cards are discarded and both players start with points from the new castle card.

"An ace dealt to either player may be one point or may be the Jingo card, but the decision must be made before the next card falls," Merrick said. "By this, the player having the ace may call out 'Jingo' and change the castle card again...but if the same suit is drawn, the *opponent* is awarded the value on the card and play continues in that suit. I would explain to the assembly that use of the Jingo card is helpful if one player feels the other might be getting too far ahead in points, yet there is a danger in using the Jingo card as well. Any questions?" This was asked of Katherine and Chamberlin.

"I could play and *win* this game in my sleep!" Chamberlin growled.

"Very well. Madam, which color beads will you be represented by?"

"I'll let my opponent have first choice," Katherine said.

"Sir, what color beads will—"

"Are you a simpleton?" Chamberlin asked.

Merrick cleared his throat and nodded. "Red for Mr. Chamberlin, blue for Madam Herrald." He began to shuffle the deck with obvious smooth expertise.

Katherine knew this game was highly valued by gamblers both in the colonies and in England because it presented so many vagaries on which to wager: who would be the eventual winner, how many hands would it take for the triumph, which would be the final suit, how many times in a single playing would the Mad Queen appear, who would call the first Jingo, and on and on. She also knew that some hands might last through several shuffles of the deck, but some could end in a flash; she appreciated the game and knew enough about it to teach Miriam as a way to pass the time, but in terms of actually playing Jingo against an experienced player...no. Therefore she sat with an outwardly stone-faced countenance and yet the inner butterflies still fluttered and flit.

"The first castle card," Merrick announced, and put forth the eight of clubs upon the table. He adjusted the abacus in the favor of both players, and then he began the deal.

A four of hearts, ace of spades, two of clubs and six of spades to Katherine; to Chamberlin the jack of diamonds, the five of spades, the seven of clubs and the six of hearts.

Katherine's eleven to Chamberlin's sixteen.

In the next hand, to Katherine the two of clubs and then the Mad Queen, which changed the castle suit to the next card Merrick dealt: diamonds. Merrick shifted the beads on the abacus back to their starting positions and a new hand of four cards was dealt.

And thus the game progressed, with another Mad Queen showing up in the following deal to change the castle card back again to clubs. Chamberlin grumbled because he'd held sixteen in diamonds to Katherine's three.

At the end of six deals, with Chamberlin calling out "Jingo" with his ace to prevent Katherine's fifteen in spades to overcome his measly four and the castle card becoming a heart, Chamberlin triumphed with twenty-four in hearts to Katherine's six.

"One down," said Chamberlin as Merrick shuffled the deck again. He grinned and mopped his brow with the handkerchief. "Can't you feel the money flying away from you already?"

She said nothing, but in actuality she did feel it. Her wealth was not substantial, though she could afford the loss of one hundred and twenty pounds…but just barely. She might have to sell Alexander to make ends meet.

Miriam had asked the question: *Why are you riskin' your own money on this?*

And Katherine's answer: *Because you hired me to do a task. The only way it can be done is this way. The truth is, you and the others will have to move and there's no alternative. I want to help you, and it's unfair to the others involved that I not help them as well. So let us hope for the best and wish that it's Barton Chamberlin who pays for your relocation and not me.*

But that was not entirely the truth.

The truth: After this much time spent with Miriam, Katherine thought that working on the farm—doing the repetition of chores that had to be done day-by-day—had given her an appreciation for the rural life that she had not possessed before. It was, in a way, an enlightening experience, and one that was so different from the life she knew that to see it destroyed in even a small way was disheartening. Had she come to think of Miriam's farm and apple orchard as part of her own holdings? Yes…a holding of the spirit, perhaps. And Chamberlin's all-or-nothing attitude rankled her. She would like—love—to see him humbled. Was progress always to be on the backs of those whom the rich man considered worthless? So…yes, it was the only way and she was risking her own money in perhaps a foolish wistfulness that she might carry this feeling of enlightenment—and actually *feeling* lighter, away from the pressures and chaos of the big town—with her for the rest of her days. She had to know that she had done all she could, and therefore the risk.

In the next playing, Katherine and Chamberlin battled back and forth with calls of 'Jingo,' particularly galling when Katherine had been ahead in the suit of diamonds by nineteen to five…but in the end the score: in the suit of spades, Chamberlin twenty-one and Katherine twelve.

"Two down," said the man across the table, with a ferocious grin that made her want to strike him across the ruddy, sweat-gleaming cheeks.

"The third hand," Merrick announced, and started to lay down the next castle card.

"If I can speak?"

Merrick paused in his upturn. Miriam had risen from her bale of hay and approached the table. "Katherine," she said, "may I have a word with you?" She motioned for Katherine to follow her to a more private location in the barn.

"What is this?" Chamberlin's voice boomed. "I protest this interruption!"

"There's nothing to stop a conference," Larrimore said, also on his feet. "Particularly as it involves one of the significant—"

"Oh, shut it!" was Chamberlin's response. "Go ahead then, and the devil take you! Lily! Go to the house and get me a glass of water!"

Lily jumped up and rushed out as if she had a forest fire on her head.

Out of hearing of the others, Miriam looked earnestly into Katherine's eyes and said, "I know the risk is on your money, but…maybe I might take a lick at this?"

"I'm in it, I should finish it."

"I hear that, but it seems to me that we've been playin' this game so much I've got the hang of it, and it further seems to me that there's a mite bit of luck in it. More than a mite bit. And like I told you…I'm mite lucky myself."

"He's an experienced gambler."

"So he is, but here's the real of it. I hate for it to be on your head, if this next hand is the last. Yes, it's your money and that's the real of it too, but… won't you let me have a try?"

Miriam's request was so heartfelt that Katherine was almost persuaded. Almost. She shook her head and started back for the table, but Miriam caught her elbow.

"You got to admit," the woman said with a half-smile, "I cain't do no worse than you, now can I?"

Katherine hesitated. Luck certainly dominated the game of Jingo. And there had to be a certain element of daring—and intuition, perhaps—to make the Jingo call itself. At the moment, with two losses behind her, Katherine felt she had not the confidence for either daring or intuition. In fact, she felt played out.

That, she had to admit.

"Speak to the others," she said. "If they agree, you can take my place."

Katherine took her time returning to the table while Miriam gave the other farmers her proposal. Chamberlin was mopping his face and waiting for his water. "Madam Herrald, you're delaying the inevitable! I am in my element and you are lost in the woods! Come on, let's finish this!"

Lily arrived, surprisingly still wearing the same hat. Chamberlin took the glass and downed the water to the bottom. "All right," he said, and gave his enormous gut a pat, "the third hand shall send you sobbing!"

"I am takin' Mizz…I mean to say I am takin' Katherine's place," came the voice from alongside.

Chamberlin looked at Miriam Lamb and his several chins dropped.

Miriam walked past Katherine and took the chair, then she levelled her gaze at her opponent and calmly said, "I am ready."

The silence stretched so hard one might have heard a squeak in it.

"A fine joke!" Chamberlin exploded. "You've had your laugh, now take your seat madam and let's get on with it!"

"Miriam is playing in my place," Katherine said, which caused another uneasy length of silence.

"Brodine!" Chamberlin shouted, as the beef-fed blood throbbed in his face. "Tell these people I will not proceed with this until Madam Herrald takes her seat! Tell them I will not sit across the table and be assailed by the smell of a savage!"

Larrimore was up again and striding forward. "There's nothing in the agreement—which you have failed to honor—that prohibits Madam Herrald from appointing a player in her place!"

"I protest this indignity as much as does my client!" was Brodine's answering squall. "He will not honor a *slave* at his gaming table!"

"Damn right I won't! This is done!" Chamberlin started to heave himself up from his chair.

"Thrash it out all you please," said Miriam, her voice soft yet still cutting through the tumult. "I suspect Mr. Chamberlin here is scairt to play me."

Chamberlin stopped in mid-heave. He looked at her as one might regard a barnyard animal, his eyelids at half-mast and his head tilted back on his neck as if fearful of catching black. "*What* did you say?"

"I fancy you heard me."

"I must be going mad or the world is! Me playing Jingo with an African savage? Preposterous!"

"I don't know what that means," Miriam said, her expression placid and the lamplight glinting yellow in her eyes, "but I'm guessin' it's just another word for scairt."

"She's baiting you, sir!" said Brodine.

"If I was fishin'," Miriam answered, "I don't think a line ever made would be strong enough to land the crappie I'm lookin' at."

"*By God, what impudence!*" Chamberlin roared, but Katherine noted that he plunged himself back into his chair with such force it was a wonder the thing was not either shattered into sticks or driven three feet into the dirt. "All right, all right!" he said between gritted teeth. "If you wish to be trounced in the same fashion as I have trounced your slave-loving friend, then I am at your service—and God forbid anyone outside this barn ever repeats I said such a thing! Merrick, reshuffle the cards and lay down the castle! Let us hurry and get this vermin out of here!"

Ah! Katherine thought as she sat on the bale of hay Miriam had vacated. Chamberlin's haste might well cloud his judgment. So perhaps already luck was in favor of the lamb versus the bull?

The first castle card was a club, the value to each player four. To Miriam was dealt the four of hearts, the six of diamonds, the eight of spades and the six of clubs. Chamberlin received the king of diamonds, the eight of clubs, the nine of hearts and the ace of spades. The abacus counted Miriam as ten and Chamberlin as fourteen.

In the following deal the Mad Queen appeared, and the new castle card was the seven of hearts.

And so the game progressed through four more deals. When Miriam was ahead seventeen to six in diamonds, Chamberlin called Jingo with his ace. The next castle card was the eight of diamonds, giving Miriam the win with twenty-five.

She said nothing and showed no emotion, while Chamberlin leaned forward to examine the winning card as if that might change the result.

"Pah!" was Chamberlin's following remark. And to Merrick: "Next hand!"

Merrick reshuffled the cards and presented the next castle card, the ace of hearts. Ten points to each player.

"Jingo!" said Miriam several deals later, when Chamberlin was ahead fifteen to five in spades. The following castle card was the king of hearts, and directly next dealt to Miriam was the Mad Queen, which changed the castle card to the six of diamonds.

And "Jingo!" once again from Miriam, when Chamberlin had eighteen to her eight in diamonds. Thus the game went on, back and forth, the Mad Queen appearing and changing the suit, the beads on the abacus rising and falling, and Chamberlin hollering "Jingo!" at one point so loudly it seemed the barn's timbers trembled. Twenty minutes passed, with neither able to gain substantial advantage. Then at Miriam's twelve to Chamberlin's sixteen in clubs she was dealt the Mad Queen. Merrick turned over a new castle card: the ten of clubs.

Miriam's twenty-two to Chamberlin's sixteen, and Katherine saw Miriam exhale her breath as Chamberlin slammed a fist down upon the table.

"Easy, sir," cautioned Brodine from his bench. "It does not help to—"

"Shut your mouth!" Chamberlin had nearly screamed it. "When I want your advice I shall ask for it!" His face had bloomed red again, and once more he used his handkerchief to blot away the sweat. "Damned hot in here!" he said to no one in particular. He glowered across the table at Miriam, who sat straight upright with a blank expression. "You're cheating at this!" he said. "No one beats me at Jingo!"

"Sir!" said Larrimore. "Mind your tongue!"

"You go to Hell, you fop!" raged the ragged reply from a ragged throat. "Wait," he told Merrick as the deck was shuffled again. "Wait, I must compose myself."

"Are you delaying the inevitable?" Katherine asked from her hay bale. In truth, she was as amazed at Miriam's turn of luck as anyone could be.

"And *you!*" he sneered. "Come here to stick your fancy nose in my business! Come here to prevent the further growth of this town and these colonies! Mark this dangerous woman well, my friends," he said, addressing the representatives from Chamberlin's Crossing. "Somehow she has taught this black slave how to *cheat!*"

"There's no cheatin'," said Miriam, her voice calm but firm. "And I am nobody's slave."

"You," Chamberlin replied, leaning slightly forward with a shard of light glinting off his teeth, "will always be a slave. You just *think* you're free. And right now the Devil must be burning the bastard who set you loose."

Before she had realized it, Katherine was on her feet. Her own face was flaming. Three paces and she was within striking distance. And strike she did, with an open hand across Chamberlin's grinning face.

"Assault!" Brodine screeched, shooting up from the bench. "Pure and simple assault! You shall pay in court for this, madam!"

"I'll show you an assault, you damned ass!" shouted Larrimore as he stood, and he raised his hand to give Brodine what he'd vowed.

"STOP!"

Larrimore's hand froze.

Katherine stepped back from Chamberlin.

Chamberlin's grin hitched and faded.

"Please stop," said Lily, her eyes huge. "I just...I can't stand fighting. No more fighting. Please."

In the silence that followed, Miriam said, "We got one more hand to play."

"Yes, we do!" Chamberlin fired back. He turned his face toward the other farmers in the assembly. "Does no one understand me but my lawyer and the citizens of my town? I'm not a *bad* man! I'm doing what I must for the *future!* The beef I raise and send to market will be a benefit to everyone, rich and poor alike! And the violence that was done...it was not my doing! It was done by an individual who lost all control and sense! Don't you understand that?"

"One more hand," said Miriam.

Katherine returned to her hay bale, her palm still stinging. Larrimore and Brodine sat down in what was obviously an uneasy truce, and Lily sat with her hands clenched tightly together.

"Deal," Chamberlin told Merrick.

The first castle card of the fifth hand was the three of hearts. It was followed by the nine of clubs, the king of clubs, the six of hearts and the four of diamonds to Miriam; then, to Chamberlin, the ten of hearts, the two of hearts, the jack of clubs and the ace of diamonds.

Miriam's ten to Chamberlin's seventeen.

In the next deal: the ace of spades, the six of clubs, the nine of clubs and the five of hearts to Miriam...to Chamberlin the ten of diamonds, the seven of clubs and...the Mad Queen.

"Turn it over," Chamberlin said to Merrick, his voice tight.

The following castle card...the eight of hearts.

Katherine gave a small gasp.

Miriam's sixteen to Chamberlin's twenty-five.

Her luck had deserted her.

"I win." Chamberlin's voice was small. Then, louder: "I *win!*" He looked to Brodine. *"I win!"* he said, louder still, and he pulled himself up from his chair and slammed his fist down upon the table. "I am the *winner!*" he shouted. "By God, I have smashed you! Dare to take me on?" He swung his red-flushed and glistening face toward Katherine, his eyes bulging. His shout beat at the rafters. "There you are, madam! Are you satisfied now? I told you, didn't I? Yes, I did! And now your money will be flying out of your—"

His shout stopped. He made a strangling sound. He clutched at the center of his chest with both hands and Katherine saw his face go gray. He took one halting step not toward his wife but toward his lawyer, and as Brodine jumped up to help a client in true distress Barton Chamberlin gave a rattling sound from deep in his throat and fell like a toppled tree, his eyes still wide in the tomb-gray face and his mouth twisted in a rictus.

At once both Brodine and Larrimore were bending over him and Katherine came forward. She saw Chamberlin's body go into several convulsions that made the head snap back and forth. With a last shiver as if in winter's grip the man was still. The others were on their feet as well, with Miriam coming up alongside Katherine and Merrick on the opposite side.

"Roll him over!" Brodine cried out to Larrimore, and together they got the bulk turned. The eyes still stared and the mouth yet grimaced. Brodine shook the body as best he could. "Mr. Chamberlin!" he shouted. "Mr. Chamberlin...wake up!" Then, to anyone: "A doctor! We need a doctor!"

Larrimore had his hand to Chamberlin's chest. He put his other hand to the throat, searching for life.

"A doctor! Hurry, someone!" Brodine urged, and one of the town's representatives ran out to get his horse.

Larrimore brought his hands away and leaned back, sitting down in the dirt. He said, "There is no need for a doctor."

"What? What?" Brodine's face had taken on its own shade of gray.

"Mr. Chamberlin," said Larrimore, "is dead."

"No! He can't be! Mr. Chamberlin...*please*...wake up!" Brodine continued shaking the body until it seemed all the strength had left his arms and his resolve to awaken the deceased had also gone.

"Dead," said Larrimore. "Dead as a post."

There came a scream that nearly made Katherine jump out of her boots.

Lily was standing and had her hands to her face. Her body shuddered. The scream shrilled up again and changed in mid-shrill, and as Lily dropped her hands away from her face it could be seen that she wore a maniacal grin, and the scream redefined itself into a laugh that would have scared the skeleton crew into fleeing from the night. As the assembly watched in a kind of shocked fascination, the girl spun herself around and around as she laughed, and she flung her hat up into the air with such velocity the multicolored paper leaves flew off and whirled down like the onset of early autumn.

"Dear Jesus!" Brodine breathed. "She's gone mad!"

"Someone take her to the house!" Larrimore commanded. The other representative of the town took her arm and led her out of the barn, but she was still laughing all the way.

"My God, what a night!" Brodine was on his feet, staring down at the body. "He just...went so *fast!*"

Not so fast, Katherine thought. A lifetime of voracious appetites had finally caught up with the future Baron of Beef. Did she feel sympathy for the man? Perhaps as for any human she witnessed die before her eyes, and it was true that maybe beef *was* the future of the colonies, but Chamberlin's stubbornness, callous disregard for those he felt beneath him and the vile way of reaching his desires...not so much. His moment of triumph had burst something inside him, and that was the fact of it.

"I cain't believe this," said Miriam in a stunned voice at Katherine's side. "I mean...I wanted to win, but...I didn't wish him *dead!*"

"No one did. I can tell you that in a way Chamberlin killed himself, over time." And she thought a lot of blood sausages and hunks of fat went into that death, as well.

"I must...I must *think,*" said Brodine. He aimed his gaze at Larrimore. "You realize Mr. Chamberlin won this contest, yes?"

"I understand he didn't sign the agreement, therefore it is null and void."

"It is not! He won! The stipulation of his winning is that Madam Herrald pay for the squatters to immediately leave! We'll take this to court if you disagree!"

"Is that so?" Larrimore's eyebrows lifted. "Well, tell me, Thomas...who exactly is your client?"

Brodine gave a sputtering sound and seemed to be looking to the body for aid. None was offered.

"You might discuss the situation with the wife," Larrimore suggested. "If Chamberlin left a will designating her as the property owner at his demise. Did he?"

There was no answer from Brodine, but it was answer enough.

"Ladies," said Larrimore to Katherine and Miriam, "the contest being over, I think you two should depart. Thank you for coming," he told the others. "Merrick, thank you for your sterling service."

"What's gonna happen now, sir?" one of the farmers asked. "We have to pack up and leave our land?"

"Do they, Thomas?" Larrimore asked.

"I don't...I think...well...I suppose in time the estate will be put up for sale. As for the herd...the same." He again stared down at the dead man, who stared back up into nothingness. "I *told* you to make out a will, didn't I?"

"Let's go." Katherine took Miriam's arm. Her last glance back showed her Brodine laying a horse blanket over Barton Chamberlin's face.

They walked out of the barn toward Miriam's wagon. A light summer's rain had begun to fall, and the woman who had been a slave for most of her life stopped to lift her face to the sky.

"Good for my apples," she said, and then she frowned toward the damp earth. "I just...it was an awful thing, wasn't it?"

"It's done."

"Yes, but...*awful*, goin' like that...like a candle just quick snuffed. Mr. Chamberlin...you have to say he built a nice bridge, didn't he?"

"It should last for many years, and I wouldn't doubt that it might become part of a new coach route, so Chamberlin's Crossing might not have needed the beef herd to grow. Just the bridge. We'll see."

"You think Mr. Hutcheson will buy from me again, after this?"

"I think fresh apples, apple cider and applejack hold more value than a dead man's promises. And by the way, I want to take some of your applejack to the taverns in New York. I believe they'd be very interested in purchasing what you make."

Miriam nodded, but Katherine could tell she was still troubled. "My luck," she said. "You don't think...it killed Mr. Chamberlin, do you?"

"No. What happened to Mr. Chamberlin was coming sooner or later. I can tell you that he was not a healthy person in his dining habits."

"He should've et an apple every once in a while," said Miriam.

"Yes," Katherine said, and she put an arm around her friend as they walked to the wagon.

Upon returning to New York, Katherine sometimes had dreams of being on the farm with Miriam...of chopping wood, of feeding the chickens, of picking the apples by the basket in the orchard, and doing all the chores that had taken her from the life she knew and put her for a time closer to nature. In her dreams she remembered the stillness of the forest and the songs of the birds, the warmth of the summer sun, the sweetness of the air...the very sensation of being alive.

She would have those dreams for the rest of her life.

And one other thing: she wondered if she might at some point stop by the house of Aurora Flinders, and find out if while Barton Chamberlin was gambling at the Fine Fellows his wife Lily had come in not only to buy her three hundred and fourteenth hat but also some potion that... say...might aid in ridding vermin from a cattle farm? That added to a glass of water might be...

...a cleverly executed murder in front of more than a dozen unknowing witnesses?

Well...she would not visit that house, and she would never know.

She didn't care to know.

With autumn just around the corner, it was time for some baked apples and a nice cup of crisp, smooth applejack.

THE PALE
PIPESMOKER

NOVEMBER, 1703

ONE

At six by the candle-clock on the white stone mantel above a politely warming fireplace, Katherine Herrald quietly said to Minx Cutter, "There is our gentleman."

The pale pipesmoker had just entered Sally Almond's tavern from Nassau Street. With him, like spectral companions, entered equally pallid tendrils of the mid-November fog that currently embraced the streets, lanes, cubbyholes, cul-de-sacs and structures of New York town. His arrival caused a momentary hesitation in the tune of "The Wandering Prince of Troy" that Sally was strumming on her guitar as she strolled amid the tables of diners at their sup, but perhaps only the two women who represented the Herrald Agency noted such for they understood the reason for fingers suddenly gone cold.

But Sally picked up the tune once more, gave a glance and a slight nod toward the table where Katherine and Minx sat entertaining their glasses of claret, and then she moved away into the tavern's second room to leave the ladies to their business and musically pursue the wayward prince.

"Hm," was Minx's comment as she took a sip of her wine. Her voice was light and easy, as if she cared not a whit for the man who'd just come in from the street, but over the rim of her glass her obsidian gaze directed at the individual was as sharp as the blades that always kept her company.

Katherine noted that a few of the regulars took a quick look at the man and seemed to shudder and shrivel before they returned to their repasts. Minx's next comment—also quietly delivered—summed it up: "Less of a gentleman, more of a walking tomb."

"Agreed," said Katherine.

They watched as he hung up his long black fearnaught coat and black tricorn on wall hooks beside the door. They noted the ebony gloves, and his other accoutrements equally dark except for a waistcoat the color of gray harbor water. Also noted was the fact that in depositing his coat and hat upon the hooks, his right hand seemed afflicted in some way, in that all the fingers did not open and close as they should. He had close-cropped gray hair that held hints of the more fulgent brown of his youth, yet it was difficult to judge his age even though firelight and lamplight glowed in the room, for his face was a haggard though craggy cliff of jagged lines across his forehead and along his sallow cheeks, as if the cracks of age and a hard life foretold a coming avalanche of flesh from the skull's bones beneath.

He gave the room a quick going-over with a pair of small and deep-set dark eyes that caught for a fraction of time red embers of light, and then he walked to a candlelit table in a corner opposite Katherine and Minx and settled himself. They noted how he angled his chair to face the door. He removed the glove from his left hand, but not from the right. He drew from a pocket of his jacket first a curved pipe and then a paper-wrapped square of tobacco. He packed the pipe while staring fixedly at the door. As he was doing this Emmaline Halett came to the table—rather nervously, the problem-solving ladies observed—to ask what he might be having for supper. He said something they couldn't hear, Emmaline scurried away to the kitchen, he flamed his pipe from the table's candle and then he sat staring at the door with the pipe clenched in the hard line of his mouth and the blue smoke wafting around the pallid cracked cameo of his face.

"Let us give him a few minutes more," Katherine suggested. She turned the wineglass between her palms. "And I will say that if you stared any more fiercely at him he could light that pipe with the friction of air."

Beneath the cocked purple riding cap that perched atop the copious blonde curls of her hair, Minx Cutter's expression had become as fearsome a thing as Hudson Greathouse's when he was about to throw himself into a fight. But Katherine mused that Minx and Hudson—who was at the moment gone to England with Berry Grigsby to find their own wandering prince by the name of Matthew Corbett—were cut from the same cloth, that is to say the same battle flags flying from their personal castles, and quick to let it be known that monsters guarded the moats and the parapets were always secured against enemies. Which in Minx's case, as Katherine had observed, seemed to be everyone else in the world...except, in a modest way, for her own self, which she took to be a compliment.

Minx averted her attention from the pale pipesmoker and seemed to be studying the burning logs in the hearth, yet Katherine knew that Minx was still actively studying their central point of being there this misty evening, and that was exactly why Katherine had decided to give Minx the opportunity to work with the agency; when the younger woman set her teeth in for a bite, she wouldn't let go until her last tooth had been broken out, and when that might occur—doubtful, if ever—Minx had her set of little sharp metal teeth that she was so expert at using, and with any one of those knives she could carve her initials on an angel's harp or a devil's hind.

It was no wonder to Katherine that Professor Fell had found Minx so useful in his criminal empire. Katherine's only question about Minx was philosophical: would the life of a problem-solver—and obeyer of the law— sooner or later make Minx raise up that battle flag in protest of everything Katherine found holy, and in so doing return to a life of hellfire endeavors?

Well...it was a question.

Katherine took her last swallow of claret. She put the glass aside and said, "Time."

They got up from the table and approached the pale pipesmoker. He didn't notice their approach until they were nearly upon him, so concentrated was his attention upon the door through his drapes of fumous consumption. Then his face turned on them as if the wind had snapped it there, his eyes lit up with red centers and he lowered the pipe from his mouth with his ungloved hand.

"Pardon us," said Madam Herrald with a charming smile. And her smile could certainly still cast a charm, even at the age of fifty-three and perhaps even more so than at thirty-three. "May we sit with you a moment?"

"No," came the voice, like a barrel of gravel being upended.

"Thanks," Minx said, already down in a chair across from him.

Katherine sat to the man's right. "Just one moment, that's all we require."

"What's this about? Who are you?" There was a stricken note now in the voice.

"We're asking the questions," said Minx.

"Tut," Katherine said, keeping the smile. She resisted the urge to give Minx's hand a pat to quiet her, as that seemed to her the equivalent of putting one's own hand into the iron fangs of a beast trap. "We have a small business to discuss with you, sir."

"I have no business with *you*, madam. Now if you would kindly remove your—"

He stopped speaking, because Minx had drawn a small curved blade from her own dark purple jacket and was admiring it as one might look upon the greatest lover.

"One moment," Katherine repeated, rather more forcefully but still with the smile at full charm.

That morning, at the Herrald Agency's office at Number Seven Stone Street, the gray-haired but lively and highly industrious Sally Almond had arrived to take a chair before Katherine's desk and say, "My problem is with a man."

"The universal problem of women," replied Katherine, with a wan smile and a quick glance at Minx, who had paused in her scribing of the recent case known to her as the Moon Maiden Murder. At the nearby desk, Minx held her quill steady over the paper to continue the previous line, yet her ears and focus of attention were held steadier still in regard to the problem being set forth by the owner of New York town's best eating establishment, that which bore the name of the famous lady herself.

"Do go on," said Katherine, bringing her cool gray-eyed gaze back upon this morning's visitor.

"I wish," said Sally, "that I might find a shred of humor in this situation, but as it is beginning to affect my business, I fail to do so. I have a repeat customer who is...shall we say...rather peculiar, and his presence—a thundercloud from whom lightning and storm is sure to strike before long, I'm certain—is making my other customers...well...*nervous*. I have had several tell me so. Some of them—all regulars—have not returned. And my serving girls...they dread to see him walk through the door. Yet walk through the door he does...exactly at six o'clock, and remains at table until the last call at nine. And he has followed this exact habit for the last ten nights, excepting the Sabbath of course."

"You know this man?" Katherine asked.

"I have never seen him before ten nights ago." Sally looked quickly toward Minx, who had moved her chair closer with a small scraping noise, and then back to the madam. "He orders fish, or chicken, with peas and potatoes. He orders coffee and a platter of biscuits. He smokes his pipe, one bowlful after another, and orders more coffee. He pays at the presentment of the bill and leaves a bit for the girls, that's no problem. But I notice that he always sits facing the door, as if he's expecting someone."

"He's always alone, then?" Minx asked, as her curiosity had been fired up for this present situation and after all the Moon Maiden affair was part of the quickly receding past.

"Always alone. And if you saw him, you'd know why. He has the demeanor of a gravedigger. That's what Emmaline said about him, the first night. Sophie says he looks more like a hangman. Anyway, to me he looks like death on a high post."

There came a heavy-sounding *thump* from across the room, loud enough to make Sally jump in her chair. "Heavens!" she said, wide-eyed. "What was *that?*"

"One of the ghosts," Katherine answered calmly. "They both dislike the 'd-word.' But never mind those two...go ahead, this interests me."

"*Us*," Minx corrected, and Katherine nodded and let it go. Minx might be valuable, if push came to kick.

It took a moment for Sally to continue. She cast a frown toward the offending spirit in its little corner of the world, cleared her throat and went on. "Well...the man...the pale pipesmoker, I call him...because he smokes all the time, and he looks as if he's never seen the sun...anyway...I fear for my business, if he continues his pattern. But, as I say, he pays promptly and I have no real reason to ask him not to attend my tavern. Yet his effect on my other customers and my girls is quite *real*, in itself."

"But even so," said Katherine, "this man is a good customer, never fails to pay for his food and drink and I would venture to say he keeps to himself in silent contemplation. He offers no trouble and recognizes the worth of your serving girls with a ready coin. Therefore his only sin seems to be the fact that he is of a phlegmatic nature. I can think of many of those in this town, yet I assume they are never refused service in your establishment."

"True enough," came the reply. "But this man...he's different. He carries something inside him. Something...I don't know what." Then she decided she did know. "Something terrible," she concluded.

"Which you believe your other customers can feel and thus is harming your business," said Minx.

"Yes. *I* certainly can. And there's the matter of his right hand."

"Oh?" Katherine's brows went up. "What's the matter with it?"

"He never removes from his right hand the black glove that hides it. I have watched him pack his pipe and eat his supper, and I can tell you that there is some affliction to the hand that demands it remain hidden."

"He's unable to use it?"

"Unable to *fully* use it," Sally corrected. "Three fingers of that hand will not bend."

Katherine spent a moment in contemplation, her own fingertips steepled together. "So," she said at last, "this pale pipesmoker, as you call him, is offensive because of his gravedigger's demeanor and the fact that he has a crippled right hand? I hardly think that calls for denying him the pleasure of meals at your tavern, no matter what your other customers think."

"I understand that position, and I have grappled with it myself. Still... from him I get a terrible sense of...well...terrible things to come. I can't put that aside, and neither can my girls nor my other regulars. I'm sorry, and I know I sound callow, but he casts a pall upon my establishment."

"All right, but what would you have us do?"

"Pay him," Sally replied without hesitation. "I will offer him ten pounds to take his business elsewhere." When neither Katherine nor Minx responded, Sally plowed ahead. "I find it disagreeable that I should myself approach him with this offer, therefore I will hire you to do the job. Ten pounds on the table for him, if he does not return to my tavern."

"And if he takes the money and does return, what then?"

"I will ask that he sign a legal document, as much as can be assembled over this. I've already contacted David Larrimore, my attorney."

"I see," said Katherine. "And you would have us witness him take the money and sign the document? When?"

"Approach him this night, if possible. Squire Larrimore assures me the document can be readied and brought here by late afternoon."

"It's a lot of money and a lot of trouble to boot someone out the door," Minx said.

"I regret having to do it, but when you see him you'll understand."

"Very well, then," Katherine said, with a slight bow of her head. "We'll do as you require. But what interests me more than booting him out the door is...who he is waiting for so patiently—not to say *urgently*—to come *through* the door?"

Thus it was that the two women sat at the gentleman's table without being invited, and as the fire crackled, the chords of Sally Almond's guitar chimed merrily from the other room, the other customers at their meals went on eating and drinking and fog pressed against the window glass, Katherine said, "I am—"

"I know you," the man interrupted. "From somewhere." His eyes narrowed. "Oh...*yes*. From London...but...it was ten years ago, at least." He nodded, as if deciding his memory was correct. "Yes. Katherine Herrald, isn't it? Richard's widow?"

Katherine felt a sudden chill skitter up her spine. How on earth did this man know her? And she was equally startled by the mention of her beloved and long-missed Richard—the creator of the problem-solving agency—who had been brutally murdered by Professor Fell in 1694.

"Yes," she replied, but her voice sounded to her slow and sluggish. "I am Richard's widow."

"Ah." Candleflame went to pipe's bowl and smoke ensued. "I do have a good memory. My wife never fretted that I would forget a birthday or anniversary. I recall meeting you and Richard at the celebratory supper Judge—" He stopped speaking and his face sharpened as the door opened. His entire body seemed to shiver with anticipation. Tendrils of fog came in first, followed by young Effrem Owles, the Master Tailor of New York, and his bride Opal, both of them bundled up and cheer-faced against the cold. The pale pipesmoker watched as the happy couple were greeted by Emmaline Halett and escorted to find a table in the other room, and then the keen—one might say *frantic*, Katherine thought—expression fell from the cracked mirror of his face. After a long pull at his pipe he continued what he'd been saying.

"The celebratory supper Judge Archer gave at the White Knight Tavern for the newly sworn constables," the man said. "Ten years ago, was it?

Twelve, possibly. I had the briefest meeting with you and Richard, a hand-shake with him and a bow for you. But afterward my wife—Laura—re-marked favorably upon your appearance, dress and bearing. Perhaps that's why I recall so clearly the occasion."

"I recall the event," Katherine said. "Richard and I were there not by the invitation of Judge Archer, who had a dim view of our business, but by invitation of the chief constable at that time."

"Jacob Mack. Yes, a very fine man. I worked with him before his retirement."

Katherine had a moment of feeling that the world was spinning away from her. She gave a look to Minx that she realized must resemble the expression of a child seeking help from an elder.

"What's your name?" Minx asked, picking up the chase in her own straight-forward runaway-coach fashion. "And what are you doing in New York?"

"I am John Kent. I arrived from London ten days ago. Here on…*invitation*, you might say, though—" He paused for a pipe puff and a curl of smoke from his mouth that looked like a blue lizard slowly emerging from a cavern crack. "Though not the same happy degree as of the White Knight event. But a momentous occasion and a great opportunity, all the same."

Katherine found her voice. "You're a constable in London?"

"Was. I encountered some difficulties that ended what I had hoped was an upward progress."

Referring to his afflicted hand? Katherine wondered. "Pardon these questions, Mr. Kent, but understand I am still in the profession of finding answers. You are in New York by whose invitation?"

Kent didn't respond for a moment. He continued to smoke his pipe, his pale gravedigger's visage aimed past the two women at the door upon Nassau Street.

At last he slowly removed the pipe from his mouth and his small, glittering and pain-filled dark eyes stared with fearsome intensity into Katherine's face.

"If you must know," he said quietly, "I am here on the invitation of one of the worst and most insidious murderers ever to prowl the streets of London."

TWO

"Your supper, sir."

Emmaline had come to the table just as Kent finished this last coldly delivered statement. From her serving tray she put his platter of broiled chicken, peas, fried potatoes and pickled beets before him, as well as a cloth napkin and silverware. "Your coffee and biscuits are on the way," she added, and both of the other women noted that Emmaline refrained from laying eyes upon him. Then, to Katherine and Minx she said, "May I get you ladies anything?"

"Bring them claret." Kent put his pipe aside and took hold of both knife and fork with his left hand. "That's what they were drinking at their table. Does that suit the both of you?"

"It suits, thank you," said Katherine, but Minx asked for a short shot of the strong apple ale that had become so popular among the younger and more adventurous members of the community.

Kent moved the fingers of his left hand so as to hold both knife and fork at angles readied to cut and eat. It was a quick and seemingly effortless maneuver, but both Katherine and Minx thought it had taken a long time and much dropped food before Kent could so smoothly fix the utensils. They watched as he began to eat, using just the one hand, though it was obvious that the greater part of his attention was still directed at the door.

He was able also to pluck up the napkin and dab at his mouth without losing his grip on knife and fork, and it was after one of these dabs that he said, "The Herrald Agency. I had no idea you were here in the colonies. As I recall, you and Richard operated on fees from clients. I have no doubt you are operating now under commission from the owner of this establishment. I am well aware of the figure I present, and of the unease I cause by being in the presence of happy, stupid people. I regret that but I cannot change it." He speared a bit of chicken and paused with it at his mouth. "I say 'stupid,' because they do not know who walks among them. I am waiting for him to show himself. I believe he eventually will." Kent gave a warped and other-wise ghastly attempt at a smile. "He is too much of a gamesman to resist." The bit of chicken went into his mouth. His teeth crunched together.

"Miss Cutter and I," said Katherine, "would appreciate hearing the beginning of this tale."

"Really?" The smile twisted further. "You dare wish to go there?" He held up his gloved hand. "I am partly an illusion, madam. I have one remaining finger and a thumb on that hand. The glove is filled out by fingerlings of wood, to give the glove a proper shape. The man I'm waiting for got hold of me with his snippers. I was very fortunate that he was unable to finish the job, as he'd done to thirteen others in the years of 1695 and 1696. You must know who I'm speaking of, it was written up in the *Globe*, and *Lord Puffery's Pin* ran on with it for two years."

Katherine's eyes darkened. She nodded. "I do know."

"Well, light *my* lamp," Minx insisted. "I had more pressing matters to tend to than keeping up with the news of the day seven years ago."

"He was called 'The Snipper' by us constables," said Kent, whose eyes had gone dead. "The *Pin* gave him the title of 'Billy Shears.' That became the popular name. He murdered six women, four men, and three children the youngest of which was eight years—" The door opened and again Kent stiffened like a hunting dog about to leap. It was the elder blacksmith Marco Ross, cleaned up in fresh clothes after a day at the forge and arrived for an evening repast; he noticed the two women and the pallid-faced man staring at him, and he nodded a greeting and claimed a table toward the other side of the room. Kent took him in a few seconds longer, but his countenance had relaxed and it was obvious he'd decided Ross was not his interest. "Eight years of age," Kent continued, as if he'd never been interrupted. "You recall his method, I'm sure," he said to Katherine.

"I do." For Minx's benefit she explained, "He snipped the fingers off the hands of his victims after he'd cut their throats. The victims were mostly people of the street: drunkards, gypsies, beggars, prostitutes and homeless urchins." She gave Kent's gloved hand a passing glance. "And almost a constable, it seems?"

"Very near. I never saw his face. He was wearing a gray hood with eyeholes cut into it. But I was a special case, you see. He wished to torture me before I was killed." Kent took a few more bites of his food before he spoke again. "I have often wondered if my wife saw his face before he slashed her throat. And what he did with her fingers. I can see him in my mind's eye, scurrying away through the alleys with his little bloody bag." He regarded Katherine and Minx with a calm, wet-lipped expression of composed horror that neither one would ever forget. Truly, in that moment his face did look like the entrance to a cracked granite tomb. "London being a city of alleys," he said. "Of people so accustomed to violence that the sight of an eight-year-old boy with his fingers sheared off and his head nearly severed from the body raises only a sigh of recognition that evil has come a'walking. And the sight of my Laura lying there on the dirty stones…the same." The agony of his false smile was as sharp as Minx's dagger. "Ah," he said, looking to the right as Emmaline approached with her tray, "here are your drinks, ladies."

After Emmaline had gone again, Minx asked, "What did you mean when you said you had an invitation?"

"Just that. The letter I brought with me was dated in August. Mailed to me from this town. Signed simply, 'S'."

"A letter from Shears? *Why?*"

"Telling me," Kent said, "that he attends this particular tavern on occasion, and that if I wish to continue our game I might find him here some night, and we might conclude our business. Therefore I am here, and therefore I wait for him at this table where I might see everyone who enters."

"But he wore a hood," Katherine said. "How would you know him?"

"As I told you, I have a good memory. My powers of observation are also quite sturdy. I will know him by his bearing...his walk...his voice. He knows I'm here. He's watching me, most likely, from some dark corner of the street. You see, part of the invitation was a directive to put a notice in your town's broadsheet on my arrival. I was to say, *Mr. Kent requests the company of the gentleman well-known to him, yet unknown.* I complied with the directive. Now I wait."

Katherine didn't reply. She took a drink of her wine and mused that there was some insanity in the pale pipesmoker. Or desperation. Or a death wish. Likely all three.

"So you understand," Kent continued, his voice following a gout of smoke, "Billy Shears has been living in this town—I would think—for the last several years. You might have seen him this day, walking about. That is to say...he is someone well-known to the citizens here...but, as I was directed to say in my notice...*unknown.*"

"Granted," said Katherine, who thought she felt yet a deeper chill emanating from this human tomb, "but how is it that he's given up his...*hobby*...if he was so proficient at such? It's my experience that a creature of this twisted nature doesn't simply stop...and we've had no incidents of murders involving snipped-off fingers."

"I doubt he's given it up completely. Oh, no. There are many small villages around, are there not? Many farms on the edge of the wilderness? Places where people might vanish and the surmise would be the act of wild beasts or Indians? And there are packet boats sailing from here to Boston and Philadelphia on a daily schedule, carrying a killer as well as the honest tradesman? No, I doubt he's given up his calling. Perhaps it's now only once in a blue moon, and he wouldn't perform the deed here in New York, but he's finding his pleasure...his challenge...elsewhere, I can assure you."

"Hm," Katherine replied. Then: "I assume that as a constable you have theories as to his personality?"

"A gamesman, of course. Probably likes his gambling and his cards. Also I would think the lower vices appeal to him. He likely lives alone and visits the whores quite frequently. I have already stopped by Madam Blossom's for a talk of whom might be her best customers, but I was turned out quite rapidly by a rather large black woman who seemed to relish the idea of bashing my head in."

"Madam Blossom is a discreet businesswoman," said Katherine. "Her list of customers would be guarded quite adamantly. As for the gambling, half the men in town are wearing borrowed shirts that the other half own."

"I want to know," Minx spoke up, "how all this came about. I mean... how he got you and your wife, and how you escaped. How you got on his track. The whole story."

Kent was silent for a while, as he finished his food. Pushing his plate aside, he repacked his pipe and touched it alight with the candle's flame. Through the drift of blue smoke he looked from Katherine to Minx and back again, and then he said, "As you wish. Imagine—"

—the streets of the Limehouse district at night, with the lamps burning both low and bright depending on what a coin seeks to buy. My district, and my responsibility. Ah, the Limehouse! The docks, the narrow ways, the nautical businesses there and all the people and situations that follow and build around men and commerce of the sea. Limehouse was at one time a swamp...which I suppose you know, Madam Herrald. It should come as no great surprise that at night some creatures crawl out from the phantom mire and walk as humans in the Limehouse. Certainly it was no surprise to me—seeing what I have seen on my rounds as constable—yet I failed to reckon with the cunning of this particular reptilian.

So...it began with the murder of a common drunkard...a man well-known in the district and looked upon as a local ragamuffin who danced in the street for a few pence. He was found sleeping in an alley...only his was the sleep that accompanies a slashed throat, and the fingers of his hands that had so readily held cups of liquor bought for him by generous idiots had been snipped off. A report was made, his body was carted away—dumped in the river, I would guess—and life went on in the Limehouse.

Pardon me, my pipe has gone out. I do so enjoy my pipe. A moment.

So then...two weeks passed. An elderly street musician was found next, three streets away from the first killing. Again, the cut throat and the snipped fingers. At that point I began to feel a cold claw touching the back of my neck. The pattern of the killings...I thought that here is someone who is killing with great stealth and with great...*joy*, I would say. And this person had found the world of the Limehouse in which to perform...a world of rapid comings and goings, of faceless encounters, of shadows seeking shadows in the taverns and alleys…a world of constant change, crews coming in and signing out and desperate women following the money trail. All this, and *my* world to patrol. My people—for better or for worse—to protect. Well, I was not the sole constable in the Limehouse, but these murders were happening on my territory. It was in the area of my responsibility, as I say, and as I had plans to continue the course of constable as far as it might take me, I was determined to act accordingly. All I could do at that point, however, was to ask questions of the locals and that got me nowhere.

A month went by, and then another. Then came the discovery of the young street urchin, eight years of age. Murdered, the same. After that, I announced in the taverns a reward of five pounds for any reliable information. I received ramblings but no leads. I was tempted to contact your agency for help, Madam Herrald, but as I was hard-pressed to apply the five pounds and my Laura held a lowly clerical job at a company that manufactured nautical rope, I was in no position to pay what I understood was your rather high rate.

"Something might have been arranged," Katherine said.

Possibly so, but the time for that went past. My announcement of a reward did not go unanswered. The next victim, a young gypsy girl who prowled around the docks telling fortunes, was found murdered the same but with a difference. There was a playing card in her mouth…the five of clubs. *Five*, you see? With that our little game began, for I realized the killer was watching me…possibly had been in one of the taverns where I made my announcement…knew I was asking questions…knew I had taken my task to heart…and possibly also was someone to whom I had asked questions, for I had made the rounds of all the shops and businesses.

I then employed four young boys to keep watch around the streets, to report back on anything they found suspicious or unseemly in their quarters of the district. It wasn't another week before one of those young gentlemen was murdered. Another playing card had been pushed into his mouth after the throat-cutting and the snipping were done…this one an ace of clubs. After that, the *Globe* and the *Pin* caught word of the crimes and I was interviewed by their agents. The stories appeared in print, and thus was "Billy Shears" born.

"A five of clubs and an ace of clubs," said Katherine. "What did you make of the cards being that particular suit?"

The same thing that is likely in your mind now. That it was of significance, and he was baiting me. The significance being, I surmised, that Billy Shears was telling me he was a member of a gambling club, of which you must know number in the many in London. So I began to visit those establishments, but what was I looking for? What outward sign would a creature of this nature show? Was there some significance in his method, as well, that there are "hands" of cards, and that human hands actually hold the cards in the playing? Well, I didn't know what sort of sign I was looking for, but still I visited all the gambling clubs in Limehouse and in the neighboring districts...and found nothing but the sense that I was being watched...played with...involved in a game that had deadly consequences.

The stories in the *Globe* and the *Pin* resulted in two more constables being assigned to the Limehouse. Their presence caused Billy Shears to disappear for several months. His next victim—another street urchin—appeared only a few days after the extra constables were taken off-duty. It was obvious to me that he was a resident of the Limehouse, and that he had his ear to the ground. As I say, possibly someone I had previously spoken to...possibly a tavern keeper or a local tradesman who knew all the circumstances and particulars. But who he was I had no clue...until his twelfth victim offered me something.

I was called to the scene in an alleyway. The killer had been interrupted in his work by a beggar who'd stopped to relieve herself in the entrance. He fled, having snipped away only six of the fingers. By lamplight the body of the prostitute was moved...and I caught the shine of a small object that had been underneath her left shoulder. It was a silver cuff button. What I had heard called a "cufflink." I surmised that the deceased pulled at her killer's arm in her throes, and so the button came loose. Upon this object—which looked quite new—was the engraving of a three-masted ship. A very beautiful object, no doubt formed by an expert silversmith. Now I can tell you that such an extravagant item was as rare in the Limehouse as the proverbial pig with wings...that is, never seen among the usual mix of dock workers, sailors and tradesmen. But I had a clue, and a track to follow.

"The silversmiths," said Katherine.

Exactly so. For the next two days I visited the local smiths with the cuff button in hand. I had no luck until the afternoon of the second day, when I visited a silversmith in Westminster, many miles and a world away from the Limehouse. This gentleman recognized the button as his work, and after I identified myself as a constable he told me it had been made on order for a young man named Davy Glennon, son of Midas Glennon whose business I knew well, his being a firm that supplied tar to the shipbuilders in the Limehouse. Therefore I visited the Glennon estate, and after some difficulty with a butler at the house I was escorted in to see Davy, who had just returned from an afternoon's ride on what is quite an admirable parkland.

Well, the young Glennon had the kind of attitude one might expect from a layabout whose father has made a fortune and expects his son to step into the role only at the pater's demise. In short, both a snob and an ass. But was he a killer? He's a slight young man in his mid-twenties. Small hands. On first impression I thought him incapable of exerting enough strength to crack fingerbones even with the adequate snipper. No, I didn't think he was my quarry…and yet there must be some connection. When I explained my reason for being there and showed him the cuff button, he recalled that some months ago he had been gambling at the Greenhalls club in the Limehouse—one of many clubs he attended weekly in which he lost copious portions of his father's money—and being short of coin put the silver cuff buttons up as a bid. Which he quickly lost. To whom? I asked.

He stated that he did not know the man's name but he had seen this individual at Greenhalls several times. A tall and elegant man, he said, but he'd seen that the hands appeared strong. Well-dressed. Age about mid-forties or so, was his opinion. The shine of a cunning intelligence in the eyes. A man silent and self-contained, and also a very able gamesman.

I knew in my bones, heart and soul…this might have been an older and more refined individual than I'd suspected…but it was Billy Shears.

My following question to Davy Glennon was…when was the next meeting of the Greenhalls? The coming Friday night, he said. I asked would he accompany me there, and point out the man who had won the silver buttons if that individual was present?

He wanted to know what might be in it for him, as he cared nothing about murders in the Limehouse. I told him that if this man did turn out to be Billy Shears, I would make sure Davy was recognized as a hero of London in both the *Globe* and the *Pin*, and from that he might win an award of some kind—either a medal or money. Certainly the *Pin* would make golden hay out of it, and Midas would have nothing to do with it. As I presumed, the thought of rising above his father's name infatuated him, and so it was agreed upon.

You might imagine my disappointment when, after meeting young Glennon in front of the building that housed the Greenhalls, he failed to identify the man at the gaming tables within. We stayed until the closing hour of three in the morning, when the last card was thrown down and the final die was rolled. Billy Shears did not appear.

And yet…he *was* there, somewhere. I believe he sighted myself and Davy Glennon meeting outside the building. He knew me well by appearance at this point, for I'm sure he'd been shadowing me. He knew I had the silver cuff button. He knew exactly why I was there with young Glennon. He knew I was closing in on him. He knew.

Therefore…he was tempted to strike at my heart. Possibly because I had interrupted his gaming evening. Possibly because he felt his luck threatened. Possibly because…he simply did not want me to win.

"Your wife?" Katherine ventured.

Victim number thirteen. Pardon me…my pipe.

There. Yes. My Laura. How he got her to venture into that alley on her walk home from her job at Brixton's…I don't know. It was not a deserted street, and the light wasn't even fully gone. How? I have tortured my mind over it. Did he call her over by saying he had news from me? Was his face hidden in shadow, or did she see it? Could he have simply said, "Come here! John has had an accident!" And her not thinking in that moment to be as careful as I'd warned her to be? What was it that drew her over there? And why did I not meet her and walk her home, as we lived only a few blocks from Brixton's rope manufacture? I had done so in the past. Why not this day? Because this day—the following Friday from my previous excursion—I was watching the door of the Greenhalls club with young Glennon again, waiting for the gamblers to arrive. As he must have known I would be.

A game. That's what all this was to him, ladies. Simply a game.

"And then?" Katherine prodded when Kent paused and took an inordinately long time to flame his pipe once more. "What next?"

Ah. Next. Next was…what I'm sure he'd planned as his final move against me, for I was getting close to him. He knew it. Also…I was preventing him from returning to Greenhalls, and I believe that heightened his desire to finish me off. I was wary, though. I understood he was out there watching my movements, and waiting for an opportunity.

A month went by. Then another. I was standing before Greenhalls every Friday night, though young Glennon had kiboshed the chase. I thought I might recognize the man by his description. I saw four who might fit… but in my heart I knew Billy Shears would not reveal himself to me so readily, and the four men I investigated were no angels but they all lived far outside the Limehouse and one was a very proper member of Parliament. I had decided already that Shears *must* be a Limehouse resident…must be, simply for what he knew about me and my questions to the locals.

I was always on guard when I made my rounds. I was not so much on guard when I returned to my little house on Narrow Street, in the shadow of the tall masts. It was just before cock's crow on the morning of October fourteenth, 1696. I unlocked my door and entered the house with my lamp before me. I was very tired, and possibly that's why I was both sluggish in mind and body. In any case, I smelled him before he struck me from behind. It was almost a medicinal smell…no…different…the smell of a predatory beast. His sweat of anticipation, I suppose.

I awakened to the twilight of my own kitchen, where Laura and I had shared so many happy suppers. My constable's lamp was still lit and sitting on a shelf. I was bound to the kitchen table with ropes around my midsection and thighs. My wrists had been tied and my arms made to be splayed out on either side of me so my hands were fully exposed. A piece of cloth had been stuffed into my mouth. I could not cry out. It's strange, though, what one fixes upon in a moment like that. I remember being fiercely angry because I could feel a cold draft from the broken window at the other side of the room, and thinking how much it would cost to have it repaired before winter set in.

Well, at that point I was surely half-insane myself.

Then...there he was.

Moving in and out of the cone of light. I was able to lift my head a few degrees. I saw something glinting in his right hand. He was wearing a gray suit with a ruffled shirt and a black cravat. I thought...yes...though he was a killer he was also sort of a dandy, and that was why he could lure his victims into the alleys, and that is why he was wearing the silver cuff buttons. The way he moved back and forth, light on his feet. Possibly had been an athlete at some point? I was still investigating, you see, even though I knew...the game was coming to an end, and I had lost.

But human nature being as it is, ladies, I clung to the hope that some-how I might get out of this...and even as the sweat steamed from my face and my heart pounded itself nearly to death some part of me remained calm...watchful...thinking of how I might literally turn the table on this monster, and avenge not only my Laura but all my dead charges.

He leaned down over me.

As I said, he wore a gray hood with the eyeholes cut out. He brushed my cheeks with his metal shears. I remember thinking how clean they were, to have been so useful.

"John," he said—and I shall never forget the silken sound of his voice, like chill death itself speaking—"it has come to this," he went on. He snapped his shears in front of my eyes. "Which hand shall we begin with?"

I tried to fight, tried to overturn the table but he slammed me in the chest and all the air went out of me. When he went after my right hand I balled it up. Again he hit me with a fist made of iron...and I felt the snip-pers close on one of my fingers.

How to describe that kind of pain? Of course the other victims had been dead—or dying—when it was done to them. Is that a thing to be thankful for? I heard the blades crunch on the bone, I heard the bone snap...and then my hand went freezing cold and the cold spread along my arm to the shoulder.

He was quick, I'll say that much for Billy Shears. The second finger was gone before I felt the blades...and, anyway, God in His mercy had dulled my senses at that point and I was falling from nightmare into dream.

Billy Shears must've sensed that, because his next move was to use his snippers to ravage most of the flesh off my next finger before he attacked the bone. My entire body convulsed. I wet my breeches. Not a very polite thing to tell, but the truth. Then I heard him gasp with either satisfaction or a darker ecstasy as he took that finger off. As I said…a beast.

The snippers closed on my thumb. I can feel its bite still, very often as I'm coming up from sleep.

There came a knock at the back door, not five feet from where Shears stood doing his work.

"John?" she called. "John, are you—"

I heard her scream and I learned that she had looked through the broken window into the room. Of course she saw what was happening, and she screamed again. My thumb, though badly cut, was spared. I think I saw him lift a knife to stab me through the heart but Doreen screamed once more and he gave up the attempt at murder to flee out the front way. I heard shouting…someone else had seen him on the street. Then I fell unconscious.

Doreen had taken to walking over from her house every few mornings to make me breakfast, knowing what time I got home. She was—is—a kindly widow, a bit older than I, whom I'd met at church. Lonely, perhaps, as I was. Her visits were not regular, thus if Shears had been watching my house he likely had not seen her visitations…and thus the remainder of my hand and my life were spared.

But after that, Judge Archer himself ordered that the Limehouse be torn apart by an army of officers searching for this monster. Not only was Greenhalls staked out and Davy Glennon forced under threat to attend every Friday night with another constable who passed himself off as a regular gambler, but records were assembled of every man who'd ever thrown a pair of dice or turned a card in that establishment. Judge Archer—a good man, that—had an artist attend young Glennon and draw a portrait of Billy Shears from his description…but, you know, by this time the memory was faulty. Was the jaw large or small? Sharp cheekbones or full cheeks? High forehead or low? Color of eyes? Color of hair? Well, dark-haired and dark-eyed was all that came out of it. Not much to go on.

And of course Billy Shears disappeared. There were no more murders involving snipped fingers. I reasoned he'd moved from the Limehouse likely to some other town in England, some place with many small surrounding villages where he might start anew, if he was so inclined. That was the end of it, until I received the letter from New York town.

How could I not respond? Knowing he is here…knowing what he is capable of. Just knowing…I could not turn a blind eye. You understand?

Katherine said after a moment of reflection, "I understand this individual may never reveal himself to you, having caused you to cross the Atlantic. You say he's a gamesman. Granted. I would think he already considers himself the winner, just letting you know he's still 'out there,' so to speak. I doubt very much he'll ever walk through that door you so ardently watch."

"I disagree," said the pale pipesmoker, with a small plume of smoke cast in her direction. "He will show himself, and I will wait for him."

THREE

KATHERINE AND MINX REMAINED AT THE TABLE WITH KENT, HAVING another glass of wine and another cup of ale, until the last chords sounded from Sally Almond's guitar, the last plate was taken away, the last customer gone and the last log in the fireplace fallen to red embers. When Sally approached the table—likely to ascertain the progress of the night, Katherine surmised—she was greeted with one word from Madam Herrald: "Later."

Outside, fog lay heavy on Nassau Street and slowly drifted like searching spirits around the roofs and chimneys. Kent explained that he had secured a room at Mary Belovaire's boarding house just across the way, and had paid for quarters with a window that looked down upon Sally Almond's tavern...thus he could watch it during the day, as well. He told the women that most definitely he would be returning to the tavern the following night for his supper. Then he bid them goodnight and went on his way, a solitary figure soon swallowed by the fog.

Minx walked with Katherine along Nassau Street toward the Dock House Inn where Katherine kept her own quarters. Though the hour was late for many, for some the night held further escapades. It could never be said that New York did not wish to become as jaunty as London, and the jauntiest citizens would be making the rounds of the more low-cast taverns until the final candle hissed out at an indeterminant hour of intoxication. Candles burned behind window glass, the occasional carriage rolled past, someone shouted here and there, dogs barked, voices went up and up in argument and then fell silent again, laughter and fiddle music played over and against each other: a town at work, meaning to be a city.

Katherine pulled the black velvet collar of her coat up around her neck, for the image of Kent's fingers being snipped off had come to her much too clearly. "It seems to me," she said to Minx as they progressed southward, "that the only way we can solve Sally Almond's problem is to also solve John Kent's. We must discover the identity of Mr. Shears. Must we not?"

"There's no proof the man is actually *here*," Minx said. "Yes, the letter was sent from New York…but that doesn't mean he's living here. He could've taken a packet boat up from Philadelphia or down from Boston. He could be anywhere."

"Certainly. This could all be simply a furthering of the game the man seems to enjoy playing. Still…there most times is a method to madness. This man—this *creature*—may wish to finish his cutting. In fact, he may be *driven* to finish it, even after this number of years. Does that make sense?"

"In a senseless kind of way."

"Yes. Well, we shall see."

"And what's next, then?"

"Tomorrow I intend to speak with Polly Blossom about her customers. Is there one who has a particular interest in hands and fingers?" Katherine gave Minx a look of rather dubious amusement. "Our creature may not be snipping, but I would imagine there are other entertainments he might desire. As for you, I presume you know the various gambling dens here?"

Minx shrugged. "I've won a bit."

"Good enough. You might do a bit of visiting as well tomorrow night. Looking for—" Katherine paused. "A man who wears cuff buttons. Possibly his habits in clothing have come with him across the ocean. In any event, it's a start."

Minx walked with Katherine to the steps leading up to the Dock House Inn's entrance and said goodnight. She waited for Katherine to go in and the door to close before she turned away. Her own abode, a room above a carriage house connected to Tobias Winekoop's stable, was about a quarter mile north on the Broad Way. She began walking, and contemplated visiting one or another of the more lively taverns and the gambling clubs tonight, as for her the night was full of opportunity and sleep before two o'clock in the morning was a waste of life.

She had turned to the east, heading in the direction of the rougher—and for her, more exciting—area of taverns that attracted the kind of ne'er-do-wells who had first planted their dirty boots on the island long before a shed had gone up. Her kind of people.

She'd gone a single block when she heard the man's voice, quite close.

"Come here."

Minx stopped in her tracks. She looked to her right and slightly behind.

He was standing shrouded by fog. Wearing a dark fearnaught coat and a dark tricorn, pulled low over the face. But she wouldn't have been able to see the face anyway; the nearest light was the yellow smear of a lantern in a window on the upper floor of a warehouse where someone obviously was either working late or stealing something.

"Come here," he repeated.

"You come here," she said, her hand going to the knife in her jacket.

He backed away, and just that quickly the fog took him.

Minx brought the blade out. She was not afraid. Knives had saved her skin many times, and she knew how to carve other skins with them. Not afraid, but rather unsettled. Unnerved might be the word. Yet still calm and composed, as was her nature. She wished she had a wall at her back; out here in the street, she was open to many avenues of attack. Her heart was beating harder, not from fear, but from the excitement of danger. Such cleared her head of all lingering traces of strong apple ale that might slow her reflexes. She was ready.

Onward she walked, pointed toward her tavern of choice, the Cock'a'Tail, which served her interest of getting a stiff drink, an inhalation of pungent tobacco smoke, hearing the kind of language that dared a spear of lightning from the hand of God, and being in the company of the roughest necks in New York. Her kind of place.

Was there movement off on her right, through the fog? Yes, there was. She realized she was being tracked. She went on, her senses both questing and tingling and her grip firm on the blade's ivory handle.

Quite suddenly, he was there in front of her.

Hidden still by the fog, yet close enough to attempt damage.

She stopped again. And said quietly, "You're in my way."

"Hear me, Miss Cutter," he replied. "I have no argument with you nor with Madam Herrald. My game is with John Kent. I would advise you—and your employer—not to interfere. Am I understood?"

The voice. Smooth and silken. *Chill death*, Kent had said. Did she know it? No.

She realized he had seen them walk out together from Sally Almond's. Watching the place, just as was John Kent. "I understand what you are," Minx answered. "Who you are...we're going to uncover that before long. Your time is running out."

"Ah." There was a long pause. "Yes. Time *is* running out. Thank you for making that so clear. Pardon me, won't you?" He began backing away. Minx saw no need to press the issue, as a knife fight in this fog was not to her liking. If she was right, the man likely had a blade in his hand as well and obviously knew how to use sharp instruments.

"Goodnight, Mr. Shears," she said, but she was already speaking to empty air.

As Minx was settling into a corner table of the Cock'a'Tail with a mug of hot spiced liquor and her blade stuck into the tabletop to discourage visitors, John Kent was awakened in his bed at Mary Belovaire's boarding house.

He lay still in the dark for a while, wondering what it might be that had awakened him. The dreams he had of Laura—both of happy times and the horrific sense that he was standing with her at the moment of her death and yet was much of a spirit and unable to raise a hand to help her—were well-known to him and constant, thus his awakening had been harkened by something else.

In another moment he heard it: a small stone striking the glass of his window.

Another followed soon after, as Kent lay struggling with the idea that he was neither entirely awake nor asleep yet on the twilight border.

He got up from bed, went to the window, drew aside the curtain and peered out.

The fog was still thick, yet as Kent peered down into the gloom from his upper-floor window he thought he was beginning to make out a figure standing in the street. Imagination? He considered it so, until another small stone struck the window glass with an almost musical *ping* and he saw the figure lift a hand in a motion that could only mean *Come out and play*.

Kent left the window. He spent a moment striking the flint and firing his tinderbox, after which he struck light to the room's lantern, a series of maneuvers with his good hand that had astounded those who'd witnessed such. By the lantern's smoky yellow glow he dressed himself, applying the fingerlings of wood to the right-handed glove and pulling it firmly over the hand with its single finger and scarred thumb.

Then he took the pistol from his travelling bag and, sitting on the bed, proceeded to prepare it for its single shot with lead ball, flint and black powder from his leather powderhorn.

He was in no hurry. He knew who was summoning him, and that the time had come. His heart was barely beating hard, yet a sheen of sweat had come up on his hangman's face and his mouth was dust-dry. The moment had arrived, and for it he must make certain Billy Shears did not again escape judgment.

He stood up, shrugged into his long black coat, wrapped a dark green woolen scarf around his throat, put on his tricorn and thrust the pistol down into the waistband of his breeches on the left side. He peered out the window once more. The figure could not be seen…but Billy Shears was there. Oh yes…he was waiting out there, somewhere, and the end of their game could not be denied.

Kent took a long, deep breath. Then he left the room, descended the curving stairway and went out the door into the murky night.

Sometime later—possibly nearing toward forty minutes—a single pistol shot was heard by only a few residents who lived up near the disused Dutch docks on the river, just off the West Ward. At most, it caused three farmers to rise up from their beds and peer out their windows, but what they could see was nothing. Then—as most people in New York town wished only to tend to their own business and not become involved in the entanglements of others—they returned to their states of rest.

And the dark went on until dawn.

FOUR

"THERE," SAID KATHERINE HERRALD, "IS HIS PIPE. OUR PROBLEM presently is…where is the smoker?"

John Kent's black pipe was sitting atop the dresser next to the packet of tobacco. Minx Cutter crossed the room to examine the implements that lay on the bed: a bag of lead shot, a small box of flints, and a leather powderhorn. "Another question," she said. "Here are the preparations, but where's the gun?"

"Do you think something's happened to Mr. Kent?" Mary Belovaire asked, holding the lamp with its three candles that lit the room. She was a thin lady with long gray hair, a sharp beak of a nose and the ability to use that proboscis to sniff out the business of just about everyone in town, though she was of generally a peaceful and friendly nature. "When he left late last night, I nearly spoke to him to ask where he was bound…but I held my tongue and now I regret it."

Katherine nodded but was also examining the implements used for loading a pistol. When Kent had not appeared at six o'clock at Sally Almond's, Katherine and Minx had been curious…when the hour of eight o'clock had arrived, they knew something was definitely amiss and thought they might be an hour late with their suspicions. They had walked across Nassau Street in the drizzling rain and entering Madam Belovaire's boarding house had heard the tale that the landlady had detected someone coming down the stairs—that eighth riser from the top always made a little *skreech* that caused the skin on the back of her neck to crawl, yet no carpenter in town seemed to be able to quiet the beast—and she'd peered out her door to see Kent leaving, and she'd known it was him because—well, she knew all her boarders, she had a quick memory and he had that nice fearnaught coat and also she caught a glimpse of the glove he always strangely wore on his—

"Yes, thank you, Mary," Katherine had interrupted. "May we see his room?"

"Is Mr. Kent in any trouble?" Mary asked as the two problem-solvers surveyed the dwelling. "He was so quiet and solitary, yet he seemed a decent man."

Katherine went to the window, drew aside the curtain and looked down upon the wet street, where a wagon carrying a cargo of barrels was just passing on its southward journey to the docks. "Mary?" she said. "Has anyone else been asking about Mr. Kent? Anyone at all?"

"No."

"Anyone you met on an errand happen to ask how your business is doing?"

"Many people do that. It's just the way of things."

"Certainly. But did any of those people ask if you ever had boarders who were in any way peculiar? Just in the matter of passing?"

"Well, I can't…" Mary paused and tapped her long chin with an index finger. "A moment. It happened some time ago…last week, it was. I happened to be in Madam Kenneday's bakery…early in the morning it was, I recall that. Then…he came in and asked for a dozen biscuits, and he said good morning to me and asked…oh, but that's nothing to remark on!"

Katherine watched drops of rain slowly running their courses down the window's glass. "Yet do remark upon it, Mary. Go on, all you can remember. And who exactly are we talking about, who wanted these dozen biscuits?"

Mary gave the name.

Katherine remained at the window, only half her face catching the light from Mary's lamp. "The rest of it, please."

"It was as you say. We began talking—just a chat, you know—and he asked that question…or sort of that question, in a humorous kind of way. He said in his profession he saw all the foibles of people and he was sure he and I shared observations on human nature. Of course I was flattered by this, him being who he is—"

"Of course," said Katherine, with a faint smile.

"Yes. So then…I recall…he asked if I had anyone recently who I might consider strange, and I told him about Mr. Kent's gloved hand. It was an innocent thing, just to pass the time. What does he have to do with this?"

Minx spoke up. "Did you tell this gentleman what room Kent occupied?"

"No, not directly. But I recall he said—and all this was just done in the most jocular fashion, you understand—that if this man had a window that looked out upon Nassau he would beware walking beneath it in case the peculiarity of dumping a bedpan onto the street was also part of my boarder's strange nature. I said Mr. Kent did, but I reminded him not to fear, that the situation of bedpans was under strict control and that Mr. Kent seemed a very civilized sort." Mary frowned and looked from Katherine to Minx and back again. "What in the *world* would have been wrong with a little joking conversation? Besides, he has been very instrumental in helping relieve the pain in my knees I sometimes suffer."

"I am glad to hear that, Mary," Katherine said as she turned from the window. She offered Madam Belovaire a smile. "Nothing whatsoever was wrong with your conversation. Please forget that I even asked." She made a show of looking around the room once more, but her investigations here were done. "Thank you for allowing Minx and myself in. As for Mr. Kent, he had asked us to do a small service for him while he was here. I'm sure he'll turn up, somewhere. And as for us...since Minx and I were working for Mr. Kent in that capacity, please keep it to yourself that we were inquiring about him. It's no one's business. Yes?"

"Certainly. But shall I expect him in the next day or two? It appears he's left all his belongings and clothes here. Even left that pipe of his! It's a mystery, isn't it?"

"Yes," came the quiet response. "But one I believe shall be solved, very soon."

"And by the by," Madam Belovaire added, "would Mr. Greathouse be returning anytime soon?"

"One hopes. I might assure you that if the money for boarding that Hudson left for you is depleted before his arrival, I shall make up the difference."

"Ah, excellent! I was just wondering, mind you."

Outside, as they walked south along Nassau Street, Katherine said to Minx, "Clever, that. He only had to know for sure that Kent secured a room with a window on the street. Then he could keep watch and see which window lit up with lantern light as soon as Kent departed from Sally Almond's. Of course Billy Shears lured Kent out last night, and Kent took a loaded pistol with him. How that lure was done is unknown, but since Kent has not returned I doubt we'll be seeing our pale pipesmoker again, unless he is lying wounded somewhere and both the players in the game are incapacitated, but I think it more likely from the history of this matter that the killer has emerged victorious."

"So," Minx said grimly, "Billy Shears has won the game."

Katherine stopped walking and looked Minx in the face. Katherine's jaw was set and red embers glinted in her eyes. "Has possibly won the game from John Kent," she said. "But *we* are now involved in the game...and he has not won from us. Now let us go get out of this drizzle, have a cup of coffee and determine what is the next move."

At the new coffee shop that had just opened a week before on Wall Street, Katherine and Minx drank from their cups of the dark elixir and enjoyed the warmth of the brown brick fireplace. There were quite a few patrons at the tables, most of whom both the women knew, but the two problem-solvers were only absorbed with the problem at hand.

"The name of the gentleman in question," said Katherine, "was given to me this afternoon at Polly Blossom's. I decided not to mention it before, until I had further information, but now I'll tell you."

She had gone to the rose-colored house on Petticoat Lane that was the abode of Polly Blossom and her garden of flowers. Here the gentlemen ventured both day and night—mostly night, unless one was spectacularly drunk or obviously aroused enough to cause a public panic—and spent their money on the damsels. All the flowers were neither particularly beautiful nor youthful, but experience had its own virtues.

Sitting in the tidy, fragrant parlor with the tall, big-boned, blonde and exuberant Polly, Katherine had explained what she wanted while several of the girls slinked around listening.

"The names of patrons," she began, over a nice cup of chamomile tea, "who might have—shall we say—a rather *different* interest in fingers and hands."

Polly paused with the cup at her mouth, her clear blue eyes wide. "Pardon me?"

"A sexual interest in fingers and hands," Katherine went on. "Possibly outlandish. Something that would definitely be remembered by one of your girls, I would think."

Polly sipped at her tea and gracefully set the pink cup back into its saucer. "Madam Herrald, don't think me rude, but that's about the strangest fucking request I've heard all month."

"It may be so, but still it's a valid line of inquiry. I can't tell you why I'm after this information. You know my work and my reputation. Also I understand you have had pleasant dealings with Matthew Corbett."

"Oh dear sweet Matthew! I pray Hudson Greathouse has found him by now!"

"As we all do. But I was going to add that if Matthew were here, he would be at my side asking this question instead of me. You must know it concerns a current situation Minx Cutter and I are—"

"That Minx!" said Polly with a laugh and a flash of the eyes. "There's one for you!"

Katherine restrained herself from asking *one what* and continued on: "Minx and I are handling. It is important that I get this information…that is, if there's anything to be gotten."

Polly took her time drinking her tea. She spent a moment telling a young dark-haired girl that if she didn't clean up her room she would soon be lodging on the street, and Katherine heard in the hard voice the stern taskmaster that such a profession desired. To Katherine, such a position would be akin to herding cats.

When the young prostitute had departed, Polly leaned toward Katherine and quietly said, "To offer the names of my customers would destroy my business. Trust is everything. If it got out that I was naming names, not only would a quarter of the men in this town be horsewhipped by their wives, but the packet boats would get rich taking those same men down to Philadelphia and up to Boston."

"I wasn't aware those towns had such entertainments."

Polly gave a short, harsh laugh. "Oh my! Such a world you must live in! Quakers and Puritans be damned when it comes to money and needs of the flesh. Where there's opportunity and money to be made...well, there will be establishments just like this one and also the castoffs in the street doing what they must do to survive. But you know all this, you're not a fool."

"I hope I'm not," said Katherine with an affable smile. "Now...to my question. Do you have such a customer? I would think he might be a regular."

"We have several with what might be called outlandish tastes. But I'm not a judge and no one else judges anyone here."

"A wonderful philosophy. Again I point you in the direction of an answer. A particular interest—an obsession perhaps—with the hands and fingers. Who might that be?"

Polly's eyes narrowed. "Well, now. Maybe I have such information and maybe I don't. What's it worth to you?"

Katherine had reasoned it would come to the purse. An agreement of six pounds was made after a few go-rounds, down from the ten Polly first proposed.

Polly gave the name.

"He's unmarried," she said, "so if this gets out at least he won't be tarred and feathered by an enraged woman. But it won't get out, will it?"

"It will not. The story, please. What is his interest?"

"It seems," Katherine said in a guarded voice to Minx as they sat at the table with their cups of coffee, "that our gentleman liked to employ his fingers and indeed his entire hand—both hands, in fact—in sexual acts that I think might cause the Devil a fright. Perhaps I'm being old-fashioned and perhaps I *am* old, but I was brought up a certain way. Such things...well, they were even so extreme that they frightened the young prostitute he liked to visit. She left a few months ago, went somewhere to the north." A hard rain had begun to drum on the roof and hiss in the hearth. "The addition to this rather sordid tale," said Katherine with a look as if she had bitten into a bitter lemon, "is that our gentleman employed the girl to do the same service to *him*."

Minx's sudden laugh was so loud Katherine feared the other patrons would think she was having a fit. It nearly knocked a half dozen cups to the floor from startled hands.

"Pardon," Minx said when she was able to speak. She wiped the tears of hilarity from her eyes. "I couldn't help but imagine it."

"My imaginings of such perversities don't end in uproarious mirth." Katherine drank down the rest of her coffee and sat staring into the empty cup. "Damn," she said at last. "Maybe I *am* old." After a silent pause of reflection upon this point, she righted herself and went on. "Your task tomorrow is to make the rounds of the stable owners. Begin with Tobias Winekoop. Ask if our gentleman has a habit of renting a horse and jaunting about for several days. They may wish to know why. Tell them it's official business. I'll give you a few pounds to play with, money being the official tongue-loosener. Also, I'd like to know if our gentleman is a regular at any of the gaming clubs. Can you take care of that?"

"Of course. There are four. I can ask Birdie to find out."

Katherine nodded. Birdie—to Katherine real name unknown and unasked for—was Minx's contact in the lower dives of the town. How she had gained the confidence and aid of an individual who evidently was part thief, part vagabond and part Sir Ears and Eyes was Minx's business, but then again there were definite advantages to employing a problem-solver of Miss Cutter's particular talents.

"If your Birdie can learn that our gentleman is a member of all four clubs," said Katherine, "and we find that he has the habit of travelling about for several days, it may be time for a visit to the man himself. Very well, then. We shall see what we shall see."

It was after four in the morning when Minx gave herself up to bed. Sometime after that, she was roused not by the sound of the rain drumming on the roof but by the aroma of burning tobacco.

She sat up, and there saw in the far corner of the room a small glow.

It strengthened fractionally. In its slightly increased light she saw the blurred image of his pallid face as smoke swirled around the visage. He was neither form nor shape, simply the pipe glow and smoke mask there in the corner. There for a few seconds and then gone.

She stared into the dark.

"We'll get him," she said to the departed phantom, if anything had been there at all. For it had occurred to her that her encounter with Billy

Shears in the fog had increased the tempo of the game and caused the killer to lure Kent out into the street, taking him to someplace where the game could be finished in favor of Shears.

Your time is running out, she'd said to the man in the fog.

Yes, he'd replied. *Time is running out. Thank you for making that so clear. Pardon me, won't you?*

And instead of putting paid to the situation right then and there, Minx had retreated to a tavern and had a drink while Billy Shears went on his way to Mary Belovaire's boarding house. If Kent was in fact dead, had his death been fast or slow? In any event, Minx felt herself to blame for spurring Shears on…she should have at least followed him…should have done something…anything…and Kent might be alive this night.

"We'll get him," she said again. She settled back against her pillow, but before she was asleep again the rain had ceased and the first somber light of dawn had begun to creep across the horizon.

FIVE

SO IT CAME ABOUT THAT ON A MORNING A FEW DAYS HENCE FROM their conversation of strategy, Katherine and Minx approached a small but well-kept white house with green shutters where William Street began to curve upward toward the larger estates of the wealthy merchants on Golden Hill.

The weather of the day was indecisive, rays of sunlight one moment and the next abolished by the movement of thick rain-heavy clouds. Katherine and Minx went up four steps to the front door. It was noted by both women that the door's knocker was a small brass hand. Katherine knocked, and they waited as a cold wind swirled around their hats and coats.

There was no response. Katherine used the brass hand again, more firmly.

A man's voice from beyond the door answered: "I am not seeing visitors today."

"We have pressing business," Katherine said. "It can't wait."

"Who is that?"

She introduced herself and Minx, but she had the idea he already knew.

"I am not feeling well. If you have an ailment, please go to the Publick Hospital."

"Yes, we understand you've not been in perfect health," Katherine said. "We have already visited the hospital." Their visit had resulted in the discovery from one of the two new physicians who'd arrived in the past few months that the gentleman in question had sent a messenger several days before stating he was feeling ill and would be taking a short leave. The timing of that, both Katherine and Minx knew, dovetailed exactly with the morning after Kent had been lured from his quarters.

"Please depart," said the man. Minx's mouth had tightened; the voice was weak, yet it held a characteristic she recognized from the speaker in the fog.

"We shall not," Katherine answered. "Open the door, doctor. Or instead of addressing Dr. Quail Polliver, should I be addressing Billy Shears?"

There was a silence. Then: "What nonsense are you talking, woman?" This time the voice carried a harsher note.

"It seems to me that the winner of any game finds satisfaction in seeing the faces of his vanquished opponents. I ask you again to open the door."

They waited. The wind shrilled around them.

In another moment they heard a latch being turned.

The door opened.

"State your business and be gone," the doctor said.

They walked past him into the tastefully appointed parlor. He closed the door at their backs and latched it again. "Ah!" said Katherine. "Minx, do you smell that lingering odor of medicinals?"

"I treat patients here," Polliver said. "Why would that odor *not* be present?"

"Of course it should be. Any hospital or physician's office would present that odor. It's the kind of thing that gets into one's clothes, I might think."

Minx knew what Katherine was getting at. When John Kent had recalled the attack on him by Billy Shears, he'd said *It was almost a medicinal smell...no...different...the smell of a predatory beast. His sweat of anticipation, I suppose.*

But Kent had been correct in his first assumption. It had been the odor of medicinals from the killer's clothes.

"I would offer to take your hats and coats," said the doctor, "but I hope you're not staying long. I am just out of bed." He was wearing a blue-and-yellow paisley dressing gown that hung to his ankles. He was gray-faced with dark hollows beneath his eyes. Still, he was a tall and stately figure, a man probably in his early fifties, with broad shoulders and a noble, handsome visage. His hair was dark brown except for a gray forelock. By the parlor's yellow lamplight, a slight sheen of sweat could be seen glistening on his forehead.

Katherine smiled. "I presume this is a case of physician heal thyself? Minx, the odor is so strong because Dr. Polliver is treating himself for..."

would it be a pistol wound? Where did John Kent hit you? Somewhere not fatal, it appears. A crease of the leg or the side, perhaps? Painful, for sure. Certainly not something you'd want the other doctors to see."

Polliver gave a gruff laugh, yet his dark brown eyes held no humor. "Have you lost your senses? And who is John Kent?"

"The question I would ask you is, *where* is John Kent? Will his body ever be found?"

"The asylum beckons you, madam."

Now it was Katherine's turn to laugh. She walked past Minx, looking at the various objects in the parlor. There were nice pieces of pottery, a few dignified oil paintings, and...lo and behold, a skeletal hand wired together and displayed on a little pedestal beneath a dome of glass. "Are you really a doctor?" she asked.

"Of course. You weren't here at the time, but you must know I tended to Matthew Corbett when he was unfortunately singed in a house fire. That whole business was a bit strange, but I can assure you I have been very successful at my profession for many years."

"Which profession, sir? Doctoring or murdering?"

"Is she always so addled in the brain?" Polliver asked Minx.

"We know who you are," Minx answered. She walked closer to the doctor until they were only a few feet apart. Polliver made a motion to step back a pace, but halted himself as the move made him wince. "We know about the trips you've been taking. Four or five days, every two or three months. You prefer to spread your business from stable to stable. We know."

Polliver stared into Minx's face.

She saw him change.

Something in his own face seemed to sharpen. The eyes seemed to sink in and the bones jutted like small blades of their own, eager for the cutting. He lifted his unshaven chin and a smile rippled across the terrible slash of his mouth.

But there only for a heartbeat, then gone.

"I attend patients," he said quietly, "in more localities than this town. In fact, I assist other physicians elsewhere, and I am much in demand. My specialty is—"

"Finger snipping?" Katherine ventured.

"Surgery," he responded, with the blankest expression. "Now, I am weakened by my poor condition. It is the weather afflicting me...no more and no less. I am going back to bed, and you are both going *out*." He moved past Minx and toward the door, and both women saw him press a hand against his left side.

"Your prostitute at Madam Blossom's," said Katherine, standing in her spot. "Her name was Miranda, I understand? Such games! What pleasure do you get from that activity?"

Polliver stopped with his hand reaching toward the latch. He turned toward Katherine with a faint smile but his eyes were deadly.

"I wish to know," Katherine continued in a calm, even tone, "what causes a man educated in *healing* to become...well, to become Billy Shears." She tapped the glass dome beneath which was held the skeletal hand. "To be so intent—driven, I would think—to murder unfortunates in such a fashion, and take their fingers as some sort of calling card. What was it—what *is* it—that drives you? May I be informal and call you Billy?" She plowed onward without waiting for the answer that she knew would never come. "Something in your past, I presume. Some incident that has caused you to become both healer and destroyer of life. Some...I suppose one might call it a *kink?* The twisted memory of a mother's or a father's hand? The hand perhaps of a minister? The hand of a prostitute when you were a child? A hand raised against you in a rage that you can never forget nor forgive? Or were you simply born of two natures, and both live in the same mind that is equally proficient at healing and desirous of killing? What is the answer, Billy? Before we leave, I must know."

"*Ha*," spoke the man, in what was nearly a strangled whisper. He looked from one woman to the next and back again, and if disgust and hatred had been a physical thing both of them would have been torn to shreds by it.

"You know," he whispered, "*nothing.* Vanquished opponents, yes. That is all you are. And *him* as well. The stupidity of him, to come over here on *my* territory. Over there, he almost had me. I knew it was a matter of time. But *here*...a different game altogether. Oh, his stupidity was his undoing! And his arrogance too...thinking he could come over here and finish me. No, no...it was never going to be."

"There he is," said Katherine to Minx. "Look at him. You can vomit when we get outside." She lifted the glass dome and ran her own fingers over the bones. "Kent made the mistake of searching low for you, when he should have been searching high. He never would've considered that a *doctor* was Billy Shears. I presume you *were* a doctor in the Limehouse district?"

"Shadwell."

"Which is adjacent to the Limehouse, is it not? Therefore you had patients who were citizens of the Limehouse, and could tell you all you wished to know in that charming way you possess of gaining information?"

"Our little conversation is over," he said.

"I doubt you're in any condition to throw us out, and I daresay you won't press an offense against us with a constable." Katherine offered him a smile that was in its own way dangerous. She returned the glass dome to its proper place. "Our case against you will not be closed," she said, "until you are brought to justice. In my true estimation, you should be killed like a mad dog in the street, but a public hanging will have to do."

"Such violent dreams!" said Polliver, with a mocking grin. It twisted into a sneer. "You're not a killer, Madam Herrald. Neither are you able to connect myself with John Kent in any form or fashion. As you have so intelligently recognized, the game is over. With not a rope's thread of evidence, I believe the hanging noose will in my case forever remain coiled in its box. Am I mistaken? You do have evidence, or is all this the wildest of conjectures that no court in this town—in these *colonies*—would entertain for an instant?"

Neither of the problem-solvers spoke.

"I thought not." Polliver continued to the door, unlatched it and opened it to the wind. "Get out," he commanded.

Katherine stood her ground for a moment more, and then she motioned for Minx to follow her out. On their way past Polliver, the doctor said, "I fear I won't be able to tend to either of you in the future, as you have such a poor opinion of me. But those new young men are very efficient, so your health will not be in jeopardy." He gave a bark of a laugh. "A healer like myself accused of being a low-minded murderer! The shame of it!"

And thus the door was closed and locked at their backs.

SIX

November chilled into December, and December shivered into January.

While hopefully waiting for the return of Hudson Greathouse with Matthew and Berry Grigsby, Katherine and Minx had no lack of problems presented to them by anxious and in some cases terrified clients. There was the case of the demonic fiddler, the strange incident of the two-headed dog, and the rescue of the kidnapped Schoonmaacher child from Captain Ballam's river pirates, to signify a few. In particular, the deadly dealings with Captain Ballam convinced Katherine that a woman with a knife was far more valuable than a man with one.

Time went on, as did the month of January.

In the last week of the month, the packet boat *George Hodel* docked at the Philadelphia wharf, having completed its journey southward from New York town. Among the passengers who disembarked in the flurry of falling snow was a tall, elegant-appearing man who wore a long tan-colored overcoat with a darker fur collar and upon his head a black tricorn with a yellow band. He carried his belongings for this trip in a leather bag that was obviously well-sewn and expensive.

In his sturdy calf's-skin boots he made his way out of the bustling harbor area and took a room a few blocks away at what was one of the town's prime inns, named the Bancroft Arms. After a short rest in his spacious room, and then a shave and a hot bath downstairs in one of the ceramic tubs afforded for the exclusive residents, he dressed again in fresh clothing, donned the overcoat, the tricorn and the boots as well as a dashing white cravat. Then he took a knife with a hooked blade, his pair of newly sharpened snippers and a small leather drawstring pouch from his expensive bag, put them into their proper hidden pockets in his coat and left his room.

Anyone who looked closely into his face would see that he was greatly excited, for it had been too long and the pressure had steadily built. But no one looked closely enough into his face.

As the snow flew, as the citizens of Philadelphia moved about their lives around him, as horse-drawn wagons and carriages passed back and forth on the long straight streets, he stopped at a tavern called the Gray Horse to enjoy an early supper, as twilight was still some time distant. An inquiry at the Gray Horse—one man to another who worked behind the bar, as well as the change of some money—sent him southward still, walking jauntily and crisply through the snow.

He was certainly a man with a purpose.

It was a walk of some distance, as the Quaker town kept the entertainments he sought at what might be considered an area of ill winds. But it was there all the same, and there he must be. The pressure dictated so.

Southward, the town became disjointed. The houses seemed crooked in their structures, and even the pallid sky and the falling snow seemed stained. As he reached a district of close-shouldered hovels, slanted roofs, broken windows and figures either huddled around open fires or slinking back and forth from alley to alley, the sun had begun to slide toward dusk.

Though the pressure was intense, he decided to have another drink, and in the murky confines of the Mossy Oak he enjoyed a cup of cider and watching for a while a game of dice. He was tempted to join in, as he liked his games and was usually lucky at them, but twilight was coming on and he had a long walk back to the Bancroft Arms and a second hot bath to wash all this filth off.

Another inquiry from the barkeep and another exchange of a few coins sent him toward the southwest, where the hovels stood raw and mottled with darkness. He began to see both women and men—those, he presumed, who had checkered histories as indentured servants or otherwise downward turns of fortune—dawdling about. Some whistled at him and motioned for his further attentions. He kept going, as the snow fell on his tricorn and his shoulders and crunched beneath his boots.

The pressure. Terrible now. But soon it would be gone.

A block further to the southwest, nearer the very edge of the town, and there he saw a slender figure in what could only be termed a ragged gray coat and an equally sad woolen cap. He approached, in the deepening twilight, and saw when she looked at him that she was not unattractive, though her face was pocked and one eyebrow was cut through with a scar that curved up into her hairline. She was perhaps fourteen years of age.

Perfect.

"I have money," he told her.

She looked at him blankly, her senses dulled by whatever she used to dull them.

"The alley there," he said, and he gave her his best smile. "Come along, I'll get you warm."

She followed him into the alley he had motioned toward. He stopped to let her pass. "Go on," he said softly. "To the end of the alley. The wind there will be less." His right hand went to a pocket but it wasn't time yet. Best while he had her to let her do her business.

She started on, dumbly.

"Run along, dearie," someone said.

Startled by the voice, both the man and the girl looked toward the alley's mouth. The figure that stood there wore a dark green coat and a cocked hat the same color, but the face was hidden by both the fading light and the falling snow.

"Run *along*," the woman repeated. "This one is mine."

The girl did not run; she hobbled past Minx Cutter, and away.

Minx spoke again to Polliver. "Are you wanting a fuck?"

"Who...the *hell* are you?"

Minx came closer. Both hands were encased for warmth in a fur muff. "I'll be pleased to fuck you," she said.

"Do I know—" And then he did know her, and he gave a small short gasp that sounded like a death rattle.

"You were right," Minx said, coming nearer still. She was smiling. Snowflakes were caught in her blonde brows. "Madam Herrald is *not* a killer. But I *am*."

And before hooked blade could be brought from coat pocket Minx's right hand came out of the muff with its own hooked terror. The knife sliced across Polliver's throat in one smooth backward arc. Minx deftly retreated as the opened throat spewed crimson. In an instant the doctor's cravat had turned black with it.

The pressure released itself within Billy Shears with a cry of anguish and a spray of piss into the expensive well-tailored breeches.

He staggered back, looking for someplace to run even as his world began to turn a darker red. His legs carried him into a wall. Twisting about, he ran into another wall. His hands came up and grasped at the dirty bricks, but they failed to hold him.

He fell to his knees. Minx wiped her blade on his left shoulder, her face as cold as the coming night.

Then he toppled forward, twitched a few times, and died in the snow-clad dirt.

Minx waited a moment, until she was sure the candle was snuffed. Then she turned the body over on its back. It paid to have connections in the offices where the packet boats signed up their customers. It paid to have someone watching the ledger for the name Quail Polliver, no matter how long it took. It paid also to board the boat the night before its departure, to take one's own supply of food aboard and stay secure in one's own cabin; no one would ever know you were making the trip.

Katherine Herrald didn't know, and never would. Better that way.

Avoiding the blood, Minx opened the dead man's coat and found the blade, the snippers and the drawstring pouch in which he'd obviously meant to carry his gory treasures for further amusement. These she left where they were. From her own coat she withdrew a roll of parchment paper tied with a red ribbon. On the paper she had written in large letters I WAS BILLY SHEARS.

She'd been keeping it since late November.

She tucked the declaration into his coat. Someone might come along and rob the corpse—likely would—but it might be someone who would recognize the name and show it to an authority. After all, she was sure there were plenty of people even here who'd just recently come over from London, and had been regular readers of *Lord Puffery's Pin*.

Someone would know, and if not…then not.

Her task was done.

Case closed, she thought.

As she stood up from her business, did she see the smear of a figure standing back there where the gloom of the alley met the dimming blue of the light? Did she see the faintest glow of flame and see a swirl of smoke spin upward through the snow?

No, of course not.

In any case, he was no longer there.

But all was right. She felt it in her bones. And she knew it in her heart.

Then she turned away and left the alley on her long walk back to the center of Philadelphia, but she thought that the Mossy Oak looked like an intriguing kind of place. She'd gotten very thirsty while waiting down the street for him to come out.

So, a hot drink on a cold evening…yes, that was the thing.

Just the thing.

Right up her alley.

WANDERING MARY

DECEMBER, 1702

ONE

"Mary…Mary…Mary," moaned the man on the bed.

At once Dr. Galbraith was out of his chair and leaning over his patient. "He's coming around," the doctor said to Matthew Corbett, who stood in the room shivering with a blanket wrapped about his body, his clothes and hair still wet from the deluge that was pounding the stone walls and whipping against the stained-glass windows.

"*Matthew*," the man whispered, his eyelids fluttering as they tried to open.

Matthew came forward to Forbes Truxton's bedside. "I'm here, sir," he said. The man's eyes suddenly opened and in the lamplight the bloodshot orbs sought Matthew's face. A hand rose, trembling, to catch Matthew's shoulder.

"Did you see her?" Truxton's voice was barely audible, his heavily lined face weary and gray. "She was *there*," he said, before the young problem-solver could reply. "She wants me, Matthew. She *needs* me. *Why?* Oh… *why* didn't you let me go?"

"I'm not going to stand idly by and watch you kill yourself. It was a close call tonight."

"I *have* to go to her! Don't you understand? Oh my God, Matthew… oh Jesus…she *needs* me. We can be together…for always and ever…that's what she wants. It is the only way, Matthew. Don't you see?"

"No, sir, I do not."

Truxton's gray-haired head lifted from the damp pillow. His hand tightened on Matthew's shoulder and perhaps deep in the eyes red embers stirred. "It is the only way," he said with an obvious effort, "that she will forgive me for *killing* her."

"Forbes," said Duncan Galbraith, who was equally as wet and miserable in his soggy clothes as was Matthew. "I want you to rest now. Do you hear me? Please…try to relieve your mind of this burden." It was an impossible request and all three in the room knew it. But the master of Truxton Manor looked up at the doctor and nodded, and though the agony coursed through him like his blood and beat within like his ravaged heart he closed his eyes and sought at least a short time of peace.

"Let us go out and speak to the others," Galbraith said, but before they reached the door he paused. "Did you see anything out there?"

"I did not." Only the sweeping rain, the wind-thrashed trees and the sea smashing itself against the treacherous cliff.

"Obviously Forbes believes he did. This idea of a phantasm—a ghost— is destroying him. That Mary is beckoning him to join her in death…it's a task for a priest, not a doctor. *Nor* a problem-solver," he added, his brown eyes peering over his square-lensed spectacles. "Why they wanted to involve you in this is a mystery to me."

"They hoped I could help." *Help* in this case being a loaded word, Matthew thought.

"You *did* prevent him from going over the cliff tonight, so thanks and appreciation are in order. That other thing we did…I'll be haunted by that for the rest of my life."

"It was necessary," Matthew said, "and now you know why."

"I understand you won't go any further into that, but if there is as you believe a malignant presence here, and you are standing in its way of destroying Forbes Truxton…it may wish to destroy you first. But I certainly have never believed in ghosts, for that matter."

Matthew almost agreed that the idea of ghosts was ridiculous, but the statement hung. He was cognizant of the spectral shades that haunted the office at Number Seven Stone Street, though they never materialized and kept their presences limited to the occasional bang, rattle and half-heard mutter. But some of his experiences with the Herrald Agency had left him wondering about the realm of the unknown, and how close—and how dangerous—it was to the realm that might be termed "normal life." It was best not to dwell on those things, but here at Truxton Manor, three days coach travel north of Boston, such had been thrust into his face. He realized that because of what he knew something far worse than a ghost might soon be at his throat.

"Let's see the others," said Galbraith, and he opened the door to the hallway.

On a morning in December over a week ago, the sun shining brightly and the air unseasonably warm for the approach of hard winter, Matthew

Corbett had been at his desk in the office, dutifully scribing a report of his last case, which had been a trifle involving a wife's pearl necklace supposedly stolen by a maid from a Golden Hill residence, but had wound up being sold by her husband on the sly to appease a business debt. It amazed him how communication between people who lived in the same house—and were both in their mid-sixties—could be so lacking. Anyway, the poor gentleman had been terrified of his wife's fury and had planted false evidence to incriminate the maid. The last of that scene had been the wife after her husband with a whisk broom.

Katherine Herrald was away in England and Hudson Greathouse—the "Great One," Matthew had started calling him, with a little respect and sarcasm mixed in together—had ridden to the west on the task of seconding a young man—a fur trader by occupation—who had fallen in love with a Mohawk maiden, and she in love with him as well, and to wed the girl it was determined by the tribe's chief that a series of tests had to be undertaken by the potential groom. Thus Greathouse had been hired to accompany the young man...and mostly to make sure he wasn't killed in these tests, or at least if he *was* killed someone would get the body back to New York.

"Just as I've always thought," Greathouse had said before he left. "Love is a walk through fire."

And here was hoping both Greathouse and his client survived the flames. The Great One was still using a walking stick to get around, but he was healing from the not-so-tender ministrations done to him at the point of a knife by Tyranthus Slaughter back in the autumn. It helped also that the Indians who'd really saved Greathouse's life had given him the name of "Gray Wolf," which somehow had worked to strengthen the man's will to survive...if just to proudly beat Matthew over the head with that title every hour of the day.

For Matthew, it was all work and no play...because in the idle hours crept not only his memory of his death struggle with Slaughter and the gruesome truth of Mrs. Sutch's sausages but also the thing he would never utter to a soul lest it become more than his fevered imagination: a certain night ride taken only the week before he and Greathouse had picked up Slaughter from the Pennsylvania asylum. So bring on the missing pearl necklaces and whatever other trivial matters that might be used as a solace to a troubled brain! Not even his nightly chess games at the Trot Then Gallop had the effect of cooling off the triple horror of Slaughter, that imagined ride to the very edge of Hell, and—oh, yes, the third horror—the fact that he was now under the potentially deadly appraisal of the mysterious Professor Fell.

But Matthew was such a hero! The *Earwig* said he was in those stories Marmaduke Grigsby kept concocting, so it must be true! Matthew thought that the way he was feeling, if he ever received an Indian name it would likely be "Fears Own Shadow," for that was about the truth.

And there was the girl.

Why did she occupy his mind so much? She and her grandfather lived right next to him and in fact Marmaduke owned the little dairy house Matthew called his abode. Matthew had promised old Marmy he would look after Berry but his vow of protection had nearly come undone with the deaths of both the girl and himself at the Chapel estate. Now this attention from Professor Fell…it would not do to let himself get too close to her, and drag her into unknown depths. She did come to the dairy house from time to time, just to say hello it seemed or to invite him to supper with them (more likely Marmaduke had directed her to visit to make sure Matthew was still among the living, since he got out early in the morn and came home with the last owl) but it was best Berry spend her companionable hours in the presence of Ashton McCaggers, who definitely had taken a shine to her.

Anyway, the girl was bad luck. It seemed every time Matthew saw Berry and McCaggers together he was always breaking a bootheel or stepping into a fresh pile of horse figs, so smitten was he by her presence it caused either an errant step or a stride into a noxious mess…which Matthew surely wished to avoid.

So, let McCaggers parade Berry around town as much as he pleased, though how she could take very much of that weak-stomached town coroner and his attic full of bones he had no idea.

Still…why did she occupy his mind so much?

It was a true mystery.

He was pondering this imponderable and quilling the last of his report when he heard the door to the street open and close. Someone was coming up the stairs…not Hudson, because no stick was in use and the footfalls were too light for his weight. Matthew turned around in his chair to face his visitor.

It was a slimly built man Matthew guessed to be in his late thirties. The gent wore an expensive-looking gray suit, a light blue shirt, a darker blue cravat and a tricorn the same hue as the suit. His black boots were polished to a high gloss. He had a handsome, square-jawed face with high cheekbones and a thin-bridged nose that tilted slightly upward. Beneath trimmed blonde brows his gray eyes took in Matthew and then the rest of the office before returning to the singular presence at his desk.

"I am seeking Mr. Matthew Corbett," the gentleman said, in a quiet and well-modulated voice.

"That would be me, sir."

The gray eyes blinked. "*You?* Well, I'd read that you were a young man but I had no idea you were merely a *boy*."

How to reply to that? If the man only knew what Matthew had been through in his young life, the word *boy* would not have been tossed out so flippantly and with an air of disrespect.

"Oh," said the man, "forgive my comment." He removed his tricorn to display a head of wavy, sandy-blonde hair. "I am taken aback at your youth, and my mouth proceeded apace before my brain. I *was* prepared that you would be a young man, though, but still…"

"I am what I am," said Matthew, who in spite of his calm demeanor felt a little reddening of the cheeks and heat at the back of the neck. "You seem to know both more and less about me."

"Quite." The gentleman offered a disarming half-smile that didn't quite disarm his target. "I am Harris Truxton, and I am very pleased to meet you."

Matthew thought the man spoke the name as if he should recognize it. He did not. "How may I help you?" Matthew asked, with no smile on face or in voice.

"You have time to hear my problem, I presume?" The man's gaze went to the quill Matthew was still holding.

"I have time." He set the quill back in its holder and returned the stopper to its inkwell. "Would you like to sit down?" A motion toward one of the two chairs before his desk took the man to it, and Matthew waited for him to settle himself.

"My problem," said Harris Truxton, "is…" He paused, frowning at the floor. "Well…first of all, I've come from Boston. I arrived by packet boat yesterday afternoon, and am staying at the Dock House Inn. Would that there might be an office of the Herrald Agency in Boston, but… alas…there is not. My younger brother Niven and myself conferred on this matter with our family physician, and therefore I have come the distance to ask your aid."

"From Boston," Matthew said; a repeat of his statement and not a question, but the question did follow: "How did my name get your attention in Boston?"

"Your town's newssheet. The *Earwig*. A copy describing your recent experience in a certain criminal matter found its way to a table at my social club. Again, I was prepared to meet a young man, but I have to say…you don't exactly appear to be the gallant hero the writer sets forth. I mean…" Truxton drew a long breath and let it slowly out. "You know, I feel I'm making a hash of this. Perhaps I should go back down to the street and come up again, if you'll still be gracious enough to hear me out and forget the prattling of a fool." He started to get out of his chair.

"You can stay where you are," said Matthew, with a shrug. "No harm intended and no harm done. I can tell you that what you read was quite embellished by the writer, but there is truth in the tale." And here Matthew had a thought that daggered him: could this obviously well-off, well-spoken and well-educated gentleman be an emissary sent from Professor Fell? Or… even worse…the professor himself? If so, Matthew's sword was locked away in a cabinet and the man could kill him at his pleasure.

"You shouldn't believe everything you read," Matthew added, and damned if his voice didn't have a quaver in it.

"I don't, but what I read was strong enough—and convincing enough—that I took the chance you would be available to help." Truxton's mouth became a grim line. "There are three possibilities in what I am going to tell you, sir. One: my elder brother Forbes is going insane from guilt. Two: someone is fiendishly *directing* his descent into madness. And three: what he sees is a reality."

"What exactly does he see?"

"The ghost," said Truxton, "of his deceased wife Mary, who appears to him in an attempt to lure him to the seaside cliffs where she met her death in September. According to Forbes, the spirit wishes him to throw himself off the cliffs onto the rocks below, thus reuniting them in the afterlife." Truxton's chin lifted. "Do you think you can help me—and I mean to say, help our family—with this problem?"

It was Matthew's turn to blink.

Truxton was waiting for an answer. When it didn't come, the man went on: "Of course…belief in ghosts is ridiculous, isn't it? I certainly do not, and neither does anyone else in the family. But the problem exists. Forbes desires to kill himself to join his lost Mary, and I am determined to see that my brother remains among the living."

Matthew shifted in his chair. If ever there was a time for the two spectral battlers who haunted the office to make themselves known, this was it. But they stayed quiet, and Matthew had the feeling they were listening to a conversation they found of great interest.

"*You* don't believe in ghosts, do you, sir?" Truxton prodded.

Matthew thought a solid *no* would bring a rattle and moan out from the nearest wall. He said, "The important thing is that your brother seems to. If I'm to help in any way, I should know the particulars. Would you begin at the beginning?"

"Yes. I *am* getting ahead of myself, aren't I? Well…it did not begin with Mary's death. I should tell you that our father lost our mother some years ago when she was run down by a coach and team in London. She was shopping for his fifty-seventh birthday. This incident unsettled his mind, just as the death of Mary has unsettled my brother's mind. The accident that took our mother was particularly harsh on all of us...because the vehicle was built by the Truxton Coach Company." Truxton paused to let that sink in. "Starting with our grandfather, our family has been preeminent in the coach and carriage construction business. It's likely that whenever you look out a window here and see such a conveyance, it will have the Truxton family seal on the vanguard. The same is true of Boston, which is now home to our business office in the colonies, and I must tell you that our business has never been better or shown a swifter profit. The coach routes are in their infancy here, as you must know. In the future we intend to have a Truxton vehicle on every route, and in time we hope to create our own carrier service."

"Commendable," said Matthew, who realized the man sitting before him was—as Hudson Greathouse would have probably put it—up to his ass in money. "And the tale of your mother's accident is a sorry misfortune but what does that have to do with your brother and this supposed ghost?"

"I am explaining that our father could not have created a better atmosphere for a haunting. Last year he went completely mad and killed himself in the house he built north of Boston. I call it a house...others call it a horror. Do you mind?" Truxton had brought a filigreed silver snuffbox from within his coat. Matthew shook his head. Truxton took a pinch up each nostril and dabbed at his nose with a blue handkerchief before he proceeded. "Our father—Whitton by name—was so disconsolate over the death of his wife and our mother that he uprooted himself from England and came here, searching for a place to...well, it turned out to be a tomb where his solitary grieving drove him to hang himself from an inner balcony. Forbes and I took control of the business when our father left England, and Niven was away studying music in Vienna. We knew Father was having a house constructed—at great expense, I should add—and from what we later learned it was as far away from people as he could get."

"Let me ask," Matthew interjected. "Your father thought himself responsible for her death? It was an accident, wasn't it?"

"Yes, a tragic accident but the fact that it was a Truxton-built coach worked on Father's mind. We knew also that our grandfather Percival, who founded the company, ended his life in a hospital raving and raging against invisible demons. Forbes and I decided to do some research on our family beyond Percival on our father's side and uncovered the rather disturbing reality that madness was a recurring...shall we call it, as you mentioned earlier...'sorry misfortune' in the Truxton lineage. We found incidents of insanity, suicide—and murder, as well—going back several generations. It would be termed, I suppose, 'in the blood'."

Matthew nodded. His next question had to be asked though it was uncertain how his visitor might react. "You and your younger brother show no signs of this mental condition?"

Truxton gave a half-smile. "If we had it, would we *know* we did? But I understand your query. Who can say what the future holds? For now, though, Niven and I simply want to help Forbes through this ordeal."

"All right," Matthew replied, reasoning that line of thought was best left where it lay. "Tell me about Mary. How did she die?"

"Another unfortunate accident. Forbes met Mary Ames at an equestrian event in England. She owned a horse in the show, and she was quite a skilled rider as well. They had been married almost two years when they came to join Niven and myself. My younger brother and I had made the voyage six months earlier to open the business office in Boston and buy residences in the town. Forbes and Mary were still looking for a suitable house. It was decided that Forbes would sell Truxton Manor—or at least make an attempt—and therefore he and Mary went up to spend some time there getting everything in order and dismissing the staff who had remained after Father's death. Did I say that Mary was a skilled rider? She was also very physically active, and was fifteen years junior to my elder brother. She enjoyed the outdoors and walking the countryside. The manor is set atop a cliff overlooking the sea. The height there is about sixty feet...not a straight drop, but quite a fall."

Truxton paused, his expression darkening. "One late afternoon Forbes and Mary were walking along the cliff's edge. He told me when they started out the sky was gray and cloudy but the wind was soft. He said that very suddenly the wind picked up and rain began pelting down. I can tell you from my experience visiting there that the weather can be very chancy. A storm may blow up at any second. It seems that very quickly the rain began slamming down. Forbes took Mary's hand and they started to run back to the house. He said he felt her wet hand slip out of his, and when he turned he realized a weak portion of the earth there had collapsed under Mary's shoes. She tumbled down amid the rocks but Forbes said she was holding on with the waves crashing below her. She called for help, he said, and as he started to climb down to her she began trying to pull herself up. He shouted for her to remain where she was, that the rocks were slippery and that he would make his way down to her...and they were looking at each other at a distance of what Forbes said was perhaps twenty feet when she lost her grip and fell. He saw her go into the water, saw her body be tossed against the rocks...and then she was gone."

"Oh my God!" said Matthew. "That's horrible!"

"Yes. And when the body—the corpse—washed up and was found by some fishermen over a month later...I can tell you, the sea, the rocks and the vicious creatures in those waters had...well, I leave that description to your imagination, though it defies imagining. Our family doctor from Boston was present in attendance to Forbes, and he blanched at the sight.

It was so bad Niven and I couldn't let Forbes see what was left. The local minister prayed over her, we had a small ceremony, Mary was laid into a coffin and Forbes had her interred in the vault."

"The *vault?*" Matthew asked.

"Oh...I didn't tell you," Truxton said. "Our father in his madness opened up the family's vault on the grounds of the estate outside London and had all the coffins shipped over to the manor. Our relatives now rest within walled chambers in the manor's lower region."

Ghastly, Matthew thought but he didn't speak it. A madman contemplating suicide and wishing perhaps to be met on the other side by his ancestors, themselves mentally deranged. "Fishermen found the body, you say," Matthew ventured. "I thought your father built the manor as far from people as possible."

"He did. During the construction there were only a few fishermen's shacks a mile or so down the coast. That locale over the years has grown into a small village called Brown's Harbor, the church of which supplied Minister Bartholomew for the funeral ceremony."

"A terrible story," said Matthew, "but I'm still not understanding exactly what I might do to help."

Truxton utilized the snuffbox and took two more pinches before he responded. Then he leveled a hard gaze at the *Earwig's* hero. "I want you to determine if Forbes is really losing his mind, or if someone is playing the part of Mary's ghost to drive him to suicide. My brother swears Mary has come into his bedroom five times and whispered to him in the night. He swears that in her last visit she has asked him to go to the cliff and join her in the eternal embrace of death. Does that answer your question?"

This was spoken so forcefully it took Matthew a few seconds to formulate his next query. "Who else is in the house?"

"My wife Simone, my brother Niven and his bride-to-be Zoya, the butler Chetley Wicks and his wife Marion who is also the housekeeper, and Dr. Duncan Galbraith. On the grounds in their own cottage is the gardener Eli Baines and his wife Ruth, who serves as the cook. In the coachhouse next to the stable lives our coachman and stable-master Caleb Clegg and his wife Leah."

"Zoya?" That name in particular had piqued Matthew's curiosity.

"She was born in the Empire of Moscovia."

"Russia," said Matthew.

"You are well-educated."

"Well-read," Matthew corrected.

"Niven met Zoya when they were studying the harpsichord at the conservatory in Vienna. Her parents left Russia and live in Colchester. Their wedding has been postponed until this situation is resolved."

"Has any one of the others seen this so-called ghost?"

"No. The delusion is my brother's alone, if it *is* a delusion."

"And if not a delusion, you suspect whom? One of the women for impersonating Mary? Surely not your own wife! And Zoya? The Russian accent would be difficult to disguise. And why would anyone in the family wish your brother dead?"

"Questions," said Truxton, "that cannot be answered in this office. I am ready to pay twenty-five pounds to you on the moment, with an additional fifty pounds to hear your thoughts on the matter after you have spoken to everyone on the estate. All your expenses will be paid, and the sum presented to you whether you have come to a clear conclusion or not." The man's brow furrowed and his eyes took on a faraway look. "This may be a situation that turns out after all to be beyond human understanding. But... Mr. Corbett...I *must* do what I can to keep Forbes from killing himself. He has taken to wanting to walk out to the cliff at night. Galbraith is giving him sleeping potions to calm him and keep him in his bed." Truxton's gaze sharpened again. "Will you aid me in this, or has my trip been for nothing?"

What could Matthew say? What would Greathouse or Mrs. Herrald have said?

It was the only thing *to* say: "I will."

"Thank God!" The man shivered as if shrugging off a heavy burden. He seemed so overcome with relief that for a moment he could not speak. Then: "I shall book us passage on tomorrow morning's packet boat voyage. I believe it sets sail at six o'clock. From Boston it is a three days' journey by coach, so we'll be stopping at inns along the way. Does that schedule suit you?"

"Of course."

Truxton stood up and returned the tricorn to his head. "I'll leave you to ready yourself. I thank you again, sir. God knows I thank you, and by the grace of Christ we might get to the bottom of this. Until the morning, then."

Matthew also stood up and the two men shook hands on the agreement.

Before Truxton left the office he said quietly, "You know...being wealthy does not insulate a man from the pressures of the mind. I think the family's riches have not helped our history, and I swear...looking back on what has gone before, I'm not sure we wouldn't have been better off as rustics making wheels for the carriages of other men. I thank you for your time and your interest. Good day."

Truxton left the office and Matthew listened to the man's bootsteps descending to the street.

It was only then that the enormity of what he had agreed to hit him. Either pronouncing a man insane, hunting a ghost or finding out who was playing at a ghost? Now he felt on his shoulders the burden that Harris Truxton had just shrugged off.

And to emphasize the point, when Matthew heard the door downstairs close behind his visitor's back, one of those damned spirits in the office gave out from a corner a half-heard, mostly muffled chuckle.

"Oh, shut up!" said Matthew from the side of his mouth, for a celebrated hero such as himself should not be afeared of a little eavesdropping specter.

TWO

IN MID-AFTERNOON OF THE FIFTH DAY THEY WERE ON THE LAST LEG OF the journey. "Another three hours," said Harris Truxton as he regarded his silver pocket watch. "We shall reach the manor sometime around six."

Matthew nodded. No matter how padded and comfortable were the sumptuous red leather seats of the coach, it had been a long and wearying trip along roads that were at best dirt tracks hacked out of a forest impenetrable to right and left. His tail end had shown him mercy by going to numbed sleep long ago, but his own sleep was fitful even though, as Truxton had told him, this family coach was the top of the line and its leaf springs were the best the company could manufacture. Still, the pitching and rocking was an assault on anyone attempting sleep, though Matthew noted Truxton managed it well enough. Perhaps Truxton's habit of snuff taking—always a pinch up each nostril followed by a dab of the handkerchief—was a soporific to him, and if that was so Matthew was tempted to try the stuff himself.

The voyage of the packet boat *Industrious* from New York town to Boston had taken two days. Truxton had secured for Matthew a very comfortable stateroom with fine linens on the bunk, a far cry from the crew's hammock quarters he and Greathouse had been stuffed into on that odious trip to Philadelphia with the Four Lamplighters in August. Upon debarking at Boston harbor, they were met by the gangly and long-limbed Caleb Clegg, their bags put into the baggage compartment of the black-and-red-trimmed four-horse coach and the road journey begun. They had stopped for each night of the trip at an inn along the way, the proprietors of which knew both Truxton and his driver well for the many visits they'd made in the past.

Matthew had rolled up his window blind to watch the forest go by on his side of the coach. The day was sunny and again cool but not seasonable for the month. A few clouds moved slowly across the sky. He was thinking again about the girl…not Mary Truxton, whom he should be considering, but Berry Grigsby.

She had come to his door the evening before his departure and invited him to supper the following night. Was she wearing a nice perfume? She did have a pleasant aroma. Her coppery red curls fell about her shoulders and her blue eyes sparkled in the lantern she held.

"We'll be having pork stew and green beans, corn muffins and apple pie," she'd said. "Please come over around six o'clock."

"I have to regret," Matthew had answered. "I'll be out of town for a few days."

"Oh. Can I ask…is it a case you're working on?"

"Yes, and I think a very interesting one."

"But not dangerous," she'd advanced. And then: "Is it?"

"Not dangerous, no."

"There are no murderous hawks and young or older killers involved?"

Matthew had had to smile at that one. "None, as far as I know."

"Well…please consider having supper with us when you get back. When *will* you get back?"

"It's a trip up to Boston and a few days beyond, so I'm not exactly sure."

She'd nodded. "All right, then. Marmy, Ashton and I will miss you tomorrow night."

Something seemed to have gotten caught in Matthew's throat, but he managed to speak: "Ashton will be there?"

"Oh, yes. You know, he's such a fascinating guest."

Matthew made a noise. Whether it was of assent or not, he didn't know. Ashton McCaggers a fascinating guest? If one desired a supper conversation about old skeletons and things best consigned to the darkest corners of the coroner's attic, then Matthew supposed he was the grandest supper guest in the entire town. He cleared his throat to rid himself of all possible obstructions. "I'm sure all will enjoy the company."

Berry had stood there silently, perhaps expecting more than this rather curt comment, until finally she said, "I'll leave you to ready yourself for your trip, then."

"Thank you. Regards to your grandfather." And he had watched her walk away from his door to her house until the lantern's light was gone.

"Musing?" Truxton inquired, bringing Matthew back to the rock-and-rolling moment.

"Pardon my absence."

"No matter. I should think this situation weighs heavily on the minds of all involved."

Here Matthew made a decision. It had seemed to him over the last few days that Harris Truxton was holding something back. Why did he think this? He wasn't sure, but perhaps it was in the man's expression or some shade of the voice. Therefore he decided upon verbal action before they reached the manor. "Harris," he said, for both had begun addressing each other less formally, "are you telling me everything I should know?"

"I believe I am."

"Search yourself," Matthew persisted. "If I'm to help in any way, I should know everything…and I simply have a feeling that at this point I don't."

Truxton peered out his window for a moment. Then he returned his gaze to his travelling companion. "I should've realized how perceptive you are. Forgive me for my lapse."

"Forgiven. But let's hear what you've omitted."

"Ah." Again Truxton was silent for a time, obviously gathering his thoughts. "Forbes is forty-eight years old," he began. "Mary was thirty-three. You might wonder about Mary's history. She had never been married before. Her life had been spent in building a business in horse breeding, and she was certainly the most independent woman I have ever met. As I've said, a strong woman both physically and mentally and also a very lovely woman. Forbes likewise had never been married. But I knew from Forbes that he thought his time to sire a child who eventually might be an heir to the business was growing shorter. Therefore one element of his attraction to Mary Ames was the desire for childbirth. She did become with child—a joyous occasion—before they left England for the colonies. Then…she miscarried in her fourth month. It happened in Boston, a week before she and Forbes went to the manor. Both Forbes and Dr. Galbraith advised her against travelling for a while longer, and you can attest that this is a tiring trip. But she was adamant that she was able enough to ride up, and Forbes gave his approval."

When Truxton paused Matthew asked, "You're saying that Mary's miscarriage caused her to be weakened? And that was an additional factor in her fall?"

"That, possibly…and another thing. This…I don't know exactly how to put, but…well, I shall have to speak it because I did omit a pertinent… if not *fact*, then observation. Forbes was the happiest Niven and I had ever seen him in anticipation of the child. In the days after Mary's miscarriage… he fell into a dark mood. It was terrible. He didn't weep, scream or rage, because Forbes keeps everything trapped inside…but he was so looking forward to the potential of having an heir…it put him on his knees. She was more settled about it, saying they surely could try again, but this didn't help Forbes's mood. Dark, Matthew. Darker than dark. We all tried to cheer him, God knows we did, but…I think going to the manor was the worst possible place Forbes could've gone with that event haunting him. I fear that…being in the place where Father killed himself, and all the darkness in that house…might have…" Truxton stopped speaking and shook his head, unwilling to venture any further.

"Might have *what?*" Matthew said.

Truxton's eyes were clouded when he answered. "Might have brought forth the first tendrils of insanity in my brother…and he is not telling the truth when he says he tried to save Mary from falling to her death. That he stood by without attempting to help, because deep inside he was enraged over the miscarriage. I hate to think that in a way he murdered Mary, and this is where his great grief and delusion comes from."

Matthew was silent because he suspected there was even more to be revealed.

"You don't understand the power of *hate*, Matthew," was the next quietly spoken statement. "Of jealousy, and wishing to forever remain among the living. That kind of ill-fated resolve can crush a child. *I know*. Whitton was not only insane, but he hated his sons because he realized they—*we*—represented an end to his domain. The brow beatings we took…the abuse… being shamed as stupid, unfit to carry the Truxton name…every horrid thing you can think of, we endured. Our mother also endured much, which likely added to Whitton's guilt. And then there was Percival, who dished out upon Whitton the same hatred and jealousy of life that our father later regurgitated upon us. So…Simone and I have spoken of birthing a child, but in truth I dread the idea of bringing an innocent onto this earth that in my own future insanity I might treat with such contempt as my brothers and I survived." He winced at that word. "*Survived*," he repeated, and he looked imploringly at the New York problem-solver. "Have we?"

"You're among the living," said Matthew.

And Truxton's response with a crooked smile: "Are we?"

Matthew settled back against his seat and Truxton directed his attention to the forest passing by his window. It seemed to Matthew that he might be in over his head regarding this situation, and where was Greathouse when he needed him? But then again the Great One wouldn't have been much help here because it was a matter of brains, not brawn. Therefore Matthew realized he was in it a pence for a pound and he would have to see this thing through to its end. Him responsible for either unmasking a "ghost" or judging a man insane? The heritage of this family was gloom itself, no matter how beautiful and sturdy were the coaches they made; the wheels had come off long before Mary Truxton's death, and really, long before her birth.

The evening came in shades of December blue, the forest darkening to black. From his window Matthew saw they were passing through a small settlement which must be Brown's Harbor. He could smell woodsmoke from chimneys and the salty Atlantic, the sea being not far to the east.

There wasn't much to the village, just a few log and stone cabins with lantern light showing from windows. He did catch sight of a trading post sign, and then the coach had swept through, the forest had closed in again and the horses were climbing a rather steep hill. Up to the top of the cliffs, Matthew thought. He pressed his forehead against the glass in an effort to see the manor as they approached, and in another moment he wished he had restrained his curiosity.

The thing was a huge dark blotch against the star-specked sky. Around it reached upward the bare branches of large trees sculpted into tortured shapes by the sea wind. His impression was of tall, straight walls, high peaked roofs, a chimney, more straight walls, more roofs, another chimney and the same again. A castle, he thought...no...a church. No...neither castle nor church though the structure had elements of both.

It was a fortress.

He saw lamplight through yellow-and-blue stained-glass windows. Up higher a red circular window bled light upon the bare treetops. A stone tower rose toward the stars...a belltower, perhaps? The dunce-cap roofs stood high above the treetops. Matthew caught sight of balconies that would give a panoramic view of the Atlantic. He noted the drive was well-tended with white gravel and curved between trimmed hedges to the manor's front steps. There were several t-shaped wooden posts spaced apart with two illuminated oil lanterns hanging from each, yet the illumination did not help: the place still had an air of grim solemnity. The dark stones of the walls glistened with moisture cast up by the waves and carried in by the wind. He was put in mind of the dampness accrued by the walls of a mausoleum.

Castle...church...fortress...

...tomb.

The coach pulled to a halt at the foot of the steps leading up to a square door of weathered oak.

"Well," said Harris Truxton, and in the presence of this death-stained manor even the simple word sounded forbidding to Matthew's ears. "We have arrived."

Up top, Clegg rang the coach's bell a few times to alert those within the manor of their arrival. Matthew figured the walls were thick enough to muffle the sound of the horses' hooves. Truxton unlatched the door on his side and swung it open, put a boot on the metal step that afforded an easier descent, and got to the ground. Matthew followed suit, finding the wind that hit him in the face both damp and chill. Clegg unlocked the baggage compartment at the rear, delivering to Matthew and Truxton the two canvas bags that each traveller had brought. At that point the manor's front door opened and there stood a thin white-haired man wearing a dark suit and holding an oil lantern. "Welcome, Master Harris!" said the man, who came down the steps—albeit carefully, for Matthew saw that the gent was aged probably past sixty and the steps were damp—and made a motion to help carry the bags, but Harris waved him off with a polite, "No need, Wicks. Let me introduce you to Matthew Corbett. He'll be staying with us for a while."

"Pleased to meet you, young man. May I carry anything at all?"

"Thank you, but I have everything in hand," Matthew said, for the elderly butler did appear frail. He had a hooked nose and deep-set, dark eyes in a very wrinkled and age-spotted face, his cloud of white hair set far back on his scalp.

"A pleasant trip, Caleb," Harris said to the coachman who was climbing back up on his seat to guide the team toward wherever they rested for the night. "I don't think we'll be needing you for the next few days."

"As you wish, sir. Goodnight to you and Mr. Corbett." With that, Clegg flicked the reins and gave a whistle familiar to the horses. The coach rolled on along the drive and out of sight beyond the lanterns' glow.

"The family has finished supper," Wicks said as they ascended the steps, "but Mrs. Baines has left a pot of chicken-and-corn chowder over the fire in the kitchen for your return."

"Very kind of her. I for one am starved."

Matthew likewise was famished, but as they neared the door he was more observant of the manor than obedient to his appetite. It had to be an astonishing achievement to build this size house atop this cliff so far from Boston; in fact, the manse had to be at least twice the size of the largest mansion atop Golden Hill in New York town, if not thrice the size. The expense had to be absolutely enormous, and Matthew figured the construction must've taken—what?—a year? Two years? In his imagination he could hear the architect say *If you have the time and the money, it can be built*. But Matthew bet the output of both time and money had quadrupled during the birth of this monstrosity. Because really it was. He felt the thing's balconies and turrets towering above him like a threat, and he had the sensation of many eyes watching him from the upper levels.

The door was open. Wicks stood just within, his lantern upraised to make a circle of light upon his wizened face.

"After you," said Harris to Matthew with a motion of his hand, and the problem-solver from New York crossed the threshold into territory unknown.

THREE

Matthew's first impression was not of the enormity of the entrance chamber, but of its emptiness. Just within the door that Wicks had just closed stood a little round table that would've been at home in Matthew's dairy house, holding a three-tapered candelabra that spread meager light; strangely, there stood a sleeping cot next to the table, but otherwise there were no furnishings and the walls were bare.

"I should tell you," said Harris, his voice echoing back and forth, "that Father built an edifice but did not consider it necessary to *furnish* the place except for a few sticks in the room he called his own. Up there is the foyer balcony."

Matthew looked up in the direction Harris had motioned. He was able to barely make out in the overhanging dark a balcony with a wrought-iron railing about twenty feet overhead.

"That's where Father fixed the rope and hanged himself," Harris continued. "It was done silently and likely after midnight. Wicks found the body in the morning. Quite a shock, wasn't it?" This was directed to the servant.

"Yes sir, quite a shock."

"Clegg was immediately sent to fetch me," Harris said. "Being of a certain age, Wicks could not pull the body up from its position. He called the gardener, Baines, who found it best to use a saw to cut through the rope. The corpse fell about where you're standing. You might still see a bit of blood between the stones, but Mrs. Wicks has done an admirable job of cleaning up the mess. Shall we get ourselves some of Mrs. Baines' fine chowder? Afterward I'll show you to your room and you can meet the others if they're not already under their covers. There are fireplaces but the manor always holds a chill."

"I presume there are at least beds in the rooms?" Matthew asked.

"Straw-mattressed cots. And those I had sent up on the market boat when it came back from Boston."

"The market boat?"

"What the fishermen use to carry their catch to market after they've salted the fish. Mackerel and tuna, most of it is. Come this way, you can leave your bags at the foot of the main staircase."

Matthew might have been following Truxton and Wicks through a tunnel instead of a manor's corridor. They came to a wide staircase that Matthew noted had no banisters. At the foot of the stairs was a second small table bearing another three-tapered candelabra, which Truxton took in hand after he'd set his own bags aside. Matthew put his down and followed the pair deeper into the house.

The kitchen seemed to be at the far side of this human-constructed cavern. It contained a large stone hearth that displayed a pot on a grill set over a bed of embers, an assemblage of pots and pans held on wall hooks along with various other cooking utensils, shelves of glassware, ceramic dishes, bowls and silverware, a sideboard bearing several copper tins and multi-colored bottles, and a large table with six chairs at the center of the room. Harris put his candelabra on the table and Wicks went about gathering up the necessary silverware as the two men took their seats.

"So," Harris said as Wicks used a ladle to scoop up chowder from the heated pot into two bowls, "has Wandering Mary appeared since I've been away?"

Wicks did not reply until he'd set both bowls before the gentlemen. "Master Harris," he said, his face impassive, "I realize Mrs. Wicks and I are soon to be discharged, but I would express this opinion whether we had one day left or one year: it is not *proper* for you to make light of a tragic situation. Your brother remains in agony, and you know how the staff felt about Mistress Mary…she was a kind and wonderful lady. Her memory should not be tainted with such a description."

Harris responded with a crooked grin. "I stand admonished! Hear the man, Matthew! We mustn't make light of any ghosts haunting the halls of Truxton Manor, because the spirit is of a kind and wonderful lady! Anyway, I'm just repeating what they call her in the village…thanks to Niven!"

"How is that?" Matthew asked, his spoon poised over what looked like a truly rich and delicious meal.

"Oh, he got in his cups down at the Red Claw and started prattling about our situation up here. He thinks he remembers calling her a 'wandering spirit.' You can imagine what those rustics down there think of us, and now for Niven to be going on about a *ghost* in the manor! It was bad enough that Father hanged himself! For weeks after that the locals reported seeing a 'luminous' figure with a rope around its neck staggering through the village after midnight. Isn't that right, Wicks?"

"Imagination knows no bounds, sir. Also I understand that the ale at the Red Claw is extraordinarily potent."

"The Red Claw," Matthew repeated after he'd had a taste of the really excellent chicken-and-corn chowder. "A strange name for a tavern."

"It suits the place," Harris said. "Have you ever seen a lobster?"

"I've read of them but have never seen one. I understand that when they come up in the nets of the New York fishermen they're quickly thrown back."

"And rightly so! Those things are the cockroaches of the sea! You couldn't pay a starving man in Boston to eat one! And here when they come up in the nets the rustics think of them as a *delicacy!* Also the same for those despicable crabs they catch at night in the cove. Well, the widow Keller who owns the tavern has a specialty—excuse my errant use of that word—of baking lobster and crab meat into pies. So popular down there that she changed the name of the tavern from Keller's Katch to what it is now, and they can have the place! But they do serve some good local-brewed ale, and you can ask Niven about that. Wicks, do we have anything to drink?"

The butler was already pouring liquid from a green pitcher into two glasses. "Lemon water, sir," he said as he brought the glasses to the table.

"I'd rather have something stronger but this'll have to do," said Harris. "Tomorrow we might walk the mile down to the tavern and get us a real drink. Wicks, is anyone else still up and about at this scandalously late hour?" It was spoken in sarcasm, since the time was just approaching seven o'clock yet the atmosphere of the manor seemed to Matthew to be long past midnight...or perhaps it was perpetually this way here.

"I am up and about, and thank you for asking."

The man who had made this statement walked through the open door-way with an oil lamp in hand. He was of medium height and build and Matthew's first quick impression was that the gent was around fifty years of age. He wore an expensive-looking and well-cut gray suit with a pale blue shirt and a darker blue cravat. His eyes behind square-lensed spectacles were dark brown and to Matthew's opinion keenly intelligent. His hair was likewise dark brown, streaked with gray at the temples and a finger's length of gray at the forehead, his hair also pulled back into a queue and secured with a dark blue ribbon to match his cravat.

"Ah," said the man, his gaze fixing on Matthew and becoming some-what stony. "You're the hero from New York."

"I *am* from New York, but I think my reputation has been a bit over-cooked. Matthew Corbett, at your service." Matthew stood up and held out a hand in greeting.

The man looked at it.

The moment stretched.

Then: "I don't shake hands. Do you realize how many diseases are spread in that fashion? I have no idea where you've been or what you've been touching."

Matthew's hand fell to his side and the smile he'd brought up also fell.

"Meet Dr. Duncan Galbraith," Harris said, "who might have question-able manners but is unquestionably a proficient medicalist...though he has strange ideas of the presence of so-called...what are they called, doctor?"

"Bacteria."

"Our good doctor has the belief that these denizens of the invisible world have something to do with medical disorders," said their host. "He seems to discount the age-old theories of bad blood being the culprit of all illnesses."

"I would correct you," Galbraith said with an icy air, "that bacteria are not invisible but one needs a powerful microscope to observe the protozoa." His gaze moved upon Matthew. "Are you familiar with the research of the Dutch scientist Anton van Leeuwenhoek?"

"I'm afraid I'm not."

"Few at this point are, but in 1676 he took scrapings from his teeth and upon examining them under a microscope of his own design discovered the lifeforms he called 'animalcules'…bacteria as they are now referred to by the educated scientist. I believe in time it will be found that these lifeforms have a profound influence on the health—and the decay—of the human body. I am presenting a paper on the subject to the medical society in Boston next month."

"I think all this proves that Leeuwenhoek should've cleaned his teeth better," Harris said. He took a drink of his lemon water, and the shine of his eyes told Matthew he was not done darting the doctor. "Denizens of the invisible world," he repeated. "Much like ghosts, don't you think?"

"I'm not fencing with you this evening." Galbraith walked past Wicks, took another glass down from its shelf and poured himself a drink. "Young man," he said, turning his attention again to Matthew, "why are you here?"

"I am—"

"No need to explain yourself," Harris interrupted. "Duncan, I've already told you why I was going to bring Corbett into this. We need the insights and opinions of someone not involved with the family." He turned toward the butler. "Wicks, you didn't answer my question. Has Forbes had any further…*experiences?*"

"No sir, he has not. At least none that he's confided in with myself."

Matthew thought it was time to interject his own statement. "I'd like to see Forbes, if that's possible."

"It isn't," the doctor replied. "I just administered his sleeping potion and hopefully he will rest—undisturbed—through the night."

"May I ask what potion you're giving him?" Matthew persisted.

This brought a cold-eyed glare from behind the spectacles. "Oh, now you're an expert on chemistry?"

"Since I'm here, please allow me to do my job."

Galbraith gave a disdainful *whuff.* His eyes narrowed. "I see you have quite the scar across your forehead. Did you sustain that playing at slingshots with the other children?"

Matthew felt his cheeks redden. He decided he'd had enough of this haughty attitude. When he spoke, it was calmly, though his innards wished him to flail out in anger. "I received the scar from a bear's claw when I suffered an attack down in the Florida country. I might have died but an Indian tribe nursed me back to life."

Galbraith wasn't satisfied. "What the hell were you doing in the Florida country?"

"I was helping a young woman accused of witchcraft escape her tormentors and her impending execution. The resolution was that she was innocent, and was being blamed for murder and so-called witchcraft due to the actions of an insidious villain I shan't care to waste any more explanation on. Oh…and I killed the bear with a blade. Anything else you wish to know?"

The doctor was silent, but Harris spoke up: "What's your boot size?"

Wicks cleared his throat and diplomatically turned away, while Matthew saw that Harris wore a sly grin. Galbraith's face remained formed of solid stone.

"I presume," Matthew went on, "that you're administering a potion only? And no bloodletting? I've had a bad experience with a friend who passed away from too much of the red treatment."

"No bloodletting," said Galbraith after another moment's deliberation, "but I do believe Forbes may be in need of balancing the humors if this condition continues. As for the potion, it is of my own concoction: chamomile, lime juice, opium, and mercury." He regarded Harris. "And I should tell you that Simone has been asking for you since long before supper. She's been in bed all day and complains of renewed pain in her joints. I have been giving her the sleeping potion as you directed with additional opium."

"My wife," Harris said to Matthew with a grave expression, "is of a… how shall I put it…sickly countenance. It's gotten worse since we've been here." To the doctor again: "Is she awake now?"

"She may be, but if so she's right on the edge. You should go up."

"Of course. Wicks, please show Matthew to his room. I expect it's been prepared?"

"Yes sir, the fire has already been laid and lighted and a blanket put on the cot."

"Good. Oh…Matthew, Father did bring his collection of books here, and you might wish to see if there's anything that interests you. Show him the bookroom, Wicks. Now excuse me, please. Until tomorrow, Matthew… and again, thank you for being here." With that, Harris stood up from his chair, took the candelabra and hurried out of the kitchen.

Galbraith swirled the lemon water around in his glass and looked at Matthew over the rims of his spectacles. "Was it a very large bear?" he asked.

"Gigantic, though it did only have one eye," said Matthew.

"Lucky it didn't take your head off."

"It did try."

"Hm. Well, then...since you're here...you should visit Forbes in the morning. A citizen of New York town, are you?"

"Yes."

"I should like to see that place someday soon. I hear a beehive is less busy."

"Always buzzing, day and night," Matthew said.

"Rightly so." He finished his drink and placed the glass on the sideboard. "I will say goodnight, then. If you perceive me as being somewhat... *cranky*...I will not defend myself except to say that I value Forbes as both a patient and a friend, and what is happening in this house has been a strain on all our nerves."

"Not to be overly bold, but what in your opinion *is* happening in this house?"

"*Delusion*," was the quick response. "Forbes blames himself for Mary's death, as I'm sure Harris told you. Did he also inform you of the nature of the elder Truxton's suicide?"

"He did."

"Harris has put it in Forbes's mind that insanity has bred and continues to breed in the family. That doesn't help his brother's condition."

"And you reject this notion?"

Galbraith scowled. "*Reject* is a mild description. Certainly a person may be of a darkened demeanor. I have heard such a state referred to as 'gloom-and-doom' but I reject the notion that insanity can infect the bloodline of a family. Forbes will pull out of this, with proper treatment, rest and *time*. Also he needs to get out of this house and to a place where there is life and liveliness."

"But he won't leave because he feels he's deserting Mary?"

"Precisely. If his construction has been more morose than others, she was a light and warmth to his soul. He feels lost without her...and thus this delusion of seeing her in his room and hearing her speak to him. But...as I say...proper treatment, rest and time will pull him out of it. I trust your visit with him in the morning will be positively productive and not negatively so."

"I don't intend to cause him any more difficulties."

"I'll hold you to that. Again...goodnight to you." Galbraith took his lantern and with a brief nod to Wicks departed from the kitchen.

"Shall we go up, sir?" Wicks asked.

"After I finish this chowder." Matthew sat down again to continue eating. He decided he might as well also continue his investigation. "Wicks, what's your opinion of the situation?"

"I'm a servant, sir," came the reply. "I have no opinion."

"A servant may observe quite a bit that others don't see," Matthew said.

"If you're inquiring if either myself or my wife have seen this apparition, the answer is definitely no."

"When was the last time Forbes believed he saw her?"

"It was the night of December ninth, one week ago. Master Harris left to fetch you the next morning."

"And how did that transpire?" Matthew asked. "What I'm meaning is...did he cry out? Did he summon someone to his room? Did he tell someone in the morning? The particulars, please."

"The particulars," Wicks repeated, in a dry and reserved tone. "Well... it happened to be long past midnight and Eli—Mr. Baines, our gardener and groundskeeper—had gone out of their house to...the particulars... empty their chamberpot, which...the particulars...evidently had become filled. He saw a lantern light at the edge of the cliff where Mistress Mary had fallen, and approaching that light he made out Master Forbes in his sleeping gown. At that point Master Forbes informed Eli that Mistress Mary had come to his room once again and asked him to join her by leaping from the cliff. Any further particulars should come from either Master Forbes or Eli."

"Did the doctor administer the sleeping potion that night?"

"He did, sir, but evidently Master Forbes had gotten accustomed to the dosage. Dr. Galbraith says that sometimes happens. He has since increased its strength."

"Let me ask this," said Matthew. "If Forbes might happen to wake up from that elixir during the night, what's keeping him from leaving his room and going to the cliff?"

"You might have seen the cot at the front door. After that very alarming episode, myself or my wife, Eli or his wife have been charged with sleeping there and keeping an eye and an ear open. As for the rear entrance, my wife and I have quarters off the kitchen and to go in and out the back one must pass through our room. Master Harris feels it's for the best to be vigilant. Last night Master Niven volunteered for the task at the front door, which was kind of him because the cot is not easy on the bones and the cold does settle in that foyer. I fear it's the same type of bedding that occupies the room I'm to take you to...but then again, everyone has them but Master Forbes." Wicks paused a few seconds before saying, "The manor was not built to entertain guests."

"Why build so many rooms at all, then? Or such a huge house?"

"I'd rather not answer that, sir."

Matthew's flag of curiosity was instantly raised to its highest altitude. "If there's something you know that I should know, I'd appreciate your telling it. After all, aren't we both attempting to secure Forbes's welfare?"

"It goes beyond that, sir."

"What exactly does it go to?"

Still Wicks hesitated, but he seemed to realize that the young man's bulldog instinct had been released and was not going back to its hutch until the words were spoken. "Your inquiry to Dr. Galbraith concerning the... instability of the family. I watched Master Whitton go to decay after the death of Mistress Deborah. Master Whitton was of a morose character, as Dr. Galbraith can attest because he has been the family's doctor for many years in England. Mistress Deborah—like Mistress Mary—gave light and life to the family estate. And she gave a softer touch to the master, though I can admit I have witnessed some very trying scenes between father and sons. Please, sir...I feel I am out of my place in telling such things."

"The house," said Matthew, to help the butler's navigation through obviously rocky shoals.

"Before Master Whitton decided to build the manor," Wicks said, "he...wished to find a place apart from people, yet...to gather his family around himself. His ancestors, I mean."

"Harris told me his father brought all the coffins over to put in the vault."

"Yes. That. But...Master Whitton wanted there to be room for...their spirits to walk freely. As time went on, and Master Whitton's decay contin- ued...he began to converse with their phantasms, as if they were really pres- ent. At the end, he told myself and my Marion that these spirits—partic- ularly those of his own father, his mother, and Mistress Deborah—wished him to join them in the afterlife. So...what is happening with Master Forbes is..." Wicks hesitated, unable to complete the statement.

"Not unexpected, considering this instability in the family?" Matthew asked.

"I have said enough, sir. Too much, I think."

"I thank you for the information." Matthew thought that he might not have received such except from a servant who had obviously worked for the family for many years. "Tell me something else, please: who was here when Mary died?"

"You mean visiting? Just Master Harris and Mistress Simone."

"And who was here when Forbes reported first seeing this apparition?"

"The same. It was the end of September. The twenty-eighth, to be ex- act. As I recall, Master Forbes had returned from a business trip in Boston on the twenty-fifth, in company with Dr. Galbraith."

"Niven wasn't here?"

"No sir. He was in Boston awaiting his bride-to-be to arrive from England. She was there visiting her family. Master Harris left for a few days with Clegg to fetch them, and Dr. Galbraith stayed to tend to both Master Forbes and Mistress Simone."

"What's the trouble with Harris's wife?"

"I'm sorry, sir," came the reply. "I can go no further."

"All right." The rest of this story Matthew would have to piece together on his own. He ate the last spoonful of his chowder and stood up. "I would like to browse the bookroom, if you please."

"Certainly, sir." Wicks took up the oil lantern and Matthew followed him into the otherwise darkened expanse that stood beyond.

With his bags in hand at the top of the stairs, Matthew stood with Wicks in what seemed to be a long corridor that the lantern showed curved to the right. Again there were no furnishings and the walls were unadorned stone. A number of closed doors marked the manor's many rooms. "This way, sir," said Wicks, who led Matthew off to the left of the staircase.

"Your room," the butler offered as they were coming up on one of the doors. "You might leave your bags."

Matthew went in and found the aforementioned straw-mattressed cot pulled up close to a healthy fire in the hearth. There was a supply of firewood in a corner and a small table bearing a candle clock, a wash basin and cloth, a clay cup and a pitcher that was presumably full of water. His host had already left a lighted lantern and a tinderbox, also on the table. On the floor next to the cot was a chamberpot, along with a wooden box that was sure to contain small dried corncobs used for cleaning up. The room held a single window made of what appeared to be dark blue stained glass by the present illumination, meaning that even at high noon the chamber would have that gloomy predication of fortress...church...tomb. Well, Matthew thought, it was just the place to be sharing with one of Whitton's ancestors, and whichever one it was he hoped there would be no snoring.

Matthew put his bags down, took up his provided lamp and followed Wicks along the corridor, again to the left of the staircase. It ended in a door only fifteen feet or so from his own room, and as Wicks held the door open Matthew entered into a chamber that held a bookcase against the wall bearing thirty or so volumes but otherwise nothing else. He did note double doors leading out upon a balcony, which in warmer weather and better circumstances would be a pleasant place to read.

"If you please, I'll go downstairs now," said Wicks. "It's my turn to be on watch until two o'clock when Master Harris takes over. Breakfast is at eight o'clock and I wake the house at seven-thirty. I trust you'll have a restful night."

Not on that cot, Matthew thought, but he said, "Thank you, and goodnight."

After the butler had gone, Matthew prowled amid the books. He was ready for sleep but while he was here he might pick out a few volumes with which to entertain himself. In a few minutes he had chosen copies of *The Heptameron* by Marguerite de Navarre, Shakespeare's *Titus Andronicus* and a tome entitled *The Worth of Women: Wherein is Clearly Revealed Their Nobility and Their Superiority To Men* by Moderata Fonte, a book Matthew thought Berry Grigsby would enjoy reading and Hudson Greathouse would throw into a fire at the earliest opportunity.

Matthew tucked the books up under an arm, retrieved his lantern and left the room...to see ahead of him an illumination of some kind just around the corridor's curve. A few more steps and he stopped solid, because ahead in the hallway was the slight figure of a woman in a white gown, her back to him, and holding up a lantern as if trying to decide if the night was right for another haunting.

FOUR

IF THIS WERE TRULY A GHOST, MATTHEW THOUGHT SHE CERTAINLY had beautiful red hair that flowed down in ringlets about her shoulders. Her head turned back and forth. Listening for something? Matthew's first impulse was to drop a book to the floor, but he quickly decided it would sound like a gunshot in the quiet and hellish chaos might follow.

Instead, he simply cleared his throat.

Did she vanish like a swirl of mist? No. She spun around, her eyes wide, and after a second of hesitation she said, *"Who are you?"*

It was obvious to Matthew who this was, because Zoya the Russian bride-to-be did speak with an accent...not very heavy, but enough to be recognizable as "different" though Matthew had never heard the Slavic tongue. Before Matthew could reply, the young woman said, "Oh...you're the one from New York."

"Correct. And you are Zoya."

"Correct also. Did you hear someone in the corridor?"

"No, I just came from the bookroom."

She held her lantern toward the other end of the corridor. "I heard someone," she said. "There was a scratching at my door."

"A scratching?"

"Scratch scratch, scratch scratch." She lifted her hand in pantomime of a claw and made the proper motion up and down. "Like that, on my door just now."

"Which is your door?"

"This one." She indicated the door to the room next to Matthew's, the door being cracked open a few inches. He came forward and with his own light examined the wood for any marks, but there were none. "I don't know what it was," Zoya went on. "I don't know if even I might have dreamed it."

"Did it wake you or were you already awake?"

"I think…I'd fallen asleep. I can tell you…the dreams one has in this house are not pleasant."

"Count it as a bad dream, then." Matthew had in the space of a few seconds taken stock of the girl. She was young, probably around his own age, was small-boned and delicately featured and was—in essence—quite beautiful. She had dark brows arched over dark eyes, the tone of her skin the lovely alabaster of which poets wrote romantic verse. Her hair was a flaming red and though it was arranged in ringlets about her shoulders she wore bangs at her forehead. Her face might have been the image of a cameo formed by an equally romantic sculptor, and she had a small beauty mark just to the left of her lower lip.

Matthew was thinking how fortunate the youngest brother was when the door past Zoya's opened and someone else came into the corridor carrying a single burning candle in a pewter holder. "I heard voices," said the man as he approached, his slippered feet sliding on the stones. "What's happening?"

"Niven, this is Mr. Corbett," Zoya said. And by way of further introduction though none was needed: "Mr. Corbett, Niven my groom-to-be."

"A pleasure," said Matthew. "I would shake hands but you can see I'm loaded up with books. You *do* shake hands, don't you?"

"You've met Dr. Galbraith." This was said with a knowing half-smile.

"Oh yes."

"And survived your first meeting! He must've taken a liking to you!"

"I'm not so sure about that…the liking part, I mean. But I did survive." As he had done with Zoya, Matthew took in quick impressions of Niven Truxton. Age, not more than twenty-five. Height and build, really about the same as Zoya's…he was definitely a slightly built man. Hair wavy and maybe a shade or two darker than Harris's. His eyes were nearly the same color gray, but they were set closer together and his face was longer, ending in a pointed chin. His nose was also wider and did not have the aristocratic upward tilt of his elder brother's. There was something about Niven's mouth that Matthew could only describe as being "mushy," as if there were a permanent wetness about the lips. Matthew was left with the thought—however wrong or right it might be—that Niven was a softer sort than the forceful and energetic Harris, perhaps made so by coming in late to a life of riches and privilege. Matthew thought that either Niven had a brilliant mind in business and finance or he couldn't tell a Truxton coach wheel from an extra-large round ginger cake.

Was that a fair assessment so early? Probably not, Matthew decided, but for now it was set in stone. Maybe it had to do with the man's choice of sleeping coat, which was blue-striped flannel, had polished silver buttons all down the front and probably cost as much as the total amount Matthew was getting for this so-called investigation.

"What're you doing up?" Niven asked Zoya.

"I was telling Mr. Corbett...I heard a scratching at my door. At least...I thought I did. I may have been asleep and dreaming."

"A scratching?" Niven frowned. "That's odd."

Zoya voiced what Matthew was thinking. "A scratching upon my door at night is *odd* in a house where a *prizrak* tries to beckon a man to his death? I feared when I opened that door I might see skull-faced Death itself reaching in!"

"Miss Smith," said Niven to Matthew, "is a superstitious sort. Forgive her."

"Don't make apologies for me! And I make no apology for my beliefs!"

"Wait a moment, please." It was Matthew's turn to frown. "I thought you were *Russian*," he said to Zoya.

"I was born in Moscow, yes."

"Your surname is *Smith?*"

"Oh. My mother is Russian. My father is Geoffrey Smith. Actually, *Sir* Geoffrey Smith, as he was knighted last year. He met my mother when he was a member—the chairman, in fact—of the Parliament's Council of Commerce and Trade sent to Moscow. I also have an older brother who is currently the chairman of the cultural exchange—"

"I think Mr. Corbett doesn't need to hear the family's accolades," Niven said, putting his hand on the girl's shoulder. "He's not here for social discourse."

"I do get carried away," Zoya said with a shrug. "But why not? I am proud of my family. Do *you* have a family, Mr. Corbett?" The dark eyes in the beautiful doll-like face fixed upon him with what seemed an intense interest.

"No," Matthew answered. "No family yet."

"But I'm sure a handsome young man like yourself must have *plans*."

Matthew offered a slight smile. Was this girl advancing upon him? "Plans, possibly. But the action is far distant."

"It's probably closer than you think," Zoya said.

Did the moment hang as if time had stood still?

Matthew kept smiling. "We'll have to see about that," he said, and instantly regretted it because he feared it made him sound open to whatever this Russian girl was advancing. He felt as if his own door had received the *scratch scratch, scratch scratch* and he'd opened it to find...a mystery amid the mystery, perhaps.

"Likely a dream," Niven said to the girl, and Matthew thought the youngest brother must not have such a high intellect because all this had flown right over the future groom's head...or was it just Matthew's imaginings? "You should go back to bed."

"Yes," she agreed, "I should. Then I shall say goodnight, Mr. Corbett."

He was tempted to say *Call me Matthew* but even that seemed a tempt too far. Zoya returned to her room and closed the door.

"Getting settled in?" Niven asked. "I trust Wicks got your fire going."

"He did. I had some chowder downstairs, I have a few interesting books, and I'm ready to turn in."

"I've never been to your town. You'll have to tell me all about it."

"I'd be glad to. And I would ask: Zoya's room is next to mine, yours is next to Zoya's but what is the arrangement further along the corridor?"

"Dr. Galbraith's room is just beyond mine," said Niven. "Then there's Harris's, and at the end of the corridor is Forbes's."

"I note that the bookroom has a balcony. Does Forbes's room have one?"

"It does."

"Well," Matthew said, "it seems to me that a leap from a balcony would be just as deadly as a leap from a cliff."

"Of course. And we've thought of that. Before he left to bring you, Harris bought a padlock from the trading post in the village. Baines already had a length of chain. We've secured the balcony doors in that fashion."

"Good. All right, I look forward to meeting your brother in the morning."

"Though you've survived meeting Dr. Galbraith I hope you survive meeting my brother," Niven said, again with that half-smile. "He is not the easiest man to speak with, and in his present condition more's the worse."

"I'll take my chances."

Niven gave a little chuckle. "You've already taken a huge chance even coming to this manor. Can't you feel it?"

"Feel what?"

"The gloom of despair. The tainted atmosphere of...well, I know Harris has told you a bit of our family's history. If any house could be said to be haunted, this one must rank high on the list."

"I don't believe in ghosts," Matthew lied, but it seemed the right thing to say at the moment.

"Neither do I, but this house encourages the thought. Harris probably didn't inform you of this, but eight workmen died during the construction. Six perished when a scaffolding collapsed and two fell from the roof. This was over the course of the three-year project." Niven lifted his lantern and shone it up and down the corridor. Matthew caught places where the walls glistened with moisture. "Quite the dank monstrosity, isn't it? Spume from the waves seeps in. It can't be kept out."

Matthew wished to get to his reading and a warm fire to ward off both the chill that was taking hold in the house and the shiver of Niven's bedtime tales. "Let us hope," he said, "any spirits that may have lingered here have departed for better climates."

"Oh yes," Niven answered. "I'm quite sure our father is in Hell. Goodnight, sir."

He turned away, walked to his room and closed the door behind him.

Matthew retired to his room. He lay on the very uncomfortable cot and by the light of the fire, his lantern and the candle clock he read about halfway through *Titus Andronicus*, but he was listening for scratching on his door or anything that went bump in the night. At last he fell asleep, only to awaken an hour or so later to add wood to the fire. For some reason other than light and warmth he felt he needed a good cheerful blaze going, perhaps in hopes of keeping at bay any phantasm that might be lurking in the shadows.

And so it went, the whole night through.

"Good morning, sir! Seven-thirty!" said Wicks behind the door after the butler had delivered three raps upon the wood.

"Thank you!" Since Matthew had slept in his clothes, all he needed to do was slip his boots on. The sunlight that streamed through the blue window was murky at best. Matthew had been awaiting the eastern dawn to arrive since his last effort at loading the fire around five o'clock. He splashed water into his face from the wash basin, obeyed his morning habit of shaving with his straight razor, combed his hair, relieved himself of lemon water in the chamberpot, buttoned himself up again and he was ready to get out of this sepulcher.

He found Wicks standing at the bottom of the stairs. "I'm to escort you to breakfast, sir," said the servant. "This way, please."

Matthew was taken through the featureless corridors not to the kitchen, but to a more formal room that actually had a long polished dining table with high-backed chairs. Upon the walls were hung what appeared to be medieval tapestries. Seated at the table already and eating dishes of ham and eggs were Dr. Galbraith and Harris. Both stood up as Matthew entered, and as Wicks departed through another door Matthew took a chair across from the pair.

The doctor and Harris sat down once more. Galbraith continued eating without a word but Harris said, "I would ask if you had a restful night but it's likely you did not."

"True," was Matthew's reply. He spent a moment admiring the tapestries. "I assumed none of the rooms but the kitchen and Forbes's bedroom had any decor."

"This is the only other. Our father wanted a dining room that was more agreeable to his guests."

"Harris, don't start that so early," grumbled Galbraith.

"Matthew should know sooner or later. Ah, here's Wicks with your breakfast! Wicks, tell Matthew about the festive suppers our father enjoyed in this chamber!"

Wicks set the plate of breakfast food down before Matthew, along with silverware and a cloth napkin. He stood with his spine stiff alongside Matthew's chair, as if trying mightily to resist his master's request.

"Go ahead, Wicks," said Harris. "Tell Matthew how you served father's guests."

"Please, Master Harris." It was spoken in a quiet voice but there was a hint of steel behind it. "I don't feel it's my place to—"

"I'll tell it, then!" Niven strode into the room, and must have been standing just outside close enough to hear the request. "Father entertained his—our—ancestors here in ghostly suppers. Wicks brought them platters of food and took the food away when it was untouched." He took the chair beside Matthew. "It nearly drove Mrs. Baines to madness herself, didn't it, Wicks? In fact, I got it from Eli that they both packed up to leave several times but the old faithful butler talked them out of it. After all, if Eli left who would be here to trim the hedges and tend the greenhouse? Who would make the grounds presentable for the spirits to parade around upon?"

"If I may," said Wicks, "it wasn't every evening. It was…only a few times."

"*Once*," Harris said, "would be enough to consider a man insane. Wicks, tell me this: why did you stay with him? Coming to the colonies with him and going through the building of this ghastly tomb? *Why?*"

Wicks looked from Harris to Niven and back again. Matthew thought the stately butler was not going to speak, but then Wicks said, "I stayed, Master Harris, because after Mistress Deborah passed away I was all he had."

Silence ruled the room for a moment. Niven broke it: "I'll have my breakfast with *three* eggs, Wicks. And tell Mrs. Baines to make me a cup of hot tea. I'm still cold from the night. Off with you!" Before Wicks could reach the door, Niven said, "Oh...Zoya will be having her breakfast at nine o'clock. Make sure she's taken care of."

"Yes, sir," said the butler with a brief nod, his face impassive, and he went through the door into the kitchen.

"What's the trouble with Zoya?" Galbraith asked, his fork poised over the last ruins of his ham.

"She told me she slept very poorly. Evidently she had bad dreams. Eat your breakfast, Matthew, before it gets as cold as my bones! God knows Whitton should've at least put a fireplace in here!"

Matthew started in on his food, but he had a question for Harris. "Your wife. Isn't she joining us?"

"*My wife*," Harris repeated, and in those words was more than a shade of...exactly what? Matthew wondered. Anger? Disgust? Perhaps both. "Simone stays in bed most of the day. She complains of stomach aches, headaches, fatigue, joint pain, ringing of the ears, pain of the heart, trouble swallowing and breathing and everything else involved in being *alive*. Isn't that right, Duncan?"

Galbraith had finished his breakfast and now he laid his knife and fork across the plate. He said, "Simone Truxton is as healthy physically as you or myself. You appear healthy enough. What I mean to say is that the lady has imagined herself into a state of wreckage, and all I can do is give her a sleeping potion. Since she sleeps most of the day her nights without the remedy can be endless. Oh, I give her potions that I tell her are helpful to these physical ailments and she perks up for a short time—"

"A *very* short time," Harris interrupted.

"But soon," the doctor continued, "she is again at death's door, because it's all in her mind. I have to say, Harris, and I've told you this before but I will say it once more with emphasis: bringing her to this house is not conducive to Simone's condition, imagined or otherwise. The cold and the wet...and it's going to get colder and wetter soon, you can mark it!"

"Yes, Duncan, you're right about the house and I will get her away from here as soon as this situation clears itself...with Matthew's help, of course. I can't leave Forbes in his present condition, and neither can I leave Simone simply with the hired help in Boston."

That made sense to Matthew, but one other issue he'd thought of did not. "Let me ask," he said. "I understand there being a watch at the front door, but why not simply set up a cot outside Forbes's room and forego the other?"

"We tried that," Niven spoke up. "In fact, it was myself who incurred my brother's wrath. It's one thing to keep watch over Forbes, and quite another to rub it in his face. At least that's what he railed at me about when he left his bed to go to the bookroom and he found me outside his door. He said he would not be treated as an inmate of Bedlam in his own home. To satisfy his anger in this matter we took up the entrance watch...which, by the way, I have tonight."

His own home, Niven had said. "Doesn't the manor belong to all the family?" Matthew asked.

"It does not," said Harris after the last bite of his breakfast. "Whitton's will was specific in leaving everything to Forbes."

Matthew continued eating. Wicks brought the tea, and had included cups for everyone. After Matthew had finished his breakfast and had a drink of the hot tea, he said, "I'd like to see Forbes now. Is that possible?"

"It is," said the doctor. "I'll go up with you."

"And I as well." Harris pushed his chair back from the table.

Matthew stood up. "If you please, I'd like to speak to Forbes alone. I'd rather my first meeting with him simply be just the two of us."

Galbraith shrugged. "As you wish. I checked in on him earlier and he was still in bed, but I imagine he's up to a visit."

Harris sat down again as well. "Go ahead, then. I'd be very interested in your impressions."

"Thank you. I'll let you know how the meeting progresses."

"Good luck!" said Niven as Matthew left the room.

Upstairs, Matthew approached the door at the corridor's end. Before he knocked he noted another open doorway nearly opposite Forbes's chamber, and within it was a staircase leading up to what Matthew figured must be a tower room.

He knocked. There was no response. Knocked again, and still no answer.

Matthew eased the door open and looked into a large bedroom that was if not lavishly furnished then certainly opulent as compared to the rest of the house, with a canopied bed—empty of its owner—a standing oak wardrobe, a dark wine-colored rug upon the floor, a table bearing an unlit oil lamp, a wash basin and other small items, and two upholstered leather chairs facing the bed. Matthew saw the double doors to the balcony were set with panes of red and blue glass, and noted the chain and new brass padlock securing those doors from being opened. Wherever Forbes was, he was not in the bedroom.

Matthew withdrew, turned and decided to ascend the staircase across the hallway. He went up through relative darkness onto a higher floor of the manor, where morning sunlight was bright enough to sting the eyes through the open doors of yet another balcony. Matthew's heart gave a jump. Could it be that Forbes had likewise jumped from this balcony just in the last few moments? And why in the world were these doors not secured?

He rushed out upon the balcony into a chilly wind and looked the long way down, but there was no corpse lying broken beneath.

At this height he had a panoramic view of the grassy cliff, the tumultuous sea with waves sparkling in the sun, a swath of forest to his right, a small cove protected by a forested headland, and then perhaps a mile away the harbor town also protected by a finger of land. He could see the dock with a few resting boats and a larger sailing craft that must be the market boat along with some structures that likely included the salting facility. Far out at sea were four vessels, the local fishermen at work. Around the dock were cabins fashioned from both wood and stone, and several more cabins were nestled into the forest just west of the harbor. At the center of the village looked to be a trading post, a church, other small structures and also situated there would be the Red Claw tavern.

Matthew took note that a trail about the width of a wagon went down the hillside from the manor, winding through the forest past the cove and to the harbor. He reasoned that this had been the road where construction materials had been brought up when they arrived by ship from Boston. He was sure it had been a daunting task, but loads of money made men shoulder any burden. And it seemed to him that Whitton's desire for solitude had actually created Brown's Harbor, for likely some of the workmen who'd labored on the manor had decided for lives as fishermen and put down roots in the shadow of the edifice they'd helped to create.

But now the vitally pressing question was: where was Forbes Truxton?

And at that moment, a rasping voice behind Matthew said, "So. You're the one they sent to put me in the asylum."

FIVE

MATTHEW TURNED TO FIND A FIGURE STANDING IN THE GLOOM WELL away from the sunlight that painted the tower's floor.

"Corbett, isn't it?" the man asked.

"Yes sir. Matthew Corbett."

"Related to the Corbetts of Manchester?"

"I wouldn't know."

"A fine family. They ran a mail service and bought an entire fleet of coaches. That was...let me think...ten years ago, I believe. I understand those coaches are still running the roads."

"I have no doubt your vehicles are sturdy."

"They are. Now if the locals would just put a mind and some money to filling the enormous potholes in the roads, there's no telling how long the axles and suspensions might last, not to mention the wheels. Those are a weak point, Matthew. May I call you Matthew?"

The problem-solver nodded into the shadows.

"The wheels," Forbes Truxton continued. "A weak point. But every creation of mankind has a weak point, don't you agree?"

"I'm afraid it's true, sir."

The man came forward into the light.

He was all gray: the Truxton head of wavy hair, his flesh, his eyes, his sleeping coat. His once-handsome face looked haggard and was heavily lined, his mouth and chin sagging. Harris had said the master of the manor was forty-eight but the man standing before Matthew might well have been mistaken for ten years the elder.

Forbes passed Matthew as if either he or the young man from New York were a ghost. Matthew saw him blink and narrow his eyes against the sun. He stood next to Matthew with his hands curled around the gray stone of the balustrade, appearing to be one with the structure as a gargoyle might be carved into its setting.

"A beautiful day," said Forbes. "My Mary would be out walking by this time of the morning. You see that path to the village?" He waited for Matthew to nod. "She enjoyed walking there, back and forth. Of course... now she walks by night." His head turned and the sunken eyes gave a fixed stare. "And of course you're like the others and don't believe me."

"It's rather difficult to believe." What else could he say?

Forbes took in a deep breath and slowly released it, his attention directed again to the scene below the balcony. "Duncan told me you'd want to speak with me this morning. You came alone?"

"Yes."

"Surprising. They watch me like the proverbial hawks. So...you went to my room and found me missing, you saw the staircase and came up, you saw this balcony and you looked over expecting to see my body lying below."

"All correct."

"Did you see the lock and chain on the balcony doors in my bedroom?"

"Yes."

"A *show* of concern," Forbes said. "If I were to jump from a balcony I have many choices of the location. This one, for instance. The balcony off the bookroom. Balconies off the rooms being used by my brothers. Why should I not use one of those when everyone is down for breakfast or supper, or in the middle of the night when someone is at the front door on their cot?"

"A valid question, sir," said Matthew. "Do you have an answer?"

"It must be the cliff," Forbes replied. "That's what she wishes. The cliff. She wishes to take my hand and guide me over. It is the clean and proper way, the way of reaching the afterlife at her side. God forbid I should leap from a balcony here and wind up confined to eternity with my father harping at me. No, it can't be related to the manor. The release from this...this *agony*...must be from the cliff."

Matthew considered his next words carefully. "Why would a loving wife even on the other side wish her husband dead?"

"For that same reason. She still loves me, and I love her. She wishes for me to unburden myself."

"Unburden?"

"From this heavy weight we call life. Over there...she says it is a beautiful place. That all sins are forgiven, and all miseries and bad memories put to rest. Young man, why is it that people fear leaving this world for a better place? Isn't that what the Holy Bible promises? You say she wishes me dead, and I say she wishes me more alive than I have ever known." The dark-hollowed eyes came back to gaze upon Matthew. "She says it is just a little pain. A little confusion...and then, the light heals and comforts you. Why don't people embrace that with great joy?"

"It's the unknown, I suppose."

"Yes, but now I *know* it! She tells me, and she has never lied to me, Matthew. *Never*." He gave a sad smile that pulled at Matthew's heart, even though he'd only been in the presence of this man for a few moments.

The smile faded and vanished. "And...I must go to her to absolve myself," Forbes said. "Because as happy as she is now on the other side, she misses me...and the truth is, I killed her."

"I understood it was an accident."

"The rain-soaked ground sliding away from underfoot, yes. But my actions directly afterward...I was frozen...and I moved too late. The few seconds I lost...I could have gotten down to her...but I did not. And she was looking at me as she fell. I killed her because I could have moved. I have seen it in my mind a thousand times over. What I could have done. What I *should* have been able to do." Forbes lifted a hand to shield his face, and he retreated into the gloom once more as if there lay his only refuge.

"It still sounds like only an accident," said Matthew. "It happened so fast and I understand it was pouring rain."

"Everyone *understands*." There was bitterness in the rasp. "But you... you don't fully understand why you are here, do you?"

Matthew was silent, thinking that perhaps he really did not.

Forbes spoke from the chamber's deepest shadow. "Can you imagine how much money went into the building of this place? My brothers and I speculate that after the tragedy that took our mother, Whitton's mind became truly unhinged if it were not already. We think all his life he hated being thrust into the demands of the family's business. Therefore the business became his enemy, and whether knowing it or not he wished to destroy it. But how, since the Truxton Company was so successful? Sell it? An army of lawyers and advisors had been set up by Percival to block such a move for the span of Whitton's life. Therefore…ruin the company by opening the coffers and dumping the money out like…like the pouring rain that day. We have obligations to suppliers and craft guilds that we can never meet, and the idea of selling this house to raise funds…I thought at first it might be possible, but being here for a length of time…it's a ridiculous notion." He gave a dry and again altogether bitter laugh. "One thing my father did for me…though he named me as sole owner of the company in his will…is that he released me from selling the Truxton line if I chose to do so. That was his only mercy. For I will tell you, Matthew, that business has driven many thousands of men into early graves, has caused those who survive to neglect their loved ones until there is no more love, and it is only the business that must be tended to…the business, first and foremost… day after day into forever. Profits, profits and more profits, and any small loss becomes a dagger to the heart and the investors shout of lawsuits, and my Mary…my Mary helped me understand that all of life should not be business…but that there are so many more important things than the tally sheet. And yet…the business comes at you shrieking every hour of the day and shrills in the night, and yes you are making profits and all the land depends on the Truxton name…you are *obligated*. You are snared in a trap created by a man much different than you yet you must still march to his drumbeat. And on and on and on…drumming drumming drumming, toward the very cliff of insanity yourself. I can hear it even now!"

Matthew saw the darkened shape lift his hands as if to cover his ears, and there was a long pause before the hands were lowered.

The voice was even more strained when Forbes continued. "Sell this manor to cover the bills? Yes it should be sold but who would buy such a thing? A castle here in the wilderness with the rustics of a fishing village your only neighbors and its tavern your only entertainment? A long and grueling journey from Boston? And the price would be exorbitant for even the most wealthy family! But the drumming goes on, Matthew, and the obligations must be met. Therefore I have made arrangements to sell the company. I roused myself in the days after Mary's death long enough to have Clegg take me to Boston, where I empowered a team of four lawyers to find a suitable buyer. It was what she wanted for me before the incident… to get us out from under the stone and find joy in life. It had to be done without Harris's knowledge, and it was very difficult since he was here and visited so often. The time was well-spent. A buyer was found and I signed the contract of intent. The deal is advancing at this moment. You are here, Matthew, because both my brothers vehemently oppose the sale. If they can prove I have become insane in the days after Mary's passing—since that is when my signature was applied—their lawyers believe they can go to court and void the contract. You are here as an impartial witness so you might testify in court on behalf of Harris and Niven, and afterward see me shut into an asylum where I might rot away the rest of my days. Understand now?"

"I do," Matthew said, though he did think that Forbes was teetering on the edge of madness. *The cliff of insanity*, indeed. "Why not simply remove yourself as master of the company and sign it over to your brothers?"

"You're not hearing what I'm saying. No matter who is 'master of the company,' the company is a hollow shell. They refuse to believe it even after I've gone over the books time and again. The holdings must be sold and at a tremendous loss! My brothers are on their journey to a debtor's prison and they are whistling on the way. But *I'm* the one who's insane! Oh, yes! Let me laugh at that! Harris with his grandiose plans and Niven about to be married and shuffling along in his shadow! Let me laugh good and loud!" Forbes suddenly clasped his hands to his face.

"Mary," he said softly. "Mary...please...come to me...get me out of this."

"Mr. Truxton," Matthew said when the man remained in that posture, "may I suggest very gently that you go downstairs and have something to eat? Also there's a pot of good strong tea."

Forbes dropped his hands away from his face. "I expect I would hear that supplicating tone of voice if I were put into a madhouse. But Mary will save me from that. Yes, very soon she will."

"Come on, I'll walk you downstairs."

"No thank you, I'll stay here a while longer. I come up here to look out on the path to the village and try to...well...try to puzzle something out."

"Something important?"

"It doesn't matter now," said Forbes. "But a few days before...the incident...Mary went for a walk to the village. When she came back, she was...I would say disturbed. In a dark mood, but she wouldn't tell me why. She said she needed time to think about it...whatever it was. But as I say, it doesn't matter now."

"You should ask her," Matthew offered.

Forbes was silent. Then: "Are you humoring me, young man?"

"No sir, only making another suggestion."

"I am not insane," Forbes said.

Matthew nodded. "I'll leave you to your ruminations. I hope we can talk again later?"

"If you wish," was the reply. And following that: "Watch your back around my brothers. They twist the truth to their own ends."

Matthew left the chamber and descended the stairs to the second level. It did seem that if Forbes wished to jump to his death from a balcony, the manor held many opportunities. The measure of padlocking the balcony doors in Forbes's bedroom was perhaps a bit of useless theater for Dr. Galbraith's benefit. Or—to take a darker view of it—a gesture from Harris to remind his elder brother that his continued obsession with Mary's death might lead to a padlocked cell in an asylum?

And all that about the Truxton Company being in dire straits and the brothers wanting Matthew to be an impartial witness to Forbes's insanity. Truth or simply more evidence of insanity?

Matthew had his chance to find out, because he met Harris coming up the main stairs on his way down.

"You spoke to Forbes?" was the man's inquiry. "Did he bite your head off?"

"Actually, we had a good conversation." Matthew recalled Niven telling him that Forbes would be a difficult interview, but perhaps Forbes was only difficult with those who gave him difficulties.

"He is obviously restraining himself around an outsider," Harris said.

"That may be, but he tells me he desires to sell the company and the papers were signed just after the accident."

"Oh, he's pursuing that line with you, is he?" Harris brought the silver snuffbox from within his jacket and took two quick sniffs. "Yes, that's true but it's another mark against his mental resources. He sneaked to Boston behind my back just days after Mary's death to hunt down a buyer for a ridiculously low price, at a time when we have the opportunity to expand the business in the colonies."

"He tells me also that the business has been broken by the construction of this manor."

"It has been *affected* but far from broken. He did go on, didn't he?"

It was time to ask the real question. "Am I here to testify in court against this sale?"

"You are here for all the reasons I specified at your office, and yes that is another reason. Our lawyers tell us that Duncan's testimony would be helpful but the testimony of a totally impartial witness would go far in convincing the judge to void the contract. Forbes's mind was disturbed by Mary's death. He signed the papers under the sway of that disturbance. Now he sees her ghost visiting him at night." Harris's brows went up. "Do you have an objection to taking a responsibility in this matter?"

"No," Matthew replied, "but I recall at the office that you said you thought either Forbes was suffering from mental instability or that someone was playing at being a ghost. There are two women in the manor. Are either of them capable?"

There was a few seconds' pause before Harris let out a harsh laugh. "Oh my God! Really? Simone can barely leave her bed for all her imagined ailments, and Zoya…well, ask Forbes if when Mary comes to him at night she speaks with a Slavic accent and she has flaming red hair! Mary's was dark brown. And I believe Forbes has said he's seen at least the lower part of her face clearly enough, because the 'spirit' evidently avoids the lamplight in his room. *Those* two women? But wait! You're forgetting Mrs. Wicks! Sixty-four years old, but she's a feisty one! She might do the trick in a dark wig and a white gown. Or Mrs. Baines, only in her forties but unfortunately walks with a limp from a childhood accident. Wait, wait! There's Leah Clegg, of course! Now *there's* your actress!"

Matthew was fully aware that Harris was having a jolly old time with this even though the idea of someone playing a phantasm had been his own in the office. Matthew said, "What about Mrs. Clegg?"

"In her mid-thirties…slim…dark-haired…an attractive woman who might certainly pass for Mary Truxton if Forbes were induced and inclined to think so! Of course! The coachman's wife is the ghost! Why didn't I think of that before!"

Matthew had not smiled or otherwise changed his expression since this little tirade had gone onto display. He said, "If someone here is playing the part of…what is she called?…'Wandering Mary'?…and it isn't your wife, Zoya, Mrs. Wicks, Mrs. Baines or Leah Clegg…then either Niven or yourself are enjoying your dress-up party."

Harris kept his rather rude grin on for a few more seconds before it slipped away. He leaned in closer to his object of intense attention. His eyes were cold. He spoke in a whisper: "It must be…*Wicks* himself!" Then he laughed again into Matthew's face but his eyes remained icy. "Matthew, beware that my brother's insanity is not contagious! Now pardon me, I need to see to my wife." He brushed past Matthew and ascended the stairs.

Matthew continued on his way, but the memory of the chill in Harris's eyes stayed with him. He found his way to the front door, where he paused to make acquaintance with the diminutive white-haired housekeeper Marion Wicks who was at work sweeping the foyer's floor. He said good day to her, went out into a wind equally as chill as Harris Truxton's glare, and walked toward the cliff's edge to see for himself where Mary had fallen. A distance from the door he turned to gaze upon the looming manor, its dark stones rising up like a mountain unto itself, the edifice a madman's refuge but also a madman's dream, and seemingly to him even a funereal presence in the bright morning sunlight. Regardless, the grounds were well-kept, all the hedges trimmed, the driveway immaculate, everything in order on that point. On his continued walk he saw situated behind the house the small stone cottage that must belong to Eli and Ruth Baines, a glass-walled greenhouse just beyond that, and further on the stable and the coachhouse that appeared to have windowed living quarters above the stall where the coach rested. Copses of oak and elm trees stood about, all sculpted into compliant shapes by the power of what must be at times a ferocious wind from the Atlantic. He went on perhaps another thirty yards to the edge of the cliff.

At that precipitous point, with the sea crashing below and the spume spinning up into his face in a cold mist, he could easily detect where a portion of the ground had collapsed and slid down. Under his boots the earth was soft and spongy, so there was still danger here. He eased forward with small steps to peer down upon a picture of tumult, for here the land came nearly to an arrowhead point and the waves hitting the wet rocks seemed determined to beat the earth into submission. Whitecaps surged and fell, seagulls whirled about, crying out in search of sustenance, salty mist stung Matthew's eyes and the briny smell of the sea was a particular perfume that some loved and others hated. He thought that Mary Truxton, being of a healthy outdoors nature, would likely have come often to this place to draw into herself the power and majesty of nature, for though it might certainly be a treacherous place it also held an allure and a resplendence that one could not experience in the harbors of New York or Boston.

He recalled in the office that Harris had said Forbes and Mary had spent *some time* here prior to arranging—or attempting to arrange—the sale of the manor. How long, he wondered, was *some time?* A few days? It seemed an awfully long trip to take from Boston for just a short visit. A week or two, perhaps? Or longer? Though the manor was pitifully empty of furniture, Forbes's bedroom was the equal of probably that in any fine Boston house, and they had the formal dining room and the staff on hand. But then again, there was the ominous presence of the manor and its dark history with Whitton. He would have to investigate this, because for some reason he couldn't explain, it seemed important to him.

And just that fast, the sodden earth beneath his right boot gave way, he lost his balance and as he pitched forward he saw his death waiting sixty feet below.

SIX

An arm clenched about Matthew's waist and dragged him back from the precipice.

"Steady sir, steady!" said the man who'd plain and simply just saved his life. "You're all right now, let's move us back a ways."

"However far you please," was Matthew's response though he could barely hear himself for the thundering of his heart and the rush of blood that sounded like Noah's flood in his ears. He let himself be dragged further back, and then he was released. He was glad to be saved but the arm that had caught him was so strong it felt as if all his ribs had been rearranged one-by-one.

When Matthew turned, he had to look *up* at the man's bearded face. The gent wasn't as tall or as broad as Hudson Greathouse but he would never have to stand in the Great One's shadow. He was looking at a man he judged to be fifty or so, the flesh of his high-cheekboned face leathery and actually turned the color of leather by the wind's burn. The beard was mostly reddish-brown, but gray at the chin and where it hung down as quite an amassment upon the chest of his well-worn brown canvas jacket. He wore a dark green woolen skullcap and below a high, seamed forehead his eyes were just a few shades lighter.

"Pardon, sir," he said. His voice was just as rough as he appeared to be. "I was comin' across the yard when I saw you. I should've hollered a warnin'." He looked past Matthew at the newly crumpled earth. "Dangerous here, sir. I ought to be settin' a rail."

"No harm done, thanks to you." Matthew didn't want to check, but he thought he might have wet his breeches a splotch. His nerves were still jittery. "I am Matthew—"

"Corbett, yes sir I know. Caleb told me. I am Eli Baines." He thrust a large hand out, and when Matthew shook it he felt as if he'd put his own hand into an oversized and hard-skinned glove. "Again sir, pardon me for not callin' your attention to the danger here."

"Of course. Dangerous, yes, but very beautiful a view."

"Sometimes the two are the same."

"Granted," Matthew said, as he thought this was an insightful statement of wisdom. "I expect Mr. Clegg also told you why I'm here?"

"He did. We're all still grieved about Mistress Mary's death and what's happened to Master Forbes." Baines stared out at sea for a time before he asked, "Do you think you can help?"

"I'm not sure, but let me ask this: have either you or your wife seen this supposed ghost roaming the grounds?"

"If we had, it'd be common news by now."

"Certainly. I understand you and your wife take turns guarding the front door? Have you had any instances where Forbes has tried to leave the manor at night?"

"No sir, that would be common news as well."

"Logical," Matthew said. "Well, I had to ask."

Baines nodded. His head tilted slightly to the side as he regarded the smaller man. "Let me ask somethin'. Caleb says you're a problem-solver. I mean, that's what you call yourself. You put yourself into people's problems and try to solve 'em for pay?"

"That's right."

"Never heard of such. Is there money in it?"

"As long as there are people, there will be problems."

Baines contemplated this before he said, "Logical."

Matthew saw the opportunity to ask some pertinent questions of this rather rough-hewn but obviously intelligent gentleman. "Do you recall the date of Mary's death?"

"Yes sir, how could I forget it? It was the eighth day of September around four in the afternoon. I was in the greenhouse when that big rain swept in, and Ruth—my missus—came runnin' to tell me."

"And besides the servants—excuse me, I mean the *help*—just Harris and his wife were here?"

"That's all."

"How long had Forbes and Mary been here before the accident happened?"

"Let's see…I recall it was likely a month or so. I believe they came 'cause they said they wanted to look the place over at first, but then they decided to stay a spell 'cause of the summer's heat down in Boston. Heatwave even up here but not so bad as there, they said."

Matthew nodded, for he remembered how sweltering August had been in New York and on that packet boat with the Four Lamplighters.

"Still unseasonable warm," Baines continued, "but it's gonna change here directly. I've always had a feel for the weather. Fact, I told Master Forbes and the mistress that a heavy rain was comin' but it swept in a day or two 'fore I expected it. I feel it comin' now."

"Heavy rain?"

"Yes sir, and more. First a fog, then the rain. Then the cold's gonna set in quick as you please, and that'll be snow."

Matthew looked out across the water at the blue sky. There were a few thin high clouds, but no indication to him of turbulent weather on the way. "How can you tell?"

"Back of my neck starts tinglin'. Then you can watch what the birds do."

"I haven't seen any but the gulls."

"That's just what I mean, sir. The birds all took wing. They was callin' and chatterin' in the trees just yesterday. I woke up with a tinglin', and them birds are all gone. Yes sir, heavy weather's comin' maybe two days off."

"Hm," was Matthew's response to this forecast, dubious or not.

"You know," said the gardener, "that we're bein' watched from the manor."

Matthew turned in time to see a figure move back from an upper balcony and into the house, but whether it had been male or female he hadn't time to tell.

"All this about Mistress Mary's ghost…it's not sittin' too well with my Ruth," Baines confided. "She's gettin' the shivers 'cause of it. Caleb tells me his Leah don't believe Mistress Mary would come back as a ghost, and she sure wouldn't want Master Forbes to…do what we hear she wants him to do. She was a kind woman, sir. She brought some joy to the house. No sir, we don't believe it."

"Neither do I," said Matthew. The cantankerous spirits at Number Seven Stone Street were one thing, this seemed something altogether different…and markedly sinister. He decided if he was going to trust anyone here, it should be this down-to-earth gardener. If his decision was wrong, then even the wrong decision would have an interesting consequence. "Mr. Baines, do you have or can you get me a dark lantern?"

"I don't have one, but I know Tom Brown has a few to sell at the tradin' post. They come up by order on the market boat. Can I ask what you're needin' one for?"

"Just to light my way," Matthew answered.

"Yes sir, I likely don't need to know. I've used one before. I borrow one from Seth Quinton when I go crabbin' at the cove with some other fellas. Catch them crabs at night and they're mighty good in a stew or soup." Baines hesitated for a few seconds, obviously thinking something over. Then he said, "I'll trade you a secret."

"Oh?"

"Yes sir. I won't tell nobody you're wantin' a dark lantern, if you don't tell nobody about the crabbin'. They'd want to know what's done with the meat, it bein' thought of as so nasty and all."

"What *is* done with the meat?"

"My Ruth and me partake most of it, but some goes to fill out the meals the family's eatin'. If they ain't never et it by name before, they don't know it from Adam's fishpot. Also…the cove is where they found Mistress Mary one night when they was crabbin', so that's another thing. See what I'm gettin' at?"

"I do," said Matthew, "and no mention of crabs or crabbing shall be heard from me."

"Thank you, sir. I'll say good day, then." Baines started to move away but suddenly stopped. "I wish you'd been here a while back, Mr. Corbett. I had a problem I needed solved and I couldn't figure it out for the life of me."

"What was the problem?"

"A robbery, sir. I figured somebody come up from the village at night and done it, but that would be the first time anything like that has happened in the many years I been workin' here, and nobody's owned up to it yet."

"Owned up to what?"

"Sneakin' in the toolshed and stealin' a shovel, a measurin' rod, a ball of heavy twine and four burlap bags. I had twelve bags I use to cover plants in the cold…now I got eight, and I use the twine to wrap the bags down."

"A measuring rod?" Matthew asked.

"Yes sir. Six foot long if an inch."

"Aren't those items likely to be sold at the trading post?"

"That's where I bought 'em all. I'm still tryin' to find out who done it but nobody'll fess, and that was in September."

The back of Matthew's own neck seemed to tingle and it didn't have anything to do with the weather. "September," he repeated. "Did this robbery occur before or after Mary's death?"

"After, sir. I recall it was a few days past when Clegg took Master Forbes on a trip to Boston, and that was…let me think…maybe four days after Mistress Mary fell."

Matthew reasoned that dovetailed with Forbes's story of going to Boston to hunt a buyer for the company. He did some mental calculations. "The eighth…the twelfth…that would make the date of the robbery around the fifteenth or so?"

"Near it, yes sir."

"And when did Forbes return from Boston?"

"I believe it was near most of the month gone. He come back bringin' the doctor." Baines gave a frown. "What're you gettin' at, sir?"

"I'm just trying to understand the time involved." Matthew thought that was about all he could get for the moment from Eli Baines, but there would likely be the opportunity to learn more later. "Thank you for your help and again, thank you for keeping me from going over the cliff. I'd hate to begin my day with a swim and a crashing headache."

"Glad to be of help, sir. Good to meet you…and good luck to you."

Matthew decided that unlike a cat he had no more lives to lose by dawdling around the precipice any longer. As Baines set off toward the greenhouse, Matthew cast his gaze toward the manor once again. If anyone was still watching, they were well-hidden. He turned away from the house and started walking in the direction of the path that led down through the forest to Brown's Harbor. In a few minutes he was striding downhill with the woods dense on both sides though most of the hardwood trees had lost their foliage probably by the end of October.

He noted the deep ruts in the path, indicative of the many wagons that had trundled up the hill from the harbor in carting construction materials to the clifftop. It had certainly been a massive and expensive undertaking... designed by Whitton to either consciously or unconsciously destroy the company his father had built? And now Forbes was trying to follow Mary's advice to sell everything and find joy and peace in a life that had been thrust upon him? It might appear that the rich had no troubles but counting their money, yet there were burdens and responsibilities that came with the high office of wealth. Forbes wanted out of it, and Mary had opened the door for him though it was highly likely he had wanted out for most of his life. The same also might be said of Whitton, who had to take on the business that Percival had created.

The path flattened out and the forest gave way to the wide half-moon shape of the cove. A wagon trail led into the forest to Matthew's left toward the sea. Out beyond the wooded headland the waves still threw foam against the rocks but the cove was relatively calm, only a few ripples lapping at a muddy shore. Hereabouts was where Mary's body had washed in, and no doubt the crabs that prowled the cove's bottom had made a feast on what were already grisly remains.

Though the harbor village itself was yet a quarter mile distant, Matthew caught sight of an unpainted wooden shack to his right and nearly disguised by the surrounding trees. The windows were shuttered and the place looked old and deserted, yet who could say that some hermit who disdained even the village wasn't living there counting his crab shells?

In time Matthew saw that the woods had been chopped away and there stood a community of cabins much better kept than the first one he'd seen. A yellow dog came running out to bark at his heels, soon joined by a brown one. They kept up a furor until Matthew paused to speak quietly to them with a few gentle admonishments. They circled him a few times but their curiosity was satisfied and they were content to follow him further with just a few yips and yaps.

And there was the harbor itself, also protected from the vagaries of the sea by a curve of wooded headland. There was the dock and the moored boats Matthew had seen from the balcony, along with racks of nets hung out to dry in the sun. Likely some of the fishermen had gone out before daybreak and had already returned with their catch. The white-painted market boat was a two-masted sloop that dwarfed the smaller craft around it. Matthew saw a few men standing beside a long gray wooden structure next to the dock that must be the salting facility. They ceased their conversation to watch him go past. He bade them good day but no answer returned, yet they continued to watch. Matthew reasoned that strangers were few and far between here, and they had to know he was connected in some way to the Truxton Manor. Even though the manor's construction had given life to the village it also had taken the lives of eight men who very well might have been the friends or relatives to those Matthew had just passed. He turned to look back up at the cliff, and saw that from here the manor made him think of a dark bird of prey with tightly folded wings…a vulture, perhaps… perched near the edge and brooding above Brown's Harbor. He imagined that living with that monstrosity over one's head was bound to affect the nerves, especially in the dark and stormy nights of winter.

He intended to find the trading post amid the cluster of small structures along what might be called a village square, but his eye caught the crudely lettered sign of The Red Claw, of course lettered in red. The tavern itself wasn't much to speak of, just a weather-beaten gray cabin. A nice touch, though: the window shutters were painted red. Smoke was rising from a stone chimney. He decided a taste of the local ale would do him good this morning, and besides he had to find a place to sit and think for a while. His question to himself was: if he were able to find and buy a dark lantern, how was he going to get it across the lawn and into the house without his possession being detected? And if it were seen…well, as it was said, the jig would be up.

Matthew entered the tavern through an equally weather-worn door that the roof's overhang had not quite sheltered from the storms. Within he found a half dozen small tables, three of which were occupied by several men all wearing long-grown beards, a serving bar with a planked top and behind it shelves holding an assortment of clay cups. A nice beckoning fire crackled in the hearth. At Matthew's entrance all conversation ceased and all attention was focused on him by seven unruly-looking customers and a heavyset gray-haired woman behind the bar. The intensity was so unsettling he tried not to trip over his own boots as he approached the woman.

"Good morning," said Matthew. "May I try a cup of your ale?"

"I don't know," the woman answered, her blazing blue eyes burning holes through him. "*May* you?"

This brought chortles and guffaws from the watchful audience.

Matthew steeled himself for another go at this. "I'd like a cup of ale."

"Well why in damnation didn't you say so?" More village hilarity ensued. Matthew thought their exposure to comedy was likely very limited. The woman picked a cup off a shelf and turned back to him. "You want the extra stout, the gut croaker or the burnin' cannonball?"

All the world seemed to await his answer.

"Give the boy the cannonball, Bess!" came a harsh voice that sounded as if the morning's breakfast had been all gut croaker. "Make a man of 'im!"

Matthew looked around to see that this unwelcome agitator was a big-shouldered, black-bearded gent who sat at a table accompanied only by his drinking cup. His wild man's mane of tangled black hair fell about his shoulders, and his flat-nosed and low-browed face had taken on the ruddy glow of strong spirits at work.

"All right," Matthew said to the barkeep, "I'll try the cannonball."

"You sure of that, sonny boy?" she asked, with a rather impish smile for her age.

It seemed the thing to do, with all these not-so-friendly eyes upon him. Anyway, Matthew felt he might need information here, and Bess the barkeep might be a fount. "I'm sure," he said.

"Your funeral. Yates, get a coffin ready!"

The black-bearded one replied with a slam of his cup upon the table. All watched as Bess reached under the bar, brought up a black clay jug shot through with streaks of red and poured a dark brown brackish-looking substance into Matthew's cup. He had a pang of remorse approaching absolute terror as she filled the cup to the brim and the stuff foamed over onto the bar's top, making a noise like bacon sizzling in a frypan.

"There y'go," Bess said. "You put all that down, sonny boy, and it's free. The fellas and me need entertainment."

"Glad to be of service," Matthew answered, instantly wondering if he should come up with something more witty as his last words. But...too late to be a poet! He braced himself as if facing not a single cannonade but an entire firing squad, and then he tipped the cup to his mouth and started drinking.

The first few swallows were bitter and strong, but nothing a man of his nature could not handle. *Sonny boy! Pah!*

On the fourth swallow the heat began prickling in his throat. One more drink and he experienced the flames of perdition that suddenly exploded in mouth and throat, made his eyes water and bulge and his nose leak. He had the sensation of the room spinning around him and his vision declining to that of peering into a tunnel. And yet the heat increased to absolute burning pain and he realized the cannonball had just struck its target.

"You ain't half done," Bess said, as if he didn't already know it.

He had broken out in an oily sweat. The fire leaped and capered behind his face. He feared his knees were going, for either his balance was flawed or the Red Claw tavern had suddenly begun to tip to one side along with the rest of the earth. Could a cup of ale explode a heart? His was hammering in his chest with dangerous abandon. Now he had to lean against the bar to remain upright, and in this haze of flaming regret Matthew realized the only thing to do was to finish the cup with the biggest swig any man had ever taken of a forest fire.

When he had forced it down he started to slam the finished cup upon the bar like a real man but instead he missed the countertop altogether, it hit one of his boots and nearly broke his foot. Then he stared at the two-headed woman behind the bar with his weeping eyes and when he intended to say "I am done, ma'am" in a voice that would've made Hudson Greathouse envious of his resounding modulation it came out like the squeak of a mouse caught under a hundred-pound anvil.

"I guess you are," Bess replied, barely able to restrain her maddening grin.

But at least there was no more *sonny boy*.

Though the cannonball was not finished with him yet. The devil's heat in his mouth and pulsating behind his face caused Matthew to shiver and jump as if his entire body were impaled on the fireplace spit along with the other hunk of ham. To this infuriating and unwelcome dance some of the men hauled themselves up with hoots and hollers and began clapping and dancing along with their victim.

In the fevered brain a thought before it was seared away: *Entertainment, be gone!*

Bess reached over the bar and with a knotty hand grabbed Matthew by the jacket collar, pulled him closer and shoved another cup into his hand. "Drink it!" she ordered, and Matthew realized that this woman's order was akin to a general's command: Obey or die. He drank.

Milk.

"Very well, you bastards," Bess said to the men as they continued to dance around and Matthew continued to douse the fire with the God-blessed remedy. "Show some respect for courage!" When they failed to respond, Bess brought a hollow bull's horn from under the bar, put it to her mouth and blew a whistle through it that rocked Matthew back on his heels and stunned the place to silence.

"Better," she said to them, and to Matthew: "That ale is brewed with Scotch bonnet peppers. A little warm, ain't it?"

He just nodded and wiped his eyes.

"Who the hell are you?" spoke up the black beard, who hadn't budged from his chair. "You come in on that coach passed through last night?"

Another nod. Maybe he could speak when his vocal cords had cooled off.

"You a Truxton?" Bess asked.

Matthew shook his head and attempted to speak. It came out as a whisper, but at least he still had a voice. "Friend of the family," he decided to say.

"Terrible about the missus. She was a fine lady. And old Whitton hangin' hisself like he did."

"House is cursed," said one of the others.

"Cursed ain't a strong enough word for it," another man commented. All joviality was gone now that Truxton Manor had entered the conversation. "What happened to Missus Mary was the Devil's work."

"The Devil had a hand in it, all right," was a third remark, followed by a slug of ale. "Had a hand in buildin' that damn house, too. Tell him, Bess."

"Leave him alone," she answered. "He still ain't breathin' right."

"*I'll* tell him, then," said the ornery gent. "You bein' a friend of the family and all. Look at that woman standin' afore you and know that damn house killed her husband and son. Killed my good friend Phillip Maguire too. He went off the roof, wasn't nineteen years old. And Bess's husband—"

"That's enough," she said, and once more it was the general's command. Her sharp gaze again returned to Matthew. "Scaffoldin' collapsed. All it was. Got paid some Truxton money for it. I started runnin' this place. They're gone but I'm still here. End of story." She put her elbows on the bartop and leaned toward Matthew. "So. Niven got hisself a bit tipsy one evenin' and spewed out the whole thing. I mean to say, he did stagger outside to puke but before that he told us about Mary. Wanderin' Mary, I'm meanin'. Forbes still seein' her?"

"I'm sorry, I can't say."

"He's still seein' her," Bess announced to the others before returning her attention to Matthew. "Hard to get anythin' out of Harris when he comes in for a drink or two, but I did get that Forbes is about ready for the nuthouse. Don't mean no disrespect, but a straight road don't have no curves. You here to take him away?"

"I'm here as a friend of the family and that is all."

"'Course, could be Forbes ain't teeched in the head," Bess said. "Could be Mary's ghost is still walkin' up there. Well, you look like you could be a minister or somethin' up from Boston. You come to bless the coffin? Have to open up the vault to get at it, don't you? That's what Niven said. She was put in the vault."

"Only way to stop a ghost from walkin'," one of the other sages said. "Bless the coffin. Ain't that right, Yates?"

The black beard did not speak for a few seconds, in which he took a long swallow of his liquor. "I don't bless 'em," he said. "I just make 'em."

"Yates Johnsey's our carpenter," Bess told Matthew. "Makes the coffins, too, when it comes to that."

Matthew turned toward Johnsey with renewed interest. "You made the coffin for Mary?"

"That's what Bess just said, ain't it?" Johnsey scowled across the room. "Made the one for the old man, too. Him with his broke neck and head all twisted 'round." He took another bracing drink. "Wasn't as bad as Missus Mary, though. What was left of her...I ain't sayin' nothin' else."

"Nobody wants you to!" Bess told him. Then, to Matthew: "We got our own minister here and he said words over the coffin. You got better words to say?"

"I'm not a minister," Matthew said, realizing this canny woman was trying very hard to uncover his role in the situation.

"By the by," Johnsey spoke up, his voice becoming more slurred, "I've got a bone to pick with Harris! You tell him he owes me money for that situation, and Drucilla is on the warpath about it!"

"His wife," Bess offered quietly. "Beats his ass with a broom whenever it pleases her."

"Tell him!" Johnsey rambled on. "Trouble if he don't pay up!"

"*You* tell Drucilla," said Bess, "to bring me some more rabbits for my stew. I'll pay you like always." And as an aside to Matthew: "His wife has got rabbit traps all out on the headland, she's a better trapper than most of the menfolk. All right, I've got you pegged now: you're a *lawyer*, ain't you?"

"I am a problem-solver," Matthew replied. "Professional, that is. People pay me to solve their problems."

"A *what?*"

Matthew shrugged at this declaration of incredulity. "I've said what I am. People come to me with their problems and I'm paid to do what I can."

"You hear that, gents?" Bess asked the others. "Ever heard the like of it?"

"Must be kind of like both a minister and a lawyer put together," said the man who had been Phillip Maguire's friend. "I suppose somebody's got to do it. You here to solve the problem of Truxton losin' his mind? Or you here to catch a ghost?" He gave a harsh guffaw. "Fella, I hope they're payin' you good and plenty!"

"It's satisfactory, thank you. And thank *you*," Matthew said to Bess, "for the introduction to a drink I plan to never again taste in my life."

"Aw, you're just sayin' that to be polite! Come on back for another one, if you like, and I'll cook you up the special of the house!"

"Something with red claws, I presume? I'd rather drink another cannonball."

"You don't know what you're missin'! Mark my words, someday they'll be eatin' 'em in Boston and smackin' their lips!"

That day seemed an awfully long way off to Matthew. It seemed also that his idea of finding a quiet place in which to think was for the moment not going to happen...at least not in this tavern. "I'll be on my way," he told the lady, and to the bearded bunch: "Good day, gentlemen."

"Come back soon for another visit!" Bess said. "We always like us a lively dance!"

Laughter and laughter upon laughter.

Yet as Matthew left the tavern in search of the trading post and hopefully a dark lantern, one of the beards in the room ceased laughing, took a last drink from his cup, stood up and said to his companions, "I'm gonna get me some air."

"Put your face over here near my bottom and I'll give you some!" hollered the friend of Phillip Maguire, who was slowly sinking in his chair under the weight of too many gut croakers.

Laughter swelled again, but the man who had announced his departure only smiled and nodded. "I'll be back directly," he told them, and then he pulled his many-times-patched brown coat about his wiry body, he situated a woolen cap upon a bald head burned dark by years of the sun off the sea, and he went out in search of a young man who was part lawyer and part minister.

SEVEN

THE TRADING POST CLERK WAS A TALL, RAWBONED, WHITE-HAIRED MAN who asked no questions of Matthew when he took the requested dark lantern off its shelf and placed it on the counter before the young man. His only comment was: "I reckon it's just right for ghost huntin'."

"If it will do to catch crabs," Matthew answered, "it might well catch a spirit of the night."

The dark lantern was made of metal and formed so that no flame from its oil-saturated wick could be seen, except through a large glass lens on the front that actually magnified and strengthened the light. The trick was a small lever on one side of the lantern that opened a shutter behind the lens and allowed what would be a rather startling illumination. Perfect to freeze crabs on their crawl at the bottom of shallow water, Matthew thought. Also suitable, as the clerk had said, to catch a ghost if the opportunity arose.

If there *were* anything to catch, or if instead, as the younger brothers believed, their elder had simply lost his mind.

"I 'preciate the business, sir," said the clerk. He brought down from a shelf behind the counter a ledger book, a quill and an inkwell. "Let me just mark down the date and the sale, also your name, please."

"Well…is that necessary?"

"It's my habit, sir. From this I get an idea of what I ought to be orderin' from Boston for the market boat to bring back. Put the names down so I know who's wantin' what, get everythin' in order 'fore the snow and ice sets in."

Matthew indulged the man, feeling that if he refused it might be an issue. "Could I have a fill of oil for this? Also that it be wrapped?" Matthew asked. A quantity of oil was applied and a suitable amount of cloth was used, which Matthew also had to pay for along with the lantern. Again the items were entered in the ledger. When that was done, twine—"free on the house today, sir, you havin' spent such a coin," said the clerk—was looped around and knotted to secure—and more importantly to Matthew, to *hide*—the purchase. Then he was out the door and on his way.

Now was the problem of getting it into the house. Anyone standing on a balcony might see him coming with a package in hand and they'd want to know what it was. They might even traipse down to the trading post to find out what he'd bought. But he was getting ahead of himself…he had no evidence anyone was playing at being a ghost to thus have Forbes committed to an asylum and overturn the signed contract to sell the Truxton company. Because this was why he had been brought here, was it not? To be a pawn in this chess game of family intrigues? He wondered when Harris was going to hand him a pen and a piece of paper to write out his witness to Forbes's insanity. Signed, *Matthew Corbett*. And that signature and Dr. Galbraith's would likely be enough for a court to void the contract, if Harris's and Niven's lawyers were top-notch and Matthew had no doubt they were. Then off to Bedlam for Forbes Trux—

"Pardon, sir. Can I have a word?"

Matthew stopped short, because while he'd been walking lost in thought through the village a man had stepped into his path.

It was one of the gents from the Red Claw; specifically, the man who'd said *What happened to Missus Mary was the Devil's work.*

"Just a minute of your time, please sir," the man said, and there was some begging appeal in both his eyes and his voice that made Matthew instantly put the matter of Truxton Manor aside.

"What can I do for you?" Matthew asked.

"I'm Zachariah Swaine, I live over yonder." He motioned toward one of the small cabins up in the woods. "Me and my wife," he added. "Been here as a fisherman goin' on twelve years, come here with my Abby and my Nora to work on the house."

"Matthew Corbett. Pleased to meet you."

"Yes sir. Well…I was over there in the tavern when you was vistin'."

"I know. I believe you danced along with my discomfort, but I'm sure I put on quite a show."

"Nasty stuff, that cannonball is," Swaine said. "You done good to keep it down."

It seemed to Matthew that this man was still dancing around some subject that gave him unease. "What's on your mind, Mr. Swaine?"

Swaine stared at the dirt for a moment, his hands in the pockets of his coat. When he lifted his gaze again Matthew could clearly see all the pain behind his face. "I'm doin' better about it than Abby is. She's all tore up, but you…bein' a problem-solver and all…I'm hopin' you can help. I ain't got a whole lot of money, but maybe we can figure somethin' out so I might pay you a little at a—"

"Mr. Swaine," Matthew interrupted. "Please tell me directly what it is that you wish to hire me for."

"*Hire* you? Oh…yes sir, that would be right. I'd wish to hire you to find our daughter Nora, sixteen years old and gone to Boston."

"Gone to Boston? How?"

"She told us she hid on the market boat that left on the sixteenth day of September, and she's in Boston doin' well and tryin' to be the artist she's wanted to be, but Abby and me have got to find her to have some peace. I went there myself twice, but I don't have no idea where to look."

"Just a moment," Matthew requested. "You say she *told* you?"

"Yes sir, in a letter come up on the boat. I mean…somebody wrote it for her 'cause she's just still learnin' how to read and write, but Missus Clegg says she's a real bright student."

"Missus Clegg? That would be Leah Clegg?"

Swaine nodded. "Yes sir, the same. She's started a school, meets at the church three mornin's a week. Teachin' folks how to read and write, and I'm thinkin' I might go myself. Abby's better at it than me, she could read most of the letter. But in it Nora says she's all right and she's made friends, and one of these friends has wrote this letter for her so we're not to worry and carry on like scatterbirds."

"Scatterbirds?"

"Yes sir, that's a sayin' Nora has. You know, every once in a while some young'un or two stows away on the market boat and they run 'round Boston for a bit but they always come back. Then they get their hides tanned. But what I'm tellin' is, they always come back. Except Nora. Now she's a girl with a mind of her own and sometimes when Abby wants her to do chores she's nowhere to be found, but she's a right good girl, sir, and she's got a level head. I just want to know why it was she didn't tell us in the letter where we could find her."

"I imagine she thought you'd drag her back. Would you have?"

"Likely I would've tried. Sixteen years old…in Boston…no tellin' what could happen to a young girl in a big town like that. Still and all, I married her mother when Abby was sixteen, but that's different. We both come up on farms. To tell the truth, sir, I fear that town might have designs on her."

"The town or the people there?"

"I mean to say the people. She's a trustin' girl. I want to know too who wrote the letter for her. She just says 'my friend'."

"Honestly, Mr. Swaine," said Matthew, "I'm afraid I wouldn't know where to start looking either. Of course I'd need a description of your daughter, preferably written down. I suppose Mrs. Clegg could do that."

He stopped himself because he realized he was opening the door to Swaine's hope and he had a ghost to either catch or banish right here. "But," he went on, "I don't know how much longer I'll be here. When does the market boat next go to Boston?"

"That would be the twenty-first, sir. Today bein' the eighteenth."

"It's possible Nora might come back on her own, isn't it?" Even as he posed the question, Matthew thought it was highly unlikely, especially since she'd already been gone for three months. "She's only sent you the one letter?" he asked, feeling that his inborn sense of curiosity was about to get him entangled in something he would rather not be roped by.

"Just the one." Swaine's troubled face regarded the blue sky for a moment before his gaze returned to the problem-solver. "Maybe I would've let her stay in Boston, but I would've made sure she was safe and happy. Abby and me can't blame her for wantin' more than what's here. Like I say, she's got it in her heart to be an artist, and she's right good at picturin'. She does things like drawin' apples and stones together, or cobs of corn and lobster shells on a plate."

"Still lifes is what they're called, I believe."

"I suppose so. Anyway, I paid Johnny Tucker to bring her a pack of colored wax sticks up from Boston on the boat. I don't remember what those are called."

"Crayons," Matthew offered.

"She does her drawin' in char pencil first, then she colors 'em in. She's a good girl, sir, that I warrant you. We figure Nora stowed away on the market boat on the night of the fifteenth, 'cause it left early the next mornin'. She took her crayons and papers with her, too. All that night we was huntin' her but we never figured she was on the boat. Please sir...might you have any idea where to start lookin' for her?"

One more statement and Matthew realized the rope had been thrown, but in spite of his misgivings his mouth betrayed him. "A community of artists, I'm thinking. I imagine Nora has sought them out for their help and direction."

Swaine's face brightened. "You'll take on my problem then, sir? I do have money, and I got more comin' in when I get my share of what the boat brings."

"I'll consider it but I can't promise. In the meantime I am under hire by the Truxton family. Before I leave, though, I'll find you and let you know."

"Oh thank you, sir!" The man actually moved to give Matthew a hug before he caught himself. "Abby'll be so pleased!"

That was about all Matthew could advance, and even so he feared he'd given the Swaines false hope. In any case, he said good day and walked on through the village toward the path up the hill, his package clasped under one arm as if it held an object formed from pure gold rather than tarnished metal.

And now as he walked on the question was: where to hide the lantern so he might get to it with ease? Give it to Eli Baines to hide in his cottage? That would mean crossing the lawn and being visible from the balconies. No, it was going to have to be somewhere well away from the manor, but near enough to—

Matthew stopped.

He was looking at the unpainted wooden shack, now on his left, and all but hidden by the surrounding trees. The windows were still shuttered. The place had a heavy silence. Where were the birds? Oh yes, Matthew recalled; they had flown before the oncoming storm Baines predicted.

The shack.

If it was abandoned—and certainly it stood far away from the other residences of Brown's Harbor and was probably halfway between the village and the manor—then it might be the proper place to hide his lantern until it was needed. How to find out?

Simply to knock at the door.

Matthew approached the shack, went up a trio of rickety wooden steps to a sagging front porch, and balled up his hand to knock when he stopped again.

Now…this was strange.

The door was padlocked. The lock itself was shining brass and certainly hadn't been exposed to the elements for very long. A fairly new lock. And was it not almost exactly like the lock that held Forbes's balcony doors chained shut?

Maybe exactly the same.

Another thing: the lockplate that held the door secured was also untarnished by the elements and had been driven into the wood by four new nails.

Matthew walked a few steps to the single front window and tried to open the shutters.

They wouldn't move. Latched from the inside?

He came off the porch and went around to the north-facing side. A second window was tried, and again the shutters would not give a half-inch.

He stepped back, regarding the other window on this side of the place. Would that one open? He tried. It did not.

"Hm," Matthew heard himself say in the otherwise absolute quiet.

Now this was a curious thing. An old ramshackle shack with a new padlock sealing the door and the windows shuttered from within. And in addition, the padlock looked to be the same as the one Harris had bought at the trading post.

A curious thing.

What was inside the place that needed to be locked away?

To satisfy his further interest Matthew went around to the other side of the shack, tramping through dead leaves and thick brush, to try the two windows there. Again, they were closed with locked shutters.

He stepped back once again.

If there was anything that ignited Matthew Corbett's fires of curiosity more than a locked box, he had yet to find it. This was a locked box that he had the feeling should not *be*. On the other hand, he wondered if he was making too much of it, and the resident of this dilapidated and forlorn structure might simply have gone out fishing and locked his belongings up for safekeeping. There was the possibility, and yet...

A new padlock and a new lockplate. Four new nails, and everything unmarked by the weather or human wear and tear.

Whether the shack was inhabited or not, Matthew thought this would be a good place to secure the dark lantern. Thus he went around to the back—no windows there, just a boil of underbrush—and spent enough time and energy to bury the package under a mound of dead leaves. To make sure he marked the spot, since it was likely he would have to return at night, he built a small cairn of stones on the northern side of the hiding place that his hands could find if he were unable to get out of the manor carrying another lamp.

When he was done he returned to the path but he regarded the shack for a time longer, and while he was standing there in the bright sunlight that streamed through the branches he realized he had heard something this morning that—like the new padlock on an old door—seemed wrong.

What was it?

Something in the tavern, he thought.

Two words.

What were they?

He couldn't put a mental finger on it at the moment, and chalked that up to a very poor night's sleep. It would come to him, but it might come when he wasn't *trying* to remember it. He walked on, following the path up the hillside, and in a few minutes he was gratified to the fates that he had decided to hide the lantern, because out on the lawn before the hulking manor two metal stobs had been inserted into the earth and Harris, Niven and Dr. Galbraith were occupied at tossing horseshoes.

Galbraith gave a toss as Matthew approached and—*clang*!—made a solid hit. "That's another guinea you owe me," he said to Harris, who along with his brother watched Matthew's approach.

"Where were you off to?" Harris asked, turning a horseshoe between his hands.

"I went for a walk and wound up in the village. Then to the Red Claw, where I met some interesting locals and had a cup of some local ale that was equally…well, *challenging* would be the word."

"Ha!" Niven grinned. "Did they pour you the croaker or the cannonball?"

"I survived the shot, but just barely. And I'm to tell you," Matthew said to Harris, "that Yates Johnsey says you owe him money for—"

And there they were, jumping into his brain.

The two words.

"*That situation*," Matthew continued. "Evidently his wife is a bit agitated."

"Oh," said Harris, "you met that damn fool. But he's proficient at what he does, though the work was for two sorry events. I've *paid* him his money already, and quite long ago."

"He seemed upset about it, but I observed he was probably on his third or fourth cup."

"I'll take care of it. Niven, you're up. Care to take a throw, Matthew?"

"No, I believe I'll go speak with Forbes again." Matthew glanced up high at the balcony where Forbes preferred to look down upon the world, but no figure stood there. "You know," he said as Niven took aim at the further stob, "that the locking of Forbes's balcony doors is unnecessary. If he's going to jump he has his choice of unlocked altitudes, and he's told me the apparition desires him to join her by leaping from the cliff."

"It's to remind him that we have his interests at heart," said Niven, who then flung his horseshoe but missed by a length. "We have had our differences, but after all…we are family."

"I see," Matthew said, though it was still unclear and Niven's definition of family was not his own. "All right, I'm off." And as he walked away from the trio of sportsmen he asked himself why he had not mentioned the shuttered shack. It was because of the new padlock and lockplate. He just had a feeling about it he could not shake, and he felt it unwise to mention to any of those three that he'd been prowling around the place.

Also…the two words in question.

Harris had stated it correctly as "the work," but Johnsey had said "that situation."

To Matthew's thinking, the task of making a coffin was a "work," or a "job," but "that situation" implied…what?

Or was he simply and completely wrong? It was picking at nits in the extreme, was it not? After all, Johnsey had been—as Greathouse would've said—a little looped, so what did it matter?

It seemed to Matthew, as he left the sunlight and entered the gloomy confines of the manor, that in the profession of problem-solving small things did matter, and perhaps might lead to larger things if investigated. At the moment the difference between a "work," a "job" and "that situation" was just a small nit, but it itched.

He ascended the stairs, went directly to Forbes's room and knocked at the door.

"Who is it?"

"Matthew Corbett, sir. Might we continue our conversation?"

There was a pause before the voice beyond the door asked, "Must we?"

"I think it would benefit both of us."

"I doubt that, young man. But come in, if you have to."

Matthew found Forbes sitting in one of the leather chairs, which he'd turned to face a robust fire in the hearth. He was wearing a dark brown sleeping coat and had resting upon his lap a slim book he'd been reading. On a small round table beside his chair was a teacup and a teapot with steam still rising from the cup and from the pot's spout. "Are you still here?" he asked, tilting his head up and looking down his nose at the visitor.

"Why would I not be?"

"I suspected that this morning you'd have signed a document of witness to my precarious mental condition and been done with it. Hasn't Harris or Niven put that in your face yet?"

"No sir."

"Don't fret, they will. Then you can have Clegg get you out of here and back to Boston. Harris has paid for your return trip to New York?"

"He has."

"Decent of him. Bills must be paid. I'm cold. Are you cold?"

It was a little chilly away from the fire, but Forbes was sitting close to the luxuriant heat. Before Matthew could reply, Forbes said, "Don't just stand there like a knothead. Put another log on the fire and sit down. Let's get this—whatever it is—over as soon as possible."

It seemed to Matthew that as the day moved on the eldest Truxton developed a darker personality, or perhaps the man regretted how many hours it was before a potential visit from the spirit world. Matthew picked up a piece of wood from a brass tub next to the fireplace, deposited it upon the other burning bits and watched the red bats of sparks fly up the chimney, after which he also turned the second chair toward the warming flames and sat down.

"May I ask what you're reading?" Matthew inquired to break what became a heavy silence.

"*The Four Idols of the Mind* by Francis Bacon. Have you read it?"

"I have."

"Then you understand it's an instruction to free oneself of misconceptions."

"I prefer to recognize it," said Matthew, "as an instruction to remain rooted in reality, no matter what misconceptions are thrust upon a man's mind."

"Each to their understanding," Forbes answered. "But perhaps you're correct." He suddenly leaned toward the young man. His eyes were sunken and dark-hollowed in the lined gray face yet they held an imploring urgency. "Listen to me, Matthew. I am neither going mad nor already fallen under the sway of madness. I *do* see my Mary."

"That's what I wished to ask you about. How is it you see this spirit when you're under the influence of the doctor's sleeping potion? Doesn't it force sleep upon you?"

"I fight it. Sometimes I win and sometimes I lose. Some nights I refuse to drink it at all, hoping I will see her again, and Dr. Galbraith is a forceful man but he can't force any drink down my throat I don't wish to swallow."

"And you're absolutely certain then that when you see Mary you're not seeing her in the embrace of a dream brought on by the potion?"

Forbes leaned back again in his chair and stared at the leaping flames. "I wasn't under any influence of the potion the first time she visited me. That was on the night of September twenty-eighth, and you can be sure I remember it very well."

"All right," Matthew said. "Describe it to me in detail."

"Detail," Forbes repeated listlessly. "Very well, then. I woke up. I suppose I had the sensation that someone was in the room with me. At first I didn't see her...until she stepped closer to the bed. She was wearing a white gown, the same as in life. She simply stood there in silence. I spoke to her. 'Mary,' I said. And then again: 'Mary.' Because I knew it was her, come back to me. At that visit she didn't answer. I have to say, my eyes filled with tears and I heard myself sob. When I cleared my vision she was gone."

"Gone how? Through a wall? Through the door?"

"I don't know. I was so overwhelmed, my senses were spinning. As I say, I wept and perhaps I cried out in both wonder and agony...that Mary was so close yet I knew she was so far."

"You saw her face clearly enough?"

"The fire had burned to embers and there was hardly any light, but... oh yes...I knew it was my Mary."

"In the house, as I understand it," said Matthew, "were Harris and Simone. It couldn't have been her?"

"Simone can hardly leave her bed. And why would she be in my room in the middle of the night? Anyway, the next time Mary visited she spoke to me."

"Detail, please."

"It was the night of October twenty-ninth. Dr. Galbraith was here and had given me some of the potion. I think I drifted in and out of sleep. I have no idea what time it was, but I heard her speak. 'Forbes,' she said. 'Forbes, I am here.' And I saw her standing at the foot of the bed, again dressed in white. This time the fire was stronger and I could make out her lustrous black hair...always beautiful, and beautiful still."

"But you couldn't see her face?"

"I didn't *have* to see her face. 'Forbes,' she said, 'I am with you always. I am always watching. My dear Forbes, I yearn for you.' And then she backed away from the bed, as again I wept. I tried to get out of bed but the potion had me hobbled and stupefied. When at last I struggled up and got a lantern lighted the room was empty."

"And you told everyone in the house about this immediately? Or the next morning?"

"The next morning." Forbes watched the fire burn. "You realize...I knew the others might think me losing my mind. I had to wonder about it myself. Was it a dream? A vision brought on by the doctor's ministrations? And then the next visit, on the twelfth of November, I knew I was not dreaming because she mentioned the child. The baby she'd lost," Forbes clarified. "I don't know if you knew that, but Mary had miscarried not long before she fell. She again was at the foot of the bed...and this time she was hazy, because Galbraith had increased the dosage as I found sleep to be my enemy. But she said, 'Do not fret over the loss of our child. Be happy that he is in Heaven, and prepare yourself to join us both in the glorious life that exists beyond. Dear husband,' she said, 'I will call for you very soon.' And then she backed away once more, as I fumbled for the lamp. I must've cried out, because suddenly Niven was in the room, and also Dr. Galbraith but my mind was so fogged I could barely make out their faces. I asked them if they'd seen her, but they had not. From then on, I've left the lantern burning bright and I've fought Duncan over the potion. Some nights I win by refusing it, but I become so tired...so weary of fighting for sleep yet dreading it because I might miss her." The heavily lined face turned toward Matthew. "I am not insane, young man. Do you think me so?"

"Continue with the timeframe," Matthew said. "The apparition visited when next?"

"The night of November twenty-second, and the night of December ninth. The former, again I was somewhat dazed by the potion but I heard her speak my name, close to the bed. I was able to pick up the lantern and lift it toward her. She drew back and said, 'The glare hurts me,' and I lowered it but I was able to clearly see the lower part of her face. It was my Mary. Oh yes...my Mary. 'Soon,' she said, 'I will come for you soon. The glorious life beyond is where we may be together forever. Will you trust me, dear husband?' And I said 'Yes, I will.' At that, she backed into the further dark and I watched her standing there for a time. I felt…so *needed*. So *loved*, that she would come back for me. I said, 'I love you, my Mary, and I always shall,' and then I suppose the potion won out over me, and I woke up in the morning."

"You never saw the apparition depart the room?" A thought struck Matthew: "When you saw the lower part of Mary's face, did you note a very obvious beauty mark?"

"No. Mary has no such mark." Forbes narrowed his eyes. "But Zoya does. Is that what you're getting at? That a *Russian* girl is playing the part of an English woman? Well, there is no beauty mark on Mary's face, and I may have been hazy but I know a Russian accent when I hear it and the girl has flaming *red* hair."

"All right, what transpired on the night of December ninth? That's when you actually went to the cliff's edge?"

"Yes. That night I had only allowed a sip or two of the sleeping potion, and it affected me but I was still in my senses. I was drifting when I heard her speak my name."

"Did you again lift the lantern?" Matthew asked.

"No, as I recalled she didn't like the light in her eyes."

A very convenient dislike for a ghost, Matthew thought but he kept his mouth shut.

"She stood in front of the fireplace, between these two chairs," Forbes went on. "That was when she said she wished me to join her from the cliff. That there was only a little pain and confusion, and then you were healed by the holy light."

Spoken by an apparition that avoided light to the face and so kept the fire's light at her back, Matthew thought. Again, his lips remained sealed.

"She asked that I go and stand there, and that she would come to me. I went, but she did not appear. I think…Mary decided for whatever reason that it wasn't time."

Or if someone is actually playing at Mary's ghost that person doesn't really want Forbes to kill himself, Matthew mused. It's all a game of proving Forbes mentally unstable in order to void that business contract. Matthew found himself staring at the chain and the new padlock on the balcony doors. Before he approached a new question that had formed in his mind he had to ask one previously born. "Does Mary whisper to you or speak in a full voice?"

"She whispers."

A nice method with which to disguise a voice, Matthew thought. He turned his attention from the lock and chain back to Forbes. "This is my opinion, sir. You see this spirit if you are either under the influence of the

potion or in fighting the potion so needy of sleep that phantasms are dancing in your head. You feel at fault for your wife's death and thus you wish to
bring her back to life. If Mary has loved you in life as you submit she has,
I see no reason why her ghost would wish to deprive you of the many years
you have left to find joy and productivity in this earthly realm. You say she
desires you to join her in the afterlife. That's not love, sir, it's selfishness, and
if what you—and others—have told me about Mary Truxton's character is
true, then the idea of leaping from that cliff to meet her on the other side is
your own fantasy, and it does a disservice to your wife's memory. Does that
strike a chord with you?"

Forbes was silent. A tremor seemed to pass over the gray face and a
muscle jumped in his jaw. He started to speak and then hesitated. Matthew
was braced to be blasted out of the room, but instead the tormented man
before him said quietly, "She probably would've liked you."

That response was certainly not what Matthew had expected, as if he'd
wished to stir the man's ire enough for him to possibly find a grip on reality
through pure anger.

"I appreciate that you speak your mind," Forbes said, "but I know that
I am not insane and I know that Mary comes to me in the night. Yes, I am
somewhat hazed by Duncan's potions and my own struggles with sleep, but
she is as clear to me as you are sitting there. And as for being selfish...Mary
was as far from that as Boston is from...well, from *Moscow*. It was she who
encouraged me to cast off the burden of industry...to find a buyer for the
company, get what I could from the result, and leave the creditors to the
new owner. She suggested selling to my brothers, but I want the business
out of the family name and as I've told you neither Harris nor Niven will
come to grips with the precarious nature of our financial condition. They
have galivanted and thrown their own money to the winds across half of
Europe while I struggled to right the ship...and now, I have sought a harbor—with Mary's blessing—and I have found it."

"Much the lesser reason for Mary to desire your death," said Matthew.
"On the verge of your finding peace in life, she wants your life to end? No
sir, that makes no sense to me...even if it come from the spirit world, which
I doubt."

"Short of you or anyone else seeing Mary, your doubt must suffice. I
would suggest you sleeping in the corner of this room for a few nights, but
I believe Mary's specter is meant for my eyes only."

Matthew pondered an idea for a moment. Then he spoke it: "If you
would indulge me, Mr. Truxton. The next time Mary shows herself to
you...ask her a question."

"A question?"

"Yes sir. The answer being something only you and she would know. Don't mention this to anyone else in the house…not your brothers, not Dr. Galbraith, not Wicks…no one. Ask that question, and find out how much this 'Mary' knows about you and herself." Of course, Matthew thought, if it was simply a matter of Forbes actually losing his mind he would hear the correct answer whispered from the phantasm in his head, would he not? Still…it was an attempt. "Would you do that for me, sir?"

Forbes stared into the fire and said nothing, his face blank of expression. Matthew considered that Forbes was allowing into his brain the thought that if someone was playing at being Mary such a question could reveal the act, and then what would Forbes do with the truth?

But for the moment Matthew knew Forbes must stay steadfast in his belief. "I can't vow to that," the man replied. "What are earthly memories to a spirit from Heaven?"

Matthew had gone as far as he could go. He regarded the padlock and chain once more, and thought that having such in Forbes's bedroom—his refuge in the manor—was pure and simply a statement of control by his brothers. Which brought to mind the question he'd skipped over a few moments before: "On my walk to the village this morning I passed a shack about midway along the path. Do you know which I mean? It's well apart from the other dwellings."

"I know it. Mary and I have passed it many times. What of it?"

"Does anyone live there?"

"I have no idea. I've never seen anyone there. Why?"

"Ah. It looked abandoned. I was just curious." Mention the new padlock and lockplate? No, Matthew decided. He stood up. "I'll take my leave, then. You'll think about what I've suggested?"

Forbes picked up his book again and opened it to where he'd been reading. "Good day to you," he said.

The problem-solver departed the room, feeling that he might rather be fighting a one-eyed bear again than becoming entangled in the world of spirits, insanity…or cunning trickery, whatever might be the truth. At least with a bear, one knew where the teeth were.

EIGHT

The remainder of the day had been quiet, marked only by Matthew being interrupted in the corridor when he was about to knock on Harris's door.

"Can I help you?" Harris asked, coming along the hallway from the stairs.

"Yes. Well...not *you*, exactly. I hoped to have a word with Simone."

Harris delayed a reply until he'd taken his usual pinches of snuff up each nostril. He dabbed the excess away with his handkerchief. "I'd rather you didn't," he said. "My wife is of a highly sensitive nature, and this situation with my brother has wreaked havoc with her nerves."

"Doesn't she ever leave the room?"

"I take her for walks when it's agreeable. Lately it hasn't been."

"Harris?" The woman's voice came from beyond the door. To Matthew it sounded weak and tremulous. "Please see to me," she said imploringly.

"Pardon." Harris reached past Matthew to put his hand on the doorknob. "I must tend to my wife."

"Understandable, but is there a better time I might speak with her?"

Harris regarded Matthew with heavy-lidded eyes. "Whatever you might ask Simone is bound to upset her further. What can I tell you that would ease your curiosity. Oh!" He brought up a thin smile. "You would want to know how a sickly woman could take on the guise of a ghost and visit Forbes's bedchamber?"

"I'm not accusing anyone. I'm only trying to pursue the matter you've hired me for."

"Pursue," said Harris, "in another direction. Supper will be served in an hour. I believe Mrs. Baines is grilling us some of the local fish tonight. Now again...pardon me." Thus saying, Harris opened the door, entered and closed the door before Matthew could get a glimpse of anything beyond the threshold.

The supper was indeed grilled fish with green beans and boiled potatoes and was as excellent as had been the chowder the night before. Forbes and Simone were served in their rooms but this evening Zoya joined Niven, Harris, Dr. Galbraith and Matthew in the formal dining room. The young woman—dressed very properly but very elegantly in a pale green gown that complimented her modest makeup and the flaming red hair—sat next to Niven and across from Matthew, and was mostly silent except to talk briefly but in admiration about the Sebestyen conservatory in Vienna where she and Niven had met when Matthew inquired about the subject. Niven picked up the conversation, talking about the Sebestyen's challenging regime of learning the intricacies of the harpsichord, and Matthew remarked that it was unfortunate the manor didn't have a harpsichord, as he was sure everyone would enjoy a little music to brighten the atmosphere. Immediately he felt this was a rather obtuse—call it *dumb*—thing to say, as another silence settled in until Dr. Galbraith took up the subject of the unseasonably warm weather and when the first snow of December might be expected.

Matthew kept his peace about this subject as well and simply continued to eat his meal and listen to the others. He found himself shifting uncomfortably in his chair as he realized he was the subject of intense scrutiny from Zoya Smith, whose dark eyes kept coming back to him time and again. She hardly seemed to pay her groom-to-be any attention, though as Niven chattered on about the social life in Boston—which he obviously relished and from his exuberance on the matter wished to return to as soon as possible—he touched Zoya's hand and arm in a loving fashion but got nothing in return.

At last Wicks cleared the dishes away and Ruth Baines made an appearance to ask how everyone had enjoyed the supper. She received compliments from everyone including Matthew. She was a short woman in her mid-forties with curly brown hair going to gray and as Harris had pointed out she did walk with a limp. Matthew excused himself while the others were taking cups of tea and retired to his room and his books. Wicks had started a new fire to ward off the chill that began invading the manor as soon as the sun began to sink, so Matthew pulled the blanket off his cot and made himself a little nesting area beside the hearth. Between the fire's glow and the light from his lantern he again indulged in *Titus Andronicus*.

But he couldn't concentrate to his full capacity because his mind kept going back to the dilapidated shack with its new lock and lockplate. An abandoned place, or not? And the same type of padlock as the one Harris had bought to chain the balcony doors. Or was it? Didn't most padlocks look the same? But it being relatively new on the shack's door…a curious thing.

It occurred to Matthew that one way of finding out was to return to the trading post and ask if the ledger book revealed the recent purchases of padlocks. So with that in his brain he was able to devote more attention to Shakespeare, and therefore he spent a couple of hours in a world that actually was more violent and depraved than he would've liked to visit, one scene being rape, the cutting out of a tongue and the amputation of hands and another being two heads baked into pies.

So much for the civilized theater of the sixteenth century. Dread that anything like that might happen in the eighteenth.

Matthew reached a stopping point, fed the fire again from the supplied amount of wood, took the blanket and fitted himself onto the cot, a tricky proposition. Hopefully this night's sleep would be more restful and complete than the night before, but he doubted it.

He got himself as comfortable as possible, shoving away the recurrent thought that in truth he was in over his head here. He was going to be asked soon to sign a document attesting to Forbes's weakened mental condition, if not outright evidence of onrushing insanity. Harris and Niven with the help of their lawyers would void the business contract, take control of the Truxton Company…and then what? Sell it themselves, thereby cutting Forbes out of any money? He imagined that if push came to kick Harris and Niven would come to blows over the future of the company, with Niven being the loser. And what of Wandering Mary? Once Forbes was in a mental institution, would he still see her? Well, was he tottering on the cliff's edge of madness or not?

Soon the document and the inked quill would be presented to him, Matthew knew. What was he going to do when that—

His mental meanderings were interrupted by a noise.

From where?

And there it was again: a quiet, creaking sound…

…and as the knob was turned in the corridor his door began to open.

He sat up. A figure holding a lantern slipped into the bedchamber and closed the door.

By the ruddy light Matthew saw who it was. "May I ask what you're doing here?"

"I heard someone walking back and forth outside my room," Zoya said. Her voice held a quaver. "I don't want to be alone right now."

"Then go to Niven. I don't think it's proper that you—"

"Niven is downstairs guarding the door," she interrupted. "Please. Let me stay with you for just a little while."

Matthew stood up. He was wearing all his clothing but his boots and Zoya wore a long plaid flannel sleeping gown buttoned all the way up to the chin but still… "I think Niven might protest this visit," he said.

"Does Niven have to know?"

The question took him aback. For a few seconds he feared he might stutter when he replied, so strong was her presence…and, really, *more* than her presence. "I am a gentleman," he replied, "unused to having the promised brides of other men in my bedchamber past…what time is it, anyway?" He checked the candle clock with the new taper Wicks had supplied: nearly a quarter after eleven, he saw by the marks.

"Still early, for me. I am what you might call a night person. Niven will be downstairs until two when Harris takes the watch." She approached the fire, holding out her hands to warm them. "It gets so cold and damp in here. I despise this place and I can't wait to get back to Boston!" She darted a glance at him and then away again. "You don't have to back up, child, I won't bite you."

He realized he had retreated before her adamant advance. "You can stay for ten minutes," he said.

"My ten minutes might not be the same as yours." She rubbed her hands together and muttered something in her native tongue.

"What does that mean?"

"It means you're an odd bird. Are you afraid of me?"

"I'm afraid of angered grooms who might have access to a pistol."

"Ha!" Zoya said with a crooked grin. "If Niven ever fired a pistol he'd take his own foot off! To ease your nerves, I won't stay very long but I'm telling you someone was walking back and forth outside my room. When I opened the door to see, there was no one in the hallway. I closed the door and went back to my wretched cot...and then the noise started again... back and forth and back and forth."

"Wasn't it accompanied by the sound of dragging chains and moaning?"

She gave him a withering look before turned her attention back to the flames. "Do you believe Forbes is seeing Mary's spirit, or not?"

"My opinion has not yet solidified."

"Perhaps not, but I suspect your morals have."

"What does that mean, please?"

Zoya once more offered up the grin, her dark eyes sparkling in the firelight. "I don't know much about you but my grandfather had a say-ing. I'll translate it for you: Time doesn't serve the timid. I think you are. *Timid*, I mean."

Was this young woman in here throwing herself at him? Matthew won-dered. At first blush it appeared so, but might there be another reason? "Which one of the brothers sent you? Harris or Niven?"

"Neither one. I told you I heard someone—or some *thing*—walking in the corridor. I don't want to be alone right now, Niven is downstairs where it's even colder than it is up here and I wouldn't dream of going into Harris's room with the way Simone is, so here I am."

"Simone," said Matthew in an effort to steer this strange ship toward a more reasonable shore. "What's her condition?"

Zoya tapped her forehead. "Weak in here. Otherwise there's nothing wrong with her, but she thinks *everything's* wrong."

"I presume she wasn't like that before she and Harris were married?"

"I have no idea. I haven't known them but these last few weeks...when Harris came to Boston to bring Niven and myself here. To this dreadful crypt," she added. She lifted her chin. "You didn't answer my question in a direct manner. Do you believe Forbes is being visited by Mary's ghost? Surely even as timid as you are, you have *some* opinion."

"I am not an expert either on ghosts or mental instabilities. Timidly speaking, that is. Now...would you please leave my room so I can get some sleep?"

Zoya remained exactly where she was. "I believe in a world beyond us. A place we can't see. I don't know if the ghost is real or if Forbes is insane, though that's what both Niven and Harris think. But in the country of my birth…we don't play lightly with the spirit world. Not after we're told the story of Baba Yaga."

Matthew started to ask *Who*? but he refrained because he had the idea she was going to tell him whether he wanted to hear it or not.

Incredibly and infuriatingly, Zoya walked to the cot, took the blanket off and used it to make a nesting place for herself next to the fire as Matthew had done.

"Are you moving in here with me?" he asked.

"Baba Yaga," said Zoya, as if he hadn't spoken. "My grandfather's tale, and his grandfather's before that and into the ancient times. Everyone in my country knows and fears the name."

"Who is it? The tax collector?"

"The terrible witch of the woods," she answered. "She is of two persons. One who is helpful and blesses the traveller, and one who tricks the traveller into ruin and destruction. She can give hope on the one hand and dash it on the rocks on the other. And…oh yes…she beckons the errant child into her house, and she may give them gifts of great worth or cook them into a stew."

"A great story to keep the errant child from wandering in the woods, I'm sure. Don't you have a lot of wolves roaming in your country?"

"Baba Yaga can be a female wolf," Zoya said. She was staring into the crackling flames and her voice had become listless and dreamlike. "What you understand as a young one is…you do not go near Baba Yaga's house… which is any house that appears to be abandoned, for that is where she waits for the wandering child…where she waits and schemes to trap the unwary and cook them in her bubbling black cauldron."

"Oh, I see," said Matthew. "The obvious scare story to keep children from entering—" *An abandoned house*, he was about to say, but he stopped himself short because his mind had suddenly veered from this room to the old shack in the woods with its still-shiny padlock and lockplate.

"Baba Yaga rides on the wind and can turn herself into an owl, a raven and a wild dog," Zoya went on. "She is everywhere and sees everything, and I know some children in the town where I grew up—just outside Moscow—who swore they saw Baba Yaga floating at night through the trees on her witch's broom, her eyes blood red in a face as white as mist." She looked up at her host. "If those tales don't make your skin crawl, nothing will. My grandparents and their parents believed, you can be sure of that. Any child who wanders too far from home, or enters a house that seems dark and deserted…*clap* goes the trap of Baba Yaga around their necks!"

"Surely claptrap," Matthew said, but as he said it he still had the image of the old shack in his head. "All right, that's your ghost story for the night. Please close the door on your way out, and be kind enough to bring the blanket back to my cot."

"You're no fun," she said, with a pout to her lips.

"At any hour past eleven I am neither 'fun' nor fully conscious." Matthew strode the few steps to the door and opened it, half-expecting to see Niven lurking in the corridor outside. "How do you say 'leave' in Russian?"

"I would say it but you wouldn't know if it was the nastiest curse I could fling at you."

"I'm sure you can command quite a few of those." Matthew closed the door again but for a crack. "My observation, Madam Smith, is that you have as much love for Niven Truxton as you have for Truxton Manor. Am I correct in what I both sense and see?"

Zoya picked up her lantern from where she'd set it on the floor. She stood up and brought the blanket back to Matthew's cot. Her expression was totally blank when she regarded the young man. "It is an arranged marriage," she said, with both ice and fire in her voice. "I have arranged to be wealthy, and Niven has arranged to enjoy the political associations my father can provide."

"You may have the short stick in that arrangement, as Forbes insists the company is near collapse."

"Even if that's true, Niven has other interests both in England and in Europe. And he will have enough to do in his goings back and forth that I will have plenty of time for my...interests."

"Not interested," said Matthew. The door was opened wide again. "To be politely blunt...*out.*"

Zoya approached him and lifted the lantern so the light hit him squarely in the face. She placed a fingertip upon his chin. "You don't know what you're missing," she said.

"Yes, I do. Goodnight."

The fingertip went away. Whether she smiled or scowled he had no idea because his eyes were dazzled. She went out the door, he closed it and that was that.

Matthew returned to his cot and though he was weary he found sleep elusive. To finish *Titus Andronicus* or not, that was the question. No, there was too much violence and depravity in that play to continue on. He lay with his eyes closed and the blanket up to his chin, listening to the popping and crackling of the very welcome fire.

He had decided that in the morning he would make another trip to the trading post and make an inquiry about the recent purchases of padlocks, lockplates and nails. The abandoned shack was much on his mind. Baba Yaga, indeed!

And thus he did fall into the embrace of Somnus but it was a rough clench. He jolted awake, the fire having burned down to embers and in his memory of a nightmare himself standing before the old shack as the cold wind whistled through the trees. Something was coming under the gray-plated sky…some terrible presence of evil…and whether it was Baba Yaga or not Matthew tried to run in his dream but within three strides found his boots mired in gripping mud. At his back this hideous thing was bearing down on him, and now he could not even turn to face it, and closer and closer it drifted…now swooping toward him with horrible intent and demonic speed, and just as it was about to fall upon the errant child who had wandered too carelessly in the haunted woods he came awake and lay staring up at the dark that hovered above his head.

He shivered a few times, sat up and drew the blanket around his shoulders.

Ridiculous! he thought when his senses had settled down and his heartbeat slowed to that of a runaway steed. *What would Greathouse and Mrs. Herrald think if they could see me at this moment, cringing from phantoms of the mind?*

It would not do.

He had no idea of the time, but obviously it was still well before dawn due to the solid blackness beyond his blue-stained window. Return to sleep, if he could? A doubtful proposition. He felt he might need a drink of the doctor's potion to calm his nerves if this kind of thing continued. Also the cot was not kind to a person's back.

Since he was awake in this chilly mausoleum with no prospect of further rest for a while, he decided he might try his hand at being a watchman. The staircase across the corridor from Forbes's room would be a good place to position himself, to be unseen yet able to see "Wandering Mary" if she had not already visited for the night. Alas, for want of the dark lantern! He could've used it in this situation, but he would have to make his way without a light. No need to frighten off any ghosts before they drifted in, was there?

And was he absolutely sure he wanted to do this?

It was his task, wasn't it? He wasn't afraid of any ghosts, and Baba Yaga was too busy cooking up children in the Russian wilderness to pay any mind to him.

Matthew put his boots on. He dashed some cold water into his face from the water bowl. Then he steeled himself, eased out of his room and waited for a while until his eyes got used to the absolute dark. There was no telling what one might stumble into in a place like this. When he was ready he moved along to the far end of the corridor across from Forbes's room. He turned to the right, seated himself on the steps—careful not to take a tumble and break his tailbone for this effort—and told himself he was doing something positive by simply sitting here in the cold dark watching Forbes's door across the hallway.

In about fifteen minutes he wished he'd had enough sense to bring the blanket. In another half hour he was ready to return to the cot's evil embrace. The manor's chill deepened. A touch on the wall to Matthew's right left his fingers cold and clammy; he could feel the damp of the Atlantic seeping through the stones. His mind moved back and forth among many subjects: if Forbes was really insane or not; why was a new padlock attached to an old door; how was *Titus Andronicus* going to end; tomorrow a walk down to the trading post for more information; what were Ashton McCaggers's intentions toward Berry Grigsby, as if Matthew cared a whit; the grueling trip back to Boston was not one he looked forward to but it beat being in this place all to pieces, and—

He jerked himself awake. Somewhere between thoughts he had drifted off to sleep, and he imagined—or did he?—that he'd heard a noise in the corridor. What had it been? Just a small *bump*, it seemed, as in things that went *bump* in the night.

And as he sat mulling this over his heart gave a kick and he thought his hair must've stood on end, because suddenly a slender figure in a flowing white gown came into his view and stood before Forbes's door.

Matthew's breath froze.

The figure simply stood there without moving, its back to Matthew. For many seconds there was no movement...and then it turned and walked directly toward Matthew and the staircase up to the tower room, as the New York problem-solver pressed himself against the wet-bleeding wall because the phantasm was going to come up the stairs and pass within inches of cringing earthly flesh.

NINE

IN SILENCE THE APPARITION MOVED PAST THE YOUNG MAN WHO HAD nearly made himself one with the wall. It climbed up the stairs, silently still, and only when it was far up ahead did Matthew stand up on shaky legs, take a few deep breaths to make sure he still was not locked into a particularly disturbing dream, and then follow the specter at a respectable distance.

What he would have given for the dark lantern at this moment! Alas, he had only his eyesight, yet he was accustomed to the darkness and he could make out the white shape ahead of him, climbing slowly but steadily upward.

The figure reached the chamber above, with Matthew a few seconds behind. He again pressed himself against a damp wall, and watched the figure as it approached the closed doors to the upper balcony. Then it stopped and went no further, once more simply standing stock still. Matthew made out the shape's long dark hair. A woman? Yes. But whether of this earth or of the realm beyond he had no idea.

The figure turned again and approached the staircase. At the point when the distance was narrowed Matthew reached out to touch the shape's shoulder as it passed by him.

"*Don't touch her,*" someone whispered, which caused Matthew a renewed shock.

The specter passed him, and the man standing in the doorway—Harris, from the voice—pushed himself back out of the way so the woman—apparition, phantasm, spirit, whatever—could descend the steps.

"Who is it?" Matthew asked, also in a whisper.

"My wife," was the reply. And then he turned and went down the stairs after her, but not so quickly that he might disturb her descent.

As Matthew reached the bottom of the stairs he saw that Harris had in hand a lantern that he must've set aside before he came up the steps. Simone had stopped again in the middle of the corridor, her back to the two men.

"What's wrong with her?" Matthew whispered, coming up alongside Harris.

"A delicate condition. She walks by night. Not every night…maybe a few times a month in Boston, but here…it's been more frequent. She's still asleep, you know."

Sleepwalking, Matthew thought. He'd heard of such a thing but he'd never witnessed it. The door to Harris's room was ajar. Matthew realized he must've come awake from his own slumber because of the noise made when Simone had opened the door. Though witnessing this phenomenon with his own eyes he still couldn't grasp it. "How did she climb the stairs if she's asleep?"

"That I can't say, though in our Boston house she once climbed the steps to the attic and spent perhaps half an hour sweeping the floor. If you saw her face you'd see that her eyes are open, so some part of her brain grasps where she is. Galbraith can explain it better than I. Did she give you a fright?"

"An understatement. Can she hear us speaking?"

"I don't think so. But if she's suddenly awakened by a touch, the application of a light in her face or a loud noise she…well, it's not a pretty sight, as I discovered to my regret. She might either lash out in violence or begin screaming in terror. We don't want to foist that upon the house at this hour, do we?"

"Definitely not," said Matthew, whose nerves still felt shredded. Simone wasn't moving, and she was between him and his room. "She can open doors in that condition?" he asked.

"And close them behind her, yes. I happened to wake up to feed the fire and saw she was gone from her cot. Galbraith has been giving her the same potion Forbes is taking, but you can appreciate that his stock of medicinals has gotten low and he's having to reduce the dosage. Thus Simone is having one of her episodes."

A thought jabbed Matthew. "Can she speak when she's in this way?"

"Not that I've ever heard."

"Could it be Simone walking into Forbes's room at night, and Forbes in his current state of mind thinking she's Mary and speaking to him?"

"Possible," said Harris, still whispering. "But not probable. Forbes contends the spirit has visited him five times. Wouldn't I have awakened at least *once* on those nights and found her either entering or leaving Forbes's chamber? Ah! Look, she's moving!"

Simone took the last few steps to the door of her own room, pushed the door open with the ease of anyone wide awake, crossed the threshold and closed the door at her back.

"I've never seen the like," said Matthew, still honestly in a mild state of shock.

"We've been married for eight years," Harris said, holding the lantern up higher between himself and Matthew. "This began in year number five. She was born into a wealthy family, her father being very successful in the indigo import business. He was aboard a ship returning from the Indies that simply never arrived back in Portsmouth. Simone was his favorite among the four children. After Simon disappeared, Simone was never the same... and then these episodes began."

"A tragic history," Matthew said.

"Yes, but there's tragedy in every family, isn't there? One is either strong enough to survive it, or too weak to..." Harris paused, conjuring up the exact word he wanted. "*Exist*," he said. "And to the marrow of my bones I despise weakness. It is my burden that I must deal with Simone day after day as she collapses further."

A harsh attitude, to Matthew's way of thinking. Certainly not the words of a loving husband. Was there any love in this family but for Wicks' devotion to Forbes and Forbes's devotion to a dead wife? Matthew had the feeling that the marriage between Harris and Simone may have hinged on a substantial dowry from indigo dye money.

"You don't like hearing that," Harris said, correctly reading the moment, "but if you were in my boots you'd likely think the same...in time, that is. You might start out with lofty notions, because regardless of that scar on your forehead you have a soft and compliant countenance, but reality soon hobbles the horse." He stared into Matthew's face, expecting—perhaps demanding—a response, but Matthew was silent.

"My wife's regrettable condition is known only to Dr. Galbraith. I trust you will keep this unfortunate incident in confidence. Goodnight," said Harris—a word with no inflection of sincerity—and he retired to his room.

Matthew felt chilled to the bone. From somewhere he could hear water dripping. In his chamber he made a bonfire in his hearth with the last of his supplied firewood, and by its heat, light and roar up the chimney he finally found sleep on the unforgiving cot.

He was awakened by Wicks's knock at the door announcing breakfast. A look at the blue glass window showed him not the sunshine of yesterday morning but what appeared to be a hazy half-light. After that perception, to Matthew's brain came the term *a soft and compliant countenance*, used by Harris really as an insult in their meeting after Simone's sleepwalking incident. It occurred to Matthew as he shaved and washed his face that *a soft and compliant countenance* was just what Harris desired when he came looking for the *Earwig*'s valiant "hero." Perhaps Harris's canny nature had told him the tales were overblown, and then to find "a boy" in the office at Number Seven Stone Street…well, it was perfect for Harris's need to find a compliant witness to his brother's insanity, was it not? Matthew wondered what the man's response would have been if he'd found Greathouse alone in the office. *My pardon, sir, I think I have the wrong address.* Likely so.

At the breakfast table the usual group—Harris, Niven, Galbraith and Zoya—had assembled, minus the afflicted sleepwalker and the tormented ghost-seer. This morning Zoya gave Matthew not a glance, and he noted she was more attentive and "touchy" with Niven, who prattled on about his interest in horse racing in England and how he'd made so much money betting on the steeds. When the breakfast dishes were being cleared away by Wicks, Harris turned his attention to the taciturn Matthew. "What are your plans for the day? We have a deck of cards available and we're setting up in here for four-handed Jingo, if you care to join in."

"Thank you but no, I think I'll walk down to the tavern again."

"Beware drinking too much of that ale," said the doctor, looking at Matthew over the rims of his glasses. "I had a taste of it and one taste took me to my own medicine bag."

"I'll go with you," Harris offered, and could not resist a smirk for the benefit of the others. "To watch over you, so to speak. After all, someone might need to drag your body back up the hill."

Being a chess player, Matthew thought the black knight had just presented its lance. "I believe I can drag myself, if it comes to that…which it won't."

"But surely you would desire my company! Those rustics down there are not worthy companions to a sophisticated young man like yourself."

A soft and compliant countenance, Matthew thought. He brought up an easy smile. "I would certainly appreciate the company, but I do enjoy solitary walks. They sharpen the thinking. Also I wouldn't wish to either deprive you of your game or of tending to Simone's condition."

Harris's smirk flagged just a little, only to Matthew's notice.

"I mean to say," Matthew continued, "that your generosity toward a guest should not outweigh a wife's needs for her husband, in case she calls for you during the day. Is that right, doctor?"

Galbraith shrugged. "She sleeps most of the day, but it's true that she becomes agitated when she calls for Harris and he doesn't quickly respond."

"But you can take care of Simone while I'm away, can't you, Duncan?" The black knight was on the move again. "I don't want our young friend to get into any trouble. He tells me that yesterday the idiot Yates Johnsey was hounding him about money I've already *paid.*"

"It seems to me," said Matthew with his smile undisturbed, "that a husband can give what a doctor cannot: love and patience."

"Well said!" Galbraith clapped his hands, as Harris's smirk dangled from a lip. "Now let's make way for the Jingo!"

Zoya said something in her native tongue while looking at Matthew.

"What does that mean?" he asked.

"A saying from my grandfather. *Each to their own game.*"

Matthew had no idea what that was supposed to mean to him particularly…unless Zoya had the idea he was going to the village for more than the tavern's ale. He suspected Harris did as well.

"Let Corbett go, for God's sake!" said Niven. "Harris, you already owe me thirty some-odd pounds on these draws and I plan to make it sixty!"

"Go about your business, then," Harris said to Matthew, a touch of frost in his voice. "Mind you, the weather's changing. I wouldn't want to be on the wagon track if a hard rain set in."

"Thank you. Good day to all."

Matthew set about his journey, and with the opening of the manor's front door he saw that the fog Eli Baines predicted had drifted in and clasped the land in folds of shimmering pale grays and blues. The air was not so much colder than the day before but was heavy and wet with the smell of the sea. He wished to go back to his room for the cloak he'd brought in his baggage but he decided that once out of the house it was best to proceed as planned.

Down in the fog-shrouded woods Matthew stopped at the old shack to see if the bundle was still undisturbed. It was, so he continued on. At the trading post he was in the company of the same clerk as the day before, and he presumed this was the aforementioned Tom Brown, obviously himself the founder of Brown's Harbor or related to the same.

In the trading post were two women buying supplies such as bacon, flour and cornmeal, and Matthew allowed them to complete their purchases and leave before he advanced to the counter.

"A quick return trip," said Brown. "What can I do for you?"

"Today I'm requesting some information. Can you open your ledger and tell me who has lately purchased padlocks and lockplates?"

Brown looked askance at him. "What's this havin' to do with?"

"As you know, I'm working with the Truxton family and this is an important point." Matthew decided from the man's hesitation that he needed a bit more gunpowder in his pistol. "I'm requesting this on behalf of Forbes himself."

"A strange request."

"Yes sir, I'm sure, but..." It seemed even stronger powder was called for. Matthew reached into a pocket and offered Brown a gold guinea coin. "I am empowered by Forbes to present this for your trouble."

"Blind me, what a shine!" Brown's eyes lit up. "Well...this is for a good cause, I reckon." The coin was accepted, the ledger retrieved, set upon the counter, opened and paged back. Almost at once Brown said, "That brother Harris bought one, mornin' of the tenth of December. Didn't buy a lockplate, though. That was my last one. Fact is, nobody needs them things hereabouts, we're all a close community and the last person done any grievances got ten strikes of the bullwhip from Burt Anson. He's what you might call our law. But...wait a minute...I had four in stock but I recall one was busted inside and wouldn't snap shut. Lemme go back some." The pages turned.

"All right," he said. "Here we are in September." He used a gnarled finger to pinpoint the scrawled and to Matthew's eye completely illegible information. "Harris bought a padlock, a lockplate and four nails on the fifteenth. The key comes with 'em, no charge."

"Ah," said Matthew in a toneless voice to disguise any reaction to this news. "I see."

"One more padlock to track down." Brown's finger moved again. "Here 'tis. Sold that one on the thirteenth. *And* a lockplate. Looky here, I forgot who bought this one! I recall he said somebody sneaked into his workshop and stole some lumber, so he was lockin' it up and he already had the nails to work with."

"Who was that?"

"The carpenter," said Brown. "Yates Johnsey. I mean...carpenter most of the time, but he *does* make the coffins too when they're called for."

"Yates Johnsey," Matthew repeated. *That situation.* The question in Matthew's mind was: *What* situation?

"Them's the three I sold." Brown closed the ledger. "I guess you could'a saved your trouble and coin just by askin' Harris about it." Once more the frown came up. "What's all this have to do with Wanderin' Mary? I 'spect that's the subject on your mind, ain't it?"

"Absolutely and steadfastly on my mind." Matthew gave the man a wan smile but behind it his brain was trying to fit bits and pieces into a whole. "I can only say," he added, "that as every padlock has a key, every *situation* also has one. It's just a matter of fitting it into the correct lock."

"You must've had some schoolin'," said Brown. "That's over my head."

"Oh, I think you're doing pretty well for yourself. Certainly the village is growing." Matthew was still mentally grappling with the information, reasoning out what step to take next because certainly a next step was warranted. "I presume Johnsey does a lot of work here," he said.

"Oh yes sir, he's a busy fella. Kinda hard to get to know, even after so many years, but he'll do."

"Does he live nearby?"

"He and his wife Drucilla got a place out on the headland by the cove. You passed the wagon road on your left as you come down the hill. Somebody up at the house needin' work done?"

"No, just wondering. I met him in the Red Claw yesterday and I have to say he was in his cups."

"Yep, he's a good worker but he's a drinker too. I'd be the same if I had Drucilla breathin' fire down my neck like she does him. Oh...sorry, sir, I'm gettin' a bit too mouthy, as my Constance tells me."

"That's all right. To be truthful, the Truxtons aren't very interesting. Aside from Wandering Mary, that is. But I prefer more earthly communications." Matthew's mind had fixed resolutely on two facts as obtained from the ledger: Harris Truxton had made his purchase of the first padlock—with its lockplate and four nails—even days after Mary's death, and Yates Johnsey had bought his five days after the accident. Was there a connection between the two purchases...and between the two padlocks?

"You're right about the village growin', sir," said Brown. "My father would be proud of it, rest his soul. But one thing we're needin' here is a regular doctor. One comes up from Boston every so often but we're needin' more than Drucilla Johnsey can give."

That added more tinder to the growing flames of Matthew's curiosity. "*She's* a doctor?"

"Well, no sir but she's the nearest we've got. Mixes up potions from plants and all and she's been known to set a broke bone or two. But she's a rough 'un and as hard to get to know as Yates. Still…she's there when she's needed—and Yates is too—so nobody can complain too much."

A self-taught female medicalist and a coffin-maker, Matthew thought. That seemed logical.

And now he had made a decision he'd been turning over and over since hearing about Harris buying the lock, the plate and the nails. Matthew said, "Oh…I am tasked to make another purchase while I'm here. Eli Baines is in need of a small chisel. Do you have anything that might do? And also I'm going to need a tinderbox, if you please. Doesn't have to be fancy."

"Don't fret," said Brown with a gap-toothed but amiable grin, "it won't be."

TEN

IN THE BLUE-STREAKED FOG THAT LAY UPON THE TRACK FROM BROWN'S Harbor to the Truxton Manor, Matthew stood staring at the old dilapidated shack. The world had the silence of winter. He had the small chisel in hand and in a jacket pocket a tinderbox—cotton, dry wood shavings, a piece of striker steel and a flint—that was in actuality a little burlap pouch tied up with brown cord.

But he wasn't yet ready to assault the lockplate. First things first: a walk on the wagon trail that would take him along the curve of the cove and through the further woods to Johnsey's abode. He was interested to see of what use the carpenter-coffin maker was making of the padlock he'd purchased. Someone stealing lumber? If it was true, was it connected to the theft of the shovel, twine, burlap bags and measuring rod from the Truxton estate?

It was time to find out.

He began walking. The fog parted before him and closed in his wake. Soon he could hear the crashing of the sea against rocks, but the forest was still thick on either side though most of the hardwood leaves were dead and gone. After what he reckoned was about a half mile he saw shapes looming ahead. Nearer, and they became a stone cabin with smoke rising from the chimney, a barn, a wagon, what appeared to be a chicken coop in the back, and two unpainted wooden structures beyond the cabin. Matthew made those out to be likely Johnsey's workshed and a windowless wooden storage hut where lumber was probably kept. He slowed his approach and kept to the forest that edged the property. Everything was quiet here but for the noise of the waves maybe a hundred yards to the east. He mulled approaching the cabin's door and simply knocking, announcing himself and taking whoever answered up in conversation of some kind just to get a closer look.

From this position he couldn't see any padlock anywhere, but the fog had thickened during his walk. A fresh cold was setting in as well. He knelt down in the brush and watched the cabin, his gaze moving back and forth from there to the workshed and smaller hut and again to the cabin. There was no sign of life but the curlicue of chimney smoke, so someone was either staying warm or cooking food.

To go to the door, or not? He decided he would give it another fifteen minutes or so while he manufactured an amiable conversation that made some sense of him being out so far from the Truxton estate. Lost? No. Enjoying the weather? Certainly not. In need of a coffin? No thank you, not to—

From around back of the cabin suddenly came a hulking figure wrapped up in a dark blue cloak. Matthew could see markedly wide shoulders and a tight brown bun of hair. Drucilla Johnsey? If so, she was well over six feet tall and had a stride like a soldier marching to battle. She was carrying something: a basket, and in it a jug and various other items he couldn't directly make out. He watched as she strode purposefully past the workshop. She stopped before the hut's closed door, and now she was bringing a small object up in her hand from the basket and...what was she doing?

He realized.

She was putting a key into a padlock.

She opened the door and went inside, leaving the door open at her back. It was as black as Satan's spit within the place, not a shard of light. A minute or two passed and she did not reappear. Matthew considered creeping closer, and as he took his attention off the hut to begin a surreptitious approach he received a shock equal to any he'd previously experienced in his young but adventurous life.

A large and muscular gray dog with yellow eyes was standing about six feet in front of him, staring at the intruder in total silence.

And as their eyes met the animal let loose with a harsh cacophony of barking that nearly split Matthew's eardrums. Panic leaped up within him. He held one hand out in front of himself with the chisel in the other to ward off a potential attack, and so doing he backed away into the forest with one eye on the shed, expecting the woman to emerge and see him at any second.

But the dog didn't follow, he got an ample amount of trees and brush between himself and the assorted structures, and as he continued to back warily away he heard a presumably woman's voice almost as harsh as the dog's bark holler "Ripper! Shut up!" When Ripper didn't immediately obey the command was followed by, "Come here! Ripper! Damn you, I said come *here!*"

Ripper seemed to know what was good for him, for he gave a few more heated barks and then silenced. Matthew slipped away through the woods and made a wide arc back to the wagon track, where he crouched in the foliage looking left and right for a time before he went on.

Then he came again to the shack.

Baba Yaga's watching, he thought. *Waiting for the errant child or the blundering fool, and she is salivating over her bubbling cauldron.*

He swept that ridiculous inkling away. He made his way around to the rear of the place, retrieved the dark lantern's bundle, removed it from its wrapping and spent a moment getting the tinderbox ignited as the air was so damp. Then he transferred the small but able flame to the lantern's wick and tested the shutter. The magnifying lens threw more than a satisfactory light. He was ready.

Before he went up to the door he chose a good-sized stone from the ground as there were many suitable choices for a makeshift mallet lying about. With that in hand and the chisel situated to be driven under the lockplate in order to pull the nails out, Matthew began the work.

It was a noisy labor. In the fog's silence the sound of the stone striking the chisel to Matthew equalled a small war in progress, musket shot after musket shot. It was truly a battle getting the chisel to gouge up the plate as the nails had been driven in by a determined hand. But slowly the battle was won and the plate and its lock could be made to surrender the door. Both combatants along with the squadron of nails fell to the porch at Matthew's boots with a ringing sound of defeat. He slid the chisel into his waistband, opened the lantern's shutter and pulled the door open. But before he crossed the threshold he smelled from the gloomy interior a sickly sweet odor that sealed his boots to the floor.

It was not a new odor, being part of the wet mustiness within, but it was there all the same: a death odor, or rather one of putrefaction. Matthew aimed his lantern's lens down, and saw upon the timbers the dark brown smears, streaks and huge stains that could only be long-dried blood. They came right up to the threshold and stopped, and were not apparent on the porch or the steps.

But here they were. Evidence of what? Matthew entered on uncertain legs, moving the light from one side to the other. He saw no body. There appeared to be a pallet of straw in one corner. What looked like a few dried apples or stones lay on the floor near a yellow plate. The only furniture in the place consisted of a single chair and a small round table, both of them overturned. The bloodstains on the floor were so plentiful Matthew thought whoever or whatever had died here had been nearly bloodless when the violence was finished. His light made something on the grisly boards gleam. He picked up the object and found with an additional shock that in his hand was a human tooth.

The lantern's strong beam showed another and another, until Matthew had picked up four teeth. Also on the floor were what appeared to be small pieces of leather clotted with gore. He realized they were bits of flesh, and this is where the death smell came from.

The scene here had been one of horrific murder, there was no doubt of it. He thought he'd better get out before his clothes caught the odor of decayed flesh and he brought it back with him to the manor, but then his light touched the far wall and the fireplace and he saw that amid the charred wood something else had been burned within.

He approached the hearth, bent down and shone the light around the ashes and the remaining shards of blackened tinder. His heart was absolutely pounding and he could hardly hold the lamp steady. He realized he had put the four teeth into his pocket…and here was something else of interest, melted upon the hearth's stone floor.

It was a puddle.

A dried puddle.

A puddle of a myriad of colors—red, blue, purple, green, orange and more—combined by the flames' heat and then preserved when the fire cooled and died.

Matthew touched it.

Wax.

He caught his breath.

In his head he heard Zachariah Swaine say she's got it in her heart to be an artist, and she's right good at picturin'. I paid Johnny Tucker to bring her a pack of colored wax sticks up from Boston on the boat. I don't remember what those are called.

"Crayons." Matthew startled himself because he hadn't realized he was speaking the thought aloud. And staring at the remains of a young girl's collection of colors he said in a voice strained by the horror of the discovery, "Crayons is what they're called."

The light picked up fragments of paper that had not been completely consumed by the fire, and he wondered in his dazed frame of mind if one of those had been a crayon rendition of apples or stones on a yellow plate.

A still life. What Nora Swaine liked to draw.

Sixteen years old and gone to Boston.

Matthew knew in opening that door he had inadvertently begun work on Zachariah Swaine's problem, and if these were the remains of his daughter here was as near to Boston as the girl had reached.

But the letter from Nora's friend saying all was well with her! Who had sent it?

Harris Truxton's lock on the door. Harris Truxton had not wanted anyone to find what was in this shack. Harris Truxton had murdered Nora Swaine, or was covering the scene of the crime for someone else?

If it was true...*why?*

This was not the house of Baba Yaga, Matthew thought as he stood up and fought back a wave of dizziness. Not the house of a Russian witch, but in truth an errant child had entered here and from the looks of all the gore a malignant evil had torn her to pieces.

He had to get out. His head was light, his senses were spinning and he feared having to spew upon the boards. When he staggered out into the fog he stood at the foot of the steps shivering in the cold and nearly frantically breathing the damp air to clear his head. It took him a long time to go back to the door, close it and work the nails back through the lockplate into their holes. He didn't care to use the rock to hammer them entirely in, as it seemed the noise was somehow the disturbance of a tomb.

Moving as if in a dream, Matthew returned the dark lantern to its hiding place and added the tinderbox to the bundle. When he got back out to the path he stood looking at the shack as the fog slid around him with cold fingers.

Another question among many questions...all the dried blood, the decayed flesh, the teeth, the puddle of crayons.

But where was the corpse?

On the way back to the manor he stopped and threw the chisel far into the woods. Then he went on, and as he walked he realized his hand was in his pocket and he had clenched in that hand the teeth of a dead girl.

ELEVEN

By THE TIME HE'D REACHED THE CLIFFTOP MATTHEW'S HEAD HAD cleared and he had a new resolve: to find out as much about Nora Swaine as possible. Thus he kept on walking past the manor toward the coachhouse. Smoke was rising from the chimney there. A set of wooden stairs on one side of the structure led up to a door above the stall where the coach was kept. Matthew climbed up and used the brass knocker in the shape of a horseshoe to announce his presence at the door.

It was soon opened by the tall and long-limbed Caleb Clegg, who was sandy-haired and wore a trimmed light brown goatee. "Master Corbett," he said, with some surprise. "What can I do for you?"

"I'd like a word with both you and your wife, if you don't mind."

"May I ask what this is about?"

"Generally speaking," said Matthew, "it concerns the current situation with Forbes Truxton. And of course his imagined visits from Mary."

A woman came to the door behind Clegg. "Let him in, Caleb, the heat's slipping out."

"Of course. Sorry for the hesitation, sir." The door was opened wider and Matthew was admitted into a warm and well-decorated parlor with inexpensive but nice chairs, a sofa, oak table, a dark green rug upon the floorboards and a white stone hearth that currently housed a robust fire.

"May I take your jacket?" Leah Clegg asked, coming up alongside her husband.

"Thank you, but I'll keep it on for the moment." Matthew noted that she was nearly as tall as the man, was of a slim build and was indeed very attractive. She had dark brown hair pinned up with little metal pins in the shape of butterflies, their blue color almost the same as the shade of her eyes. She was wearing a prim and unostentatious lilac-hued dress with a white lace collar and cuffs. Her gaze upon him was cordial and confident and he thought both she and her husband were people to be trusted. At least he fervently hoped so.

"Please, sir, sit down," Clegg said. "We have a pot of tea, if you'd care for a cup."

"Again thank you, but no." Matthew sat in a chair close to the fire and turned it so he could take in both of them. Clegg and his wife remained standing and appeared a mite uneasy. "I am not here as a *master*," Matthew said, reading their consternation. "I am here as an *equal*. I am in the employ of the Truxtons just as you are. So please…let's not have any formalities."

They both seemed to breathe a sigh of relief. Then they sat down on the sofa and Clegg leaned slightly forward. "What may we do for you, sir? I mean…what may we do for you?"

"Just call me Matthew, if you please. A question for you: when you are here and Harris desires to come to the manor from Boston, how does he travel?"

"He has his own coachman. A very able gent name of Andrew Bryce. When he's here Andy sleeps in the spare room."

"And has Harris made that trip very often? Specifically before Mary's accident?"

"A few, yes. He was in the habit of visiting Master Whitton from time to time, and after…um…the hanging…he continued to occasionally visit."

Clegg shifted in his seat and shot a glance at his wife. Matthew could tell that the unease had returned. "Sir...I mean, Matthew...not to be impertinent, but exactly what is this about?"

"You know I've been hired by Harris to investigate this unfortunate situation. In that capacity I must leave no stone unturned." *Or door unlocked,* Matthew thought. He imagined he could still smell the reek of the dead up his nostrils.

"If I can pose a question?" the woman asked, and she waited for Matthew to nod. "What do Master Harris's trips here from Boston have to do with...as you put it...this unfortunate situation?"

"I am interested in the comings and goings of everyone, not just him." That was a lie but it had to be said. "Harris has presented to me three theories: one, that Forbes is insane; two, that someone is playing the part of Mary; and three, that there is an actual ghost haunting the manor. Which theory I tend to believe I have yet to decide."

"But surely you don't believe there's really a ghost!" Clegg said. "No, I think the poor man began to lose his mind when Mistress Mary fell. Probably before, knowing what I do of the family." He blinked. "Sorry sir, I've let my tongue get the better of my manners."

"Not at all. I appreciate the candor. To continue turning the stones, how many visits here would you say Harris has made in the period before Mary's death?"

"Many," said Leah.

And there was something about the word that instantly made Matthew lock eyes with her, for the expression of her face had changed...not overtly...but there was now a hardness about the mouth and her shoulders had come forward slightly as if in a self-protective gesture.

"Many?" Matthew repeated as a question. "As in...four...eight...ten? How many?"

"Over the period of five months before Mistress Mary's accident," Leah said, "I would count that Master Harris visited the estate seven times and stayed about three or four days each trip. On those occasions Mr. Bryce brought him and took him back."

"Hm," Matthew said. "Seven trips. Three or four days each. And Forbes and Mary did not arrive here until August, I understand. Did Harris's wife accompany him?"

"On some visits, yes. On others, no. I heard from Marion that they used Master Whitton's bedchamber."

"Sensible," said Matthew. "But what is there to do here in that empty house for four days for a sophisticated gentleman from Boston? I know Mrs. Baines is a good cook, but that's certainly a long trip to take for some chicken chowder. Don't you think?"

"Master Harris very much liked to hunt," Leah offered. "Often he went out in the woods with his musket to shoot deer. Eli, Caleb and Andy hauled the carcasses back and Ruth cooked the venison. And I know he's killed fox for the sport of it. Otherwise, I have no idea."

"Are you sure about that?" Matthew asked.

The couple were silent. Then Clegg cleared his throat to say, "It's not our place to be talking like this, sir. We are not of their social order and should not be *speculating*."

"Understandable, but this matter of a wandering ghost should for the moment banish the boundaries between master and servants…unless, that is, you *want* to see Forbes Truxton committed to an insane asylum."

Clegg sat up a little straighter and the concerns of his position were made apparent by the furrowing of his forehead. "Is *that* what's going to happen to him? I didn't know."

"It's possible, so please tell me anything that you think might be of importance, even if you *don't* think it's important. Nothing will go past this room."

They were silent again until Leah spoke up. "Why is it you want to know how often Master Harris visited?"

"I am putting together a list of dates and I'm finding some peculiarities." Matthew did not go further, but he was thinking of four particulars: Harris buying a lock for the old shack on the fifteenth of September seven days after Mary's death; Yates Johnsey buying a lock on the thirteenth of September and obviously using it to secure a windowless shed; and—very disturbingly—Nora Swaine not coming home on the night of the fifteenth, supposedly the eve of her stowing away to Boston on the market boat.

And add an additional event near or about the fifteenth of September: the theft from Eli Baines's toolshed of a shovel, a six-foot measuring rod, a ball of heavy twine and four burlap bags.

The smell in Matthew's nostrils was now not so much of a murder victim's decayed flesh but of a plot hidden within another plot.

"Master Harris," Leah suddenly said, speaking hesitantly but firmly, "has…accosted me on several occasions."

"Leah!" Clegg said sharply. He grasped her hand. "We vowed not to mention that to *anyone!*"

"I know we did…but as Mr. Corbett implies, anything might be important." She gave Matthew a steady gaze. "On several occasions Master Harris touched me in inappropriate places. The first time it happened he insisted on walking to the village with me…to the church where I teach reading and writing. While we were on the path he said…" She paused to gain a bit more courage, for speaking on this subject about a master was a sure route to dismissal and disgrace. "He said I was far too attractive to be married to a coachman, and if I desired it he could make me a very happy woman. Then he placed one hand on my arm and the other…just below my left bosom."

"And you responded how?" Matthew asked.

"I moved away from him, of course. And I told him I was already very happy, but thank you for your interest."

"Did he continue with you to the church?"

"Not that morning, no. But on some others he did. He always sat in the back and watched."

"On other occasions he touched you inappropriately?"

"Please, sir!" said Clegg. "Must we—"

"It's all right, Caleb," she said gently. "I think we can trust Mr. Corbett. On other occasions," she said to Matthew, "he touched my hips…my bosom…my private area. He became very flagrant about it, but I did my best to avoid him. In fact I haven't set eyes on him since Mistress Mary's death."

What Leah was describing was not in itself a crime, Matthew thought. He guessed the number of serving women either beguiled, cajoled or forced into sexual situations by their wealthy masters was in the legions. Courts cared not a whit about such subjects. Harris Truxton's wife was probably not a willing partner most of the time due to her conditions either real or imagined, thus the buck must gallop after any doe in the field.

It was time to inquire about another subject that was pressing weightily on Matthew's mind. "One of your pupils has been a young girl named Nora Swaine. Is that correct?"

"Yes. Nora has been a very attentive student." Now Leah's forehead furrowed. "Why do you ask about *her?*"

Matthew ignored that for the moment. "What do you know of Nora?"

"Well…very attentive, as I've said. A pretty girl, all of sixteen and interested in drawing. She's shown me some of her work and I've told her she has a talent for it."

"She uses different colored wax crayons?"

"Yes." Puzzlement surfaced in the blue eyes. "I don't understand why you're asking these questions. Could you explain yourself before we go any further?"

Again Matthew chose to ignore the inquiry. What could he say? Begin by showing her the four teeth in his pocket? "You do know that Nora has stowed away on the market boat and gone to Boston? I met her father in the village yesterday, and he—"

"*Wait,*" Leah said. "Just a moment." She shook her head. "No, that's not right."

"It's what her father believes, and it's written in a letter he received."

"Oh. Yes...the letter," she said, and in those last two words was...what? Surprise? Wariness? Mistrust? Matthew waited to hear what must be revealed next.

It took a while. Leah looked at her hands as she worked them together.

"What is it, dear?" Clegg asked, putting an arm around her shoulders. "Something's wrong?"

The woman's chin lifted and she looked into Matthew's face. "Yes," she said. "Something *is* wrong. Nora was not planning to stow away on the market boat. She was supposed to be taken to Boston by...someone. I don't know who. She wouldn't tell me. When Nora went to Boston she was two months with child and she was terrified to let her parents find out. She asked me for advice. Of course I told her to tell her mother and father and get it all out in the open. I asked her also who the boy was, but she wouldn't say. All she told me was that he was taking her to Boston and she was staying there until she had the baby. Then she would come back afterward."

"My God!" said Clegg. "Why didn't you tell me this long ago?"

Leah sighed and shrugged. "It's just...that it was *female* business. Nora trusted me not to tell anyone, and I promised. It wasn't something that should've concerned you."

"Admirable that you kept your promise until now," Matthew ventured, "but how would Nora have been taken to Boston by a young man in the village if not by the market boat?"

"She said he had his own way to get there, and it definitely was *not* the boat because I asked. She wouldn't say more." Leah put a hand to her face for a moment. When she brought it away she said, "I didn't know *what* was the right thing to do. I mean...about betraying Nora's trust and telling her parents, or keeping a silence when I knew the girl should stay here and have the child. Drucilla Johnsey has a reputation for being rough-handed, but she's birthed many babies. Of course I was worried about Nora and what might happen to her in Boston. Then Zachariah showed me the letter written for her and asked me to read it to him. In that letter was pronounced that she had hidden aboard the market boat...but that's not what she'd told me was going to be done. I was confused...I thought perhaps she *had* been a stowaway...but no young man who might've gone with her is missing. It just doesn't make sense!"

Matthew nodded. He kept his focus on her and would not let her look away. "I want you to think very hard. Did you see Nora with any young man in the village on a regular basis? I am asking...who might have been the father?"

"I saw her with no young man from the village," was Leah's reply.

But she kept working her hands together…working and working, as if trying to fashion another answer from the air as one might knead a shape from shapeless clay, and Matthew again waited.

Her hands stopped moving. "One morning…months ago," she said. "May, it was. A warm day. Master Harris was here with Mistress Simone, and he said he needed some air…away from her, he said. He walked to the lessons with me. He didn't touch me. He hardly spoke. He sat at the back and watched the students. When the lessons were done, he stood up and walked out. I spoke to the students for a while and answered the questions they always posed to me. Afterward…when I left the church, I happened to look around for Master Harris…and he was standing in the shadow of the oak tree just off to the right. And…I saw him walk up alongside Nora…talking to her, smiling…and I thought *Nora, don't stop.* I thought *Nora, keep walking. Nora, Nora, go home to your mother and father, and don't come back to that oak tree after dark.* I should have said something…anything…out loud, but I did not…because it was not my place, even knowing…what I knew."

"And what was that?" Matthew prodded.

Her reply: "How much Master Harris enjoyed the hunt." She blinked, her blue eyes hazy. "So…no…I saw Nora with no young man from the village."

Matthew couldn't let this sit. He said, "Therefore you might speculate—" He stopped, because that was the incorrect word. "You might *imagine* that Harris and Nora were…how shall I put it?…*involved?*"

"Imaginings are beyond our station, sir," said Clegg, his expression stony. "We perform our services here and that is all."

"All right." A glance at Leah showed Matthew that her face was drawn, her eyes downcast and her hands again clenched together. He knew that was all he was going to get. "I thank you for your time and confidence." Matthew stood up. "Oh…Mrs. Clegg…I might ask…when do you next go to the village for the lessons?"

"Tomorrow morning."

"Do you carry anything?"

"I have a bookbag, yes."

"A large bag?"

"It is canvas and accepts as many books as it can carry. Why?"

He offered her a warm smile, though it was difficult to manufacture because the murder scene in the old shack was still so terribly clear to him. "Would you consider bringing an item back for me when you return tomorrow? And making sure there's room for a bundle about this size?" He demonstrated with his hands. "It's very important." he said to her once more puzzled expression. "Also it means digging through some dead leaves, but it's not far off the path. Would you?"

"I...suppose...I could."

"Excellent. And would you bring this bundle here to your house and keep it until I call for it? To add also...you would make certain you didn't mention this bundle to anyone? And I do repeat...not to *anyone*."

"You make it sound so mysterious," Clegg said, and it was obvious he had a sudden jolting thought. "It's not *dangerous*, is it?"

"Only to ghosts," Matthew answered, and he left it at that.

TWELVE

RIPPER.

As Matthew washed his face and cleaned his teeth before the call to supper, he remembered Tom Brown saying that Johnsey had bought his padlock and plate because someone had stolen lumber from his workshop.

With a watchdog like Ripper, how the hell would anyone dare to creep in there at night and try to steal *any* damn thing? The Johnseys might take the dog in at the evening, but still...with the prospect of Ripper bounding around in those woods, only a huge fool would play thief on that property.

So...why had Johnsey really bought the lock and plate?

Matthew knew of two reasons to put a padlock on a door.

To keep someone out...and to keep someone *in*.

In thinking about it, Matthew reasoned that Drucilla Johnsey was taking a basket of food and drink into the shed after she'd unlocked the door.

Who was inside the shed?

After leaving the Cleggs he had walked for a time around the estate, just making circle after circle as he pondered a task that he knew was outlandish—insane in its own way, perhaps—but he thought had to be done, and done as soon as possible. While he walked he kept turning the four teeth over and over in his pocket. Then he had stood in the darkening air at the cliff's edge, watching the waves crash in, and made his decision.

He had found Eli Baines tending to plants in the greenhouse. When Matthew explained what he wanted done, Baines had stood open-mouthed and unable to respond.

"You do know the area, don't you?" Matthew had asked.

"Yes sir, I did the work there...but...what you're askin'...it's an unholy thing, ain't it?"

"It might be. In this case it's a necessary thing."

"I don't know, sir...I don't think I can vow to do it."

"Eli," Matthew had said, "much depends on *you*. If you can't or won't do it, just bring what is necessary and I'll do the work. I will speak to Wicks about letting you in through their quarters. I am thinking one o'clock. Do you have a pocket watch?"

"I have a candle clock, sir."

"One o'clock," Matthew had emphasized. "Bring the tools and then leave if you like, but bring the tools."

So that had been his conversation with Baines, and now there was one more—a harder case, to be sure—to convince of this unholy mission. That would have to wait until the quiet hours after supper.

Matthew prepared himself, which meant making sure his resolve was strong enough to keep a good face on. He would have to sit at the same table with Harris Truxton. It was not going to be easy or pleasant.

He had come to the conclusion today—the only conclusion that made any sense to him—that Harris Truxton had been the village buck who got Nora Swaine with child. The shack had likely been their place of many assignations over the summer months before Mary's accident. A pallet of straw in a corner could do as well as a bed if it had to, and where else would Harris have taken the girl? Had he murdered her because she was pregnant? The child might have been a problem. Matthew thought that Harris might be more dependent on Simone's family money than he let on, and thus… disaster for him if Simone found out.

Forbes's voice in Matthew's head: *A few days before the incident Mary went for a walk to the village. When she came back, she was…I would say disturbed. In a dark mood, but she wouldn't tell me why. She said she needed time to think about it…whatever it was. But as I say, it doesn't matter now.*

No, Matthew mused. It doesn't matter now. But on that particular walk on that particular day had Mary seen Harris and Nora either going into the shack together or leaving it? And she had died before telling her husband what she'd seen. Had she told Harris?

Did that matter now?

One thing that really and vitally mattered: the fact that Nora's corpse—brutally mangled as it must have been—was unaccounted for. What had Harris killed her with?

All that blood, the teeth and the clots of flesh. Too much for a knife.

An axe at work?

Or the hard edge of a shovel?

Beaten to death when she was thinking she was going to be taken to Boston in Harris's care and deliver the child there. And her crayons brought along to accompany her on the trip. Likely she'd done some artwork there in the shack, and Harris had burned the evidence in the fireplace as well as throwing the crayons in.

Matthew ran a hand across his forehead. He was going to have to steady himself to face that man at supper, and if he cracked one fraction of an inch the cunning and conniving killer would see it. And Harris might sense it without even a crack.

If Harris had taken the shovel from Baines's toolshed to kill Nora Swaine…what about the other missing items? The six-foot measuring rod, the ball of heavy twine and the burlap bags…what of them? Had Harris used the shovel to bury Nora when the work was done? Then from Boston he'd gotten someone to write the letter to her father. Who was that someone? A willing accomplice or a person who was unaware of the crime?

And another thing that worked on Matthew: the padlocked shed on Yates Johnsey's property. Johnsey had bought the lock and plate on the thirteenth of September. Harris had bought the one on the shack on the fifteenth. Obviously he had killed Nora probably the early evening or night of the fifteenth and he already had the materials in his possession to seal the shack up.

But what did he use the rod, the twine and the bags for? If she was already dead—and God knows it wouldn't have taken long, losing all that blood—he wouldn't have needed twine to tie her down with. Maybe there'd been a blanket or coverlet of some kind for the straw pallet, so if that were the case he could've wrapped the corpse up in it and dragged it out so that was why there was no blood on the porch or the steps.

I've got a bone to pick with Harris! the half-soused Johnsey had yawped at the Red Claw. *You tell him he owes me money for that situation, and Drucilla is on the warpath about it!*

The hulking Drucilla, unlocking the shed with her basket of food and drink.

That situation.

What was it?

Matthew reckoned he was as ready as he could ever be. He took his lantern and as he left the room he caught sight of Harris—also with lamp in hand—just descending the staircase to his right. He stood stock-still in the doorway, his heart thumping, until Harris had gone down out of sight, and then he took an opportunity he'd been hoping for.

He walked along the corridor and knocked softly on the door beyond which lay Simone Truxton.

"Who is it?" came a weak and tremulous voice.

"Matthew Corbett, ma'am. May I enter?"

After a pause, there was a "Yes" that was perhaps even weaker and more tremulous.

Matthew went in.

She was lying on her cot covered with several blankets but propped up on a mound of pillows to face the fire in the hearth. At her side a double candelabra burned on a small table that also held a teapot and cup, and on the floor was a stack of books and what appeared to be several items of needlepoint in progress. Beside that—many feet away from Simone's cot, Matthew noted—was the cot Harris used, and in the room also was a single leather chair.

He closed the door behind him. As he approached the woman, Matthew had the impression that she once had been very beautiful but now was sallow and hollow-cheeked, her dark brown eyes sunken in lines of either real or imagined pain, and her entire demeanor one of hopeless suffering. She lifted up slender white hands to touch her long hair as if in an effort to better present herself to the visiting gentleman, but it was a futile gesture and not much came of it.

"Good evening," he said, standing at the foot of her cot.

She nodded. Her eyes narrowed as if having difficulty seeing him. "You are...the young man Harris hired. From New York town."

"That's right."

"Here to testify to Forbes's insanity." It was a statement. "The poor man. I remember when he was lively and vibrant. And Mary...such a treasure she was. But life can be terribly cruel, don't you think?"

"Unfortunately it's true."

"I know how true it is. I lost my dear father...it seems like only yesterday but then again an eternity. Can you understand that?"

"Yes."

"Will you sit for a while and keep me company? Harris says Wicks will be bringing my supper soon, but please stay." She motioned toward the chair. "Dr. Galbraith sits there," she explained. "He's another treasure. Without him...I'm not well, you know."

Matthew took the chair. "I doubt the atmosphere of this place agrees with you. I doubt it agrees with *anyone*."

"Yes, it's frightful isn't it? I long to get back to Boston but I dread the trip. I had to come with Harris though. I couldn't bear to be left in the house. In Boston, I mean. We do have servants but that's not the same as having a husband near. A wife does need her husband's attentions."

"Of course," Matthew said. "I understand your husband has made many trips here, both before Mary's accident and afterward. Did you accompany him on most?"

"A few. Not all. He's energetic, my Harris is. I have to admit I can't keep up with him...always moving, always here and there...forceful would be the correct word. In truth he wears me out. My father was like him. A businessman, always in motion…always with a plan that had to be carried out. It's *life* for that kind of person, isn't it?"

"Absolutely."

Simone struggled to sit higher on her pillows. Matthew got up to help her but she waved him away, got herself situated, and Matthew returned to the chair. "It was a wise man who discovered fire," she said, staring into the flames. "I wonder who that might have been."

Matthew had no idea how to answer that. He said, "You are part of an interesting family." She didn't respond but kept her gaze on the fire, and the blankness of her expression made Matthew fear she was already in the trance of sleepwalking. He was about to repeat his statement when she tore her attention away from the hearth and said, "A sad family. There is very little happiness in it."

"The business makes harsh demands. You know that from dealing with your father, I'm sure."

"Oh yes. But we do have a happy occasion ahead, after all this unpleasantness is done. The marriage between Niven and Zoya. Will you be staying for the wedding?"

"When will it be?"

"I don't know, Harris hasn't told me yet." Simone gave him a look that he might equate to that of an eager puppy after a meatbone. "What does she look like?"

"Zoya? You haven't met her?"

"No. I have asked Harris and he simply says she's very young and very pretty. I understand she's Russian. Or partly, Harris says. I think on her mother's side. Describe her to me, if you please."

"She's very beautiful. She has dark eyes and red hair. Fiery red, I'd say."

"Hm," was Simone's response.

"We've only had a few instances to speak," Matthew continued, "but she seems—"

"That's a strange thing," Simone interrupted.

"Pardon?"

"A strange thing," the woman repeated. "Fiery red."

"I'm sorry. Why is it strange?"

"Because of the play. At the Winthrop House. It was showing for many nights. Harris took me and I commented on her hair. Just like that. Fiery red."

Matthew leaned forward. A pulse had begun beating at his temple. "I am very simple this evening. What play do you mean?"

"The one that showed at the Winthrop House. *The Russian Widow.* The actress who played…I forget her name…had that fiery red hair, and I commented on it. Well it wasn't a large part…she was a handmaiden to the main character. I do love the plays. My father did also, and he took me to many in London."

"Ah!" said Matthew. "A grand entertainment! But that's quite a coincidence, isn't it? Tell me…in all the time you've been here, you've never set eyes on Zoya? Miss *Smith*, I might say. You didn't accompany your husband on the trip to Boston to fetch them?"

"Oh no. Sometimes on that journey I feel my spine is about to break, with all the jostling. I have asked to meet Zoya but…you see…I'm not well. My strength comes and goes and I am not out of bed very often. Harris says I *will* meet her, though. Isn't it funny? I understand she is just in the room down the hall and it might as well be a world away."

"Funny," said Matthew.

"The engagement announcement came as such a surprise," Simone said. "Niven sent us many letters from Vienna but we never heard a word about Zoya. Harris takes me for walks sometimes, down toward the village, but I can't go very far because my legs are unsteady. It seems that I miss meeting Zoya at every turn."

"Her loss, I'm sure," Matthew replied.

"It does get lonely, and Harris is away so often. I do have books and my needlepoint, though. May I ask if you're married?"

"You may, and I am not."

"When the time comes," said Simone, "choose wisely. My father always told me one cannot fully know another's heart, thus part of a marriage is a leap of faith." She suddenly winced and reached back to rub her neck. "I have pain sometimes," she said, her voice strained. "It comes upon me like a dagger to the bones."

"Is there anything I might get for you?"

"No, it's simply what I must bear." Through the obvious—or imagined—discomfort she managed a faint smile but her eyes remained dark-hollowed. She sighed deeply as her fingers worked her neck. "This world is heavy on me," she said.

Matthew again had no response to such a statement but he was saved from imbecilic silence by a knock at the door.

"Wicks, Mistress Simone," was the announcement.

"My supper," she explained to Matthew. And she said in a voice made pointedly weaker than Matthew had previously heard it: "*Come in.*"

The elderly butler entered bearing a tray on which was a plate holding two links of sausage, boiled potatoes and a corn muffin, along with silverware, a cloth napkin and a glass of what was likely lemon water. He placed it on the table beside Simone's cot. "Is there anything else, mistress?"

"No, that's all. Thank you."

"Master Corbett," said Wicks. "I brought Master Forbes's supper up to him a few minutes ago. He told me he wishes to speak with you."

Matthew stood up and took his lantern. "All right. And I need to have a word with you as well." To Simone he said, "Thank you for your time. I hope we'll visit again soon."

"Delighted," she answered, and proceeded to pick up her fork as if it were the weightiest instrument on earth.

In the corridor, Matthew said quietly to Wicks, "At one o'clock in the morning Eli Baines is going to come to your door in the back. I want you to let him in, no questions asked. And no questions now, either. Just do as I request."

"I am on duty at the front door until two o'clock, but I will let Marion know. Is this so important, sir?"

"Vitally. For the benefit of Forbes and to help clear this matter up."

When Wicks had gone down the stairs, Matthew knocked at Forbes's door and was immediately bade entrance.

"I knew it would be you." Forbes was in bed with his tray of food at his side. He was still as gray and haggard as Matthew had last seen him. "I wanted you to hear that Mary came last night. She told me she would come for me soon…for the last time…and that the afterlife would accept me joyfully just as it has accepted her." His eyes glinted in the firelight either with great hope or terrible madness. "I will be free of all burdens, Matthew. It is a wonderful thing to be so blessed…and so forgiven, for my part in her death."

"You had no part in her death, sir. It was simply an accident."

"My hesitation killed her. I see you'll never understand that." Forbes started to cut into one of the sausages but began picking at it instead. "I have no appetite," he said, and pushed the plate away. "I am too excited at what the future holds for myself and my loved one."

"You should eat," Matthew urged. "I doubt the meals in the afterlife are as satisfying as Mrs. Baines's cooking."

"It will be the satisfaction of the soul," Forbes answered. He cocked his head to one side. "For your information, I took your advice and asked Mary something only she and I would know. I asked her what had disturbed her so much when she returned from her walk to the village that day. You recall I mentioned it?"

"Yes."

"She said she saw an injured fawn limping in the woods, and it hurt her heart to see one of God's creatures so harmed."

I'll bet, Matthew thought. It was a nice maneuver, though. Score one for the "ghost." "Was this after Harris shot it?" he asked. "I understand he's quite the hunter."

"This has nothing to do with my brother. Anyway, I asked and she answered and there you have it."

"What now? You wait to be summoned to the cliff so you may throw yourself to your death?"

"So I may submit myself to eternity and life everlasting." Forbes gave Matthew a fearsome scowl that made the younger man think this gentleman in his prime and right mind had been a hard brick to handle. "And *love* everlasting," Forbes added. "Haven't you ever been in love, boy?"

"No." A champion to Rachel Howarth, but only that.

"How could you understand me, then? There is a far chasm between us. Go on about your business, and take this food out of here on your way."

"You *are* my business," Matthew replied, but the man *whuff*ed some air at him and said nothing more.

Matthew obliged the master of the manor by taking the tray. But on his way to the stairs he stopped and regarded the sausages. After a moment of thought he took the tray into his room, wrapped the sausages in the napkin and put them on his table. He also removed the corn muffin for later consumption, but he dumped the potatoes into the hearth's fire because he'd be having his fill of those downstairs. Newly ready to comport himself carefully before the watchful eyes of both Harris and Niven, he descended the stairs with the emptied plate on its tray and joined the others at the table.

It was all Matthew could do to look Harris in the face when asked about his walk to the village. Suspecting what he did, to him Harris had taken on a vulpine appearance, akin to a predator stalking its victim. "A nice exercise," Matthew answered, and then turned the conversation toward their game of Jingo.

Galbraith and Niven conversed about the date of his and Zoya's upcoming wedding, which Niven said would be set in stone as soon as "this untidy affair" was settled. Matthew mused that an untidy affair had been settled very untidily about a half mile from where they sat, and in recalling the scene and the death odor he could eat no more. Zoya bubbled up and started talking about the beauties of Vienna, the architecture and so forth, and Matthew wondered which book with drawings she'd gotten that out of. In the meantime Harris ate slowly and carefully, bite after bite, and more often than not Matthew found himself the object of the man's sharp-eyed stare.

When Harris had finished his meal, he put aside his knife and fork and said, "We all agree life must go on, don't we, Matthew?"

"It must, yes."

"Duncan, what's your verdict of my brother's mental condition?"

"Precarious," was the doctor's response.

"And your verdict, Matthew?"

"My *verdict*? Are we already in court?"

"Your *opinion*, then." Harris laughed and swept a hard gaze across the others at the table. "By God, you New Yorkers are a quarrelsome bunch!"

"Not quarrelsome. Exacting."

"There you go! Just as I said! All right then, what do you *think* of my elder brother's mental health? And I will go one further…are you ready to sign a document declaring yourself an independent witness and attesting that Forbes Truxton should be housed in an asylum? Or let me restate that: a *sanitarium*, I believe, after the Latin. The difference between an asylum and a sanitarium being a yearly expense of several hundred pounds."

"I am still on the fence," Matthew said.

Did the ruddy color of anger rise up into Harris's cheeks, and his eyes shine with it? If so it was only for an instant, then gone.

"Hang your fence," he said in a quiet and tightly controlled voice. "You'll have to decide one way or another, Matthew. Once you do we can all get on with our lives and quit this miserable place."

"I'm for that!" Niven spoke up, and put his arm around Zoya's shoulders. This time she smiled across the table at Matthew and seemed—or pretended—to welcome the touch. "And the sooner the better," Niven went on, "so our wedding preparations can commence!"

Don't lay it on too thickly, Matthew thought. He said to Harris, "I'll let you know."

The meal proceeded in a kind of agreed-upon silence. Matthew ate his fill and retired to his room, fed the fire and began reading *The Worth of Women,* which he found both fascinating and revolutionary for its time. He was surprised its author was not threatened with burning at the stake as Rachel Howarth had been.

As he read he ate the corn muffin and kept an eye on the clock candle as it burned down through the hours.

When the mark on the candle indicated twelve o'clock, he put the book aside, stood up, took his lantern and as quietly as possible went out into the corridor. He had reasoned it might take him the better part of an hour to state his case. The house was silent and not a wandering ghost in sight. What he had to do gave him some urgency, but again moving as quietly as he could he knocked at the doctor's door. If Harris, Niven or the girl heard this he was sunk, but he had to hope that in their misdeeds they did sometimes give themselves over to genuine sleep.

He had to knock a second time.

Then the door came open and a bleary-eyed Galbraith in his blue-striped sleeping coat peered out, adjusting his spectacles as he did. He said, "What the *hell* are you—"

Matthew put a finger up to command quiet. Whether the doctor liked it or not, Matthew pushed his way in and closed the door at his back. Galbraith was sputtering like a pump gone dry.

"We have work to do," Matthew said.

"*Work?* What work? Have you gone mad too?"

"We're going down to the vault and exhume the corpse that came out of the water," Matthew answered. "And you're going to examine it and tell me if it's really Mary Truxton."

"*What?* My God, boy! Am I still asleep and dreaming this insanity?"

Matthew reached into his pocket, held his hand up before his lamp's light and showed Galbraith what was in it.

"Specifically," he said, "you're going to see if these four teeth fit the mouth."

THIRTEEN

THE FIRST STRIKE OF THE PICKAXE SOUNDED AS LOUD TO MATTHEW AS a cannon's blast.

"Dear God, that's a noise!" he said. His voice echoed back and forth from the chamber's arched ceiling and brick-walled corridors. "Can it be heard above?"

"All that stone over our heads?" Eli Baines had paused before the second blow. The first had cracked the gray bricks directly below a small, tarnished brass plate on which was engraved *Mary Truxton, Loving Wife—January 11, 1669—September 8, 1702*. "We're down thirty some-odd feet," Baines continued. "Not even the ghosts'll hear it. Pardon my sacrilege, doctor."

"Don't mind me," Galbraith said behind the lantern he was holding up in a black-gloved hand. "I will be due for a minister's forgiveness after this sorry endeavor."

"You gents ready for me to go on?" Baines inquired. The doctor remained a scowling statue, but Matthew nodded though he wished to squeeze his eardrums shut. The pickaxe struck again, chips of brick flew into the lantern's light, and they were that much closer to the coffin behind the wall.

It had been a hard pull in Galbraith's room an hour before.

"Teeth," the doctor had said. "All right, where did you find them?"

"I can't say yet. I will at the proper time."

"*Now* is the proper time, young man! Rousting me out of my sleep—such as it was—and barging in here with these things! So you have four teeth in your hand, what am I to make of it?"

"Tell me what kind of mouth they came from."

"What kind of *mouth?*" Galbraith backed away a step as if he really did fear he was in the presence of a lunatic.

"I mean…the age of the mouth. The teeth look fairly young to me. Not a lot of wear."

"Oh, for the sake of Christ! Just a moment! If I catch my death from these I'll haunt you to your grave!" The doctor strode across the room to a wine-colored bag on the floor and came back wearing black leather gloves. He adjusted his glasses, grudgingly accepted the teeth and held them closer to Matthew's lamp. In a few seconds he said, "I agree, they're from a young mouth. Fourteen or fifteen years old I'm supposing. All incisors. This one is badly chipped, but the others are in pretty good shape." He gave them back and held his gloved hands before him as if they carried the pox. "I've told, now you tell: what is this about?"

"What it's about," said Matthew, "is that in *about* an hour we will be meeting Eli Baines at the back entrance to the Wicks' quarters. He'll be bringing a pickaxe and an iron crow suitable to pry open a coffin. He will lead us to the door beyond which he says are stairs leading down into the vault, and then he will proceed to—"

"*Stop*. I've heard enough. Too much. Get out of here before I call Harris to skin you alive."

"You don't want to do that. These four teeth make me suspect that the corpse in Mary's coffin is *not* Mary. It was never fully identified as her body, was it?"

"Mary fell from the cliff on the eighth of September and the corpse was discovered in the middle of October. No one else fell into the ocean in that span of time. The voracious sea life hereabouts showed no mercy on her flesh, and I can tell you that it was a horrific sight. The broken bones, the gashed and gaping wounds…she had no *eyes*, young man. The crabs had feasted like never before on that body."

"And you being somewhat abhorrent to bacteria, you kept your distance except for a cursory inspection?"

Galbraith's mouth worked for what was likely going to be an angry response, but when the voice emerged it was quiet. "My father was a rounder. He died of creeping syphilis. When you witness something like that, eating the flesh away day after day, you are never the same. It was a double-edged sword that got me interested in medicine, but still…I do what I can, the best I can. All right, I looked the corpse over and then I stepped aside to let the village minister and that coffin-maker do their work. But if it wasn't Mary's corpse, *whose* was it?"

"I will speak three words that are not to leave this room. Do you understand that?"

"I understand *nothing!*"

"Three words: a murder victim."

"*What?* Whose murder?"

"I've said all I'm going to say. Doctor, I need your help and I'm trusting you."

"Well why would you *not* trust me?"

"Because," Matthew said, "some in this house are *untrustworthy*, and likely highly dangerous as well. I am taking a chance even bringing this to your attention, but it has to be done in the pursuit of justice."

"The pursuit of further insanity, you mean! Opening Mary's *coffin?* It's a blasphemy!"

"It would be if it was really the corpse of Mary Truxton," Matthew agreed. "Which I believe it is not."

"The corpse," said Galbraith, "was already water-swollen, had burst open and was ravaged beyond recognition. Now she's been months in the coffin. Do you have an idea what the further decomposition will be? How am I to determine anything from the...and I shall put this as gallantly as possible...*remnants?*"

"Are you afraid to look?"

The eyes glinted red behind the lenses. "No, but *you* should be."

Matthew waited for the flash of anger to subside before he said, "I *am* afraid, but I'm not going to let that stop me."

Galbraith started to remove his spectacles but hesitated and Matthew thought it was because of the teeth-tainted gloves. "I wish to God you'd never come to this house."

"Others will feel the same, but you may recant that statement before we're done. Now: will you *please* do as I ask?"

In the gray-gloomed vault, the brick chips continued to fly and dust hazed the air as Baines struck with the pickaxe, each blow a nerve-shredding assault to Matthew's ears. The portion bearing the nameplate collapsed. Baines used one fork of the pickaxe to pull loose bricks out upon the floor and then kept up the steady work.

"Hell of a thing," said Baines as he took a breather. "I didn't know I set them bricks so firm. Sad to see such work go to ruin, but—" And once more he set to the destruction.

A hole was made as more bricks collapsed. Musty, long-contained air wafted out from the dark beyond. The space widened. A few more strikes and there was enough space to admit a living body. Galbraith had brought his washcloth from his room and used it to shield his face from the swirling dust. Matthew wished he'd brought his own. Baines set the pickaxe aside. "I believe that does it," he said, and he picked up the iron crowbar that leaned against the far wall. "Will one of you light the way?"

Matthew went in first with his lantern, ducking his head and pulling his shoulders in to get through the opening. Within, the coffin stood on a stone dais about three feet off the floor. It was simple, of plain unvarnished wood, and it bore on its lid the burned-in outline of a Christian cross. Matthew had to bend over, for the space was tight and his head brushed the roof. Baines entered next and then the doctor with his lamp.

At the sight of the coffin with its emblem on the lid Galbraith said behind his makeshift mask, "I feel the flames of Hell torching my ass. By God, this is a crime against nature!"

"Go ahead," Matthew told Baines, before any of them lost their nerve.

Baines took a long breath, exhaled and drove the crowbar's business end into the seam between lid and casket. As he worked the bar, nails began popping free with noises like little pistol shots.

"I am damned for this business!" the doctor muttered, but to his credit he did not flee the chamber.

Nail after nail popped. "Jesus!" said Baines, pausing in the struggle. "How many nails did that bastard drive in this thing?"

"Enough to seal it forever," Matthew replied. "Do you want me to try my hand?"

"No, I'll manage it."

Which was all to the good, Matthew thought, because he was about to lose his nerve himself and his runaway heartbeat must be as loud as the nails coming loose. It was amazing how one could sweat in the cold.

Then Baines got the bar well under the lid and started working it up. There came a noise like a dozen demons shrieking their rage as their bones were broken. Galbraith gave a choking sound and started to retreat but Matthew snagged his sleeve and held him. With a last horrific *crack* of splintering wood the lid came up and fell to one side and into the chamber roiled the dry, vomitous odor of old death.

No one moved, and no one looked into the coffin.

Galbraith spoke, his voice now that of the calm professional: "Add your light to mine, Matthew. And if my eyes have to witness what's in there, yours will too. Step forward."

Matthew braced himself and obeyed.

Life.

It was so shocking and so sad, really, that life eventually through its twistings and turnings, its dark days and light, and year in and year out came to this: a moldering husk, a scarecrow, a thing barely recognizable as ever having been human much less alive, and dressed in a crypt-yellowed gown with an embroidery of small faded red roses around the gaping hole where the throat had been and below the jawless and eyeless brown face that was no longer a face but a shapeless mass like the melting of a wax candle this had once been *someone*…a girl, a loved one, a treasure…now more a shriveled bundle of broken sticks and no telling of the age, the beauty, the history, the talent, the hopes or the dreams.

Matthew stood looking down upon the hideous visage, with its scalp laid to the bone in patches by the hungry denizens of the sea, just a few dark scraggly lengths of hair remaining, and whatever horror he felt at the sight was overwhelmed and pushed aside by his will to see justice done.

Galbraith said behind his cloth, "You can tell that the four items in your pocket are of no use here, since the upper jaw is gone and the lower one broken into pieces." He leaned past Matthew for a closer look, Eli Baines having retreated to give the pair more room. "I don't see how in the name of God I can identify anything from this."

That was the point, Matthew thought. "Those wounds and the shattered bones…the rocks did all this damage?"

"The rocks began the damage and the sea life went to work…crawling, winnowing and squirming into the corpse. After the internal pressures caused the body to burst open, it was all the worse."

"The gown. She wasn't wearing that when she fell, was she?"

"Don't be dense," the doctor scolded. "The waves took all her clothing. This gown was Mary's in life. Harris took it to the coffin-maker."

"It seems very large for the body."

Galbraith straightened up and regarded Matthew with heavy-lidded eyes. "Death does have a way of shrinking a body, young man. Your education is lacking in the way of mortality."

But not necessarily in the way of murder, Matthew almost replied. He watched and kept the lantern aloft as the doctor leaned in again. One gloved hand kept the face cloth in place and the other moved here and there, gingerly as if in respect to the sleeper.

"This is pointless," Galbraith muttered. "Worse than a fool's errand."

"Is there nothing you can examine that might give you a clue?"

"Nothing." He started to straighten up again and then stopped. "Well…something, I suppose. The bones of the right wrist are not broken. Let me look there."

"Looking at *unbroken* bones?"

"Hush," the doctor said.

And then, perhaps fifteen seconds later, came from him a soft "*Hm.*"

"What is it?"

"Interesting, this is." He leaned closer and then away again. "Mary told me some time ago that at age fourteen she was thrown from a horse. It resulted in a severe fracture of her right wrist. There were two breaks, she said. In cold weather her wrist tended to ache and I applied liniment for the discomfort. I could feel the calcification where the breaks had healed."

Galbraith lifted his face toward Matthew. "There is no evidence of calcification here. None whatsoever."

"Meaning?"

"Meaning, young man…unless in my older age I am losing my memory and all sense of sanity…this right wrist does not belong to Mary Truxton. I am nearly stunned beyond speech but I have enough wind left to ask: Do you know who I'm looking at?"

"Yes, but I can't say at present. May we get out of here to speak further?"

Baines placed the lid back upon the casket as well as could be done, and the doctor and Matthew left the crypt. In the chamber outside, Matthew addressed both men: "I don't think I need to ask either you not to reveal any of this. The time will come but it's not yet here."

"I wouldn't breathe a word, sir," said Baines.

Galbraith grunted. He peeled his gloves off with obvious distaste and put them in a pocket. "I'm sure I'm going to run upstairs and tell Forbes I assisted in an opening of his wife's coffin *without his knowledge* that resulted in finding his wife wasn't in it! I leave this dirty business to you!"

They went up the stone stairs to the door that led to an inner hallway, Baines leading the procession. Just before the door was opened there came to the ear a muffled shout, and as Baines pushed through the shout became a startling and strident cry of *"Help! Someone help! Master Forbes has gotten out!"*

"He's gone for the cliff!" Matthew cried, just as stridently as Wicks had done though it was something all already knew. Baines dropped the crowbar and pickaxe to the floor, and at once the three ran for the foyer and front door, where they found a broken lantern spilling its burning oil across the stones and the cot turned on its side. Through the wide-open doorway Matthew could make out a running figure, either Forbes or Wicks. With his own lamp in hand he ran in pursuit, with Baines a few paces behind and the doctor last.

A cold and rising wind bit into Matthew's face. He passed Wicks, who stumbled and staggered to one side wheezing for breath. *"Stop him! Stop him!"* the butler managed to get out before his voice was finished. Then Matthew caught sight of a figure perhaps ten yards away standing right at the cliff's edge, and just that fast there was a dull basso rumble somewhere in the clouds and an icy rain suddenly hammered down from the dark.

Forbes Truxton jumped.

His nightcoat was almost torn from his body as Matthew grabbed hold of it with both hands, his lantern lying back where he'd dropped it. At the same time Matthew felt himself being carried over the edge by Forbes's forward impetus, his bootheels digging furrows in the earth. He might have been dashed into the rocks and crashing waves with Forbes but for his savior

Eli Baines again, who not only grasped Matthew but whose long arms caught the master of the manor at the sides as well and whose strength in the desperate moment heaved them both to one side like a child's jackstraws.

Matthew sat up in the downpour, the water streaming through his hair and down his face. Forbes lay on his back, his hands pressed to his eyes and his body shivering. Baines stood to one side as Galbraith and Wicks came up. The doctor immediately knelt down to give aid to Forbes, who waved him away and curled up as if wishing the whole world would disappear.

"I tried to stop him!" Wicks said against the storm. "He rushed past me, but I tried!"

"No one's blaming you," Galbraith answered. "Let's get him back to the house."

Both Harris and Niven were at the door, with Zoya behind them, as the rain-soaked group trudged in. Baines and Matthew had firm grips on either side of Forbes, who was muttering incoherently and whose legs kept threatening collapse. "What the hell happened?" Harris demanded. "He got past Wicks? Forbes, this madness has got to end! Do you hear me?"

"That doesn't help," Galbraith said. "Forbes, can you make the stairs?"

"Mary," Forbes answered in a low voice, his head hanging and water dripping to the floor. "She was there. Mary...my Mary...calling me."

The doctor gave Matthew a quick glance and then away. "Harris, you and Niven help me with him. Someone close the door, for God's sake!"

Matthew hung back and obeyed Galbraith's command as Forbes was taken up the steps. When they were out of sight and hearing Matthew said quietly to Baines, "Best retrieve your tools. I believe you dropped them in the—"

"This is yours, I think." Marion Wicks in a white flannel nightgown and cap appeared through the corridor holding the bar, which she'd seen when Baines had entered through their quarters. "I didn't ask what it was for then, and I won't now. I tripped over those things and nearly broke my neck when I heard the shouting and came to the door a moment ago. You can get the pick yourself." She gave the crowbar to its owner and regarded her sopping-wet husband. "I knew it was a matter of time before Master Forbes got out. Is he injured?"

"Rain-soaked and somewhat delirious," Matthew said. "But thank God that's all. Also thank God for Mr. Baines being quick to act."

"Are you all right, Chet?"

"Unnerved, wet and winded. I tried to stop him but he was just too fast."

The woman's gaze then fell upon the glass on the floor from the broken lantern, the oil still showing blue flame but in no danger of catching anything alight. "I'll fetch my broom from the closet and sweep that up." She shook her head. "Poor Master Forbes. A man who wants to leave this life so much…God help him," Mrs. Wicks turned her attention to Matthew, and in her stony stare he reckoned that the small, elderly white-haired woman could be a formidable power if her hackles were raised…and they certainly seemed to be up at the moment. "May I speak freely, sir?"

"Of course." Matthew was starting to shiver from the cold and wet, but he figured when this lady had something to say it was best to give her an ear.

"Neither Chet nor I feel that Master Forbes is seeing Mistress Mary's ghost, though it's likely some unhappy spirits walk here. Neither do we feel that he has been driven mad by the accident. Oh, he's carrying a burden for sure…but it's a burden that's been made all the heavier by…how shall I put this and remember my place?…*human* interference. Whoever is doing this to Master Forbes is evil to the soul, young man. Mistress Mary was a delight…a wonderful woman, God keep her. The idea of her returning from the dead to take Master Forbes with her is pure…I shan't say the word."

"No need," said Matthew. "I share your sentiment."

"I have my suspicions but I won't speak them." She stepped closer to Matthew and he had the impression even Hudson Greathouse might have retreated from the fire in her eyes.

To him she spoke three more words.

"*Catch the bastard*," she said. And then she addressed her shivering husband: "Come on, dear, let's get you out of those wet clothes and then I will clean up this *mess*." With that her gaze went up to the foyer's balcony, and Matthew thought she was recalling a hanging man and blood that had dripped down upon the stones for a loyal housekeeper to blot away.

FOURTEEN

"MARY…MARY…MARY," MOANED THE MAN ON THE BED. AT ONCE Dr. Galbraith was out of his chair and leaning over his patient. "He's coming around," the doctor said to Matthew Corbett, who stood in the room shivering with a blanket wrapped about his body, his clothes and hair still wet from the deluge that was pounding the stone walls and whipping against the stained-glass windows.

"*Matthew*," the man whispered, his eyelids fluttering as they tried to open.

Matthew came forward to Forbes Truxton's bedside. "I'm here, sir," he said. The man's eyes suddenly opened and in the lamplight the bloodshot orbs sought Matthew's face. A hand rose, trembling, to catch Matthew's shoulder.

"Did you see her?" Truxton's voice was barely audible, his heavily lined face weary and gray. "She was *there*," he said, before the young problem-solver could reply. "She wants me, Matthew. She *needs* me. *Why?* Oh… *why* didn't you let me go?"

"I'm not going to stand idly by and watch you kill yourself. It was a close call tonight."

"I *have* to go to her! Don't you understand? Oh my God, Matthew… oh Jesus…she *needs* me. We can be together…for always and ever…that's what she wants. It is the only way, Matthew. Don't you see?"

"No, sir, I do not."

Truxton's gray-haired head lifted from the damp pillow. His hand tightened on Matthew's shoulder and perhaps deep in the eyes red embers stirred. "It is the only way," he said with an obvious effort, "that she will forgive me for *killing* her."

"Forbes," said Duncan Galbraith, who was equally as wet and miserable in his soggy clothes as was Matthew. "I want you to rest now. Do you hear me? Please…try to relieve your mind of this burden." It was an impossible request and all three in the room knew it. But the master of Truxton Manor looked up at the doctor and nodded, and though the agony coursed through him like his blood and beat within like his ravaged heart he closed his eyes and sought at least a short time of peace.

"Let us go out and speak to the others," Galbraith said, but before they reached the door he paused. "Did you see anything out there?"

"I did not." Only the sweeping rain, the wind-thrashed trees and the sea smashing itself against the treacherous cliff.

"Obviously Forbes believes he did. This idea of a phantasm—a ghost—is destroying him. That Mary is beckoning him to join her in death…it's a task for a priest, not a doctor. *Nor* a problem-solver," he added, his brown eyes peering over his square-lensed spectacles. "Why they wanted to involve you in this is a mystery to me."

"They hoped I could help." *Help* in this case being a loaded word, Matthew thought.

"You *did* prevent him from going over the cliff tonight, so thanks and appreciation are in order. That other thing we did…I'll be haunted by that for the rest of my life."

"It was necessary," Matthew said, "and now you know why."

"I understand you won't go any further into that, but if there is as you believe a malignant presence here, and you are standing in its way of destroying Forbes Truxton…it may wish to destroy you first. But I certainly have never believed in ghosts, for that matter."

Matthew almost agreed that the idea of ghosts was ridiculous, but the statement hung. He was cognizant of the spectral shades that haunted the office at Number Seven Stone Street, though they never materialized and kept their presences limited to the occasional bang, rattle and half-heard mutter. But some of his experiences with the Herrald Agency had left him wondering about the realm of the unknown, and how close—and how dangerous—it was to the realm that might be termed "normal life." It was best not to dwell on those things, but here at Truxton Manor, three days coach travel north of Boston, such had been thrust into his face. He realized that because of what he knew something far worse than a ghost might soon be at his throat.

"Let's see the others," said Galbraith, and he opened the door to the hallway.

Harris, Niven and Zoya were just outside, both the brothers holding lanterns. "Will he sleep?" Harris asked.

"I hope so," the doctor answered. "Though it will have to be on his own, since the last of the potion has been used between Forbes and Simone. I need to place an order for more chemicals with the market boat's captain."

"You should do that in the morning," said Harris. "I understand the boat sails on the twenty-first." He looked from the doctor to Matthew and back again, and Matthew could see his eyes almost imperceptibly narrow. "You two got after Forbes very quickly. Were you downstairs?"

Matthew suffered a freeze of the brain. Galbraith luckily did not; he said, "I wished for a glass of lemon water and found Matthew in the kitchen. It was fortunate we were that near to the door."

"I see. And where did Baines come from? He was also wanting lemon water well after midnight?"

Galbraith showed a calm face. He shrugged. "I imagine Baines was doing what Baines sometimes does. Emptying a chamberpot in the middle of the night. Again...fortunate, wouldn't you agree?"

"Very fortunate," Niven spoke up. "But I don't know how much longer we can bear all this." He put his arm around Zoya, whose own expression was bland and Matthew thought somewhat detached from the scene. "We want this to be done," said Niven. "Our marriage awaits."

"Our *future* awaits," Harris added. "Listen, Matthew: I have the proper document of witness ready, prepared by my lawyers in Boston before I came to New York town. Will you sign it tonight and let us move past such horrible events? Really, it's for Forbes's good that he be taken somewhere for recovery. Wouldn't you agree, Duncan?"

Before the doctor could speak, Matthew said, "I hear what you're saying. I *will* sign...but I want to be absolutely certain I'm doing the right thing."

"How can you *not* be? The next time Baines might not be out there emptying his pot, and neither you nor Duncan in the kitchen after midnight!"

"I'll sign," Matthew replied, "if tonight Forbes has the delusion again. One more night. If 'Mary' appears to him, I will gladly and readily do as you ask."

"Thank God!" said Harris, throwing up his free hand. "Finally, some sense! Well, I'm fully awake now and have no chance of going back to sleep! It's my time to be on watch, anyway…though I doubt Forbes is up to another jaunt. Matthew, you will be doing a great service to the Truxton family. I will make sure you are rewarded beyond our initial agreement."

Matthew said, "Thank you. I'm glad to be instrumental in this affair." He also didn't know if he could sleep the rest of the night, but he had to try because he had an early morning ahead and he had to be sharp. "I'll say goodnight, then. Dr. Galbraith, I thank *you* for your help."

"*Pleased*," Galbraith answered…a shade grimly, but not enough to be noticed except for the one who knew.

All the rest of the night the rain slammed against the window in Matthew's room and made the search for sleep almost impossible. He thought from the torrential noise that Noah must be out there somewhere building a new Ark. But by the first dim gray light the sound had ceased and Matthew rose from his cot chilled to the bone, though he had changed from his wet clothes into a sleepcoat he'd brought in his baggage and had the benefit of a dry blanket. He could see his breath plume out—a ghost of its own—as he dressed in fresh clothing also from his bags. He decided to wait, shave—oh that water in the bowl was going to be icy!—feed the fire and warm himself as much as possible until Wicks came up to announce the serving of breakfast. That would mean Harris was no longer on watch duty at the front door, and it was imperative that Matthew get out of the manse without being seen.

At seven-thirty the knock and call came from the butler. Matthew gave it about ten more minutes, and then he picked up the little cloth bundle he'd prepared and tucked it into the inner pocket of the wine-colored cloak he donned over his dark brown jacket. A lighter brown woolen cap went on his head. A furtive opening of the door and a look into the corridor—empty—and he was out, down the stairs and headed across the foyer, which he noted had been swept clean by Marion Wicks's industrious broom.

He walked out of the house into both bitter cold and a heavy falling snow. The lawn was blanketed white by the depth of at least two inches and the flakes were coming down so hard by the time he'd strode to the forest path he could make out the manor only as a shadowlike shape in the swirling curtains.

Would someone look out and see his footprints? Matthew was gratified to realize they had already been covered over in the space of a few minutes. He pulled the cloak tighter around himself for warmth and hurried to his task.

When he'd reached Johnsey's property the snowfall had strengthened and the frigid wind was blowing hard into his face. Around him the woods were a phantasmagoria of wet black tree trunks, skeletal white branches and equally white underbrush. The flakes hissed down through the trees, his boots crunched through the crust and occasionally a burst of wind shrilled past his ears. He smelled smoke from the cabin's chimney. As he neared the snow-freighted structures he had a sudden start: would this raw weather prevent Leah Clegg from going to the village for her lessons with the students? If so, she wouldn't be fetching the dark lantern for him, and how was he getting that safely into the house?

Well, he was sure a heavy snowfall wasn't an uncommon event up this distance north of New York, but still…he had to hope she would put on a suitably warm coat and brave the weather if not simply for the benefit of her pupils but for his own—

And here he stopped thinking of Leah Clegg, her lessons and the snowfall because with the cabin and the locked shed in sight he was faced with the silent and ominous form of Ripper the dog staring fixedly at him.

The animal was going to start barking at any second, and the snow might muffle the noise but surely not that much.

A hand dove into his cloak, within the inner pocket, and winnowed into the cloth napkin there.

And as Ripper tensed to set up a barking barrage heard from here to Philadelphia Matthew dropped at the dog's front paws a piece of the sausage he had salvaged from Forbes's supper plate.

There came an abbreviated bark that turned into a guttural growl nearly like a question being asked. The yellow eyes fixed now not upon the human meat but upon the pork.

"Take it," Matthew breathed, his voice as calm as could be manufactured from a throat that seemed to have been seized by a metal clamp. "Go ahead."

Ripper sniffed the sausage. Made another low guttural growl…and then *snap* went the jaws and the meat was history.

Matthew dropped another piece from his cloak.

This time there was no growl to preface the meal.

After the fourth drop and the last of the sausage, and Matthew quietly saying, "Good boy! Good Ripper!" in hopes his offerings had done the trick…Ripper looked up at him placidly and the tail wagged. Not by much…but a wag was a wag, wasn't it?

Now to test movement toward the shed, and pray it didn't set Ripper off again. "I'm going this way," Matthew said, pointing in the desired direction. "Easy, easy. All right?"

The first forward step made Ripper back up, but there was neither growl nor bark. The look in the animal's eyes was not angry or ferocious… in fact, there seemed to be a playful gleam.

So far, so good.

Another few paces and still Ripper had not barked. Matthew reached out to touch the dog for reassurance but Ripper gave a low grunting sound and backed further away; the animal was having none of that and Matthew thought it had been a stupid gesture anyway.

He made it to the padlocked shed without noise or incident. Once there he balled up his fist and—again praying this sound would not touch off the cannonfire—he knocked softly at the door.

From the shed there was no answer.

He tried again, heard Ripper give an alarming half-bark that died in the throat, and then from inside the shed came the voice of the person he knew was locked within.

It was very weak, but the woman said, "Drucilla? Drucilla…I beg you for a lamp. Please. And another blanket. Please, for God's mercy."

Matthew could not reply to Mary Truxton's plea. No mercy could be given this morning, yet he intended it to be soon delivered. She had survived the fall and might be in a broken condition, but she was alive.

The situation.

Here it was. Either Drucilla, Yates or Ripper had likely found Mary washed up on the headland. Had the two miscreants immediately reported the discovery, or had Drucilla used her homegrown medical skills to keep Mary alive and therefore approach Harris for a sizeable reward? In any case, *the situation* was that Harris was evidently paying the pair to keep her here so Wandering Mary could haunt the bedchamber of Forbes Truxton.

A dark plan. But something darker still: the Johnseys knew the coffin Yates made was not for Mary. Did they know Harris had decided that Mary's fall and subsequent discovery would be the perfect cover for the murder of Nora Swaine? A corpse was needed, and a child to further complicate Harris's ambitions was not.

Matthew realized that from the very first, when Harris had entered the office, he had sensed the presence of a predator. After all, one of his initial thoughts had been that this dapper man in the expensive clothes might well be a killer sent from Professor Fell.

So it was there, but he hadn't fully grasped it until he'd walked into a shack that would've terrified even Baba Yaga.

"Drucilla?" Mary called, her voice so tentative—hopeless would be the better assessment—that it was nearly inaudible. "Answer me, please!"

Matthew could not. If Mary realized someone had found her and she was in a fragile state either physically or mentally she might reveal it to the

Johnseys and Matthew was not ready for that. He had to draw away from the shed, with Ripper following his path, and merge once more into the snowy woods. Ripper did give the courtesy of only starting to furiously bark in his direction when he'd gotten far enough away not to be concerned.

Next: if Leah couldn't retrieve the dark lantern, he was going to have to chance it. Could he tuck and hold the bundle up under his cloak? Possibly, but again it was a risk. Before he'd left the Cleggs he'd told Leah how to find the hiding place, beside the small cairn of stones he'd built just on the northern side of the mound of dead leaves. With all this snow—and now it was whirling sideways in white sheets that portended a true blizzard before a harsh and rising wind—the stones might be covered over. He reached the shack, went around to the back and found that all the vegetation there was buried beneath white drifts that took his legs to the mid-shins. With a sense of both urgency and panic Matthew started digging in the area he thought the bundle might be.

Nothing.

He shifted his search a few feet more to the north, digging again through snow and leaves.

Nothing.

"Oh my God!" Matthew said aloud. Without the dark lantern he could turn the trick, but its intense glare would give him the extra few seconds he would need.

He shifted again, trying more to the south.

This time he found the stones, all iced together.

But the bundle holding the lamp was not there.

With frantic energy he kept searching, digging and digging, until the cold both burned and numbed his hands and his strength simply collapsed. Then he sat back on his haunches resembling a snowman in repose and nearly wept in frustration. The only thing keeping him from doing that was the knowledge that his eyelids would freeze shut.

He couldn't stay out here much longer. He had to rouse himself and get back to the manor, for better or worse.

He stood up. All of winter seemed to be weighing heavily on him. The sky was as gray as the walls of the Truxton vault. A person could die in this kind of weather, and he hoped that the Johnseys were not so evil or stupid that they wouldn't make sure their captive remained alive.

But another question: after Matthew had signed the necessary document and Forbes was carted off to an asylum...what was to be done with Mary?

He pulled his cloak tighter about himself and realized there was something in the pocket...a lump against his side. He reached in and found he'd missed one remaining piece of sausage folded in the cloth napkin down in there.

So with a grave countenance and a face whipped by wind and snow he had a late breakfast as he walked, and he shivered all the way back to the grim tomb on the cliff.

FIFTEEN

NIVEN TRUXTON ENTERED HIS ELDER BROTHER'S ROOM WITHOUT knocking. He lifted his lantern toward the bed, where Forbes lay staring up at the canopy above him. His hands were clenched over his chest atop the bedding. Wicks had come in a few minutes before, at half-past nine, to feed the fire. The roar in the hearth was not enough to blank out the more tremendous roar of the snowstorm that had raged all through the daylight hours and now fearfully had strengthened with the fall of night.

"Do you need anything?" Niven asked.

"Don't speak to me," was Forbes's terse reply.

"Forbes, I'm not your enemy. Neither is Harris. We want what's best for you."

"That's a damnable lie."

"You need *rest*, in a place where you can be taken care of properly. And you need peace of mind, Forbes. You surely can't get it here." Niven walked over to the hearth to warm himself. A whine of wind made the glass in the chamber's windows shudder. "Listen to that! We're in for hell before this is over."

"Snowed in with you and Harris *is* my idea of hell."

Niven turned from the flames. "If you want to rid yourself of the company so badly, why not just sell it to Harris? That would have been a simple—and sane—stroke of a pen."

"I've tried to tell you a dozen times that we cannot keep the business going. Our funds are depleted and we have to get what we can. The building of this house finished us off as a wealthy family; it's all for show now."

"But Harris could—"

"Harris is the one who's insane!" Forbes sat up on his pillows, his face strained and his eyes bloodshot. "No matter what he's made you believe, he's living off Simone's wealth! I know, I've seen the bills! And I know also that he's bleeding that poor sick woman dry!" He nodded at his own declaration. "You understand why she's sick, don't you? She loves him and she knows how he's using her! So better to keep to a room and a bed and beg for some morsel of affection, because even that small bit Harris despises to give!"

"My God," Niven said calmly. "You're turning into Father. Will we have to start guarding the ropes in the village?"

"If you're following Harris's track he's leading you right over the cliff out there," Forbes answered, his own voice stone cold. He waved a dismissive hand. "Get out."

"I'm going. I wanted not only to check on you but to remind you that I am on door watch duty tonight, so please behave yourself, refrain from seeing ghosts and stay in your bed as that last incident badly disturbed Zoya. She's beginning to wonder what she's gotten into."

Beginning? She should've realized it when she met you in Vienna!"

"Dear, dear brother," said Niven. "So much love to give." And with that statement and a thin, bitter smile he left the room.

The night and the storm went on.

In the dark chambers windows rattled and the cold made wooden doors crack. The damp walls bled, and in some places far from a fireplace silver spiderwebs of ice spread across the stones. Up high amid the chimneys and the dunce-cap roofs inches of snow thickened and frozen stalactites grew like fangs, and on this night the ghosts that walked the halls of Truxton Manor paused in their journeys between worlds to listen to the keening and crying of the wind, for that strange music made them remember all the sorrows and hardships of the fragile condition called life, yet they yearned to know it again and thus having lost it they hung their shapeless heads and drifted on.

"*Forbes,*" the woman's soft voice said. "*Forbes, my darling.*"

The white-gowned figure with long black hair came nearer to the bed. She was a form silhouetted by the last crackling tinder of the fireplace, and she moved with a light step befitting a wandering spirit of the night.

"Forbes, are you awake?" With the stirring of the figure under the blanket, she said, "Hear me, my dearest. Let the day arrive and go, and at the next one o'clock I shall be waiting at our place of meeting. Our wonderful place, my loved one…where we shall never, ever be parted a—"

There was a small *click*. Instantly a bright light hit her in the face, making her gasp and stagger back.

At once Matthew was out of the bed, and rushing upon her he grasped hold of the black wig and pulled it off to reveal the fiery red beneath. Zoya's dark eyes were terrified, and Matthew saw that her face had been further whitened with makeup and the beauty mark covered.

Before she could cry out, Matthew held a finger to her uncolored lips.

"Don't say a word," he told her, as quietly as the ghost had spoken. "Just listen. Do you realize you and Niven are involved in a murder?"

"A *murder?* What are you talking about?" Alas, all trace of the Slavic accent had vanished along with Wandering Mary but there was true fear in her voice. "I haven't murdered anyone!"

"Keep silent. I don't want anyone to know this has gone wrong. And if you *tell* either brother, I'll make sure you swing from the noose just as Harris is going to swing."

"Harris? What?"

"You leave this room and try to run, you'll wind up frozen to death in the woods," Matthew continued. "And I daresay if you do decide to be a fool and tell Harris or Niven, your life will be ended before…as you put it…the next one o'clock. Likely Niven will join you in the grave, because I don't think he realizes what the second part of this plot was."

"The second part? Listen, I'm just an actress! I'm being paid to—"

"I know what you're being paid to do. Pretend to haunt Forbes Truxton so Harris might secure a witness to his presumed insanity. And I know all about *The Russian Widow.* I should've realized something was amiss that first time I met you and you started spouting off about your Russian mother and your father being an English member of Parliament. Niven stopped you from going further because you were *overacting* the play."

She blinked in the hard light from the dark lantern's magnifying lens. It was set on the table next to the bed where Matthew could readily reach it and open the shutter when the time was right. Leah Clegg had not left the coachhouse for morning lessons due to the weather, but in obeyance to "Master Matthew's" request Caleb had gone out at six o'clock before the worst of the snowfall and found it where Matthew had indicated. Matthew had brought the item in through the Wicks' quarters, and it had served its purpose very well.

"How do you know about *The Russian Widow?*" the actress asked, starting—or at least pretending—to regain some of her composure.

"A spirit told me. I believe Harris and Simone saw the play and later he reasoned that an actress who could speak with an accent would be useful to this chicanery. What's your real name?"

"Gwendolyn Jennings. Listen…Harris is going to be coming to my room at any minute to ask how the visit went. I'd better be there when he comes in. Tell me…who's been murdered?"

"I'll spare you that for now. But *you* listen to me, and you'd better hear me well: your life may depend on your next job of acting, which is returning to your room and telling Harris that all went as planned tonight. Let me say also that if you show one *crack* of indecision, the blade for your neck will start being sharpened. Do you understand?"

She nodded, her eyes wide.

"Say it."

"I understand." She looked toward the bed. "Where is Forbes?"

"We switched rooms. I convinced him that if Mary came tonight she could find him wherever he slept." Matthew didn't reveal what else he'd told the master of the manor between the time Niven had left the room—leaving the door conveniently ajar for the silent appearance of Wandering Mary, as must have been the usual custom by the brothers—and Matthew's preparing the dark lantern and swaddling himself in the covers. "Come to breakfast as usual," he added, his voice commanding. "Show no sign of distress. Now go along, and take this." He held the wig out and she took it, putting it on in case she ran into Harris in the corridor. To oblige the danger of discovery, Matthew closed the lantern's shutter so the intense glare would not get out, the room being lit now only by the fitful firelight. Just before Gwendolyn Jennings left the chamber Matthew said, "All that goulash about Baba Yaga. Was that a real story?"

"The character is real in folklore," she replied. "But that was part of my speech in the play. And I have to tell you...Forbes *is* losing his mind, because I didn't come to this room last night."

"All right. Now go and do some more acting, and you'd better be good."

When she was gone Matthew fed the fire to fever heat. Wind yet screamed around the manor and made the blue glass window tremble in its frame. Matthew returned to the bed and relaxed in its comfort as opposed to the cot's merciless grip; he hoped Forbes could get a wink of sleep out of that hard monster.

Matthew closed his eyes. There would be no more wanderings of Mary tonight or evermore. On the morrow, though...he declined to dwell too long on that oncoming dawn, because much hung in the balance.

Much.

At last he did himself wander into the blessed realm of sleep even with the storm howling outside, but if one could sleep tensed to awaken at any instant Matthew Corbett was at present the master of that precarious twilight.

When real twilight did arrive, Harris Truxton answered the insistent knock at his and Simone's door preparing to blast Wicks for an unnecessary disturbance when the regular announcement for breakfast would've sufficed. Instead, he faced the New York problem-solver, freshly shaved.

Matthew said, "I've decided. If you'll bring the document down to breakfast I'll sign at the table."

"Thank God you've come to *your* senses! Very well, I'll get dressed and be downstairs in fifteen minutes."

Matthew nodded assent. He had spent the last twenty minutes in productive activity, so another fifteen was no hardship. He went downstairs wrapped in his cloak, for a biting cold had invaded the manor and might expect to live there through February. Matthew entered the formal dining room and sat at the table to wait.

As expected, Harris came in with Niven and the once-Zoya-now-Gwendolyn-Jennings a few paces behind. Matthew ascertained that Miss Jennings was in fact a good actress because only he noted in her eyes the look of a deer in the stagelight.

With a parchment document in one hand and in the other a wooden box containing the inkpot and quill, Harris pulled up short as soon as he was in the chamber. "What is *this?*" he asked, looking from side to side.

"Oh, since this is such an important moment for the future of the Truxton family I thought it agreeable to have witnesses to the signature," said Matthew.

"*All* of them?" Harris asked.

He was indicating the other persons standing in the room: Duncan Galbraith, Chetley and Marion Wicks, Ruth Baines and Caleb and Leah Clegg.

"As either friends or in the Truxton employ, all should be present," was Matthew's answer. He motioned to the space on the table before him. "Shall we proceed?"

"Shouldn't we bring Forbes down?" Niven asked. "And if you're including everyone, where's Eli Baines?" In continuing the performance he put his arm around Miss Jennings, who showed her teeth in a grim smile while the rest of her face remained lifeless. Matthew felt a little pity for her, getting involved in this family's mess and having to be touched by that sorry sack. But only a little.

"I understand both are indisposed due to the rigors of last night. I think we can get this done without them."

"Agreed!" Harris set the document down before Matthew, smoothed it and placed the wooden box alongside. Moving as one triumphant, Harris opened the box, removed the silver inkpot, unscrewed the lid, put the pot down, and dipped the quill in the ink. Then he offered the instrument to Matthew with a huge false smile. "You see at the bottom where your signature should be," he said.

Matthew did see. Also he saw that Harris and Niven had already signed. As Matthew started to touch quill to parchment, Galbraith suddenly said, "Harris? I'll do everything I can to make sure Forbes is comfortable and taken care of. You can count on that."

"I shall, Duncan, and your help through this unfortunate affair has been of the utmost value."

The exchange, engineered to divert Harris's attention for the time it took Matthew to write in the assigned space, was ended and Matthew handed Harris the document.

"There," Matthew said. "All done."

"I thank you. The entire Truxton fam—*what?*" Harris's jaw sagged because he'd seen the writing. "What's the meaning of this, Corbett?"

"Read it to the room, if you will. It may make more sense to you then."

Harris read aloud what Matthew had scribed: *"You are caught."* His cheeks flushed and there was a red gleam in his eyes as he looked down upon the young man in the chair. "What game are you trying to play?"

"I'm not playing a game, I'm ending one that really began well before Mary's fall." Matthew stood up and Harris backed away a few paces, nearly bumping into the Wickes behind him. "I thought of asking Simone to join us, Harris, but I decided that would be unnecessarily cruel. She had no idea you were coming up here from Boston so often to enjoy a dalliance with Nora Swaine."

"Who?"

"If you've forgotten, the young girl you murdered."

There was silence in the room, as Matthew had warned them all to remain quiet no matter what was revealed here…and, he'd said, much was to be revealed.

But the one person he'd not warned sputtered and nearly cried out: *"Murder?"* Niven's face had gone almost as pale as the makeup Miss Jennings used to mask herself as a ghost. "What's all this about?"

"It's about your brother being a cunning predator who realized he could knock down two birds with one stone," said Matthew. "He feared gallivanting in Boston, as there Simone did sometimes get out and about—to plays, for instance—and as I believe Harris is living off her family's money any whisper of scandal would not be wise. Therefore he found the prey here, got her pregnant and killed her…not just because a child would've been a problem, but because he needed a body to *solve* a problem."

Harris interrupted Matthew with a harsh laugh. "My God, Corbett! We should be signing a document of insanity for *your* admittance to Bedlam! Duncan, have you ever heard such lunacy?"

"That's exactly what Matthew predicted you would say," said the doctor. "I fear I am looking at the lunatic, and he's been right there before me for many years."

"The problem needing to be solved," Matthew went on to Harris's shocked silence, "was that Mary Truxton did not die in the fall." He paused while Marion Wicks gasped and Leah Clegg held onto her husband as if she might faint. "In fact, Mary is still alive and was evidently discovered by either of the Johnseys or their dog. She's been kept locked up on their property since she was found a few days after the accident. What condition she's in I don't know, but as I understand she was always physically strong from her equestrian activities and likely that has aided her survival. Well, we'll know more soon because Forbes and Eli Baines have gone to get Burt Anson and then they're proceeding to the Johnseys' place."

Harris had removed his silver filigreed snuffbox from his jacket pocket and now took a pinch up each nostril. Did his hand shake? No, not in the least…which put Matthew on guard for any sudden movement.

"Madness," Harris said. "Mary is dead. No one could've survived that fall."

"Actually, my opinion is that she *slid* down most of the way after losing her hold on the wet rocks," Matthew replied. "She may have suffered broken bones and painful injuries…but then again, Drucilla Johnsey is the village medicalist, is she not? I imagine she tended to Mary as best she could to keep her alive, and you were paying them to keep the secret after either Yates or Drucilla let you know they'd found her. And they were not going to let you kill her, because they were making money from the situation and I think even in their twisted hearts they're not murderers. Only they had to know that *someone's* body had been found…and, of course, Nora Swaine being the only girl who had supposedly run off to Boston…well, they figured that out. My question to you is: after I'd signed this document, what was to happen to Mary? Were they going to close their eyes and let you do what was necessary? But I imagine that by this time the Johnseys might suspect that after Mary got the blade their own necks would be next."

"Is he *mad*, Harris?" Niven asked, and in his voice was a note of pleading. "The truth, Harris! *Please!*"

"Oh, you weren't supposed to know anything about this," Matthew said to Niven. "You were just supposed to be the front for this young actress standing beside you. How could you know that around the fifteenth of September Harris killed Nora Swaine in the little shack they used for their meetings? And that subsequently Harris beat the body to pieces with a shovel he'd stolen from Eli Baines's toolshed? He paid special attention to the face, I can tell you. Then he dragged the body out on a blanket or some spread used to cover a pallet of hay in the corner of that shed. At the cove where he knew the crabs were plentiful he filled four burlap bags full of rocks and tied the corpse's arms and legs to the bags with heavy twine. He then dragged the body out to a sufficient depth where it would hang at the bottom and the sea life could get at the poor girl's remains, and he left it there until he decided it had been ravaged enough to drag back onto shore for some crabber or fisherman to find. That was a period, I believe, of about a month."

"More wild insanity!" Harris countered. "How would I ever *find* the body if I dragged it into the cove and left it moored underwater?"

"Easily," Matthew said. "With the use of a six-foot measuring rod you also took from the gardener's toolshed. You plunged it into the mud to mark the body. If you recalled the general vicinity from some landmark on shore, you could find the rod and thus the corpse. But you should've gotten rid of Nora's artist's crayons some other way than by throwing them into the fire, where they melted into a sadly colorful puddle—now solidified—which I found when I broke the door's lock and entered the place. That last work of art—yours, from a killer's brash hand—spoke for her, when she could not."

"Wait, wait!" Leah spoke up. "What's this about an *actress?*"

"Miss Gwendolyn Jennings should answer that," Matthew said, and nodded toward the girl with the fiery red hair.

"Not a word!" Harris had nearly shouted it, and now in his voice Matthew did catch a quaver.

"I think it's a bit late to try to silence anyone. If you please, Miss Jennings?"

"I was hired," she began tentatively, "to play a part. That's all. I didn't know anything about a murder."

"Nor did I!" Niven said with such vehemence the spittle jumped from his mouth. "My God, Harris! We were only supposed to get the sale can-celled! I thought the body *was* Mary's!"

"It isn't," Galbraith said. "I can attest to that."

"They came to me after a performance of *The Russian Widow* in Boston," the girl continued, directing her attention to Leah. "They took me to a room at the Sentry Hill Inn and told me what they wanted and how much they would pay. I was given information about Mary's life with Forbes and told to continue to speak with a Slavic accent when I was pre-sented as Niven's bride-to-be. They said also that in the dark or in low light I would pass as Mary's ghost because my shape was similar and with a black wig and pale makeup…well, a job is a job and one must eat. All I knew was they wanted Forbes out of the way…but they told me he wouldn't really try to kill himself, no matter how I presented the part. They said he would be declared insane long before it reached that point…and I believed them."

"I think you mostly believed in the money," Matthew said. "Acting on the stage is one thing, but playing on a desperately unhappy man's emotions is a criminal act in itself. I would say, though, that Harris is clever in a very twisted way. I believe he got the idea of Wandering Mary when Simone sleepwalked into Forbes's room on the twenty-eighth of September—the first reported visitation—and just stood there silently, making Forbes think he'd been visited by his supposedly dead wife. But by that time Mary had been found and Nora Swaine was in the water."

"They should all be strung up!" The statement had come from Marion Wicks, who looked as if she might be ready to crunch into an oil lamp and spit both jagged glass and searing flames. "I had my suspicions about *that* blackguard!" The finger she aimed at Harris trembled with emotion. "Niven and this…this *actress*…betraying Master Forbes as they've done… they should all hang!"

"I'm not a murderer!" Niven protested. He was proof that even in a chilly room a man's face could glisten with sweat. "Harris…killing the girl…did you *have* to do that?"

Harris Truxton took two more pinches of snuff and ran his finger around in the powder before he speared his younger brother with a damning glare. "You total fool," he said, his voice remarkably restrained for one Matthew knew was destined to the gallows. "Yes, it had to be done. When Yates Johnsey came to me about his wife finding Mary and demanding money to tend to her…what else was I to do? That girl was pregnant…I couldn't allow a birth, so what else was I to do? And you readily agreed to the plan, dear brother, therefore remember your *place* in all this."

Harris swung his gaze about the assembly in the room. Matthew saw his lip curl, saw the strangely luminous shine in his eyes and thought that the idea of madness as an infection of the Truxton line was not so far-fetched.

"You people…doctor and servants…you have no inkling of what it means to be *wealthy*," Harris said, with a reptilian hiss in his voice. "To be *someone* in this world. Respected…bowed down before…treated like royalty. To ride instead of walk. To be ushered through any door you choose to open. *Yes, Mr. Truxton, by all means, Mr. Truxton, anything you wish, Mr. Truxton*. And I'm supposed to stand aside and let a sobbing weakling destroy that for me? To stand aside and let all the pleasures of wealth slip away? Now *that* is truly insane. I will not let a traitor to the family name wreck us back into…" He hesitated, his mouth smiling but his eyes frigid. "*Irrelevance*," he continued. "Oh, no. I will see Forbes placed in a madhouse and I will stop that contract from being honored, and I—I, Harris Truxton—will save this company from ruin. I'm the savior, don't you see? The hero of this play! If there is a ghost in this manor it is that of my father, and he watches me from every nook and cranny. He tells me…stop Forbes, that weak link in the chain. Stop him…have him put away where he can do no harm…and keep what this family has spent *decades* in building. And Forbes…bending to the wishes of a *woman*? A *woman* not born of our blood is going to convince Forbes to give everything away? Isn't that insanity?" His gaze turned upon Matthew. "Isn't it? Answer me."

"You will have to find an answer for yourself," Matthew said. "You might come up with one as they put the rope around your neck."

"I think...*not*," Harris answered, and with that last word he flung the contents of the snuff box into Matthew's eyes.

Matthew staggered back, blinded and trying to clean his vision. He heard a shout, a scream, a chair going over and what sounded like a body hitting the floor. When he got his eyes back, though burning and fogged, he saw Galbraith and Clegg helping Wicks up, the elderly butler having been standing next to the threshold beside his wife and now bleeding from the nose due presumably to a blow from Harris. Niven and Miss Jennings had drawn back into the room, both of them needing no makeup to be as pale as ghosts.

"He's gotten out!" Galbraith said to Matthew. The doctor's spectacles were crooked on his face. "Shoved me aside when I tried to hold him! Wicks got a grip and he threw a fist!"

"That bastard!" Marion seethed at her husband's side. "Oh, dear Lord look at the blood!"

Matthew had no time to look. Though his vision was still in jeopardy he ran out of the room and followed the freezing air to the wide-open front door. Beyond was a world of white.

"Let's run him down!" Caleb Clegg said, coming up alongside Matthew, and with no further hesitation they set off in pursuit following the snow tracks of a murderous madman.

SIXTEEN

"I'VE KNOWN YOU FOR YEARS, DRUCILLA," SAID THE GRAVEL-VOICED, brown-bearded man who held a knife to her throat, "but if you swallow that key I'll cut you open as I would the basest stranger."

The hulking woman held her lips tightly clenched. Her deep-set gray eyes beneath an overhanging forehead looked from Burt Anson to Forbes Truxton, to her husband being held with his arms behind him by Eli Baines, and back to the village's lawman.

"Give it up," Yates Johnsey said, his own mouth bleeding from Baines's hard fist as he'd tried to block the door. "Ain't no use gettin' sliced."

Forbes nearly reached out to seize the woman by the neck and strangle her for what they'd seen her pick up from a table and put into her mouth, but then Drucilla's lips parted, the purple-tinged tongue extended, and there was the key.

Anson's gloved fingers snatched the object up. He gave Baines the knife. "Either of 'em move, you've got my nod to cut 'em. Come on, Truxton, let's get to that shed."

Outside snow was still swirling down before the freezing wind. The boots of the two men crunched through seven inches of white crust and deeper drifts tried to defeat their passage. Ripper was yet barking furiously as he'd begun when the invaders had arrived but he had taken a stance and obviously decided it wasn't worth the effort to move; in any case, Anson had told Forbes and Baines when Ripper had started his alarm that the dog was sold as a pup from the litter his sister's mongrel had birthed, and before Ripper was Ripper he was named Creamcake.

"I want to open it," Forbes said as they reached the shed.

Anson handed over the key.

Forbes struggled to fit it into the padlock. His hands were trembling, and not only from the cold but from both great anticipation and great fear of what he would find beyond the door.

Don't cry out or make any exclamation for what I'm going to say, Matthew Corbett had told him last night. *Mary is alive, and I know where she is being held. Hush, I said! Make no noise! You have been the target of a most wicked game. It ends tomorrow morning. No, I won't tell you where she is or what I know right now. Just listen to me. At six o'clock I want you dressed and out of here. Go out the back way through the Wickes' quarters. Eli Baines will be there waiting. I said...just listen! Baines is going to escort you to the village. He'll know what he's supposed to do. You just follow along with him. In time he'll tell you where you're going, who you're to meet in the village, and thereafter where your next destination will be. No, Mary is not in the village. How do I know all this? Because I determined that the spirit world is not as cruel as the world of the living. Now no more questions and I realize sleep will be impossible for you tonight, but do not leave this room. Speak to no one until you see Baines in the morning. Do you understand? Nod your head if you can't find your voice. All right, then. I would say good night but it would sound like a mockery of the emotions I know you must be feeling. Six o'clock. Baines at the back door. Dress warmly, it's as cold as a witch's curse out there. That's all.*

Forbes's trembling hand could not fit the key into the padlock. Anson grasped the other man's wrist, took the key, told Forbes to stand back, pushed the key into the lock and sprang it open.

Then Anson opened the shed's door.

From the darkness within came a strengthless gasp, as the wintry light streamed past the two men and illuminated the scene before them.

Anson spoke. "Mrs. Truxton, we've come to free you."

And from Forbes, a hushed and quavering: "*Mary.*"

With an obvious effort the figure that had been huddled under a tattered brown blanket stood up from a mound of hay pushed back against the far wall. A thin arm reached out and retrieved a tree branch carved to serve as a walking stick, and with hesitant painful steps the figure approached

Forbes and Anson, the other arm up to shield the pallid sun-starved face and squinting eyes from what must surely be a blinding glare.

"Oh my God," whispered Forbes, as he realized the torment his wife must've been subjected to in this hideous, bitterly cold hovel. And as Forbes pushed past Anson and rushed the few steps to Mary—the longest steps in his life—the emaciated woman with the jutting cheekbones, glassy eyes and mass of dirty dark hair cried out either in renewed hope or terror that she was having another dream of rescue which always became the reality of darkness, silence, hunger and cold. Her spindly legs—both broken in the fall and set without any tender mercy by the rough hands of Drucilla Johnsey—betrayed her, and down she fell once more, this time to be caught by a man whose tears were already freezing on his cheeks.

Matthew and Caleb Clegg were trudging through the snow, following the set of deep bootprints that led away from the manor toward the cliff's edge. Snow spun into their faces. The hilltop had turned into a white room whose walls shifted with the wind. Matthew still couldn't see at his best, the tobacco powder yet stinging his eyes.

A few more paces forward, and a figure lunged through the wintry murk at Clegg. Double-clasped fists swung and struck the coachman across the back of the neck. He fell with a muffled cry of pain...and as Matthew turned to respond Harris Truxton got an arm clenched around his throat and began dragging him toward the treacherous edge.

Matthew fought. The arm clenched tighter. Matthew felt the blood pounding in his face and he could hardly draw a breath. "If I'm to swing for one murder," the man said through gritted teeth into Matthew's ear, "I might as well make it two."

They were nearing the precipice. Black spots whirled before Matthew's eyes; he still fought but his strength was ebbing fast. Through the hiss of blood in his head he heard the thunder of the waves and what sounded like ice grinding against the rocks below.

Matthew tried to get Truxton's arm away from his throat enough to draw air but it was a hopeless effort. He was dragged right to the edge...and there Matthew saw another figure emerging from the white walls, coming straight at them.

It was Baba Yaga, snow in her hair and her eyelashes, her face death-pale except for red whorls at her cheeks and crimson glints of pure rage in her eyes. Baba Yaga, come to witness a second murder with Matthew Corbett as the unfortunate victim.

Truxton's head turned toward the oncoming witch.

A broom lashed out.

It struck the man in the face, and just that fast his grip loosened on Matthew's throat. The young man whooshed in a breath and pushed away, and as he fell to his knees he looked back to see Baba Yaga strike again with the broom. This time Truxton was thrown off-balance...he took one step back...a crust of snow broke and fell...and his face was contorted into an expression of silent terror as he went over the edge.

Matthew sat in the snow, his chest heaving and his head still pounding from the exertion of staying alive.

Marion Wicks leaned on her broom and peered over the cliff's edge. "No one hurts my Chet, not even a master," she said...perhaps to Matthew, perhaps only to make a statement to whatever humans, ghosts, witches or goblins that might be lurking about. Then, positively addressing Matthew: "You all right?"

Matthew nodded, though he was still unable to stand. At that moment Clegg staggered up, rubbing the back of his neck and working his head from side to side to clear the cobwebs. He eased to the edge beside Mrs. Wicks and looked over.

"He's already gone," the woman said. "Bastard like that...best the sea takes him and plants him ten fathoms deep." She regarded her broom, which possibly was the same with which she had cleaned the remnants of Whitton Truxton's suicide, and then she wiped it back and forth in the snow as if ridding it of any lingering trace of Master Harris.

Clegg helped Matthew to his feet. He, Matthew and Marion Wicks walked back toward the manor. Duncan Galbraith, Wicks and Leah Clegg had come outside, and it was the doctor who pointed out the figures in the white haze, coming up the hill from the direction of the village. There were three walking, and one pushed a wheelbarrow with a fourth figure curled up in it and covered with at least one blanket, if not several.

As the others went down to meet them, Matthew stood with his face upraised to the flurries of snow and thought that Mary's days of wandering had come to an end. She would likely need further medical attention, but she was alive...a ghost no longer. He looked back at the house and could make out both Niven and Gwendolyn Jennings standing in the doorway. When they obviously realized what the aftermath of "this situation" had been, they retreated out of sight...first Niven, and then the actress. Exiting the stage, so to speak...but not getting out of the criminal charges that Matthew was prepared to insist be weighed upon them in Boston.

"Matthew! Matthew!" It was Forbes calling for him, still a distance from the manor that was at the same time a castle, a church, a fortress and a tomb.

"Yes sir?" Matthew answered.

"Come meet my wife!" Forbes said, and his voice did break just a little bit.

Matthew started toward them, thinking that today the manor would be much more than castle, church, fortress and tomb.

This day it would be the most welcome and happiest of homes.

A coach back to Boston, business with the legal authorities there in concert with Forbes Truxton, a writ for Matthew to return on a certain date when Niven Truxton, Gwendolyn Jennings, and Yates and Drucilla Johnsey (both of whom had received a dose of their own hospitality by being locked for a time in that miserable shed by Burt Anson) were to appear in court, a packet boat journey back to New York, and Matthew arrived in town just as another tremendous snowfall swept through the streets.

But drinking ale and surrounded by friends at the fireside in the Trot Then Gallop, Matthew didn't mind the weather. He had done his job, been nicely rewarded from Forbes's wallet, and the matter resolved to his satisfaction. The worst part of it, really, had been his visit to the Swaine house, to inform Nora's parents that the task of locating their daughter had been accomplished, and it was a sorry thing he had to report.

After it was done, a tearful Zachariah Swaine had actually offered Matthew some coins in exchange for the information, which almost made Matthew weep for the waste of it all...a daughter lost at the hand of a man who while protesting the onset of insanity in his elder brother was himself in need of the padded walls of Bedlam.

A loose end was the letter the Swaines had received attesting to Nora's well-being. Had Harris written it by his own hand or paid some other confederate to do so? Niven and Miss Jennings of course knew nothing about it. So that had to be laid to rest without any positive solution.

In time Matthew learned from both the trial in Boston and from Forbes himself that Drucilla had discovered Mary while visiting her rabbit traps with Ripper. The dog's barking had alerted her to a nearly naked shape washed up in the cove. Mary had two broken legs, a gash on her head and was spitting up blood. For the first month, Mary had been unable to remember who she was or what had happened. It had been a close-run thing, with Mary nearly perishing twice before Drucilla could revive her with some self-made medicinal potion. But Mary had clung to life, and was now regaining strength and health and was as far from being a ghost—said Forbes in one of his letters—as could be imagined.

Forbes reported that after a suitable—but short—period of mourning, Simone Truxton recovered her stamina and in Boston became hostess to a number of parties that put her at the pinnacle of social life there, proving that once a harmful bacteria was removed a return to vitality might be the result. Matthew figured Duncan Galbraith would have a theory on that.

The judgment from Forbes on himself was that his despair over losing Mary and his belief that he'd not acted quickly enough to save her had unhinged his mind enough to *want* to see her wandering phantasm, and to believe she wished him to join her in a glorious afterlife where he would be forgiven and their love remain eternal. He reported to Matthew that Mary simply considered her fall the unlucky placement of a foot and the unluckier weakness of that section of earth. To that matter, Eli Baines had constructed a railing to guard the precipice.

Though Forbes was successful in selling the company—though indeed for pence on the pound—he informed Matthew that he and Mary were soon leaving the colonies to return to England. She was interested in her equestrian sports and he was determined to find a small but comfortable homestead in the country where they might simply enjoy the rest of their lives in peace. Matthew wished them well, and long productive lives.

The future of the Truxton Manor was unknown, and Matthew never did learn if it had been sold or not. In his estimation it might still be a brooding hulk of itself in a hundred years, and passersby on vessels going up the coast might wonder at its history, and who had ever wanted to live in such a place…because from the look of it, it was obviously haunted.

One thing Matthew did learn.

Harris Truxton's broken and frozen corpse had washed up six days after his fall.

And as a courtesy to the family name, Forbes had him buried in the vault.

Dear Reader,

We have come through seven shades of evil, yet another tale has come to my attention that must be told. We cannot forget one character who has suffered much and survived quite an ordeal, and thus this tale speaks to this person's bravery and strength in the face of…well…much evil on one's own.

So here is the eighth tale in our journey of seven, with our not-to-be-forgotten character and yet another shade of evil, perhaps the very worst of the lot.

Yours Truly,
Robert McCammon

INCIDENT ON THE *LADY BARBARA*

FEBRUARY, 1704

ONE

SHE HAD HAD ENOUGH OF IT, AND SHE WASN'T GOING TO TAKE IT ANY-more.

Therefore upon rising from her bunk in the morning and dressing her-self in warm clothes—since any place onboard the ship but the galley was cold enough to give musical chatter to the teeth—Berry Grigsby left her compartment and marched with defiant purpose along the lamplit passage-way to the door at its stern end.

With two sharp knocks that cemented Berry's determination, the door was opened. There stood on the threshold the imposing figure of Captain Henry Stoneman, who appeared more suited to climbing mountains than mastering a ship since he was so tall and the overheads were so low. Berry had noted him banging his bald noggin several times in the first week of their voyage, which brought forth the kind of cursing that he had also mas-tered but for which he was quick to apologize to the ladies aboard.

"Mornin', Miss Grigsby," the brown-bearded mariner said. He was wearing his usual working attire of a dark blue fur-collared jacket over a red-and-blue-plaid shirt. Buff-colored trousers with brown-patched knees and sturdy black boots completed the outfit. "What can I do for—"

"You likely already know," Berry interrupted, for the problem was plain to see. "It concerns Mr. Reginald Goolbie and his continued attentions, which I have never encouraged and which now have moved into the realm of what might be called the 'touchie-feelies'."

Stoneman nodded but said nothing, obviously waiting for the next burst from the copper-haired—and quite lovely, in his estimation—firebrand.

Berry did not disappoint. "I'm sure his reputation as 'Rowdy Reggie' is well-known in England, but I refuse to add to it except on the side of revul-sion. I do recall you mentioned to Matthew Corbett before we left harbor that you would see after me." She added something else she recalled. "As you would your own daughter." And then, witnessing the little sad retreat in the captain's eyes, she added again, "If she were still living, I mean, and pardon my clumsy attempt at reminding you of your word."

Stoneman nodded again, a silent enigma. Then he opened the door wider and stepped back. "Come in," he said.

Berry entered and Stoneman closed the door. As far as she knew, none of the other passengers aboard the *Lady Barbara* had yet been invited into the captain's private quarters. She quickly understood one reason was that the cabin was very small and the other reason was that all space was taken by a bunk that looked far too short for Stoneman's length, a desk that appeared to have been saved from the flotsam and jetsam of a previous sea wreck, and a cupboard holding a number of rolled-up documents that must be charts. Add to that a cow's-hide chair at the desk, a second chair facing the desk, an oak chest, two oil lamps fixed to the wall on gimbals, a wash basin and a little oval mirror on a stand and the place couldn't have held a pickled herring more. In fact, pickled herring was a staple of the galley meals, as was other salted fish, beef, dried potatoes and corn boiled, baked, fried and creamed in just about everything. Occasionally there was fresh fish hauled up from the frigid depths, but it took a steadfast crewman to stand out there in the Atlantic wind of February and cast his line hour after hour.

The *Lady Barbara* was one month out from harbor on her voyage to New York. *A ship is always a lady,* the captain had informed all once underway, *so treat her with respect and sensibility, for I can tell you she remembers slights and pays them back tenfold.*

As one of the four ladies aboard the *Lady,* Berry had been at first annoyed by Rowdy Reggie's unwanted attentions and then infuriated by the repeated "accidental" passing of the hand across the hips when Berry was trying to get past the man in the narrow passageway. It seemed that her sister passengers Cara Dixon and Jessica Rinehart had also been accosted in the same manner. Though Miss Rinehart was travelling alone, Mrs. Dixon's husband Drake had recently told Goolbie in the galley before all the others that one more "accident" of such indecency and the Rowdy One would find himself swimming the rest of the way to the colonies. Berry reasoned that Goolbie would've also had designs on Glennis Hammett—wife of Galen Fitzroy Hammett—if the woman hadn't been sixty years old, though indeed she was well-maintained—well-bred would be also correct—and quite witty in her conversations.

Stoneman leaned against the desk. The ship was rolling, which was a common occurrence and took much getting used to in the first week out but by this time everyone aboard had sea-toughened stomachs. "No one has to remind me of my word," the captain said. "When I give it, it's my bond.

And to the problem you're bringin' up, I've had two talks with the man and I think it's cooled him down some."

"Really? I presume you spoke to him before last night, when he just happened to…well, I shall say it…graze my bosom with a strategic elbow?"

"Some grazings can't be helped, sorry to say. It's in the nature of everybody bein' at such close quarters."

"Of course I understand that," Berry countered, "but it's him…and him…and him, again. He's taking advantage whenever he can."

"Many men do."

"*Some* men do. From that very first morning before we left London, Goolbie has continued to come at me like a rutting bull…pardon my language. If it's not physical, it's his…again, please pardon…suggestive statements. Or his staring at parts of the anatomy until it seems his eyes are about to burst from his head. I swear the man drools over the shape of a woman's throat and he goes into near ecstasy when a feminine coiffure passes near his nostrils."

"I wish I could command Mr. Goolbie to refrain from seein' and smellin'," said the captain, with a heavy-shouldered shrug. "Them things are beyond my capacity."

"Can't you do *anything*? It seems trying to talk civility into the man is pointless!"

"Might be, but I'll try again." He frowned at his own proposal. "I doubt it'll do any good. He's high on himself and he's got a history of livin' high off the ladies, is what I figure. All that mishmash about his jewels and such, that's supposed to intrigue the birds and bring 'em flockin' to his tree."

Berry thought that was an earthy way to put it but it was probably true. She recalled Goolbie's statements the first morning she'd met the man on the dock, with Matthew at her side.

"Rowdy Reggie to my friends," the fox-faced, brown-mustachioed-and-goateed gent had said by way of introduction. "Buyer and seller of fine jewelry. Your neck, dear one…would seem created for a string of the most magnificent pearls."

"Which you happen to have in your baggage?" Matthew had asked. He'd started to put his arm around Berry but she beat him to it by putting her arm around him.

Goolbie's eyelids had flickered only the faintest bit. "But of course, sir. You and this beauty are travelling together to New York?"

"This beauty," said Matthew, with a stiffening back, "is travelling alone, but I intend on asking her to marry me when I also return to New York."

"Oh. I see." *Tap tap* went his gloved fingers on his pursed lips. "Meaning you have *not* yet asked her to marry you? That's a pity. And when, sir, will you be travelling to New York?"

"Soon," said Berry. "Very soon. And whether Matthew has asked me or not, the answer to that question will be yes, yes, a thousand times yes."

"A pity," Rowdy Reggie repeated. "I do have many samples of beautiful items in my belongings." He was speaking now directly to Berry. "I understand there are only six or seven other passengers. It's a long journey." He gave a slick smile. "There will be plenty of time for you to see what I'm carrying." At the same time he'd shifted his balance, just so his rather grotesque meaning would be applied like a hammer to the forehead.

"I'm sure I'd rather not see," Berry had said.

"Oh, but I am an expert at the delight of women! Knowing what sort of jewels give them the most excitement, is my meaning. Yes, very much the expert. May I ask your name, since we shall be travelling companions on the long journey ahead of us?"

"Your bad luck," she'd replied.

His face didn't lose the slick smile, but there was a shade of caution in his eyes when he answered, "Pardon me, then, I shall say it was a pleasure meeting the both of you and…sir…I do hope your return to New York will not be too late."

"Too late for what?" Matthew had inquired.

"For *everything*," was the rather tight-lipped response, and then Rowdy Reggie had motioned with a disdainful hand for his wagon-sized trunks to be hauled up the gangplank and he strode away.

He hadn't gotten very far before it hit him.

The slip of a boot on a smear of cow flop might only discomfit some individuals. For Reginald Goolbie it spelled the disaster of destroying his balance as if he'd been blunderbussed at the kneecaps, making him stagger three steps, careen off the pig's crate and then stagger three more…though unfortunately for him, only two of those steps had timbers beneath them. With a hoarse yell he'd toppled over the other side of the dock into the cold and dirty water. Matthew and Berry could only stand and watch as Captain Stoneman ordered a rope to be thrown to the flailing figure, and when the dripping mess came out Rowdy Reggie was more of a Sad and Soggy Sight, minus his fur-trimmed tricorn and with his hair plastered down over his face like one of Professor Fell's tentacled sea curiosities. Berry could not restrain a little giggle which she hid—mostly—under her hand, and she felt badly about it afterward but in the moment not so much.

The excitement over, and Rowdy Reggie raging and stamping about as if in a bizarre dance with the gypsy girls who capered around him, Matthew and Berry went aboard the *Lady Barbara*. Captain Stoneman himself led them to a forward hatch, down an angled ladder that served as a stairway, past a storeroom full of barrels of more victuals and kegs of fresh water, and along a short passage to an open door and a small but comfortable pink-painted cabin. Within there was a bed, as narrow as it was, a clothes stand and a dresser with her own wash bowl and a supply of clean towels. Fresh linen on the bed, Captain Stoneman said, and also he indicated a key upon the dresser top that fit the door's outside lock. "Inside is this here latch, good and proper," he said, with a pickle-sized forefinger on it. "The crew's to be trusted. Been servin' the *Lady Barbara* back and forth six trips now, most of 'em's been with me the lot. Ain't need for a worry about your safety. And you can have your meals brought to you in your cabin, if you please." He'd given a rather embarrassed grin. "Ol' Henry's never been paid the number offered for this space. Used to be a pen where we kept the goats, but you see we fashioned it up, put a door on it and cleaned it out to a very spot."

"Commendable," Matthew had agreed. There was not a bit of goatishness in the cabin, it was true. Everything clean and quite stylish, in its own nautical way.

"I'd prefer to take my meals with the others," Berry had asserted. "A long voyage...no need not to be sociable."

"Very well, then!" said the captain. "I like that spirit! 'Minds me of my own daughter, bless her soul." Something sad had passed across the rugged face. "No longer on this earth, but I have her here." He put his hand against his heart. Then in the next second he was again all scrimshaw and hardtack, obviously proud of the work done here for the lady's comfort. "Lantern's there for the convenience." He pointed to it on a shelf beside the bed. "Supply of wicks for you, and your own tinderbox. Beg your pardon not to set my ship alight, so if you're needin' I'll have someone come by and flame the lamp for you."

"I can handle a tinderbox, but thank you for the offer."

"Chamberpot under the bed," he'd continued. "So's you won't have to share with nobody. I'll have someone clean it for you every day or so. Will you be requirin' both those trunks?"

"No, only the one with the blue leather grips."

"Yes'm. I'll have it brought in from the hold after we set sail. Shore bell will be rung in near an hour," the captain had said to Matthew. "'Til then, I'll leave you to your own." He'd given Matthew his own form of slapdash salute, bowed creakily for the lady and took his departure, cannily closing the door at his back.

One month ago. And Berry recalled the captain's statement of *I'll treat her as I would my daughter* as Matthew had been about to leave the ship...a sad moment of parting that Berry still felt like a hole in her heart.

"The man's a rounder for sure," Stoneman said, as the problem of the present came back into Berry's consideration. "Not much you can do with 'em, when they've got that kind of set to the mind."

He's more likely to be minding my set and those of the other ladies, she almost said, but decorum forbade the impulse. "I try to stay as far away from
him as possible," she replied. "Unfortunately that is not far enough to avoid
him, since we are thrown together on this voyage. And another month to
go, wouldn't you say?"

"We're runnin' a good clip. If the wind holds, we'll make port toward
the middle of March."

An eternity in the presence of Rowdy Reggie, Berry thought. But what else
was there to do but bear it? "I do hope you'll speak to him again."

"My word on it."

And that was all she could do. She said good morning to the captain
and departed. On her way to the galley she passed the second and third
cabins, which were occupied by the Hammetts in the former and Mr. Coy
Chandler in the latter, and then the area of living quarters that were separat-
ed from each other by canvas curtains. In this area dwelled the other passengers Mr. Micah Halliday, Mr. Morgan Stout, the Dixons, Jessica Rinehart,
and the dreaded jewelsman Reginald Goolbie. Past this area was her own
cabin, a storeroom and the forward ladder leading up to the deck, and
beyond that was the galley. Toward the ship's bow another ladder led down
to the crew's quarters, the *Lady Barbara* employing eight who handled the
ropes, sails and wheel and an additional man who served as the cook.

At their first meeting on the dock, Goolbie had said he thought there
were six or seven other passengers but he'd been incorrect by one, since
the corpulent trader in botanical medicines Morgan Stout had been a late
arrival. From what Berry had learned of the others—and on a journey of
this nature, one did learn a lot about one's companions in (it must be said)
misery—Miss Rinehart was on her way to meet her fiancée in New York,
the Hammetts were going to visit their two sons and families, the Dixons
were relocating from Lancaster to open his accounting firm, Mr. Chandler
was in the building construction business and Mr. Halliday—the youngest
of the others, being only twenty-three—was on what he called a "great adventure" to tour the colonies.

Berry's concern with Rowdy Reggie's behavior was a single nettlesome
thorn, but it carried not the weight of the thornbush of worry she felt for
Matthew. It was on her all hours of the day and night, and dogged her now
as she moved forward toward breakfast in the galley.

*I have bargained with the professor to help him in his efforts to find the
mirror.*

Sixteen words, spoken by Matthew at their last dinner together. Sixteen
words, equal to sixteen tons of torment for her.

Was the man she loved *insane?* Bargaining to help Professor Fell find
a mirror somewhere in Italy? And not just *a* mirror, oh no! An object

supposedly created by a sorcerer for the purpose of calling forth a demon from the Nether Reaches? And this book of demonic summons and such that would put the creature at your command...unless you made a mistake in the summons, and then it would likely tear your head off!

But she thought herself insane for entertaining that a mirror like this could even exist. No, it could not. Matthew was going to find the mirror, all right—and God knew he could find a pence in a pigpen if he had to dig through the mud to the center of the earth—but it would simply be an object of furniture, likely already broken and of no use to anyone. Then, that ridiculous quest done, he would have satisfied his bargain with Fell and be on the way home. No matter that the bargain had been with her own life and sanity and that of Hudson Greathouse, who was stupid enough to actually *volunteer* to help Matthew.

No, no...that was wrong! God bless Hudson Greathouse! If Matthew could be kept from danger by anyone, it was that big ox of a man. Not that she didn't like Hudson, but the fact was that he really *was* a big ox...and just what Matthew needed to shield him from...exactly what?

And again the worries flooded in. A book of spells...a mirror fashioned by a sorcerer...the very God-forbidden idea of calling a demon up from Hell to do the bidding of a sinister criminal...and who could say what might happen to the searchers on the *way* to Italy, or once there what might befall them?

For it had occurred to Berry in the midst of her sleepless nights, as the *Lady Barbara* sailed along and the miles between herself and Matthew grew longer and longer, that if Professor Fell had learned of this mirror so far away in England, who else might have learned of it there in Italy?

She shivered to wonder. With this on her mind as she lay on her cabin's bed she sometimes felt as if a cold hand had been drawn slowly along her spine.

The hand of death, a portent of what might be waiting for Matthew and the others on their journey...for if this mirror was real...if it could actually draw forth a demon...then others of even more sinister intent than Professor Fell might be in search of it, and those monsters who walked as human beings would have no hesitation in killing—

"Ah, the love of my life!"

Berry abruptly stopped just short of the doorway into the galley, for there before her stood Rowdy Reggie Goolbie, who as usual wore his slick smile like an invitation to debauchery.

TWO

"PLEASE REMOVE YOURSELF FROM MY PATH," BERRY SAID WHEN SHE'D regained her equilibrium. She saw that Goolbie was holding a corncake from the galley's table, one bite missing.

"The love of my life," Goolbie repeated, as if Berry had remained mute. "My life begins every morning, fair one. And so, here you are."

"I've asked you—" She changed that: "I've *told* you to move."

"So you have," he answered, but he did not move.

Berry regarded him as one might consider a particularly nasty insect that had crawled into one's way, though it was true that Rowdy Reggie would be thought of as very handsome by many women...likely a multitude of women. Berry surmised that he was around forty years of age, and by all appearances was well-maintained and quite fit. He had smoothly combed brown hair held back in a black-ribboned queue, a trimmed brown mustache and goatee and blue eyes in a sharp-nosed, foxish face. Obviously his jewelry business was doing well, for during the days and nights at sea he wore what looked to be a parade of stylish suits in pastel hues, with clean white ruffled shirts, usually a cravat of a darker hue, a patterned waistcoat and brown or black boots of exotic leathers. In passing him—usually at unfortunately close quarters—Berry had not failed to detect the pleasantly spicy scent of either the man's special soap or hair tonic, another gentlemanly touch that would win a lady's attention.

But there were always the groping hands, the face, chest or lower regions thrust too close for comfort, and the entire demeanor of one who intended to demean by way of attitude. In short, Berry was disgusted by him and over the course of the past weeks had worked hard to avoid him, but on a ship less than a hundred feet in length it was a problematic task.

And here he was, refusing to budge as he took another bite from his corncake.

"You're interfering with my breakfast," Berry said.

"Oh? How so?"

"You're causing me to become queasy and lose my appetite."

"Well, it must be that you're still not accustomed to the roll of the ship. My, you have a lovely color in your cheeks this morning! That fellow of yours must be a fool to let you travel alone!"

"As you've said to me several times," Berry pointed out.

"True, and each time I mean it all the more. I haven't asked, for the sake of decorum, but what does that young man do for a living?"

The phrase *for the sake of decorum* had almost made her laugh out loud, but she compressed her lips until the urge had passed. She saw no need to discuss any of her own or Matthew's business with this cretin but it came out anyway: "He is a very responsible and adept problem-solver in the employ of an agency that…well…solves people's problems. Now would you remove yourself?"

"A *problem-solver?* Hm! How interesting! You mean he undertakes what might be called *mysteries?* As in the finding of lost objects and such?"

"Much more than that. Listen, Mr. Goolbie, I want to get to the galley for breakfast. If you don't move, I shall call for—"

"I'll move," he replied, and Berry noted that something in his voice and expression had become less playful—or playfully foolish—and more serious. "But one moment. I wish your young man was with us to solve a problem, for I think we have a prowler aboard."

"A prowler? What do you mean?"

"I mean—" And here he looked past Berry along the corridor, behind himself at the galley's door and up at the closed forward hatch before he proceeded in a more subdued tone. "That someone has been prowling around in my quarters. Two nights ago, it was. I came back from supper to find my boots disturbed."

"Your *boots?*"

"I line my four pair of boots up beside my bunk. My habit is to place them in exactly a straight line. I have done so for years. In any case, when I returned from supper I found my boots in disarray…at least, moved enough for my notice. My belief is that someone aboard is looking to steal my jewels."

Berry had the feeling that all this was leading to what she had heard called a "punchline" but she took the bait anyway. "Your boots might still not be accustomed to the roll of the ship."

"Not a laughing matter," he persisted. "I think someone may have thought I'd hidden some of my merchandise in my boots, and went through them with a clumsy hand. Whoever it might be doesn't know most of it is in my baggage in the hold, and a small pouch of it is always carried…well…" And here he actually did motion toward his meadow of manhood.

Made you look, Berry thought his next grinning statement would be, and her cheeks were ready to flame red-hot as well as her tongue to throw fire.

But instead the Rowdy One continued quietly, in such seriousness as Berry had never witnessed from the man. "I'm in that area of curtained quarters because I lost my cabin on the ship I was *supposed* to be taking to New York. I was informed by messenger from the company that the *Briana Halsey* had been unfortunately overbooked and I was out on my ear because of some doddering wealthy couple paying double for my space. Then…at the last minute along comes Mr. Morgan Stout, who evidently made his payment *after* I was transferred to this ship. I wonder if he wasn't aboard the *Halsey*, and decided to jump ship there when he'd found from the passenger list that I was aboard here. I did note that both Stout and Miss Rinehart left the galley that night before the rest of us. They might even be working together to rob me." Goolbie raised his brows. "What would your problem-solver make of it?"

"He would tell you to abstain from the nightly portion of rum because it's inflaming your imagination."

"I vow it's not my imagination that my boots were disturbed!"

"All right," said Berry, who decided to play along for the moment. "Two nights ago?" She thought about it. "You might recall that Mrs. Hammett was ill that evening and neither she nor her husband came to the galley. Also, that Mr. Chandler entered after everyone else…except for myself, who dreaded sitting at a table with your lecherous face hanging about, so I was the last. I can swear on a hundred thousand Bibles that I would not dream—or entertain a nightmare—of bothering your boots."

"They're very, very *large* boots," he said, and that lustful smile slid back again as if it were as much a part of his wardrobe as his current gray-checked waistcoat. But in the next instant, as Berry's expression turned to absolute solid stone, Goolbie's smile vanished and he lowered his gaze. "Pardon," he said. "It comes upon me and I can't help it."

"Help what? Your incessant flirting and otherwise outrageous behavior?"

"It's who I am, Miss Grigsby." He lifted his chin. "It always has been so. Why? Who can say? All I know is, I have the power to twist a woman into any shape I please. I have the power to lure the fair sex to any den I choose, and it is as addictive as that gin raging the rounds in England. White Velvet, I think it's called. Yes, I have that power but it is also a power over *me*." And here a shine of what might have been anger glinted in his eyes. "You believe I think very highly of myself, don't you?"

"Yes, and too highly for one whose manners are so low."

"Granted. I have been bent over and whipped. Now…will you do me a favor?"

"No," Berry said.

"A small favor. Your Matthew being a problem-solver, some of that essence may have rubbed off on you. I do recall you and he spent some time together in your cabin before we left harbor, so the rubbing might have been…well, there I go again, but what I'm asking is simply for you to keep your eyes open."

"They *are* open, and watchful for *your* attempts at rubbing."

"*Ouch.*" He offered a smile that was this time a bit curdled on the lips. "We should as fellow passengers admit that we understand each other and let it go at that. I am asking you to watch my back."

Berry expected some further off-color jocularity to be made of that, but Goolbie did not proceed along a sordid avenue. He said, "You might be alert for anything you overhear or see that could be deemed suspicious. That's all I require of you."

"You can keep your requirements to yourself. If you imagine that someone is scheming to rob you, you should notify the captain. Also consider to cease bragging about the value of your merchandise."

"Here, here!" someone said loudly, approaching along the passageway from behind Berry. "Miss Grigsby, is this so-called gentleman accosting you?" Berry turned just as Drake Dixon reached them.

"Not in the least, sir!" Goolbie protested. "We are only having a decent discussion!"

"Like the one you had with my wife about the—as you put it—enchanting shade of her eyes?" Dixon was about five or six years younger than Goolbie, was dark-haired and dark-bearded having stopped shaving during the duration of the voyage. His deep brown, nearly black eyes glared arrows at Goolbie from a craggy though handsome face with a nose that appeared to have been broken more than once. And more than appearances, for Dixon's wife Cara had told Berry that in his younger days Drake had been involved in boxing matches as a way to pay his fees at the King's School in Rochester. Unfortunately this activity had involved gambling and the young man was dismissed, but he had joined a notable accounting firm in Lancaster, had become its chief operating officer and now was preparing to open an office in New York. Cara had told Berry they'd tried to secure a cabin, because Drake could certainly afford the expense, but at the present time there was such a movement of business people headed to the colonies for investment opportunities they had to take what they could get, therefore they were in what Cara called the "curtained estates," each "estate" being a bunk or double bunk, a small writing desk and chair, a little table to hold the wash basin and sundries and that was about the size of it.

Dixon's expression was fierce, but Rowdy Reggie did not flinch or draw back. "Sir," he said, "what affront is there in complimenting a lovely woman on her lovely color of eyes? It is rare to see such vivid blue."

"I can make you see a darker blue if you'd like," Dixon growled, as he lifted a big fist in front of Goolbie's face.

Berry decided to step in before the Rowdy One went down for the count. "Mr. Goolbie wasn't bothering me," she said. "In fact, he was just moving along. Weren't you?" She gave Goolbie a stare that meant *if you have any sense, start walking.*

If nothing else, the man did have good sense. "Pardon me," he said to both, and with great care pushed past them. But perhaps his sense was marred by his affinity for risk, because only a few paces away he turned again and said, "Mr. Dixon, can I help it if when I look into your dear wife's eyes I am transported to the warmest, most cheerful days of summer? And there resides the blue sky of morning, and the softest breeze that takes me away for one moment from this cold and dreary ship? Am I to be *blamed* for appreciating such a miracle of God's hand, that He should give your Cara the power to spread summer with only a glance? My, my, Mr. Dixon! How you fail to understand the gift you hold in your fist...I mean *hand*."

Dixon said to Berry, "Tell that jackass to get himself along before I decide which hand to make into the fist."

"Going, going!" said Goolbie, and off he went along the passageway.

Dixon and Berry watched him depart until he entered the area of curtained mansions on the port side of the ship. Then Dixon said quietly, "He's got a mouth and an attitude, but he's right about Cara. Still...it's his 'accidental' brushing of hip against body that we object to. It's happened far too many times, as I'm sure it's happened to you."

"It has, but then again the passageway *is* narrow."

"What? Making excuses for that creature?"

"No, simply stating a fact. Now...I am starved for breakfast, so you'll forgive me for wanting to dismiss Mr. Goolbie in favor of some food."

"Absolutely, and as I like nothing more than a hardy breakfast myself, I am going in the same direction."

Dixon held the galley door for her as she entered. It was blessedly warm in the chamber due to the red brick oven which was now in use by the dour and rather crabby Scottish cook named McKeague, who though was best left undisturbed in his labor was a master at cooking whatever was available a dozen ways, including his specialty of oat porridge. The galley appeared to be a hodgepodge of stacked barrels, pots and pans hanging on hooks, plates and cups on shelves and everything crammed into a small space with a table and chairs enough for six people at a time, but McKeague moved about his kingdom with the supple grace of maritime royalty. He gave a nod to Berry and Dixon as they entered, though his baleful gaze and outthrust juggernaut of a chin said *Welcome, but stay out of me way.*

Seated at the table having a breakfast of fried potatoes, red beans and corncakes with cups of coffee and additional cups of sweetened lime juice were Micah Halliday and Coy Chandler, the former the young red-haired adventure-seeker and the latter a stocky square-shouldered man in his fifties with a square jaw to match and light brown hair going to gray on the sides.

Good mornings were said all around. As soon as the two new arrivals took their places McKeague brought their food and drinks over, as usual without a word.

"Should we wait for Cara to join us?" Berry asked Dixon.

"It'll be a while. You should know by now that I'm an early riser while my wife enjoys spending the midnight oil at her reading. Also the fact that she doesn't want to get out of that warm blanket on these cold mornings."

Berry nodded. One nice surprise aboard the *Lady Barbara* was an ample supply of books, and the passengers had entertained themselves as much as possible playing games of cards and different variations of draughts.

"Just like a woman," said Chandler, whose voice was a sawblade rasping on stone. "Hard to get 'em into bed, hard to get 'em out."

"Careful there, sir!" Halliday warned, with a quick glance at Berry. "We've already got one obnoxious cad aboard!"

"Oh, my apologies, Miss Grigsby." Chandler's heavy-lidded eyes made Berry think of a big lizard sunning itself on a rock. "Sometimes my horses get loose before the barn door closes. He was in here just a few minutes ago, talkin' up his merchandise and such. Showed Micah and me some blue sapphires from that pouch he's always carryin', said they was worth a hundred pounds apiece and not a pence less."

"I'm pleased to have missed that demonstration," Berry said, thinking that Goolbie was such a fool that if someone aboard was really plotting to rob him his peacock strutting was begging for the theft.

Dixon said, "Probably blue *glass*, is what they were." He took a drink of his hot coffee. "I'm not sure the man could be trusted to sell a child's marbles much less precious stones. Ah, here's our Miss Rinehart! Good morning, madam!"

The door had opened and Jessica Rinehart had entered the galley. She was a slim young woman who had turned twenty-four two weeks after they'd set sail—as she'd told Berry in one of their conversations—and was always elegantly dressed in a nice gown even on the roughest of sea days. She had a peach-colored complexion, ash-blonde hair styled with tortoise shell pins, and a lovely face with a slightly upturned nose and gray eyes that were likely the shade of the ocean today but in her case they shone with youthful energy and the excitement of one day closer to her beau in New York. His name, she'd told Berry, was Timothy Batson and he was a first-year lawyer in David Lattimore's office.

"Good morning, all," she replied, and with a greeting nod at McKeague she took her place at the table next to Berry. "Everyone sleep well?"

"Thankfully, Cara and I did," said Dixon. "Unlike *some* nights in the past."

Berry agreed with that but didn't speak it. Some days and nights the Atlantic seemed an enemy to the *Lady Barbara*, lifting her up over one wave while the wind moaned and thrashed through the rigging and then slamming her down again with a force that made the passengers hang on to something—anything—for dear life. In the last week though the journey had been relatively smooth but the sun had become a stranger. Every morning if one dared to bundle up for a perilous excursion on deck, the intrepid explorer found the ship glistening with ice on timbers, railings, fixtures and ropes, and members of the crew would be put to work chipping the dangerous weight of it away.

McKeague brought over Jessica's breakfast. She thanked him and he gave his usual grunt, then moved back to his work.

She took a sip of coffee and a spoonful of beans before she asked, "Is *he* up and about yet?"

"We have already had our morning encounter," Dixon said. "He was accosting Miss Grigsby before she could get into the galley."

"A minor accosting," Berry said with a shrug. "Actually he just stopped me to have a word."

"A *word?*" Jessica looked incredulous. "What could he possibly have to say of any interest?"

"He was—" Berry stopped because she realized she was about to reveal a confidence, and no matter how detestable was Rowdy Reggie to her, it was not the right thing to do. So she said, "Just a minor complaint about his quarters. I advised him to take it up with the captain."

"Strange, that he should bring that up to *you*," spoke Chandler's rough voice. "Don't seem like the man's ways."

"Likely he had some idea of getting Miss Grigsby to his quarters for a look at what was bothering him," Halliday said, and he followed this statement with his habit of tugging at his right earlobe, as if this were somehow an aid to his thought processes. "That gent's a fox but he's not near as clever as he thinks himself to be."

Berry said, "Exactly," and let the matter go at that.

The conversation thankfully turned away from the human irritant aboard to the constant concern of every mariner and passenger upon the sea: the weather, and how cold it was yet to become before February was out. As they were discussing Chandler's memory of a four-foot snowfall in the second week of March, the galley door opened once again and in strode the self-proclaimed empresario of botanical medicines, Morgan Stout.

It had come to Berry's mind over the past weeks that Mr. Stout did not simply enter a room: he *arrived*. In a violet-colored suit with a wine-red cloak about his huge shoulders and an equally huge belly preceding all else, he was to the other passengers as a galleon was to a schooner. His head was bald, his eyes were intensely blue (though wintry as compared to Cara's summer hue), his chin looked to be a fleshy battering ram and his jowls were, to say the least, well-fed. Berry thought the thickness of his neck could've supported two heads. All in all, he was a formidable arrival, and yet to come was his voice, which when directed to the others sounded as if he deemed them all to be idiots not worthy of his presence. If Rowdy Reggie hadn't been so blatant in his excesses, the tide would've turned against Mr. Morgan Stout but as it was the big man was simply tolerated…though it was true, as Berry had found, that Stout exhibited an amazing intellect, had evidently read hundreds of books and could talk about the civilization of ancient Egypt as easily as the latest London gang murders, and it seemed to Berry that he had a rather pointed interest in crimes…the more bizarre, the better.

Did he also have an interest in jewel theft? It remained to be seen.

"Morning, Mr. Stout," Halliday said, but the big man did not deign to answer. He sat down in a chair that made a mewling noise of protest like a cat being tortured.

"Coffee!" thundered the order, which was made every morning about this time, and every morning McKeague gave him a look like a Scottish Claymore sword being driven into the massive gut and took his own sweet time doing any damned thing.

Halliday's pleasant nature persisted. "Have a good night, sir?"

Stout turned his frigid gaze upon the young man and sat staring for an uncomfortable few seconds before he said, "I am aboard a ship that moans and groans like an old man being tormented in a nocturnal visit by the Devil himself, and I am squeezed into a bunk that contorts me into a shape heretofore unknown to the citizens of this earth, so how could I *not* have a good night?" From a pocket of his jacket he removed a small blue vial, uncorked it and held it under his nose. His nostrils flared. "Ah!" he said. "The essence of orchids! A cure for nerves, the palsy, indigestion, corrupted humors and headaches!"

"But no use for irritability, it seems," Berry had to say.

Stout's cold attention fixed upon her, but he brought up a smile so thin it might have cut some of McKeague's hard-cased sausages. "A cure for almost *everything*," he said, "though impotent against ignorance masquerading as companionship."

What response there might have been to this weighty sentiment was never to be known, for into the galley came Captain Stoneman, wearing a woolen skullcap and heavy coat. Flecks of ice clung to his beard. He gave them all a gravelly *good morning*, took a cup of coffee from the pot, swigged some of it down and then addressed the group. "I've advised one and all against venturin' on deck until about midday when the ice is cleared but we have quite a sheen on us today and the wind's beyond bitter. I would warn 'gainst goin' up, though I know some of you are wantin' the fresh air. If you do go, make sure you wear your gloves and keep hold of the safety ropes. Got me?" He waited for nods and sounds of agreement, and then he regarded Berry. "My word's my bond," he said. "I've laid down the law like you asked, and I hope it's done some good." He finished his coffee, took two corncakes and left the room.

"Laid down the law?" Dixon asked when the door had closed. "What was that about?"

"I requested that Captain Stoneman speak again to Mr. Goolbie about his atrocious manners and disregard for the ladies aboard," Berry replied. "I don't wish to go another month avoiding the man's hands and whatever else he thrusts into one's way."

"A toast to that!" Dixon lifted his cup. "Cara will be glad to hear it! But if I had my way I'd forego the pleasantries and toss the scutter over the side."

"Well," said Berry, "since the *Lady Barbara* is Captain Stoneman's ship, it's up to him to enforce the rules of civilized behavior. Let's hope the talk sticks."

"Doubtful," rumbled Stout. "The man's a crashing boor and what's bred in the blood cannot be expelled."

On that sour note, Berry finished her breakfast and left the galley. In her cabin she put on a heavy fur coat—purchased in London, she realized, from Professor Fell's bloody pocketbook—her leather gloves and a snugly fitting woolen cap, as she was determined to go up for at least a few minutes for air. It did not have to be said that the combined odors of humans at close quarters, the livestock of cows, chickens and pigs aboard, and the lingering perfumes of chamberpots were no walk through Kensington Gardens. Thus the need for a few uncontaminated though lung-freezing breaths, and though the deck would be treacherous there were safety ropes all along the railings to grip hold of but gloves were necessary on the ice-filmed lines.

At the height of the forward ladder she pushed open the hatch and was immediately almost forced back down again by the wind. Bitter was too soft a word for its hard attack. Still, one could not curse a strong wind on a sailing ship, for above her the full sails on their tall masts were spread in majestic glory against a dull gray sky, and the vessel was cutting a thoroughbred's clip across a seascape of argentine waves shot through with threads of green and topped by flying white foam. The *Lady Barbara* was pitching, waves breaking at the bow and flinging up mist that became the glossy ice shrouding all surfaces, but the ship's action was nothing out of the ordinary and far less rough than on some more stormy occasions.

As Berry came up from the hatch she gripped hold of the red-painted rope to her starboard side that was secured to the railing and extended along the entire length of the ship and, proud of her hard-won balance against the sea's challenging instability, she made her way past the galley stove's flue that protruded above the decking to the starboard rail amidships, which was probably just above her own cabin.

The sea and the distance…gray upon gray, and seemingly going on forever beyond the walls of the morning's murk. Looking to her right, she could make out as hardly more than a shadow the figure of the helmsman at the ship's wheel. He would be wisely bundled up and wearing a woolen facemask as was the usual protection in this kind of cold. To her left, the spray coming up over the bow could be felt like needles to the cheeks. She could not stay here very long, but she would enjoy it while she could.

Rowdy Reggie Goolbie. Someone planning to steal his jewels. Or so he believed. Of what merit and truth was that? Still…the man had seemed highly concerned about the formation of his boots upon the floor, maintaining that a prowler had been visiting his own curtained estate. But again…what of it? The man was imagining hands searching for his jewels, and if any man likely had experience with hands going for jewels he was certainly the one.

But in a way, Berry felt sorry for him. He seemed to be a man whose nature would not let this amorous and braggartly effigy of himself become human. He seemed to be—the worst kind of affliction, she thought—a man who could not make friends. But it was on his own head, was it not?

She recalled Goolbie saying *Your Matthew being a problem-solver, some of that essence may have rubbed off on you.*

Well, that was ridiculous.

Wasn't it?

She suddenly realized that since her meeting with Goolbie outside the galley she had not been assailed by worry about Matthew.

What I'm asking, he'd said, *is simply for you to keep your eyes open. You might be alert for anything you overhear or see that could be deemed suspicious. That's all I require of you.*

Her doing anything to help Rowdy Reggie? It was unthinkable!

Or was it?

After all, her concern for Matthew could not aid him in any way whatsoever and only served to rend her heart and spirit all the more…but here before her was a problem that even Matthew might have found of interest.

No, there was *no* problem! Goolbie was imagining the whole thing!

But what if he wasn't?

Berry faced the wind, as the sea thrummed against the ship's hull and the entire world was made of sky and water.

There was yet a long way to go to harbor, she thought. Perhaps…just a little alertness on behalf of Rowdy Reggie would help make the voyage pass more quickly, whether he was imagining a prowler in his quarters or not.

Time would tell.

She breathed in the frigid air for a while longer, and then with a clear head she returned to the forward hatch, lifted it and descended the ladder into the depths.

THREE

AFTER BERRY'S BRIEF VISIT TO THE DECK, SHE HAD SPENT HER DAY IN much the same manner as everyone else aboard: enclosed in her cabin and reading, or napping, or otherwise entering a state of dreaming about land-fall and how excellent solid earth was going to feel under the feet. In the early afternoon Jessica Rinehart knocked at her door and invited her to join in a game of draughts in the galley, as they had played nearly every day about this time.

Thus during the game Berry had the opportunity to further advance not only her pieces but her curiosity, for Jessica had mentioned previously that not only was she eagerly looking forward to being Timothy's wife but that she also was going to try her hand at—of all things—writing a novel.

"An interesting ambition," Berry commented as she watched the other woman deliberate over the arrangement of pieces on the board. "Do you have a theme?"

"Oh yes," Jessica said. "*Mystery.*"

"Pardon?"

Jessica looked up from her study. "Mystery," she repeated. "I suppose one may say…who did it, why, and how?"

"I'm sorry, but…who did *what?*"

"Whatever was done," came the still-puzzling reply. "I have always been fascinated by such things…the culprit in the night, the missing bag of money, the unseen stalker." She gave a sweet smile. "Those and more. The mystery of it. You see?"

"I don't think I do."

"Well," Jessica said, as she folded her hands together, "I believe you would agree that the criminal will always be with us, and in the future it will be the same as now: the element of a criminal act that makes people want to know who did it, why and how. In my estimation it's a timeless subject, going back to the mists of history. And an exciting subject for books, also in my opinion."

"How so?"

"Because of the questions themselves. Because they challenge the reader to solve the mystery before the final page, thus the reader is...shall we say...intimately involved in the outcome. And the writer's task is to shade the subject...to offer bits and pieces of the solutions...not so miserly that the reader does not have a chance to answer the questions, yet not so overtly as to...how shall I put this?...spill the beans. You see?"

"I see you've spent much time considering this," Berry said.

"And gladly so! I think in the future much praise should go to the mystery writer, for lighting the candles of imagination and intrigue in a world that can sometimes seem so dreadfully dark."

Berry smiled. "A noble calling, it seems. Miss Rinehart, I hope your ambition results in the lighting of many candles. Now, if you'll look more closely at the board you might find the answers as to who will win this game, when and how."

Berry took the first game, Jessica the second and third, and Berry the fourth. As they played, Micah Halliday entered and sat down to observe, and Goolbie came in, stood watching for a few minutes without a word—which was highly unusual for his habit—and then left the galley. At the end of the fourth, Berry said she was retiring to her cabin and Halliday offered to play Jessica another game. Then Berry departed...and in the passageway Goolbie suddenly emerged from the little passage that led into the curtained estates.

He said quietly, "Miss Grigsby, may I have a word with you?"

"What is it?"

"Please...would you come to my quarters with me?"

"Certainly not!"

He held up his hands, the palms open. "I swear to you, this is not a trick of some kind. I need to speak to you in my quarters. It is *urgent*. Please."

"You can speak to me right here, sir."

"If I am less than gentlemanly, may God strike me dead. I have a proposal I wish to make."

Berry's mouth crimped. "Of that I'm sure!"

"No, no...a decent proposal. Please...one minute of your time, but it must be made in private."

What to do about this? Berry would never have dreamed of entering Rowdy Reggie's domain, yet the man seemed really distraught. A trick to get her in there behind his curtain? Possibly so, but—

"It's about my jewels," Goolbie said, interrupting her deliberations. "The ones in my pouch. Please, miss. One minute."

She gritted her teeth to this request, but her answer was: "One minute and no longer, and if I am touched I shall either scream for help or slap you across the face so hard your eyes will have to be returned to their sockets."

"Granted," he said, his head downcast in unusual acquiescence, and led the way.

His compartment was the third down the passage to the right. He drew the heavy canvas curtain aside, revealing the small space. Berry noted his collection of four pairs of polished and probably expensive boots perfectly lined up beside his bunk, which was made up as if no one had ever slept upon it. There stood a little round table with a few drawers next to the bunk holding his wash basin and oil lamp, a rattan chair and a wooden rod bolted to the bulkhead that supported a number of his pastel-hued suits and two cold-weather coats on pegs.

Goolbie drew the curtain closed behind her, opened the table's bottom drawer and drew out the purple velvet pouch that had likely been recently kept near his repellent manhood.

"I am asking you to hide this in your cabin," he said, and held it forth in offering.

Did she take a backward step? Possibly so.

"I mean it," he continued. "Hide this until the end of the voyage. Would you? Please?"

"I want nothing to do with that pouch," she managed to say.

"Do you know the worth of what's inside? At least four hundred pounds," he plowed on. "Two sapphires, an exquisite uncut emerald, two moonstones, three opals and three silver bracelets of fine quality. They're what I display to potential customers."

"And potential victims?" she asked.

"Forget about that for the moment, I beg you." An expression of grave concern had surfaced upon the man's face and fixed there. "I told you that someone was in here prowling about, probably looking for this pouch. What I did not tell you is that in the last few days I have felt myself to be watched. It is just…the feeling that someone here is observing me in se-cret…sliding away just as I turn to look…a shadow where there should not be a shadow. Do you understand?"

"I understand that again your imagination is at work."

"It is *not!* Listen…I am well aware of how to shadow a person, because I've done it many times. Following women, I have to admit. Seeing a lovely one in a dress or a hat shop, and strolling along to find out where she lives and if she might be attached or not…just keeping out of sight enough to learn what I need to know and planning my approach. Now…someone here is doing the same to *me*, and I fear the approach will end in violence."

"Thank you for the report on your execrable history."

"Think all you wish of me, but the current situation demands help from one fellow passenger to another. One fellow passenger I can *trust*, I mean."

"This is outlandish!" Berry said. "If you believe someone may attack you and take the pouch, give the item to Captain Stoneman so he can lock it in his quarters."

"I don't even trust *him*," Goolbie answered. "You I trust because I saw you with your Matthew and from what you've told me…well, it rings true to my ear."

"No one here is planning to steal your merchandise. And if you were attacked, how would your attacker get away without the law being called as soon as we reached harbor? Anyway, I understand that even on a ship of this size there's a brig down below where a troublemaker would be locked in."

"Fine for that." Goolbie's mouth had become a thin grim line. "But what if there's no victim to report the trouble?"

"*Murder?* Aboard this ship? I doubt your absence wouldn't be missed, and it wouldn't take very long for someone to find the body. *Your* body, I mean. Listen, Mr. Goolbie—"

"Please. *Reggie*. We should at least be on a first name basis if we're to be compatriots."

"*Mr. Goolbie*," Berry repeated with some force to it. "In my opinion everyone on this ship is exactly who and what they say they are and mean no harm to you nor do they wish to grab your jewels. Your *merchandise*, that is."

"Everyone? You forget the nine members of the crew. How do I know one or more of them don't have wicked designs? That McKeague looks like he wishes to put a knife in me. And Captain Stoneman has given me the evil eye, too. The shipping companies don't pay these nautical louts very much for their efforts, so how do I know one of them is not lurking around, biding his time to strike? And I still say I don't trust that Morgan Stout, scurrying aboard late like he did."

Scurrying was not a word Berry would ever have used to describe the laborious movements of Stout, but she made no comment on Goolbie's choice of language. Her next comment was more direct and final. "I will not accept responsibility for your merchandise. And I believe the one minute has long passed."

"You refuse to help me, then?"

"I do refuse."

Goolbie nodded, staring down at the floor's timbers. "I hope," he said in a strained voice, "that you do not have to accept responsibility for any violence that is done to me, and for the theft of my precious merchandise."

"I repeat: take the pouch to Captain Stoneman and have him lock it away. I will now say good afternoon."

He offered nothing more, as Berry pushed aside the curtain and left Rowdy Reggie's estate.

At promptly six o'clock the galley bell rang, as usual, to summon the "first list" of passengers to supper, as the table was only suited for a sextet. The "second list" would be served at seven, and this had been drawn by lots soon after they'd left the dock. The lists were not adhered to at breakfast, as that meal was not as demanding of McKeague and one could come and go as one pleased, finding table space as available. The crew had their own supper area down in their quarters. Berry entered the lamplit and blessedly warm compartment to find already there Jessica and the Dixons, being served dishes of sausage, rice and the familiar red beans by the ever surly and silent McKeague. Berry took her place at the table, was served and began to eat. Across from her sat Cara Dixon, who likewise had suffered the indignities of intentional leering and "accidental" groping from Goolbie. She was a pleasant and expressive lady a few years younger than her husband, with light brown hair and the vividly blue eyes that had so entranced the Rowdy One and led him into dangerous waters with her husband. The supper conversation centered as always around the length of the voyage and the challenge of finding something constructive to do with one's time—Cara's was intricate needlepoint, a particular challenge on a wave-tossed ship—the anticipation of reaching New York, and the vagaries of the winter weather.

The ponderous and pretentious Morgan Stout entered about fifteen minutes after six, and this was the last of the first list. He did not speak during the entire event, as this sterling specimen of civilization was too busy stuffing his face in a most uncivilized manner.

As the meal was being finished, the passengers were served a drink of rum in small brown clay cups, which in truth most looked forward to as the delight of the day. Particularly delighted in this—as they had told her so—were the slender duo of Galen and Glennis Hammett, who would arrive in the second list along with Mr. Halliday, Coy Chandler and Goolbie. Though both in their sixties, the Hammetts were as bright as new silver coins to match the color of their hair, they were always dressed as if out on a London evening, and they eagerly looked forward to the adventure and pleasure of visiting their two sons and their sons' families first in New York and then in Charles Town, albeit they lamented having to leave their little dog Astrid at home in the care of servants.

The rum downed and the supper done, Berry returned along the passageway to her cabin, passing Mr. Chandler on the route as the bell for the second list was sounded. Then she settled in with her lamp lit to continue her reading of Lady Margaret Cavendish's *The Description of a New World, Called a Blazing World* which she'd chosen from the well-used library shelf down near the captain's cabin. In time the bed in her pink-painted abode beckoned her, she took off her gown and shoes and put on her heavy woolen sleeping coat, got under the very welcome weight and warmth of two blankets, extinguished her lamp and sought sleep.

The dream that came she knew was a dream yet was striking in its solidity. She saw Matthew also aboard a ship, but one that was tossed by an angry sea. Behind the ship was darkness, but before it was a strange reddish mist that undulated above the waves. In her dream she saw Matthew standing on the deck, looking ahead toward that strange horizon…and then there were two figures approaching him, one on either side. As they neared her love she felt her heart beat harder and the breath quicken in her lungs because there was something both fearsome and terrible about them, and she tried to call out a warning but her voice was frozen in her throat. She could not make out their faces but she could tell that one was a man with a tight, glossy cap of hair and one was a woman with long tresses…and here the strangest of the strange, for the male had hair black on the right side and red on the left, and the female red on the right side and black on the left. They reached out to grasp Matthew's shoulders, and he was yet unaware of their presence… and again as Berry tried to call out a warning nothing would emerge, and just as the hands of these two creatures closed upon him the ship was engulfed in the mist and—

Thump.

Her eyes opened in the dark.

A noise above her.

Hadn't it been?

Quite a noise, it had seemed. Enough to jar her from the dream, which she was glad to get out of. Something above her cabin on the deck.

She lay still, listening. There was nothing now but the incessant sound of the sea hissing around the hull, with an occasional fist strike of an obstinate wave.

But this sound had been over her head, like possibly a weight of ropes falling to the timbers on the starboard side.

Well, what of it? As long as they weren't sinking. She might have imagined the noise. She thought the night's portion of rum might have fueled the dream, so it might have also made mental bumps and thumps in the night seem very real.

Nothing to be concerned about, she decided. That, no…but the dream. Disturbing. And meaning what?

That she needed to get back to sleep, and perhaps not read further in the rather chilling and unsettling *A Blazing World*, which had as its premise a young woman being kidnapped into a world populated by bizarre talking animals, fish men and bird men and becoming involved in a war for the fantastical Kingdom of Esfi.

She wished she had one of Miss Rinehart's "mysteries" instead.

Berry closed her eyes, and the *Lady Barbara* sailed on.

FOUR

BERRY HAD TO ASK. "DID ANYONE ELSE HEAR A STRANGE NOISE LAST night?"

"Oh, I hear a strange noise *every* night," answered Glennis Hammett, who sat next to Berry at the breakfast table. "It emanates from the nostrils of this gentleman seated to my left, and presents a wonderful serenade."

"Anything for you, my dear," Galen Hammett replied, with a fork's spearing of ham before his mouth. "I do know how you miss the musicales at the Stork Club."

"Thank you for the thought, darling, but I fear your style of musicale went out of fashion with the barbarians."

Galen leaned forward to give Berry *that* look: half-ironically indignant and half jolly old fun, and then he returned to his morning repast.

"What strange noise?" Seated across the table from Berry was Coy Chandler, who had entered about ten minutes before. The others had not yet made an appearance.

"It sounded like a weight falling to the deck, nearly above my head. I don't know what time it was, but it had to be very late."

"Hm." Chandler rubbed his jaw. "Maybe I did hear somethin'. I recall I came awake all of a sudden, but I went back to sleep quick enough. I don't remember much beyond that." He looked toward the cook. "Mr. McKeague, that hard-boiled egg ready yet?" He had asked for one directly upon entering.

McKeague paused in his work long enough to give Chandler the dirty eye. "I'll let ya know," he said in his foggy brogue.

"I have to tell you, Miss Grigsby, I saved you last night," Chandler confided.

"Oh? How?"

"Halliday, Dixon and me played some games of Newmarket in here 'til after eleven. I was on my way to my cabin when I saw somebody standin' with a lamp at your door. A little closer and I made out it was…you know…*him*."

"Oh, yes, the dreadful *him!*" said Galen, knowing exactly who the *him* was.

"Double dreadful!" Glennis added.

"Yeah," Chandler agreed. "Anyway, I saw he had his fist balled up ready to hit your door."

"One thing I can't abide," Galen said. "Violence to an innocent door."

"So I called out to him to ask what he thought he was doin'," Chandler said, "and he dropped his fist and looked like he was…I don't know…confused, maybe. I told him he shouldn't be botherin' anybody so late, and in particular not you."

"Thank you for that."

"He went on to his quarters, I suppose. I didn't see him after I turned my back and went in my own cabin. But before he moved on he asked me somethin' I can't quite figure." He interrupted himself to take a drink of the coffee McKeague had served him.

"Don't leave us dangling, young man!" Glennis said. "What did he ask?"

"He asked if I'd left him the note."

"High C, I presume?" asked Galen.

"Low F," Glennis corrected.

"The *note?*" Berry frowned. "Was anything else said?"

"I told him I didn't know what he was talkin' about, and that's the whole of it."

"Not quite the whole." Galen leaned forward again to cast a sharp eye upon Berry. "May I inquire as to why Mr. Goolbie would be attempting to knock at your door after eleven o'clock? I had the impression you'd asked our captain to…shall we say…dissuade Goolbie's further attempts at communication?"

"Put the strong arm on him, you mean," Chandler said.

"Exactly that, though it appears the strength of the arm weakens after all doors are closed and curtains drawn. What might Mr. Goolbie have wanted with you?"

"Isn't that obvious?" Glennis asked, with a sardonic smile. "Darling, you're showing your age."

"Pardon my curiosity, Miss Grigsby. Too much rum in my cup last night. Or not enough. I shall make amends at tonight's offering."

Berry felt a little heat beginning to rise in her cheeks. "I can vow to you that Goolbie was not invited to my cabin, and I have—" *No idea of what he wanted*, she was about to say, but she realized she did have an idea and it concerned his fear of theft. "I have no intention of inviting him," she finished.

"Puzzling though, isn't it?" Galen steepled his slim fingers together. "Why in the world would the man attempt to knock at your door, late at night, after you—and the other ladies, of course—have made it clear to him to keep his distance?"

"I'm glad I don't have to worry about him," Glennis said.

Galen put his arm around her. "Oh I told him very firmly on the dock not to go after that beautiful, elegant and sophisticated lady who is the light of my life and the apple of my eye."

She looked askance at him. "You forget that we left Astrid at home." But she kissed him anyway.

"Hard-boiled," said McKeague as he put the egg in its ceramic cup before Chandler.

"Just as I like it," Chandler replied.

Berry finished the last few bites of her breakfast and left the galley, greeting the Dixons as they were entering. In her cabin as she bundled up for a breath of air on the deck, she reflected that she was in what her Grandda would have called "a pickle." She did not wish anyone to think she was carrying on clandestine meetings with Rowdy Reggie while pretending to recoil from his advances. And what was this about a note? Whatever it was, it had to have been unsigned. Should she ask him about it? No, certainly not! She wished not to be involved in his affairs, and she still thought he was imagining being watched or followed or whatever else his inflamed mind concocted.

A climb up the forward ladder and through the hatch to the deck showed her the sky still thickly clouded and gray the same as yesterday, the wind bitingly cold and sleet flying into her face. But upon the deck on the starboard side about amidships stood a monster.

A familiar monster, however. She'd seen Morgan Stout wearing his hooded black bearskin coat many times before. The coat made him appear to be of monstrous size. As she gripped hold of the safety rope and moved carefully toward him over the ice-glossed deck, she saw the man lean down—and how he could fold at the middle being so huge was either a miracle of nature or a case of mind over matter—and work something up from the timbers at his boots.

"Good morning," she said as she reached him.

As was his habit, Stout did not answer. He was examining something he held in a bear's claw of a glove.

"What did you find?" she inquired.

She thought that again there would be no reply, but the hooded head turned toward her and he held up an object that was curved and about as long as a finger. "A piece of broken glass stuck in the ice," he said. "I stepped on it and heard it crunch." He wafted it back and forth under his jutting slab of a nose. "The chimney from a lamp. I can smell the whale oil. Also one can see a residue of soot." He leaned forward, his free hand on the safety rope as the *Lady Barbara* performed a graceful pitch against an oncoming whitecap. "Ah, here's where it broke. You see the soot mark there on the rail?"

Berry edged closer, also holding firm to the rope. Where Stout indicated she made out just the slightest dark smear under the pale white film.

"Someone's lantern broke here last night, I'd say, from the accumulation of ice upon this glass and the soot. This wasn't here yesterday, as I make morning and afternoon rounds of the deck my regimen. Exercise, you see." He offered her his version of a smile, which in truth was a rather frightening grimace.

"I heard a noise about here last night," she said. "It sounded like something fell to the deck, but it was much larger than a lantern."

"Really?" The big man's lips pursed and his head moved from side to side, the eyes searching. "My question is, where is the rest of the lamp?"

"Possibly a crewman broke his lantern's chimney by accident and took the rest away."

"And left broken glass on the deck? I doubt Captain Stoneman would approve of such negligence, and why not get the glass up before it became seized by the ice?" Stout nudged the frosted accumulation below him with the toe of a boot. "I'd venture there are smaller bits frozen in there. If one would make a study of the depth of ice, one might say the lantern was broken sometime last night…likely a late hour. Interesting, wouldn't you say?"

"Someone's accident, that's all."

Stout said nothing, still examining the piece of glass. Then, abruptly, he replied, "Quite correct. Someone's accident," and he tossed the shard to the waves. "Pardon me, miss. I'll continue my rounds."

He moved away, holding fast to the red rope. Berry remained where she was, regarding the faint smear of soot beneath the railing's ice. Did this have something to do with what she'd heard last night? She looked up and saw two crewmen working in the rigging above, which had to be a nasty job on a day like this but such tasks had to be done. It could've been that a crewman in the rigging had dropped his lantern last night, and it had broken here. But Stout was correct about Captain Stoneman not allowing such negligence; from what she'd seen, the master of the *Lady Barbara* was meticulous in keeping his ship in order, and the allowance of broken glass on the deck so near to where the passengers would be walking was out of character. Someone could fall on the deck and be badly cut. If the lamp had fallen from above, surely the man who'd dropped it would've made sure the shards were cleared away.

It was strange…that this evidence of a shattered lamp chimney should be so near to where she thought—imagined? dreamed?—hearing a weight fall to the deck.

The sleet was coming down with greater force, hissing through the rigging and pelting her face. She gazed out at the limitless gray sea and suddenly felt very lonely, wishing that she could reach out and grasp Matthew's hand. But it would be a long time before she saw him again, and that was the hard reality of it.

After a while Berry turned away from the sea and brooding sky and returned to the forward hatch to get out of the bitter weather, but for some reason even when she went down into the relative warmth of the ship she still felt cold inside.

FIVE

As the first list of supper-goers finished their meals and left the galley that evening, Berry found herself waiting in the passageway outside the door as the bell for the second list was rung. Here came Chandler, followed by Micah Halliday. A few minutes later the Hammetts came along the passage, Glennis laughing at some remark made by her husband, who Berry thought must have been quite the rascal himself in his youth.

Berry waited.

Reginald Goolbie did not appear.

She had not seen him the whole day through. Was that unusual? No, there were some days he stayed to himself in his quarters, but today…after that business of wanting to knock at her door so late at night and a note of some kind…well, she decided she would wait a while longer, because she wanted to ask what that was all about.

Reginald Goolbie did not appear.

From beyond the door she could hear the others conversing in the galley. Heard the sounds of utensils at work. Heard Galen offer some other witticism, and then Glennis laughed again. Those two did enjoy their rum.

The time moved past, and Reginald Goolbie did not appear.

Again she felt the chill of winter, and it was not just the temperature of air. She gave it a few more minutes, and then she walked to the passage that led into the curtained estates. Lanterns hung from pegs on the overhead illuminated her way. Her short journey halted before the third compartment on the right.

"Mr. Goolbie?" she said, speaking in a guarded voice so as not to bring anyone else looking out in curiosity. "Are you there?"

No reply came. *He's not there*, Berry thought. *He's not…anywhere.*

"Mr. Goolbie?" she tried again, and this time she drew back the curtain.

By the light from the passage lamps she saw that indeed he was not there. His bunk was unmade, as if he'd possibly attempted sleep and gotten up, or slept restlessly and then left his blankets. On the floor were the four pairs of boots, perfectly lined up. She noted that his lantern was missing, and so was one of his heavy coats.

Ah! she thought. *He's gone up on deck!*

But instantly she knew that was not true, because after sundown when the real cold set in none but the crew dared to go up and they were being paid for it.

She entered the compartment but left the curtain open so she might see what she was doing.

She looked down at the perfect row of boots.

It had to be done to satisfy her own curiosity. If Goolbie were going to hide the pouch, might he have hidden it where he thought the prowler had already searched? Of course he might have kept it on his body, but the way he'd spoken last night—wanting Berry to take charge of it—he feared being assaulted and having it taken from him by force, so…

She knelt down and reached a hand into the first boot.

Her fingers found it pushed into the toe of the second boot of the second pair. As she pulled the velvet pouch free something else came with it, and when she withdrew her hand she was looking not only at the pouch but a small folded piece of paper with a ragged edge that told her it had been torn from a larger piece.

She could feel the stones and bracelets through the velvet, so it was likely all of Goolbie's allurements were there. Placing the pouch on the bunk, she unfolded the paper and saw what was printed upon it in black ink.

Twelve midnight, starboard deck. Susan P.

"Can I ask what you're doin' in here, Miss Grigsby?"

The voice at her back caused her to jump so hard she thought her skin had left the bones behind. Looking around she saw the mountainous figure of Captain Stoneman standing there, and instantly she stood up with the note in her hand.

"I'm concerned about Mr. Goolbie," she said over the noise of her pounding heart. "He's nowhere to be found."

"*You?* Concerned about *him?*" Stoneman's eyes found the pouch. "His jewels?"

"Yes."

"Sittin' right out in the open?"

"No, the pouch was hidden in one of his boots."

"And you knew that? How?"

"I searched, that's all." Her heartbeat was thankfully returning to normal. She took a few deep breaths to clear away the remainder of the shock Stoneman had given her.

The captain nodded at her assertion, but Berry could tell he'd become somewhat suspicious in his speech, manner and expression. "I went to the galley for a cup of coffee and saw that Goolbie wasn't there," he said, his eyes narrowed. "Decided to look in on him myself, figured he might be ill. Never reckoned I'd find *you*. What were you plannin' on doin' with that pouch?"

"Giving it to you, if Goolbie can't be found." She took it up from the bunk and held it out. "Here."

"Hold on, now. Let's don't drop anchor on this too quick. Could be he's wandered off somewhere he ought not to be, like down below to the crew's quarters."

"Doubtful," Berry said. "Why would he do that?"

"You did lock your own cabin 'fore leavin' it, didn't you?"

"I always do."

"What's the commotion?" Drake Dixon appeared in the passageway alongside Stoneman. "Is our good friend up to his—" He saw Berry in the compartment and for a few seconds seemed surprised into silence. Then he said, "Miss Grigsby! What the devil are you doing in *there?*"

"Mr. Goolbie's missing. I came to see if he was here."

"You don't know he's missin'," Stoneman chided. "Could be he's up on deck."

"No one but the crew goes up on deck after the sun sets. I've never spoken to any of the others who did."

"Could be a first, the fella's a downright fool anyway." Stoneman's gaze caught on the paper in Berry's other hand. "What's that?"

"A note Goolbie received last night. He put it in his boot with the pouch." She offered it, and Stoneman took it.

"Susan P?" he said after he'd read the lines. "Who in thunder is Susan P?" In a sharper tone he asked, "How do you know Goolbie got this note last night?"

"Mr. Chandler found him outside my door last night sometime after eleven. Goolbie asked if Mr. Chandler had left him the note."

"Chandler left it?"

"No. What I'm saying is that Goolbie was just asking. Evidently Goolbie received the note—from someone unknown—after supper. It was probably left in here for him to find while he was at the table."

"What's all this *about?*" Dixon asked. "Somebody's written a note to that cad?"

"*Printed* a note," Berry corrected. "So it can't be certain if a man or a woman did the printing."

"What's the matter?" Cara Dixon had come to her husband's side, and behind her was Jessica Rinehart, who had already donned her blue flannel sleeping coat.

Dixon said, "I'm still trying to get the sense of it. It appears we're missing a certain unpopular passenger."

"He must be here somewhere," Stoneman insisted. He looked again at the note and then put it into his jacket pocket. "All right, a search'll be made of the ship from bow to stern. I'll go down to the crew's quarters and have a look, and I'll have a team go up on deck. If Goolbie's up there, I can vow he won't be stayin' long."

"What about *this?*" Berry again held up the velvet pouch. "I don't want to be carrying this around."

"I'll lock it up in my cabin, then." Stoneman accepted it. "Let's not disturb the others at their supper. Just *yet*, that is. I'm thinkin' Goolbie's gonna be found as soon as we start really lookin'. Miss Grigsby, you meet me in my cabin in about fifteen minutes, after I've had a look down below."

"Morgan Stout," Berry suddenly realized. "Where is *he?*"

"Not in his compartment," Jessica reported after opening his curtain next to Goolbie's.

"Someone mention my name and going through my quarters?" Stout appeared, coming along the passageway with four books from the library shelf in his arms. "What's happening here?"

"Goolbie's missing," Dixon said. "Have you seen him?"

"Not since yesterday evening."

"A search is gonna be made of the ship," said Stoneman. "We'll turn him up."

Stout gave a grunt. "If Mr. Goolbie is not 'turned' up in the next half-hour, I would suggest that he is never to be found."

"What's that supposed to mean?" was the captain's quick response.

"It means, sir, that if Mr. Goolbie is not found aboard the ship, logic dictates that he is no longer *on* the ship. Meaning also that since surrounding us is naught but frigid ocean and I doubt the gentleman has the Christ-like ability to walk on water, he has gone beneath the waves. Let me ask if Goolbie's lantern is still in his quarters."

"It's gone," Berry said.

"You recall the broken lamp chimney glass I showed you this morning? I suspect it was Goolbie's lantern, broken when he slipped upon the ice, somehow lost his hold on the safety rope—if the fool had a grip on it at all—and went over the rail at that precise point where the smear of soot stained the glaze. The remainder of the lamp followed him down. So...do search for the gentleman and I hope that for some strange reason he has winnowed himself into a crevice that would strain a mouse, but I believe he has been in the ocean and left behind for nearly twenty-four hours." Stout shrugged his massive shoulders. "All done. *Finis*. Rest in peace."

"You don't know what you're talkin' about!" Stoneman said, nearly with a snarl. "What's this about broken glass and such?"

"Leave it to the young lady to explain. I am going to my deliciously uncomfortable bunk and try to do some reading so as to remove from my mind the fact we have at least thirty more days and nights to be confined in this floating prison." And off he trundled to his curtained estate, where he closed the curtain with a decisive *snap*.

"That loon don't know what he's babblin'," said the captain, but in his voice Berry caught a quaver. "I'll look in on the galley again and if Goolbie's not there I'll go down to the crew's deck. I'll have a couple of men go up to check with the night crew. The rest of you just settle down and go about your business. No word yet to the others. Miss Grigsby, in my cabin in fifteen minutes and I want to hear the whole story."

After Stoneman had hurried away, Berry was surrounded by the Dixons and Jessica. "I can't believe it!" Jessica said. "Goolbie possibly gone over the side?"

"If he did he wouldn't have lasted but a few minutes in that water," said Dixon. "Miss Grigsby, you found broken glass on the deck?"

"Mr. Stout found it. He examined it and said in his opinion it was from a lantern's chimney."

"And this note," Dixon prodded. "You say someone likely left it for him while he was having his supper last night? Do you know what it said?"

Berry repeated what she'd read.

"Susan P?" Cara asked. "There's no Susan P aboard...at least not using that name."

"A moment," said Jessica. "Are you saying one of the women here is like...an imposter?"

"Whoever it is," Berry said, "the note was written to entice Goolbie to the starboard deck at midnight...and at the starboard railing about amid-ships is where Mr. Stout discovered the glass."

A silence fell, and in it Berry realized the weight of what she'd just said.

Dixon spoke first, in a low voice. "You know you're suggesting that someone among us wrote the note to lure Goolbie to the deck, possibly guided him over to the railing and…what? Pushed him over? I doubt a woman could've done that."

"A man working *with* a woman could've done it," Jessica ventured.

"But there's always a night crew of two or three on deck, isn't there?" Dixon looked as perplexed as Berry felt herself to be. "Wouldn't the man at the wheel have seen something?"

"You'd think so," Berry agreed, "unless the weather had closed in, it was sleeting and the visibility was low. The man at the wheel might not have been able to see much in the dark, with the weather in his face."

"We're leaping ahead," Dixon decided. "No matter what Stout believes, we don't know that Goolbie fell off the ship."

"Or was pushed off," Jessica said.

"I have an appointment with the captain," Berry said, for this round-about was going nowhere and she had her own theory that she didn't wish to share. "Pardon me," she told them, and left them standing still discussing the situation.

Stoneman's cabin was locked and when she knocked there was no answer, therefore she waited for his return. She was pondering the noise she'd heard last night. The sound of Goolbie's body falling to the deck? Which meant violence was done to him before he went over, and he was probably unable to cry out. The lamp had been dropped from a nerveless hand, the chimney broke, and whoever—one person or two—had tossed the lantern over the side to follow the body.

But that was all wild conjecture. Stoneman might possibly return with news that Rowdy Reggie was found playing dice down with the crew. Still… the note…the enticement…and the name.

Susan P. Who was that? Someone who Goolbie knew, and that was why he'd gone up? Berry realized that the man had likely come to her door late last night to show her the note, and possibly to ask her opinion of whether he should respond to it or not.

And there was this thought: if someone had actually murdered Goolbie, the theft of jewelry that the man had so feared was not the purpose, because whoever did it might have searched the body as it lay on the deck and then, not finding the pouch, had all day to go through Goolbie's quarters.

Which had not been done, since the pouch was still there.

Above Berry the stern hatch opened, admitting a blast of sleet and freezing air. Captain Stoneman in his heavy coat and cap shut the hatch over his head, descended the ladder and without a word to Berry unlocked his cabin. He said, "In," and closed the door at her back.

Within, the mariner's two oil lamps on their wall gimbals burned to illuminate the chamber. Stoneman shrugged out of his coat, took off his cap and sat down behind his desk. He motioned for Berry to take the second chair, but she said, "I'll stand. You didn't find him, did you?"

"No."

"What does that mean?"

"It *means*," he said with more than a hint of sarcasm, "that Stout is right. Rest in peace, Reginald Goolbie. Now: tell me everything you know about this, startin' from the first."

She did. At the end of it, she said, "I believe I heard his body fall last night. That means he was perhaps knocked senseless, and he had to be picked up and thrown over."

"Two people, then." Stoneman reached into his jacket pocket and brought forth the note. He set it down before him on the desktop. "Lurin' him up to the deck. Did more than shadow him, that's for sure."

Berry said, "If this incident happened around midnight, who was at the wheel who might have seen something?"

Stoneman stared up at her for what seemed an uncomfortably long time before the answer came: "*I* was at the wheel. I went on at eleven to spell Godwin, my first mate. I was on that duty 'til four."

"And you didn't see anything?"

"Sleet was comin' down, the sea had roughed up and the ship felt jumpy. My attention was on my job, but I did see a lamp's flame in that area of the deck 'round midnight. I couldn't leave the wheel to look closer. All of a sudden I saw it go out and I figured whoever it was had turned a back to me and gone on to the forward hatch and down again. As for hearin' anything, that wind and weather takes your ears."

"You only saw *one* flame?"

"Just the one."

"Were there other crewmen on deck?"

"A single man," Stoneman said. "And he wasn't what you might call 'on deck.' That was O'Hara, up in the crow's nest, and a worse place to be on the nights like we've been havin' couldn't be found. To the next question I reckon you'll ask: O'Hara's job is to keep a lookout in a forward arc, not to look down at the deck. Now." He pushed the note toward her. "What do you make of that?"

"It's an obvious ploy to get Goolbie on deck at that particular time but I have no idea who 'Susan P' might be. I would venture that Goolbie knew the name or he wouldn't have gone up."

"Yes," the captain said, his eyes on the paper. "Must've known the name."

"Whatever this is about," Berry said, "it doesn't have anything to do with Goolbie's merchandise. Would you agree?"

He nodded. "'Pears it wasn't about thievin'."

"So…what *was* it about?"

"'Susan P,'" Stoneman answered. "Somebody maybe that Goolbie used to know. I'm thinkin' 'Susan P' is not herself aboard, but maybe it's somebody actin'…you know…*for* her. That make sense?"

"Yes."

Stoneman sighed heavily and ran a hand across his face. "Never lost a passenger this way before. I've had 'em sicken and pass…even little children, which'll break your heart when you see it happenin', but not an overboard. It *does* happen from time to time. I've heard it from other captains. Just the bad luck of the draw, and some think the sea demands payment every so often. Neptune's Due, they call it. That's why I ride everybody so hard about not goin' up 'til that ice has thawed some or been chipped at, and always to hold tight to the safety rope." He sat for a few seconds staring into empty space, and then his vision returned to the here and now and he focused once more on Berry. "I don't know that there's anything left to do tonight."

"I agree, but you can't let this sit. One or more of the persons on this ship murdered a man. What are you going to do to find out who it was?"

"Miss Grigsby, I'm listenin' to whatever you might suggest. This is a new one on me."

She spent a moment thinking over the possibilities. One struck her as potentially valuable. "Everyone aboard could individually copy what's written on the note without seeing the printing. It might be difficult for the original writer to disguise his or her hand…and I think this should include the crew as well as the passengers. But I'll tell you, captain, from what I know of the others it escapes me that any of them could be involved in this."

"You never can tell what's deep in a person. Not from appearances, anyway. All right, I like that idea. We'll start it up in the mornin'. Do you think you can get any sleep?"

"Do you?"

"No," he said.

"I'll at least try, and you should too."

With that, Berry left Stoneman's cabin and proceeded along the passageway. When she reached her own door, with the key in her hand, she decided that sleep tonight was a far distant prospect. The ship was quiet but for the usual creaking of timbers and the noise of the sea along the hull. She walked on and entered the galley.

The chamber was empty but for McKeague, who was scrubbing the night's dishes with sand over a large iron pot. He nodded a greeting at her but kept at his work.

"Might I trouble you for a cup of coffee?" she asked.

"Down to the dregs, it is." This sounded like a warning.

"I don't mind."

Berry sat down at the table. Above her head a pair of lanterns swung with the ship's motion. McKeague drew her about a half-cup, all that was left, and set the wicked-looking ebony stuff before her. One taste of it and she figured she might be awake for the next two days.

McKeague returned to his scrubbing. Suddenly he said quietly, "Heard there was an overboard last night."

"Yes."

"Goolbie, it was?"

"That's right."

His gaunt-cheeked face turned toward her, then away again as he worked. "Shame of it, but you can be sure he went quick."

"A small mercy." It occurred to Berry that the crew did not know about the note...or that is, only the person or persons behind the note knew about it if it had come from the crew's complement.

"Happens once in a while," McKeague said. "Somebody gets careless, do'na understand how dangerous a rollin' ship and an icy deck can be."

Another sip of the coffee and that was about all Berry could manage. "I hope we'll get out of this weather soon."

"Yes'm."

She pushed her chair back, stood up and started to return the deadly cup to him.

"Had an overboard...let's think...two years ago," McKeague said. "Old man, it was. Comin' 'cross from New York. Captain thought he might've decided to go over, 'cause his wife had just passed."

"A pity. What ship was that?"

"This one, miss. I've never been workin' on no other."

Berry stopped where she stood. "*This* vessel? I just understood from Captain Stoneman that there'd never been an overboard on his ship."

McKeague stopped scrubbing. He put the half-finished plate aside and turned toward her. "Somethin' you said yesterday rankled me, miss, and I've got to get it off my spleen. You said this was Captain Stoneman's ship. Well, it 'inna. This ship's master is Captain Doyle, pure and proper."

"Captain Doyle? I don't understand."

"We don't rightly either. Us below, I mean. Just 'afore the loadin' started up, we got word from the company that Captain Doyle was standin' down this trip and Captain Stoneman was runnin' the helm. It was Captain Doyle had that nice cabin of yours all prettified and pink-painted, so you can thank *him* for that. Fact is, none of us below ever worked with Captain Stoneman and we ain't even *heard* of him, so to say this is his ship...you see how it cuts a man."

"Yes," said Berry. It had been spoken listlessly. What was in her mind was Stoneman's statement when he was showing Matthew and herself the painted cabin that had been altered from a goats' pen: *The crew's to be trusted. Been servin' the* Lady Barbara *back and forth six trips now, most of 'em's been with me the lot.*

Hesitantly, Berry said, "You mean…this is Captain Stoneman's first voyage on the ship?"

"Yes'm. Not sayin' he 'inna fine at his craft, but Captain Doyle…well, he's the true master." McKeague spied the coffee cup in her hand. "All fueled up?" he asked.

"To near explosion," she managed to reply. She gave him the cup. "Thank you."

"Yes'm. Good night to you."

"Good night," Berry said, and somehow she got out of the galley without staggering.

SIX

At long last, there was light.

Through stinging sleet and gusts of snow, the dull pearl of morning dawned. Standing at the bow of the *Lady Barbara*, Berry Grigsby stood bundled up in heavy coat, cap and gloves, watching the sullen break of day.

Around her the ship had come to life: crewmen working in the rigging and already chipping at the new ice that had collected, the sails filled with the wind that pushed the vessel closer and closer to New York, and further and further away from Matthew Corbett.

She had asked herself many times during the sleepless dark what Matthew would have done, if he were here at her side. She knew. It had to be. But if this was the lot of the problem-solver, she would gratefully give it up to the young man she loved.

When she was ready, she went through the stern hatch and descended the ladder there, and standing before Captain Stoneman's cabin door she steeled herself for what was ahead. She had decided she would not see any of the others this morning. Not until this was over.

She knocked.

When he answered, his voice was rough and ragged. He, too, had been through a dark night. "Who is it?"

"Berry Grigsby."

There was a long pause. Did he know? Possibly.

"It's unlocked," he said at last.

She entered and closed the door behind her.

Captain Henry Stoneman was sitting at his desk as she had left him. He was wearing the clothes of the night before. His face was drawn and haggard and his eyes were bloodshot. On the desktop stood a squat brown bottle with a wide bottom, and at his right hand was—surprisingly, instead of a well-used clay cup—a glass of cut crystal holding two fingers of tawny-colored liquid.

He said nothing as she took off her coat, cap and gloves. She draped the coat over the back of the chair before his desk, put the cap and gloves aside, and sat down.

"I have another glass," he said.

"No, thank you."

"Have you had your breakfast?"

"I'm not very hungry. Also, I didn't wish to speak to anyone else this morning."

Stoneman took a drink and turned the glass between his hands. "I didn't sleep. I expect you didn't either."

Berry plunged in. "How did you manage it?" When he remained silent, she went on: "How did you manage having Goolbie transferred from the *Briana Halsey* to this ship, and then replacing Captain Doyle as the master?"

Stoneman contemplated his drink, his expression suiting his name which by now Berry knew must be false.

"How long," she said, "had you been planning to kill him?"

He took another drink and continued to stare into its depths. Then: "Years."

"Susan P," Berry continued. "The deceased daughter you told Matthew and me that you keep in your heart? What's your real name?"

"Henry Parr." His sunken eyes had taken on a shine in the cabin's lamplight. "Yes, my daughter Susan. How'd you figure it?"

"No matter. The point is I have. What were you looking for when you entered Goolbie's quarters and happened to disturb the line of his boots? Not the jewels, I know that for sure."

"Don't care 'bout the jewels," he said. "I was just in there lookin'. Takin' stock of the belongings of the man I was gonna kill. Saw the boots and the fine clothes. Saw the nice expensive coats. I thought…this man buttons his jackets just like you do, Henry. Puts on his boots the same way. He's a human bein', just like you, Henry. Can you really do it, when the time comes? I almost said to myself…no, let it be. Let the past die in the past. But then I was thinkin' of him lustin' after you and carryin' on as he did, and there was no stoppin' him no matter what I said…and like I told your young man…I was gonna treat you like you was my own. So…it had to be done."

"I could take care of myself very well without having him murdered."

"It wasn't just that." Parr finished his drink with a quick swig and poured himself another. "It was his way. His *life*. You asked how I managed things, and I'll tell you. There are three partners in the shippin' company you chose."

"Chosen *for* me," she corrected.

"All right, chosen for you. I'm one of the three. It might not 'pear so, but I'm what you'd call well-heeled. I just don't live high on the hog, and my education is the sea and ships more than anything. When I saw the passenger list for the *Halsey* I recognized his name. I had the accountin' department show me his bill, which he'd signed with that same fanciful description of himself he was so proud of. So it was the same man, and it was a simple thing to have him moved to this ship. Then I asked—gave a professional request, I reckon it would be—to Tommy Doyle to take the *Lady* to New York. I used to captain long years before I joined the company. Told Tommy I missed the action. The challenge. Told him it was time I got some salt in my skin." He hesitated, as if in his weariness gathering strength to carry on. "A bottle of good whiskey, a steak dinner, and ol' Tommy was fine with it." He looked up from his glass and gave a faint, sad smile. "Easy done."

"I should've known this wasn't your ship," Berry said. "The first week at sea you kept hitting your skull on the overheads. If this had been your ship—for six trips back and forth, I remember you said—you'd have known every fraction of every inch."

"True enough. I suppose I…what would be the educated gent's word… embellished? Well, the first job of any captain is to inspire confidence in the passengers and crew, so I was doin' my justs."

"Also hiding your intent. My God, Captain Stoneman…I mean, Parr! Why did you have to commit *murder?*"

He leaned back in his chair and for a time simply stared up at the timbers. "When he came up and I saw his light," Parr recounted, "I was ready to lash the wheel down. I knew it wasn't gonna take very long. What I'd waited for…for years…not long, now. I went to him, and I said, 'I'm Susan Parr's father,' and he said, 'Who?' I said 'Susan Parr. The girl you ruined. Don't you remember her name?' He answered…'I've known many Susans,' and he gave a smile that…well, I had a belayin' pin behind my back. I hit him across the side of the head. He went down hard. The lamp broke right then and the larger part went over the side. Maybe he was dead outright, 'cause when I hauled him up he was loose. There was no blood. Over the rail, and he was gone. I went back to the wheel, unlashed it, corrected a few degrees, and…I wondered later where the note was, but I figured maybe he had it on him. To be honest…I didn't care." Parr turned his red-eyed gaze upon her, and Berry thought his face seemed almost misshapen by inner torment, so horrible she nearly had to look away. "I don't care now," he added. "And the thing is…did my killin' him bring Susan back to life? Did it do any damn good in this world at all? Oh, maybe it saved some other girl from gettin' with child and bein' abandoned to the street. Maybe it saved some other from jumpin' off the London Bridge and drownin' in the Thames, like my Susan did on the fifth night of January, 1700. Maybe it did. But you see, miss, Reginald Goolbie wasn't the real villain in this piece. The real villain is *me*."

His voice choked. "Before I murdered him, I killed my daughter. Killed her with neglect and anger and turnin' away when she needed me. Killed her by givin' her up to that fine fella called himself 'Rowdy Reggie' Goolbie the jewel merchant who was gonna give a rich life to a barmaid, and me takin' the next ship out 'cause I am the *captain*, and because the sea and the freedom of it meant more to me than my girl."

Parr leaned slightly forward. His eyes were damp and a pulse beat at his temple. His mouth opened and closed, opened and closed again like a gasping fish hauled up on a strange and brutal shore. "My wife passed of the fever when Susan was a little girl," he said. "Right then is when I changed…when I was lookin' to escape the world. I was hard on her, caused her to leave home too early and go out where the sharks swim. She wasn't ready. I didn't help her get ready. And when she was with child—his child—she begged me to let her come home and I said she had to row her own boat on the river she'd made, 'cause I was goin' to sea again. I found out later the baby died. That man wouldn't have nothin' more to do with her after she was tainted. She went down…how could a girl not go down, when her own father pushed her aside? Maybe…maybe she looked too much like her mother…maybe I was stabbed in the heart whenever I looked at her…but I was hard…I was a man of stone, and just like Goolbie maybe couldn't help what *he* was, I just went on gettin' harder 'cause I couldn't think no other way."

A trembling hand lifted the glass. The mouth drank. Two tears slowly trickled down along the seams and creases of the captain's face.

"The worst evil," he said. "The worst. Turnin' your back on somebody who loves you. Not listenin', not carin' when they call out for help. When they need you, and they've got nobody else. She tried. God knows she did. In the end, I think she was just wore out with tryin'." The face contorted again under inner pressures. "The bridge is so pretty at night, with all the hangin' lamps," he said. "You could look at it and think it could take you 'cross to a better world. Me…I always had a ship to command. No, she couldn't come back home…'cause there was no home for her to come back to. You know they buried my girl in a pauper's field? And the hell of it is…

just a worn-out old sail canvas wrapped 'round her in the dirt. Well, I had her moved and right then over her headstone I thought that if I ever found Reginald Goolbie I would make sure he remembered my girl. And there was his name on the list."

Parr's eyes squeezed shut and he kept them closed. His cheeks were wet. "Maybe if he'd said he remembered, maybe I wouldn't have struck him. I don't know. But it was the smile. It was that my Susan was just nothin' to him…same as I'd realized too late that I'd let her become nothin' to me, and it cut me to the soul."

His hand found his mouth. The last drink from the glass went down. When he continued, his voice was strained and further weakened. "I said Goolbie ruined my girl…but it was *me* that ruined her first. Nobody in this world can live without somebody somewhere givin' 'em love and care, and a place to belong to. That's my evil, miss. Yes. The worst."

The eyes opened, and in them Berry could see a small portion of Hell.

"The others," he said. "Will you tell them?"

"I won't. You should."

"I will," he said. "In the galley tonight."

Berry had to ask something else. "Am I safe?"

"Yes, miss. But *I'm* not. Now that it's done, I see how many ropes are aboard a ship that could get caught 'round a man's neck, or how slick that deck is in the middle of the night. But I am the captain and the passengers and crew of this ship are my responsibility. I figure there are just as many ropes in New York."

Berry stood up. Her heart ached as she watched Parr attempt to pour another glass from an empty bottle. "It'll be up to the others to decide what to do when we reach harbor. You know that, don't you?"

His crooked half-smile was a horror to behold. "As I said, now that it's done…I don't care."

"I'm sorry," she offered.

"Way past that," he said.

She took up her coat, cap and gloves. It was time to leave the captain of the *Lady Barbara* to that most fearsome judge…himself.

"One more thing, miss." Parr opened a desk drawer and held out the purple velvet pouch. "This is yours."

"I don't want it."

"Neither do I, but I think Goolbie would've wanted you to take it as well as whatever's in his baggage in the hold. From what you've told me and what I know, you may have been the nearest thing to a friend he ever had."

Berry hesitated, but then she took the pouch from his hand. She recalled Goolbie saying that the greater portion of his merchandise was in his baggage. Trinity Church would appreciate the offering.

As she left the cabin and closed the door she heard Parr give a single broken sob, but she had no doubt that after he addressed the group tonight he would adhere to his duties and get them to their destination, as befitted a true master of a ship.

She put on her weather clothes once more and went up through the stern hatch to the deck, where she stood at the starboard railing near the point where Rowdy Reggie had gone for his final plunge and thought about the very slim line between life and death.

After some deliberation, Berry opened the pouch and let the gemstones and the silver bangles fall into the sea. This Neptune's Due was as much about asking for Matthew's safety as for their own uncomplicated progress. When the last of it was gone, she held the pouch into the cold wind and let it fly away.

For the remainder of the voyage she would simply be another passenger and no one's problem-solver. After all this had settled down and the conclusion was likely made—with her urging—to allow Henry Parr to approach the law in New York freely and by his own choice, she would look forward to further meals and conversations with her shipmates.

She also had no doubt that Micah Halliday would find many adventures in his tour of the colonies, that Coy Chandler would construct an edifice substantial and important, that the Dixons would find favor in their new life in the New World, that Morgan Stout would continue his affinity to the essence of orchids, that the Hammetts would enjoy visiting their family and likely find new situations that befitted their aged youth, and that Jessica Rinehart would be happily married and might someday indeed write a "mystery."

She wondered if in that future tome there might be a character named Berry Grigsby.

Because it seemed to her that by a writer's pen a person could live forever.

But...she didn't wish to live forever, not without Matthew. The next few months—possibly a year, an eternity—were going to be difficult to get through without knowing exactly what was happening to him.

That dream she'd had. She could still see it in her mind: the two figures, male and female, with their bizarre black-and-red-haired heads, converging on him from both sides as if to—

What?

Destroy him?

She did not believe in premonitions, but if she did believe she would think that those two figures somehow were a portent of the future, and that they represented some terrible danger beyond what Matthew had ever faced.

She couldn't dwell on that, as it was too horribly unnerving. She would take one day as it came, no more and no less, and trust that Fate would send Matthew back safely to her arms.

Berry looked up at the sky.

In this moment—just this one moment in time—she was glad.

The sun was coming out.